REDEMPTION

Books by Vincent M. Wales

Wish You Were Here

One Nation Under God

The Many Deaths of Dynamistress

- *Book One: Reckoning*
- *Book Two: Redemption*
- *Book Three: Renaissance (coming soon)*

REDEMPTION

THE MANY DEATHS OF DYNAMISTRESS

BOOK TWO

Dinah Geof-Craigs
with
Vincent M. Wales

DGC PRESS • SACRAMENTO

Model photo by Lisa Charrie Photography
Cover concept by Vincent M. Wales
Cover design by Iana Petkova

ISBN 978-0-9741337-6-8

First DGC Press printing, April, 2015
Printed on acid-free paper

Acknowledgments

Thank you to my wonderful test readers: Rich Barr, Jacquie Jean, Lisa Kiner, and Mike Krumm.

The character of Bloodmoon was co-created by Jacquie Jean.
The character of Bronwyn Couch-Jones was co-created by Susan Wales.
The character of Fabian was co-created by Brent McKeehen.
The character of Half-Life was co-created by Amanda Brewer.
The character of Macy Zhang was co-created by Joe Martinez.
The character of Nexus was co-created by Claudia Silva.
The character of Quanta was co-created by Lisa Kiner.
The character of Resonator was co-created by Kiet Nguyen.
The character of Sinta was co-created by M. Young.
The character of Transcendant was co-created by the late Tre Chipman.
The character of Vesper was co-created by Roland Martinez.
The character of Zero-Point was co-created by Miguel Tarrats.
My deepest gratitude to you all for allowing them to live in my world.

And thank you to my sister, Sue, for helping to make this happen.

Dedication

This book is dedicated to lost friends, especially:

Wayne Himes, a fellow comic book lover and gamer who would have loved seeing this series. Thank you for your friendship.

Sherry Jennings, my dear cousin. Thank you for all the wonderful memories and long talks.

Tre "Ascendant" Chipman, whom I sadly knew only in the virtual world. Thank you for the joy you brought to so many.

Parke Godwin, author of so many wonderful books. Thank you for your kind words and for reminding me of who I am.

"Everyone is necessarily the hero of his own life story."

~ John Barth

Introduction

"Super of the Month" Interview
January 2008
Supers

Supers: Dynamistress, thank you for your time and hospitality.
Dyna: My pleasure, but please call me Dyna.
Supers: Dyna, most of our readers will probably not know your name, yet.
Dyna: Which makes me wonder why you're sitting here in my living room.
Supers: Well, as I mentioned to you on the phone, we often receive unsolicited mailings from teams when they add a new member. One of these was from when you joined the Bay Scouts.
Dyna: Where it clearly sat in your slush pile for a while.
Supers: True, but unlike the vast majority, yours made it out. We generally feature only metas who are already famous, as you know. But I just had a good feeling about you.
Dyna: Meaning that you learned of my involvement in the Nevada Incident and thought that would be a good hook.
Supers: That was part of it, sure. But I was actually more interested in the background profile that came with your submission. I believe it was written by the leader of the Bay Scouts.
Dyna: Scoutmaster.
Supers: Who is now retired, I understand.
Dyna: Due to a crippling injury, not by choice.
Supers: Right. The Nevada Incident. By now, everyone knows about the strange gateway into another dimension. An alternate Earth, so to

speak. It was one of the metas from that world who injured Scoutmaster, right?

Dyna: Yes.

Supers: And she later killed another member of the Bay Scouts.

Dyna: Listen, that whole episode isn't something I care to dwell on, if you don't mind. It's still too recent.

Supers: All right. So let's go back in time. You have a doctorate in genetics, and you used this expertise to give yourself your abilities, manipulating your own DNA to become a meta.

Dyna: After a fashion, yes.

Supers: That's an accomplishment many scientists have attempted, but without success.

Dyna: So I've heard.

Supers: What do you say to those who insist that such attempts at manipulating DNA are an affront to God?

Dyna: *[Laughs.]* I say if you have that sort of view, you'd have to consider the entire field of medicine to be the same sort of "affront." Is it an affront to God to use genetic treatments to restore hearing to the deaf or sight to the blind? To cure hemophilia?

Supers: Giving meta-abilities, most would say, goes well beyond correcting birth defects, which are not the norm.

Dyna: And in another ten or twenty generations, being born *without* meta-abilities may be considered a birth defect.

Supers: So you view it as the next stage in human evolution?

Dyna: *[Long pause.]* Honestly, it would be hard for me to say that. Evolution is adaptation in order to survive, driven by an outside trigger, such as a changing environment. But I can't see any particular stressor that's currently creating a need for meta-abilities.

Supers: The tendency toward meta-mutation is inherited, if I understand correctly, in a recessive fashion. Like someone having blue eyes even though their parents have brown eyes?

Dyna: That's right.

Supers: So tell us about your abilities.

Dyna: I generate a bio-plasma type of energy that I can expel from my body in different ways. Blasts. Propulsion. Even something like a force field around my body. And energy-enhanced physical strength.

Supers: That sounds awesome.

Dyna: It's pretty cool, yeah. *[Laughs.]*

Supers: But the actual experiment itself didn't go quite as planned. You performed your work on your off-hours at the lab where you were employed, without your company's knowledge. There was a fire. The lab burned.

Dyna: Yes. I was found culpable and had to pay restitution to the company.

Supers: Do you know how the fire started?

Dyna: *[Hesitates.]* No.

Supers: The court record indicates that you were drunk at the time.

Dyna: *[Hesitates.]* That's what they said, yes.

Supers: You worked as a bartender in college and here in San Francisco. I see you have probably a hundred different bottles of liquor in your home bar. Dyna, do you have a drinking problem?

Dyna: No.

Supers: What are you drinking right now?

Dyna: Dr Pepper.

Supers: Maybe a little Bacardi in there?

Dyna: Sorry, is this an interview or an intervention?

Supers: There just seems to be a trend.

Dyna: *[Silence.]*

Supers: Okay, so why did you do it in the first place? Most people probably couldn't comprehend the level of commitment you showed.

Dyna: Let's call it what it was: an obsession. I grew up dreaming of being able to do incredible things. And of being famous.

Supers: Lots of kids do.

Dyna: I know, but... *[long pause]* Let's just say that I spent too many years of my life being a child.

Supers: So, as a child, what other ambitions did you have?

Dyna: At one point, I wanted to be a singer.

Supers: So you're a frustrated rock star?

Dyna: Well, this was during the seventies, so...

Supers: So if you hadn't pursued your work in genetics, and didn't become a disco queen, what do you imagine you'd be doing, now?

Dyna: I dunno. Roller derby looks like a lot of fun. Can you make a living doing that?

Supers: I don't know, but the Bay Scouts kind of sounds like a derby team name.

Dyna: *[Laughs.]* It does, doesn't it?

Supers: Did you skate a lot as a kid?

Dyna: Just up and down our street. The rink in my town was torn down before I was born.

Supers: You grew up in a rural area pretty much devoid of metas, isn't that right?

Dyna: If there were any in those parts, they quickly made off for places with actual crimes to fight. Or opportunities to commit them.

Supers: And you ended up in San Francisco, where you soon became a member of the Bay Scouts, which was disbanded around the time of the Nevada Incident.

Dyna: Yes. And let me say what a great bunch of people they were. It was an honor being with them.

Supers: Let's hear about your very first assignment with the Scouts. I bet you were excited.

Dyna: *[Laughs.]* You'd lose that bet. My first assignment as a full member had us sent to investigate a stench over in Marin.

Supers: You're kidding.

Dyna: I wish.

Supers: Did you figure out what was causing it?

Dyna: Yeah, a cave full of slime molds and other fungi. Not the most exciting thing, but the worst part is that this investigation took me out of commission for months. I got really sick after accidentally inhaling some spores. Cryptococcal meningitis, it's called.

Supers: Anything with "crypt" in the name sounds unpleasant.

Dyna: *[Laughs.]* It was, but I got over it, with treatment.

Supers: So after the Bay Scouts disbanded, you joined the Gatekeepers. How did you score that invitation?

Dyna: Scoutmaster put in a good word for me. As did Captain Shepherd, who was the Bay Scouts' liaison to the Coast Guard. And Kimera was my "in." She's my sponsor in the team.

Supers: "Sponsor?" Sounds like an AA meeting.

Dyna: It means she's the one who felt I was a good fit for the organization and nominated me. Therefore, she was the one responsible for helping me become acclimated to the group itself.

Supers: Kimera was one of those replaced by the other-worlders.

Dyna: *[Silence.]*

Supers: Right, we're not talking about that. So let's look at some of the things that have changed as a result of that event. Is it true that it was your idea to convince the government to reveal the existence of the portal, and to use telepaths in the effort to return the imposters to their own world?

Dyna: Not sure how you learned that, but yes.

Supers: Public opinion of metas, and telepaths in particular, appears to be easing. Do you think that's a good thing? Many think we have every reason to be afraid of metas, and telepaths especially.

Dyna: I don't really pay close attention to these things, but yes, I've heard the rumblings. These seem to be the same folks, though, who are afraid of pretty much everything. They're afraid of immigrants. They're afraid of non-Christians. They're afraid of pretty much anyone different from themselves.

Supers: Can you really include metas in with those other categories, though? Metas can be quite dangerous.

Dyna: *Anyone* can be dangerous.

Supers: True, but most metas are inherently dangerous.

Dyna: So are non-metas, to varying degrees. An adult is inherently more dangerous than a child.

Supers: I think many parents might disagree with that.

Dyna: *[Laughs.]*

Supers: I see your point, but you have to admit there's a difference. Metas are far more dangerous than non-metas.

Dyna: A non-meta with a gun is far more dangerous than one without.

Supers: But nearly anyone can get a gun. Evens the scales.

Dyna: Yes, and that's a disturbing thought in itself. There are plenty of people I know that I wouldn't trust with a gun, all of whom have no restrictions on their ability to legally own one. So my question would be to ask why it is that the thought of any nitwit or misfit being allowed to have a gun doesn't scare these same people? There are far more of them than there are metas.

Supers: I don't think that's how they look at it.

Dyna: Of course not. Because these people are driven by fear, especially of things unfamiliar to them. They don't fear guns, because they're familiar with guns. Yet it never seems to cross their minds that they don't know gun *owners*. They keep chanting, "Guns don't kill people; people kill people," but are at the same time opposed to background checks of the people who want to buy guns.

Supers: Not everyone in support of gun rights opposes background checks, but I'll agree there are plenty who do. But you're not taking into account that if a person commits a crime with a gun, they can lose the right to own one. If a meta commits a crime with his or her abilities, we can't take those abilities away from them.

Dyna: But that's not the same thing at all. Taking away meta-abilities isn't like taking away a person's right to own a gun. It's like cutting off the person's hands so they can't fire a gun.

Supers: But people aren't born with guns built into their hands. Metas essentially are. And you must agree that, far more than metas who can "shoot" you from their fingers, telepaths are the ones to most be feared.

Dyna: And why would I agree with that? Because it's "scary" for someone to have the ability to read our thoughts? For a *very* tiny number of them to be able to manipulate those thoughts?

Supers: Yes! And that they can do these things without us knowing about it. That we could become someone's puppet. A telepath could, for example, walk into a bank, control the employees and security guards, wiping from their minds any memory of the person having been there, and walk out with a fortune.

Dyna: Do you realize just how few telepaths have that kind of ability? A ridiculously small number. You have more chances of being struck by lightning – twice – than ever encountering a meta with powers of that magnitude. To be afraid one of them is going to directly affect you would qualify as blatant paranoia. And you, as a researcher of metas, should know this.

Supers: I'm simply voicing a common thought among the non-meta population, no matter how paranoid it may seem. What you're saying is probably true, if you don't live in a metropolitan area. But metas congregate in the big cities, as you well know. Wouldn't chances be significantly higher, there?

Dyna: To encounter a meta, sure. But even with that, the fear of telepathic metas is still unfounded. I *am* a meta, and I've personally only ever met three telepaths.

Supers: That you know of.

Dyna: What do you mean?

Supers: How do you know all telepaths have admitted to being one? I mean, we can detect metas with testing, but we can't determine what abilities they have. Of all metas, telepaths would be most likely to lie, in order to protect themselves. Beyond that, how do you know for certain that one of the telepaths you've met hasn't mucked about in your head? Can you say with any kind of certainty that you haven't been programmed by to be a sleeper agent, ready to be remotely activated to act at their whim?

Dyna: I think you read too many spy novels. Look, let's get back to what started this. You wanted to talk about the way things are changing. So how about the fact that police departments and the FBI are utilizing telepaths in beneficial ways?

Supers: Such as?

Dyna: Finding kidnappers, child molesters, rapists, murderers, and so on. Haven't you wondered, for example, why the number of AMBER Alerts has dropped considerably over the past few years?

Supers: I wasn't aware they had.

Dyna: The government has been employing metas for such things for a long time, but has never made much effort to let the public know it. Some say it's because they think the public would freak out over it. Others say it's because the government is fine with the public maintaining a fear of metas.

Supers: There's also the issue of telepathic abilities being a violation of the civil rights of those upon whom they're used, especially the ones who turn out to be innocent.

Dyna: Sure. But let's be honest. That's *status quo* for police work. It routinely abuses the rights of the innocent. And to some degree, it's probably unavoidable. So why choose to be offended by just this one type of offense?

Supers: So you're saying that because the system is already flawed, it's okay to add new types of abuse to it?

Dyna: Consider that the use of telepaths could *decrease* that abuse, by determining someone's innocence right up front. If a quick scan can verify an alibi, that person will never be dragged through a trial, never face that humiliation, never have to deal with all the repercussions, including incurring all those costs, let alone being found guilty for something they didn't do. It's not like our current system compensates those people when they're found innocent, before or after. If you're found innocent, say by DNA testing, after twenty years in prison, do you think you're adequately compensated upon your release? In probably half the states, there's no guaranteed compensation whatsoever.

Supers: I did know that, and I agree that it's outrageous. So, okay. Let's say you're right about all of this. So what's to prevent telepaths from being used to monitor everyone? As the expression goes, who will watch the watchmen?

Dyna: Who's watching them now? Who has *ever* been watching them? The debate about personal freedom versus security has been raging for a long time, but it seems to me that whenever you institute any form of "watchmen" – whether police, military, or meta – you are sacrificing a certain level of freedom. Is it even possible to ensure public safety without such a sacrifice?

Supers: Obviously, this isn't a question we're going to resolve, so let's switch topics.

Dyna: Good idea.

Supers: You said before that your focus was to be famous. But you didn't exactly jump on my interview request. Why is that?

Dyna: *[Hesitates.]* It just didn't seem right.

Supers: In what way?

Dyna: As I said earlier, I spent much of my life being childish. I've grown a bit since then and I suppose I didn't reply right away because I didn't feel I was deserving of appearing in your magazine. I hadn't done anything to actually earn any fame.

Supers: So what changed your mind about the interview?

Dyna: *[Laughs.]* Vanity, probably.

Supers: Obviously, your career hasn't gone as you'd anticipated. Are you disillusioned?

Dyna: I suppose I am. But that's a good thing. I mean, who wants to live an illusion?

Supers: Tell us about what's different.

Dyna: Everything! Other metas are nothing like I'd expected them to be. The work certainly isn't what I expected. But the main thing that's different is my outlook and what I want to get out of all this. Or maybe a better way of putting it is that I don't really know what I want to get out of it, anymore. I just know it's not what I'd wanted before.

Supers: So what keeps you doing this?

Dyna: I dunno. Maybe just to embarrass my mother.

Supers: And if you couldn't do this anymore?

Dyna: I guess I'd go back to research, work in a lab.

Supers: But doesn't that pale next to being a hero?

Dyna: Oh, please. I don't consider myself a hero.

Supers: Why not?

Dyna: *[Shrugs.]* I suppose... because... I'm still not sure what that word means.

One

"I think the promise of fame and what it holds to you as a child and dreaming of it is not what it is. What it is, I'm not complaining about, but it's just different than the reality you dreamed."
~ Rosie O'Donnell

Once upon a time, children entertained themselves by using imagination to live out their fantasies of other lives. They would play out simplistic scenarios of good guys versus bad guys. Sometimes it was a clearly delineated case of stopping the bad guy. "Cops and Robbers," for example. Sometimes it was a situation in which "good" and "bad" depended on a particular point of view, like playing "Army" or "Spies." And sometimes it was a twisted version of good and bad, warped by history books written by the "winners" and the exaggerations of the entertainment industry, such as "Cowboys and Indians." And of course, often it was what every kid viewed as the ultimate in good guys against bad guys – playing "Superheroes."

Oddly enough, I didn't engage in such games. But then, I guess that's what comes of growing up with virtually no friends. The few I did have were other girls, interested mainly in playing with Barbies. I'd play along, but at some point, I'd tear off my doll's clothes, revealing the colorful costume underneath that I'd applied with my brother's model paint, and announce that I was ready to save the world. Then my friends would yell at me for ruining the game and not play with me again for a month.

And that's what I thought the metas did – save the world. I wasn't ever quite clear on how. The news never revealed any incredible threats like the ones in comic books. There were no super-powered megalomaniacs out to dominate the world (at least, that we knew of), no teams of "super-villains" on rampant crime sprees, or anything else grandiose and obvious. It was always mundane stuff, like thwarting muggings or rescuing people from some minor catastrophe or another. Important, to be sure, but not big. Not glorious. Not things that would make people adore them. Except, I suppose, for the people saved from harm.

Despite this obvious reality, I never honestly believed it. I just *knew* there were teams out there given assignments that never made it onto the news because they were just too big or sensitive, against threats so heinous that they'd cause the populace to freak out. Like alien invasions. But in fact, the alien invasion happened on my watch, and wasn't like any I'd ever imagined.

Project Echo. That's what the Department of Homeland Security named it. But the press referred to it as the Nevada Incident, so that's how it's known. Much as I wanted to forget about it, it fills my dreams with death. In my dreams, everyone dies, and always due to my own negligence or outright stupidity.

It seems wrong to think about my own happiness when people died, especially when two of the deaths were my doing. But the ironic truth is that two events came out of the Nevada Incident that brought a lot of joy to my life.

The main one would be my friendship with Sinta, my Bay Scouts teammate who became my roommate after the group disbanded. In truth, she's almost like a daughter to me. But since I'm pretending I'm not twenty years her senior, I'll say she's like a little sister to me.

The other event would be my membership in the Gatekeepers. In the month following her return from the other world, Kimera and I spoke at length about the Nevada Incident. When she learned of my role in the clean-up of that mess, including my recommendations to DHS, she passed it on to the leadership of her team. They verified everything with Captain Shepherd and Scoutmaster. And that's how I ended up getting the invitation.

The Gatekeepers is a very different sort of group than the Bay Scouts. For one thing, the pay is way better. My base salary was a good bit more than what I made even with active mission bonus pay with the Scouts, so my active mission pay with the Gatekeepers was quite attractive.

Another difference is that the Gatekeepers is much larger. The Scouts never had more than a dozen members at any given time. During my tenure, it had nine, including me. The Gatekeepers' roster averages around forty-five.

One advantage to having a large roster is that you have a wide array of abilities, making it likely that the Gatekeepers can handle just about any situation that arises, and have the ability to pair the less experienced, new members with more seasoned metas, ensuring that the newcomers are kept relatively safe while learning the ropes.

The main disadvantage, though, is considerable downtime. Because there are so many members, assignments don't come all that often for anyone who hasn't got a certain level of seniority. Generally, the longer you've been with the group, the more assignments you receive. So a good bit of my time was spent doing what I'd have been doing as a solo agent – going out to find trouble. Except now I was at least drawing a salary for it, not relying on bringing in bail jumpers, as I'd once had to.

One of the more interesting differences between my two teams would be the organization structure. Daniel was the leader of the Scouts. Period. We all had input, but he was the decision-maker. The rest of us followed. The Gatekeepers, though, has a distinct hierarchy. The top guy of the group holds the title of Legate. Under him are two Prefects. Under them are six Tribunes. The "Romanclature" is a bit silly, in my opinion, but they've always used it. Each year, nominations are made for the officer positions. Self-nominations are not allowed. There is no overt campaigning, since the members know each other well enough to make a decision. From the nominees (including those already serving), eight are elected by the group as a whole. From these elected Tribunes, two are selected as Prefects by the Legate (which itself is pretty much a life position), similar to how a president chooses his cabinet. There are no restrictions on how many times an individual may be elected. The current Legate, Invictus, has held that position for nearly two decades. In fact, he has been with the Gatekeepers since its inception and rumor has it that he was the one who suggested using the Roman names for the leadership ranks in the first place.

Invictus isn't a young man, obviously. He's at least a dozen years older than I am, and I'm not likely ever again to be carded at a bar, despite looking younger than my years.

As for my former team members, I visit Daniel a couple times a month. His speech eventually recovered to mostly normal, but he's never regained full mobility. And while still emotionally devastated at his forced retirement, he's made the most of his time by doing a lot of volunteer work, much of it with disadvantaged children. He is also frequently requested as a speaker for schools, scouting groups, and similar organizations.

Jack took a job with a robotics company, while continuing his study of zero-point energy on the side. Ping Song essentially left the "hero" biz and continued working with the University of California in computer science.

And speaking of science, one entire floor of Golden Gate Citadel, the Gatekeepers' headquarters, is nothing but a variety of different scientific labs. Very handy for my continued work, even though none of them have a focus on genetics.

And yes, I do need to continue with my work. Every few years, I need a "booster," so to speak. Of course, I not only reinvigorate myself with these updates, but I also work on new enhancements. After joining the Gatekeepers, I worked on an enhancement that would boost metabolism efficiency and energy storage capacity. While it's awesome to eat anything and everything without worry of blimping out, having to consume so many thousands of calories per day can become damned inconvenient.

Fame is a funny thing. I'd craved it from the time I was a little girl, and foolishly thought I deserved it. Now, on the cusp of thirty-seven, I knew I hadn't earned it, but here I was, about to be famous, even if temporarily.

When the issue of *Supers* with my photo on the cover was released, Dana came down from Sacramento for the weekend and took me out to celebrate. It was the January 2008 issue, which means it was released in mid-December of 2007, since the publishing industry has never been able to read a calendar.

Dana began the weekend by yelling at me.

"You did *what?*"

"I bought a stock," I repeated.

"*A* stock? One single stock?"

"Is that bad?" I said as I brought coffee from the kitchen.

"Well, what happens if it tanks? You're screwed. It's better to have a broad portfolio, for safety." He accepted the coffee as I sat down next to him.

Feeling progressively embarrassed, I said, "Well, the shares were only like five bucks each."

"Mm. So how many did you buy?"

"Fifty thousand," I said.

"*Fifty thousand dollars' worth?*" Dana nearly choked on his coffee.

"Um..."

His eyes widened. "Tell me you didn't buy fifty thousand *shares.*"

"Okay. I didn't by fifty thousand shares," I lied.

He sighed deeply and shook his head. "I had no idea you even had that kind of money."

Immediately, I felt guilty, remembering how much I owed him for all his help over the years. "I'm sorry. I should have finished paying you back, first."

He dismissed that with a wave. "I just didn't know that DynaPaste was selling so well."

"PowerPaste," I reminded him. "But yeah, it is. The company has marketed it pretty aggressively to all the GNCs, Vitamin Shoppes, and other such stores all around the world, not to mention supermarkets, department stores, and pharmacies. If even half of those stores buys a few boxes of the stuff each month?" I shrugged. "That's a hell of a lot of sales the company is making. And that's not even figuring online sales. Sports nutrition is something like a thirty billion dollar a year business."

"Wow. I had no idea. So what piece of junk did you buy?"

I stirred half-and-half and sugar into my coffee. "I heard of a company last year that's producing an anthrax vaccine. Jumped out at me because of that cousin of ours who was killed by it back after 9/11."

Dana frowned. "How were we related, again?"

"Oh, I have no idea. Some twisted branch of the family tree. Fourth cousins twice removed, or something only a genealogy freak like our mother would know."

Dana nodded, then sighed again. "I just hope you don't lose your shirt."

I looked down and shrugged. "Not one of my favorites, anyway."

We spent the weekend going out for meals, hitting the bars, and so on. At one point, Dana said, "This might be the last time you're able to go out in public without being swarmed by fans."

I just laughed. That might have been true if I'd already had some fame before the magazine's release, but I was an unknown. Probably only one percent of readers in San Francisco would have heard my name before picking up the issue, and no one outside of California would have, other than my friend Rhonda and her family back in Pennsylvania.

I'd been in a mild state of shock since the interview. It had been one surprise after another. I'd been surprised to be asked in the first place, further surprised that the interview was in-person, and that there was also a photographer. Even then, I didn't expect it to be published, so it was a surprise when the editor-in-chief not only accepted it, but also chose me as "Super of the Month." And I suppose I shouldn't have been, but I was surprised by the immediate attention it garnered.

I wasn't approached at all during my weekend on the town with my brother. But soon after, people started recognizing me on the streets. Most were cool about it, limiting it to, "Oh, hey! You're Dynamistress!" and asking for my autograph or to take a picture with me. I didn't mind that at all. Though the public attitude toward metas had improved, there were still plenty who reviled us. I got a lot of fearful looks.

My occasional employer, the Red Devil Lounge, asked me to do a stint behind the bar. They'd lost their main attraction when Rachel, their for-real "Devil Girl," moved to L.A. They obviously wanted to use my new celebrity to pull in lots of customers. I was open to the idea, but told them I would not be held liable if anyone decided to attack the bar in order to get at me. Unsurprisingly, they chose not to pursue the idea. They also said I should probably not expect any more shifts, even though I hadn't worked one in months. Nothing personal, of course.

I'd never been great at the whole secret identity thing, so it wasn't long before I got my first phone call from a fangirl, a spunky kid named Macy. I actually got quite a kick out of it, spending at least half an hour talking to her the first time. She called often, and one day she said, "There should be a Dynamistress fan club, I'm thinkin'."

I laughed at the idea. "Why?"

"Because you're cool! And you've been so nice, always taking my calls and stuff. I just want to do something nice for you."

"Mace, I think you may be my only fan, but if you really want to spend your time on that, you have my blessing. Though it's totally not necessary."

"I'm *not* your only fan, and I'll prove it! Your club will have fifty members inside a month."

"Unlikely."

"Bet you ten bucks."

"You're on."

"Awesome! I'm gonna send you an email, okay? With some stuff I'll need from you."

"As long as it's not a blood sample."

Of course, it wasn't just fans who'd call. The occasional male caller would ask if I wore panties under my tights. I'd get calls asking me to be a spokesperson for a particular group or product.

Eventually, I got rid of my landline and utilized my cell phone exclusively. Got a different email address, which I gave to Macy, along with my cell number. She texts me. A lot.

Access to our apartment building is only by key or by a tenant inside buzzing you in, so no one showed up at my door, but occasionally I'd see people outside who seemed to be waiting for someone. If I suspected that person might be me, I made my exit via the fire escape. My apartment was at the back of the building, with the fire escape hidden from street view.

Truthfully, though, I wasn't worried much about my identity being so easily discovered. The only living people I considered my "enemies" were in prison. And of those, the only one who might pose any sort of threat was Hellion. But as I'd always told Rachel, he was a punk. I wasn't afraid of him.

There was always the possibility that some up-and-coming villain would try to make a name for himself by taking out Dynamistress in her sleep. But to be honest, my name wouldn't give anyone much street cred.

There was a bigger downside to my fame, though, which was that it caused some issues among the ranks of the Gatekeepers. I still had only the barest familiarity with probably half the team, and there were several I only knew by what I read in our database. And every last one of them had been at this business longer than I had. Though the group itself was mentioned frequently in *Supers* and other publications, only a few of the current team, such as Invictus, had ever been "Super of the Month." He'd even been "Super of the Year," back in 2001. He'd taken a dozen of the Gatekeepers with him to New York City after 9/11 to help in the recovery.

It would be nice to say that these renowned metas were above pettiness, to say there was no envy, but some of them weren't and sometimes there was. It didn't make for the best working environment.

Fame is a fleeting thing, of course, unless one works to maintain it. The popularity I enjoyed by being "Super of the Month" in January would last, I figured, perhaps six months, with each month bringing less attention than the one before. The memory span of the average reader seemed to be about that long. The memory span of my teammates, however, seemed to be infinite.

There was, actually, one other surprise that came out of the *Supers* interview. I fell in love.

K.T., the girl who'd interviewed me, was an adorable brunette with big eyes, freckles, and a sparkling demeanor that was positively infectious. After the interview, we'd talked casually as the photographer packed up his equipment and headed out. We'd joked about some story that had then recently been in the news, and she ended staying for pizza and some of Dana's latest batch of home brew.

Over the ensuing weeks, we spent a crazy amount of time together. We met for lunch, movies, and such as often as possible when I wasn't on assignment with the Gatekeepers, sometimes spending entire days together.

She had a goofy sense of humor that I found cute beyond words. Her laugh made me melt. She got the biggest kick out of some of the simplest things. One day, we idly roamed the aisles at the supermarket, not shopping, just pointing out to each other what our favorite foods were. We discovered we both loved Fig Newtons, Yoo-Hoo, and Honey Nut Cheerios. And we both disliked crunchy peanut butter, ranch dressing, and radishes.

"I knew the first time we met," she told me one day, "that we were soul friends."

"Soul friends?"

"You know those friends you have where years can go by without communication, and then you see them and it feels like you just saw them yesterday?"

I'd never had a friend like that, but I just smiled and nodded. I smiled a lot with her. Falling for K.T. was so easy. It was a crush of the first order, the sort that made me giddy and stupid. The problem was, my heart was still hurting from Rachel's abrupt departure. Even though our relationship hadn't been what you'd call romantic, I still missed it. I missed her. And I'd become convinced that I simply wasn't any good at relationships and shouldn't even put myself out there, anymore. So I didn't tell K.T. of my feelings. I just enjoyed her company, loved her without saying so, and pretended this was an acceptable substitute for romance.

We talked shop a lot. She'd been working as a stringer for *Supers* for more than five years and her knowledge of metas put mine to shame. My obsession with knowing everything about them took a back seat to my studies in college, after all, and never really returned to the same degree.

The public's opinion of metas was slowly improving, and we agreed that the main reason was that they knew about the other world. They regarded it as more of a threat than Earth's metas and viewed the existing super-teams similarly to how they viewed the police. Many distrusted them, but sure as heck wanted them around when something bad was going down.

Possibly in an effort to reinforce the positive view of metas, teams began to take on different duties than they previously had. Many groups, including the Gatekeepers, help out during earthquakes, fires, and other disasters, typically with search and rescue. Of course, this didn't mean our reputation was pristine. There will always be people who use their abilities to help themselves instead of others.

Case in point, sports. For years, all players had been tested for evidence of the meta "gene." Any who tested positive were barred from playing. But as the world soon learned, it wasn't just the players who needed to be tested.

The previous year, for example, there had been a huge scandal in football. A coach for the New England Patriots was a telepath. During a game against the New York Jets, he was caught (evidently by another telepath in the stands) reading the thoughts of the Jets' coach and using that knowledge to the Patriots' benefit, such as changing formations to match the Jets' planned play. It was a highly contentious incident that resulted in large fines and penalties against the Patriots.

More and more scandals came to light, the most recent of which was that the caddy of a professional golfer was discovered to be a minor telekinetic. A little mental tap here or there while putting turned out to be crucial to winning many championships. He was a very highly paid caddy, until his talent was exposed.

While the sports industry was rocked by all this, the real surprise for many was the discovery that so many metas in the U.S. were unregistered. It caused those tracking such things to raise the estimated number of metas by almost twenty percent.

There is no consensus on what effect this had on public opinion. On the one hand, knowing there were more metas in the world made a lot of people uncomfortable. On the other hand, the knowledge that these people had been living among them with no ill effects made other people shrug their shoulders, deciding it wasn't such a big deal, after all.

"She sounds great!" Fabian said as he worked on my hair. I sat in the chair, staring at my reflection as he clipped and combed.

"She is," I said, smiling. Fabian had been my hair stylist since Sinta and I moved in together. He knew more about my life than most people, simply because there's not much else to do but gab when you're having your hair done.

"Have I told you that you're my favorite client?" he said.

"That's because you see me so often," I said. "And I'm a big tipper."

"True. I swear you must grow an inch a week."

"I don't think it's quite that fast."

"Never contradict your stylist," he said, flicking a lock of my hair from his bright pink shirt.

"Have I told you how weird it is to have a bald hair stylist?"

Fabian laughed. "I shave my head because it's just not possible to have hair as fabulous as the rest of me."

"I see," I said with a chuckle.

"So you're going to tell her you're into her, right?" he said, turning the conversation back to K.T.

"I... don't think so."

"Then you're the dumbest member of the Gatekeepers I know."

"How many do you know?"

"One," he said, with a flourish of spray to finish my new 'do. "All done."

"Love it," I said, rising from the chair. "As always." I gave him a hug. "See you in a couple weeks."

I walked a few blocks down Haight Street on my way home. I loved the eclectic shops and eccentric people. I couldn't imagine a place more different from my tiny home town in rural Pennsylvania. My white hair didn't really stand out, here, though I did occasionally have someone ask me where I have it done.

At home, I checked my email. Among them was a short one from Macy: "D: You owe me ten bucks!"

I went online and Googled myself. And there it was, my own website, in blue and white, adorned with a border of big, white double-helices. There were photos of me, a bio put together from the *Supers* interview and Macy's conversations with me, and a sign-up for the fan club.

On the Contact page was a photo of Macy and a blurb introducing her as the webmistress. It was nice to know what she looked like. Macy had the Asian features of her father, but the Spanish skin tone of her mother, with long, dark hair and almost-black eyes. Cute kid. There was a post office box address, too, which I hoped already belonged to her family. I didn't like the idea of her spending money to maintain one for this silly page. For that matter, she had secured a domain name and, since there were no ads on the page, it seemed she was paying for hosting.

I wrote her a check for five hundred.

In February, Sinta and I celebrated our seventeenth and thirty-seventh birthdays, respectively. Jack and my brother joined us and we went out to lunch, then had a Pixar movie marathon on DVD at home. Dana brought cake and ice cream, both of which he claimed to have actually made, himself. I told him he'd make someone a nice little wife one day.

That jab, though, was inspired by a bit of jealousy on my part. When I'd first moved to California, Dana and I spent all kinds of time together. He'd come to the city every weekend, making sure I was getting settled in and acclimated to this new life of mine.

But as time went on and I became more involved with the Bay Scouts, I'd see him less and less frequently. We'd talk on the phone a good bit, but that was never the same. Lately, we'd been going weeks without talking. Life had become busy for both of us. He had his counseling practice and I had my new team, but more significantly, he had a new relationship that seemed to be serious.

Aside from a brief fling he'd had the year following his divorce a decade before, this was the first relationship he'd had. And despite being busy myself, I resented that this woman was stealing from my time with my brother. He was the only family I cared about, and I missed him.

But, I reminded myself, at least I had family. Sinta didn't. The Bay Scouts had been her family. I guess that's part of why I asked her to live with me. The other part, of course, is that I just find her to be a delightful girl.

She seemed younger than her years. So childlike in many respects. Despite the terrible life she'd had, she was so full of joy. I didn't understand how that was possible, but was grateful for it.

Sinta did, however, sometimes suffer from nightmares. She'd never discuss them, but I always assumed they were memories of the bad things she'd experienced while in foster care. It took her a while, but eventually she learned it was okay to come to me after these dreams. She would climb into my bed, curl up beside me, and pull my arm around her.

It reminded me of when I'd do the same thing as a kid, climbing into bed with Dana after one of my own nightmares. And I was still having plenty of those.

In April, I had a check-up with my physician. I was relieved to have health coverage again through the Government Employee Health Association. Most meta teams are parts of various government departments. Today, most of them are under the Department of Homeland Security, but groups formed before DHS was established have generally stayed with whatever department they'd previously been attached to. So the Gatekeepers are still part of the Department of Justice.

We ended with a spinal tap to check my cerebrospinal fluid for the presence of fungus. I'd been having this procedure done quarterly ever since recovering from my bout of cryptococcal meningitis. But that didn't mean I was used to it.

In truth, it's not very painful, since they numb me up pretty well. But any injection for me is tricky. My subconscious mind detects the needle as a threat, so I have to deliberately suppress my energy shield for it to penetrate easily. And occasionally, the positioning of the needle isn't just right and has to be done over. I hate that.

"Everything seems to be in working order," my doctor said when he was finally finished.

"For a change," I said, as I lay there waiting for the clotting to finish after the tap. "No major trauma, lately," I joked.

"Let's keep it that way," he said. "We should have the results of your CSF test tomorrow. I'll send you an email." He hesitated, then said, "I hate that I'm about to say this, but can I ask you for a favor?"

"Uh, sure."

"Thanks," he said, slightly embarrassed. "It's actually for my daughter. She's going through a phase of fascination with metas." I chuckled as he pulled out the magazine from under his clipboard. "Would you mind?" he asked as he handed me a pen.

"Of course not!" I said, turning to the photos inside. "What's her name?"

"Jenna."

"How old is she?"

"Eleven," he said with a smile. He pulled out his wallet and removed a photograph, holding it out for me.

I looked at the girl, who wore an enormous smile on her face, eyes twinkling. "Wow. She looks a lot like I did at that age," I said.

"We signed her up for your fan club," he said, tucking the photo back in his wallet.

"Cool," I said, and made a mental note to talk with Macy about being more active in the fan club, beyond approving the emails she'd send under my name. I shook my head and turned my attention back to the magazine. I inscribed a little message to her and scrawled my signature before handing it back to him.

"Thanks," he said. "This might make up for her not receiving a letter from Hogwart's."

When I got home, I pulled out an old photo album from the depths of my closet. I flipped past the baby pictures until I found some from when I was about Jenna's age.

The resemblance really was striking. One photo in particular was a somewhat embarrassing shot that Dana took of me. I was dressed as a superhero. On my blue shirt was pinned a big, white letter "D" that I'd cut from a piece of felt. I had a blue domino mask that was too big for my face. Dana had let me use his terrycloth wristbands and headband that he wore when playing tennis. And a white towel "cape" completed the ensemble. I was striking a heroic pose.

I thought about the feeling I'd had when looking at Jenna's picture. I'd never seriously thought about having children, for any number of reasons. But I couldn't deny that I really did think of Sinta as a daughter, sometimes. I've always liked kids, but had never desired to be a mother. It was always a "maybe someday" thing, with "someday" being far in the future.

But I was fast approaching forty. And while I was in excellent physical shape, certainly healthy enough to carry a pregnancy to term, my eggs weren't young, anymore. And that's the real factor when it comes to the dangers of pregnancy at a later age.

I put the album aside. Then I got online and researched egg harvesting and cryogenic storage. Just in case the maternal urge ever became strong. And if it didn't, they could always be donated to someone in need.

There was one other factor that caused some of my teammates to resent me, and that was my involvement in the Nevada Incident. I was called upon every so often to assist in returning a discovered "replacement" to the other world. In a sense, I was still working for DHS, and possibly always would be, given the debt I owed them for not holding me responsible for Dr. Gray's death.

In mid-May, I was contacted by Captain Shepherd. "We have a bit of a problem," he said and explained that DHS agents had recently located another of the "replaced" and had attempted to take him through the portal, only to find that they could not pass through.

"You mean the portal is gone?" I asked.

"No," he said. "It's there, and our monitors show no change in the readings, but no one can pass through. Our team is stumped. I was hoping you and Jack could check it out."

"Why us?"

"Because you got it working again once before, I guess. I know it was different, but you're sort of our last resort."

"I see," I said. "I'll contact Jack."

"Already done," he said. "A car will pick you up at oh-eight-hundred tomorrow."

I didn't know why, but I hung up the phone with a feeling of dread.

Two

"All changes, even the most longed for, have their melancholy; for what we leave behind us is a part of ourselves; we must die to one life before we can enter another."

~ Anatole France

Joining a new team is like starting a new job. Lots of new faces. Lots of new policies and procedures. And lots of new toys.

Probably the coolest toy in the Gatekeepers' box was a private jet, a Cessna Citation X. This is one of the fastest passenger jets in the world, topping out in the neighborhood of 700 miles per hour. Kimera is one of five pilots on the team. As part of my orientation, she flew us from San Francisco to Los Angeles in little more than half an hour. We spent more time on the tarmac than in the air.

To be fair, ours isn't as cushy as the ones shown in the Cessna catalog. We sacrifice some luxury for utility, installing banks of equipment, a RoboDoc, and plenty of emergency supplies.

But since the flight to Groom Lake was a DHS endeavor, the jet wasn't an option. Instead, we were in the Sikorsky Jayhawk, a medium-range helicopter with a maximum speed that was a crawl, compared to the Cessna. Not that I was in a great hurry to get there. Jack didn't seem eager, either. He sat silently as Shepherd gave us a deeper understanding of the situation.

The portal had, of course, been under constant observation for the past year. But no one else ever came through from the other world in all that time. Most of the monitoring by this time was done remotely, in fact, as the machinery did all the data capture.

DHS teams had investigated the other world before the portal stopped admitting them, and verified that there was no apparent threat level. There was no sign of anything but desert anywhere around the portal on the other side. Because of these facts, the DHS physical presence in Nevada was scant.

In truth, I was more concerned with us invading that world than of any hostilities from their side. But I kept that to myself. I also wondered why it was that none of them ever reported an encounter with my double on their trips through the in-between. Doubtless, she had a monitoring system in place for just such eventualities. It wouldn't be hard for her to get out before they could locate her.

Shepherd and I caught up on personal matters during the flight, too. He had earned my trust and I genuinely liked the man. I was grateful for all he'd done for me in the time since the Bay Scouts disbanded. I'd even become friendly with his family.

"Sydney asked about you, the other day," Shepherd said. Sydney was Shepherd's older daughter, now in her second year at UCLA. His younger daughter, Layla, was a sophomore in high school. She wanted to follow her old man into government work, which didn't thrill her mother, Helena.

"Give her a hug for me," I said.

Shepherd smiled at me and then Jack. "When are the two of you going to settle down?"

I think Jack nearly swallowed his tongue. His eyes widened and he flushed a deep red. I said, "Oh, you know, I'm not the settling type."

Jack didn't speak for the rest of the flight.

As Shepherd had described, the portal looked no differently than it had when we'd last seen it. I looked over the exterior of the frame as Jack reached up and pushed his hand against the swirling interface. And, again as Shepherd had described, it sank in about an inch, but didn't go through.

"How odd," he said, pulling his hand back. "Let me see the monitor readings."

As he moved over to the computer, I stood next to Shepherd. And because I'm one of those people who has to see things for herself, I did as Jack did. I reached out and pushed against the swirl.

And I sank inside up to my forearm. I yanked it back, shocked, as Shepherd offered an astounded, "What the hell?"

Jack dashed back as I stared at my hand. Then he tried again, with no different result than before. "Do it again, Dyna."

So I did. And once again, my hand eased into the gelatinous miasma. I removed it, taking a step away from the machine. The men looked at me, just as confused as I was.

"What does this mean?" Shepherd asked.

We both turned to Jack, who frowned. "What are you looking at me for?"

"You're the physicist," I reminded him.

"Yeah," he said, "but I have no idea whatsoever, here. I mean, except for the obvious."

"What's obvious?" I asked.

"Well, that there's some way to make the portal selective. She wants you to come through, I guess. And only you."

I looked at both of them, eyes narrowed. "Yeah, fuck that." I turned and strode down the ramp from the portal to stand near the computer, arms crossed resolutely.

Eventually, the guys joined me.

"Dyna," Shepherd began, before I cut him off.

"No!"

He sighed. "We still have people who need to be sent back."

"Me going through won't let *them* get through."

"But you could find out what's going on with it, perhaps."

I glared at Shepherd, not liking him one bit at this particular moment. Then I let out a deep breath and hung my head. "Fine."

I hated the idea of going through and being cut off from communication with them. DHS had tried everything over the past year to maintain real-time contact with operatives who went through. Obviously, anything radio-based wouldn't work. They even tried wired communication, essentially a high-tech version of two cans connected by string. But for whatever reason, there was enough interference from the portal that made communication impossible. The best they could do was pass through a note on a long stick and wait for a reply. But that wouldn't be an option for me, as a stick could no longer pass through.

There really wasn't any preparation I could do for this. So, once Jack was sure the computer was all properly monitoring, I stepped up and oozed on through.

I emerged on the other side of the portal, my arm cocked and surging with power, ready to send flying anyone or anything that might be waiting. But there was no threat to greet me.

It was as I remembered it – the book cases, the computer desk. But it wasn't exactly the same. For one thing, the computer monitor was active. A screen-saver scrolled a string of letters – G O B A G – across the monitor's face. Paperwork lay scattered across the desk, in the form of spiral-bound notebooks, sticky notes, and scraps of various sizes. Several empty mugs sat near the keyboard, and the stench of coffee dregs was acrid in the air. On the floor near the desk was a large duffel bag, zippered shut.

I looked back at the portal, frowning at its noise. It was thrumming and knocking like an MRI, much louder than its counterpart on the other side, in my world.

"You get used to it," came a voice from behind me, sending a chill down my spine. I spun, energy flooding into my forearms, ready to blast forth with a thought. But I held it in check.

My other-self stood calmly in the doorway at the far end of the room, leaning casually against the door jamb, a steaming cup in her hand. I took in the image, letting the energy subside from my hands. This was the first time I'd seen "myself" in person. And it wasn't a pretty sight.

It wasn't the spiky, shag haircut, which I wouldn't be caught dead wearing. It wasn't the searing white tendrils of energy that flickered from her eye sockets, obscuring her eyes. Rather, it was the circuitry embedded in her flesh. It was in her face, and I could see it trailing down her neck, disappearing under the red blouse she wore. It ran up her arms from her hands, vanishing under the sleeves.

My feelings must have shown, because she nodded and said, "Yes, it was very painful." She took a sip from her cup. "And no," she continued, "it wasn't worth it." She gave a grim smile. "But it does work," she said. "Once the surgery was complete, my ability to control my energy flow increased dramatically. Recovery times were halved." She shook her head. "But still not worth it." She nodded toward me. "Nice outfit. It looks good on us."

Despite myself, I looked down at the blue cable-knit I was wearing with white Capris and silver belt. Then I frowned and looked "myself" in the eye. "Why did you bring me here?"

The woman raised an eyebrow. "I didn't bring you here."

"I don't mean literally," I snapped. "But you did something to the portal so that no one but me could come through. Obviously, you wanted me to come."

"I have no idea what you're talking about," she said. "Though I'm pleased to see you're doing well."

The simple compliment threw me, and I hesitated. Why was I being so confrontational? She hadn't done anything to me. In fact, if anything, I owed her thanks. But I was scared. I hated what had happened in this place, the last time I'd been there. Its very existence – *her* very existence – creeped me out.

"Thank you," I said. "And, I'm sorry. I'm not angry at you."

"No? You were ready to blast me into next week when you turned around a minute ago."

I just shrugged. "Sorry." I turned my gaze away. It was hard to look at her, to see the way the skin puckered where it was scarred around the implanted metal.

"Come on, then. Let me show you around."

"That's okay. I'm pretty familiar with the place." I forced myself to look at her again. "I just want to know what's going on. We've still got people to bring back here and no one but me is able to come through."

"Mm," she said. "Do you need to understand it right this minute? Aren't there some other things you're wondering about?"

She had me, there. Of course there were. Nearly everything about this world was unknown to me. The fact that I was having a conversation with another "me" freaked me out more than just a little. "Well, yeah," I said.

"Let's talk somewhere away from that noise," she said, and abruptly turned and left the room. I followed her down the hallway, through an open blast door, and around the corner into the main area of the facility. It looked much the same as when I'd last been there, with rack upon rack of weaponry. But we went off to a side corridor, into the kitchen, where she poured herself more coffee. She offered me some, but I declined. She leaned against the counter, cradling the cup near her face. "Look," she said, "I'm willing to answer your questions, but believe me when I say you really don't want to know some of the things you're going to ask."

Her voice was filled with an echo of pain, but there was one question I needed to ask, no matter what the answer was. Just the thought of it made my heart race. "Tell me," I said, "about the madness."

Even though I couldn't see her actual eyes, I knew she was staring into her cup. She was quiet for a moment, then nodded. "It's not really possible to say what the actual cause was," she said softly. "I mentioned the meningitis in my note to you. Then there's the addiction to painkillers I developed after this." She indicated the embedded circuitry with a sweep of her fingers across a cheek. "Or it could just be that I'm nuts."

"You don't seem nuts."

She nodded, then sipped her coffee. "It comes and goes. I've developed a sort of treatment. It helps when the meningitis flares up." Here she dropped her hand to her belt, which was studded with metal ampules about three inches long and half an inch wide.

"Anti-fungal drugs didn't help with your meningitis?" I asked.

"Did they for you?"

"Yeah."

She was silent for several seconds, looking at me with an expression I couldn't read. The energy leaking around her eyes made it nearly impossible. "I'm glad," she finally said. "Anyway, the medication keeps it fairly minor. It's my own concoction, based on years of experimentation." She smirked. "Some things never change, eh? But I do need regular injections."

I nodded, and since it was on my mind, said, "What's with the..." And I wiggled my fingers near my eyes.

She chuckled. "Freaky, right? I produce too much energy. More than I can contain. This is part of how it vents." And before I could ask, she said,

"And yes, it makes normal vision pretty difficult. I can repress it, with effort. But I typically see things differently, anyway."

I thought of my own ability to detect organic energy patterns and assumed she meant something similar. "So you live here, now?" I asked.

She nodded. "It's comfortable enough. It has power and the plumbing works. Just don't ask me where the power comes from or where the waste goes, though. These in-between spaces are really weird. Most importantly, it has a lab. I can make my medicine. Besides, I really don't have any other home to speak of."

"Wait. You said 'in-between *spaces*.' Plural. There are more?"

"Well, of course there are more. There are innumerable universes. Stands to reason more than one would intersect, doesn't it?"

"I guess," I said, my stomach turning.

"They're not usually as elaborate as this, from what I understand."

"You've been to them?"

"Not personally, no. But Ping Song said she'd been to five, including your world."

"How?"

"She built a machine that was able to detect the overlaps, somehow. I've no idea how she did it. Her abilities are far beyond my understanding."

"And are they... are we...?"

"They're all fairly similar, from what she saw. All of them are "earth," with the same countries, cities, and so on. Same gravity, the same atmospheres. The differences are mostly socio-political in nature, and in that regard, the others she visited were more like your world than mine. One of them, in fact, appeared to be devoid of metahumans altogether. Naturally, that's the one Valora wanted to invade. But that portal collapsed not long after Ping Song's return. Probably a good thing for that world, I'd say."

I was boggled. I'd been having a hard enough time accepting the existence of another Dinah Geof-Craigs. Now I had to accept that there could be a nearly infinite number of me out there. The one in front of me stared into her cup, then softly asked, "How's Rachel?"

A slight pang shot through my chest, but I forced a grim smile. "She's doing well, it seems. She went back to L.A."

"Oh. I'm sorry."

"It's okay. It's what she wanted. And it seems she's going to be in a movie."

Her eyes flashed. "A movie?"

I nodded. "A sort of remake of her old TV show, but with her as an adult, obviously."

"TV show?"

"Yeah. Wasn't your Rachel a child actress?"

She shook her head. "No. No, she wasn't." After a moment of silence, she said, "And Sinta?"

"She's great. She lives with me, now. She'll be glad to know you're doing well, too." She smiled, then I said, "Can we talk about the portal, now?"

She hesitated a moment, then said, "Sure." She put down her cup. "Let's go."

I turned and began following her back to the portal room. The conversation had crossed a line in my head, becoming too personal. I didn't want to like this woman.

We reached the blast door, and I noticed something I hadn't when we'd first passed by. The control panel on the base side of the door was destroyed, nothing but a slag of melted wires and broken circuit boards.

A little warning went off in the back of my mind, but before I could react to it, I was hit with a familiar feeling. My stomach fell and my brain spun. It felt as though I was being pulled in every direction at once. My vision blurred, and when it cleared, I was facing my double, who now stood next to the undamaged control panel on the other side of the doorway, while I was a few yards back from where I'd been.

I was utterly disconcerted. I stared at her, noting that she didn't seem surprised at all. And then she said simply, "Sorry, hon," and hit me with a blast that sent me flying backward. I crunched into the wall behind me and fell to my knees. I recovered quickly, but by the time I did so, the thick door was almost closed. I screamed and let loose with the heaviest blast I could muster, aimed dead center at the door. But it didn't put so much as a nick in the metal.

Three

"Perhaps everything terrible is, in its deepest being, something helpless that wants help from us."
~ Rainer Maria Rilke

I was an emotional little boy. A mama's boy, I suppose. So I certainly have never fit the stereotype of the cool and aloof scientist, unmoved by emotion. Of course, like most stereotypes, this image of emotionless people in white coats isn't accurate. The truth is, most scientists –including me – are quite emotional. We're simply moved by emotions of a different nature. We're in an almost constant state of amazement of the world around us. The more you know of how it works, I think, the more likely you are to be this way.

I'm a physicist who is emotional not only about my work, but about pretty much everything. My stoic front is an affectation many years in the making.

Of course, sometimes it's quite evident just how fragile that front is. "*I'm not the settling type,*" Dyna said on the flight. And it was like a gut punch. I knew she was aware that I was developing what were probably inappropriate feelings for her. And I knew she said that to Shepherd so I wasn't put on the spot by his question about us settling down. But it also reinforced the idea that she was out of my league.

I took a ribbing from friends who said she was gay, but held out hope that she wasn't entirely opposed to men. Foolishly optimistic of me, I suppose. But I've always been drawn to intelligent women. It didn't hurt when their brains were housed so attractively, of course.

In truth, I hadn't realized how strong my attraction to her was until she'd disappeared along with our other teammates, more than two years previously. I was worried about all of them, of course, but my concern for Dyna was almost crippling.

So when the other-world Dyna came through the portal, my heart caught in my throat and panic seized me. I was alone in the room, Captain Shepherd having gone to answer nature's call and grab us some coffee.

She stood on the platform, gazing around, a duffel bag slung over her shoulder. "Hello, Jack," she said when she saw me. She said it casually, familiarly, and it made my stomach churn. I was too flustered to reply, though I did manage to make my way over to her as she descended the ramp.

"What's going on?" I finally blurted.

"I need to get to San Francisco," she said, as though giving instructions to a cab driver.

"Where is she?" I asked, realizing how foolish the question was as soon as it was past my lips.

"She's fine, Jack. Let's just leave it at that."

"If you've hurt her..."

"Seriously? Are we going to waste time with all that? The sooner you help me, the sooner she comes home. She said you'd understand."

I was stunned by her bluntness. But I quickly realized that we were at her mercy. No one but she, apparently, could go through the portal to bring "our" Dyna back, so threatening her would do no good.

"What the hell?"

It was Shepherd. I turned to see him standing in the doorway, two paper cups of coffee in his hands and an expression of utter confusion on his face. I quickly explained. Captain Shepherd is a smart man. He understood the predicament as well as I did.

Twenty minutes later, we were aboard the helicopter, flying to San Francisco. And I wasted no time in trying to get as much information out of her as I could.

To my surprise, she told me things she couldn't have known, unless Dyna had told her, such as the fact that Dyna and Sinta shared an apartment. Or that Rachel was in Hollywood. I'd been concerned that Dyna had been attacked and imprisoned – or worse – in the in-between zone, but this was evidence that their meeting was at least semi-cordial.

Could she have gotten this information in another fashion? Maybe. She wasn't telepathic, though it's conceivable that there could have been a telepath with her. Beat it out of her? Not likely. Dyna would have given as good as she got, and this woman showed no signs of injury.

I said, "You'll understand if we're a bit concerned with why you're here."

She nodded. "Of course."

"And I hope you'll also understand that I'd prefer to remain with you, during your time here."

She turned and looked at me, her face inscrutable. The flickering plasma in her eyes made it impossible to read any feelings. "I do understand, Jack, but no."

"Why not?"

"Because I don't trust you." Before I could voice any offense, she said, "I am too familiar with your counterpart in my world. And, while I know you're not him, it's something I can't seem to get past." The Jack in her world had been consort to that world's Valora. I didn't have fond memories of him, myself. "Still," she said, "I have no wish to cause any paranoia on your part and company would be nice. I would like Sinta to be with me."

When Jack and Captain Shepherd showed up at the apartment with the "other" Dyna, I was surprised, but excited. I really liked her. She was always nice to me.

Jack tried to explain what was going on, but I don't think he actually knew. I knew he was worried about "our" Dyna. He really liked her. Like, *a lot.*

I wasn't worried. I knew she'd never do anything to hurt our friend. But I think I was the only one who felt that way.

So I agreed to be with her. We both knew I was supposed to watch whatever she did and let the others know about it. And that was okay, since I knew they were just being suspicious.

After the guys left, I made tea for us and we sat and talked. She asked me what I'd been up to since her last visit and I told her. When I asked how she'd been, all she would say was, "Just fine, kitten." And she told me about meeting "our" Dyna and said she was glad it finally happened.

"Why are you here?" I asked.

"Well," she said, "it's a bit complicated. I'm looking for some things."

"Like what?"

"Samples. Specimens. I'm doing some scientific research," she explained. "About your world."

"Why?" I asked, thinking that was weird.

She sipped her tea. "Oh, you know. Curiosity."

I didn't think she was telling me everything, but figured I couldn't make her say more. "So where will you get these samples?"

I was surprised when she said, "In the cave where your friend encountered the spores that made her sick."

So that's where we went, the next day. I had to check the old Bay Scouts logs to remember exactly where that cave had been. When we got there, it was all sealed up, but she blasted it open. Then she opened her bag and pulled out a big spray bottle. "This is an anti-fungal," she said. "When I come out, spray me head to toe with it." Then she pulled out a shoulder bag, a flashlight, a respirator mask, and a pair of those blue, stretchy gloves that doctors wear. She put on the mask and gloves and slung the bag over her shoulder. She made me stay behind as she went down inside.

She was in there for about an hour. I got a little nervous because, of course, we didn't have any communicators. But finally, she came back out.

As she'd asked, I sprayed her down, especially her face. Then she removed everything she'd taken with her, putting them back in the duffel. I put the bottle back in. "I really need a shower, now," she said.

"Did you find what you were looking for?" I asked as she closed the bag and lifted it.

"Maybe," she said. "We'll see."

She was quiet on the way back and didn't look very good. She seemed really tired. Back at the apartment, she took a shower and changed clothes, cleaning the ones she'd been wearing in our washer and dryer.

I'm not as smart as a lot of people, but I knew what was going on. She was still sick with the same disease that "our" Dyna had gotten in that cave. And she was trying to find a cure.

Over the next few days, we talked a lot. Mostly about me, because she never wanted to talk about herself or her world. And we did a lot of sight-seeing. She loved the water, so we went to the beaches. We went to Muir Woods, too, so she could see the redwoods.

"When will you be going back?" I asked her. We were sitting in the living room, playing cards.

"I don't know, kitten. I'm having such a good time here with you."

"I'm having a good time, too, but don't you need to work on your medicine?"

"I do. But that can wait."

I didn't understand that. How could she think it could wait? Wasn't she sick? Didn't she care? I looked at her belt, which had these metal things that held her medication. I only saw her use one once, and that was the day after she'd gotten here, just before we'd gone to the cave. And she was starting to talk a little funny.

She put down her cards. "I'm tired of this," she said. "Let's go out."

"Okay," I said. "What did you want to do?"

"I don't care! I'm just tired of being inside." She made a face, like she found the apartment unpleasant, all of a sudden.

So we went out.

I watched her as we walked along Page Street. I was worried. I remembered what she'd been like sometimes when she first came here. I noticed that, when she walked, she would play with the metal things on her belt, popping them off and snapping them back on.

"Isn't it about time for more medicine?" I asked.

"Doesn't feel like it," she said.

"Well, because you don't quite seem like yourself," I said. She didn't answer.

I'd been telling Jack everything we did, and that she was starting to behave strangely. He asked me to let him know if it got worse. I had a feeling I was going to have to tell him that, very soon.

"You know," I said, "Dyna shared with us the note you left her."

"Did she, really?"

"Mm hm."

"Can't say I remember a lot of what I wrote in that," she said, frowning. "But I do remember saying some nice things about you."

"Too nice, I think." I was embarrassed by what she wrote about me.

"You think wrong," she said, and reached over to give me a friendly squeeze.

We'd walked about a dozen blocks when she stopped by the elementary school on the corner of Webster. Some kids were playing on the basketball court behind the building. We watched them for a while. Or rather, she watched them. I watched *her*.

She looked so sad. I knew almost nothing about her life. Not much more than what she'd put in the note to my Dyna. So I had no idea what she was thinking as she watched the kids playing. And it didn't feel right to ask.

"Poor kids," she whispered, and I didn't know if she meant for me to hear it. "No idea what's coming."

Just then, a ball ricocheted off the edge of a backboard and came bouncing over at us. A boy chased after it. As it rolled up against the fence in front of us, he looked up and saw us. I'm used to people looking funny at me, and he did. But when he saw Dyna's face, he looked scared. He grabbed the ball and ran away, glancing back over his shoulder, like we were going to chase him.

"Don't stop!" Dyna yelled. Then, to herself, "Never stop running." Then she hung her head, looking suddenly tired.

"Dyna?" I said. "Are you—"

"I'm hungry," she said, turning away from the fence. "Where can we get a pastrami burger?"

"Um, let me check," I said, and pulled out the smartphone Dyna had bought me for my birthday. I already knew where to go for burgers. What I was really doing was texting Jack, letting him know where we were going to be and that she was acting weird. Then we set off for the restaurant.

My stomach sank when I read Sinta's text message. For her to say the other Dyna was acting "weird" meant we had a big problem. Sinta had previously told me that the woman hadn't been taking her medication. I didn't know how often she needed it, but assumed it was more frequently than "never."

Shepherd and I had discussed what to do in this eventuality. Both of us believed Sinta was too emotionally attached to this Dyna to judge whether she was dangerous or not, so it was up to me to make that determination.

We'd notified Kimera, as well, believing that someone from the Gatekeepers needed to know what was going on. Before leaving to meet Sinta, I relayed her message to both Kimera and Shepherd.

I found them at Burgermeister. It wasn't crowded, as it was mid-afternoon. Dyna's back was to the entrance, but Sinta saw me from their table. I strolled back to join them. Sinta was nibbling on some fries and Dyna had an enormous pastrami burger.

"Well, hi," I said. "Small world."

Sinta greeted me with feigned surprise as I sat with them. Dyna ignored me and continued eating. I sat there awkwardly, waiting for some reaction from the woman. Glancing around, I noted the stares aimed at them by patrons and staff alike. I wished Sinta hadn't brought her to a restaurant.

"Not eating?" Dyna finally said.

"I ordered," I said.

"No, you didn't. You came straight to our table."

I frowned at being caught in the lie. It's not that I'd forgotten that our Dyna had the ability to sense others without looking at them. I just didn't know this one could also do that, or that she'd be able to identify me, coming from behind her at a distance.

"And you have Kimera waiting for us outside."

Sinta glanced toward the window, a look of alarm on her face. "Jack?" she said, a look of betrayal in her eyes. My heart began to race.

"It's okay, kitten," Dyna said, putting down her burger. "I expected nothing less. And I don't blame *you*, Jack," she added. Then she frowned and rubbed her temples. "Still, I don't know what you hope to gain."

I decided to cut to the chase. "When's the last time you took your medicine, Dyna?"

She turned those awful eyes upon me and, despite myself, I pulled back slightly. "Why so concerned? Afraid I'll have one of my episodes and wreck the restaurant? Or disappear, so you'll never see my weaker self again?"

I bristled at her description of our Dyna. "Well, now that you mention it..."

With a disturbingly casual shrug, she said, "Not that you'd be seeing her for much longer, anyway." Before either of us could question what she meant by that, she pushed her food away, wiped her mouth, and dropped the napkin on the table. "Excuse me a moment," she said. Then she stood and walked toward the exit. Sinta and I exchanged glances, then followed her.

No sooner were we out the door than we saw Dyna lash out with a heavy blast that took Kimera by surprise, knocking her off her feet and into the street. Traffic screeched and swerved to avoid hitting her. Then Dyna took off into the air.

We ran to Kimera. "*Gae saeki*," she swore in Korean as she got to her feet, rubbing her ribs. "That hurt."

We stared into the sky after her, but Dyna was quickly out of sight.

I felt terrible. Dyna was gone and it was all my fault. I should have told Jack sooner that she'd been acting funny. We stood there in front of the burger place, people staring at us. Kimera got on her communicator and told her teammates what was going on.

Our Dyna had told me that she and Kimera got along great, but that some of the other Gatekeepers weren't so friendly to her. I wondered how those people would think of her now, given this whole situation.

She told us the Gatekeepers would take care of looking for Dyna and that she'd let both of us know when she was spotted. I told her they shouldn't hurt her, since she wasn't dangerous. She said she couldn't make any promises. I understood that, but it bothered me.

I hadn't met many other members of the Gatekeepers since Dyna joined them. Kimera was a little scary looking, with her snakey eyes and the big horns. At least her fangs didn't show all the time. She seemed much nicer than the version of herself from the other place. Some people make fun of me because my face looks like a cat, with the fur and whiskers and everything. But at least most people like cats. Not many people like snakes. I bet Kimera got made fun of a lot more than I did when she was little. Unless the other kids were too afraid to tease her.

As she left, Jack said to me, "What did she mean when she said we wouldn't be seeing our Dyna for much longer?"

I looked up at him, my heart hurting. "It means she thinks our Dyna is dying," I told him. "Just like this Dyna is." I felt bad for saying it. Jack loved Dyna, after all. But he did ask.

I wanted to find her before the Gatekeepers did. And even though there were a whole bunch of them and only one of me, I figured I had a better chance, since I knew her better. We'd spent a lot of time together when she was here, last, and I knew what areas of the city she liked.

I went home, first, but she wasn't there. Next, I checked Kirby Cove. We'd gone there a few times. The view of the Golden Gate Bridge from there is really great. And she liked its beach, too. But she wasn't there, either.

I went everywhere I could think of. All the beaches. Most of the parks. But of course, all these places were big. Even if Dyna had visited them, the chances of her being there at the same time as me were pretty small.

I got home that night, worn out, hoping she'd be there. But she still wasn't. And in the morning, I took my bike and did it all again, feeling more and more frustrated and sad with each hour.

In the middle of the afternoon, I got a text from Jack. "The Gatekeepers want to see us," it said.

I'd never been to the Gatekeepers' Citadel, before. But Kimera told us their team felt they needed to be involved in this. So Sinta and I met her at their headquarters, on the west side of the Presidio, where a small leadership meeting had been called.

Dyna had told me about their base and I admit I was envious when she described their lab facilities. The building was just as impressive as she'd described it, the great entrance hall adorned with many columns, mostly Ionic, as well as paintings and Romanesque sculptures of current and former members of the Gatekeepers. Oddly, the sculptures weren't plain white marble, but brightly painted. "I guess they're more concerned with making the statues look more like today's metas than like historical sculptures."

"No," Sinta said. "They were painted back then, too. Or a lot of them, anyway."

"That's right," Kimera said.

"What?" I looked between the two.

Sinta nodded. "The Greeks and Romans painted a lot of their sculptures in bright colors. The only reason most people don't know it is because the paint has worn off most of them."

"Interesting," I said, having forgotten how much Sinta likes to read.

"In fact," Kimera said, "the outlandishly painted statues then would make today's most garish meta costume look positively pedestrian."

Kimera escorted us into the elevator, where she held her thumb on a scanner and pushed the button for the top floor. We got off and went into the Legate's office. There were three other Gatekeepers present, in addition to Invictus. We were introduced first to a gray-eyed, auburn-haired woman around my age who spoke with a London accent. She went by the name of Nexus and wore royal blue leggings with a black, iridescent top that sparkled in rainbow colors with every movement. Next was one of the Prefects of the group, a woman called Bloodmoon. She stood about six feet tall with dark hair pulled back under a red bandana. Her darkish skin spoke of a mixed background. She had a friendly demeanor that seemed out of place on someone with what looked like a shotgun strapped across her back. The final Gatekeeper was the Legate himself, Invictus. He wore a white, knee-length tunic, decorated with purple and gold trim, cinched with a gold belt. The tunic, I knew, hid Kevlar armor underneath. He was even more impressive in person than in the news clips.

After introductions, Invictus hit us with the question I knew was coming. "Why was this woman not more closely guarded? No disrespect to Sinta, but she can't fly, after all."

I nodded. "Given her somewhat spotty behavior and her potential for violence," I said, glancing at Kimera, "we didn't want to do anything that might upset her. We need her to return to her world, which is something we cannot force her to do, under the present circumstances. To make her feel at ease, I thought it best that she stay with Sinta, as she'd requested." Anticipating his next question, I said, "She would destroy any tracking mechanism we placed on her. She's a proud and stubborn woman, much like our own Dyna."

Invictus nodded. "As I understand it," he said, "the return of Dynamistress is dependent not only upon getting her double to go through the Nevada portal, but also through a second portal into her own world."

"That's correct," I said. "And we can't get in, so the only way this will happen is of her own accord."

"Just how dangerous is this woman?" Invictus asked.

"I wish I could give a definitive answer," I said, "but she is mostly an unknown."

"Your reports indicate that she herself was not actively involved in the Nevada Incident," he said.

"Not in the same respect as the others, no," I confirmed.

"And yet," Bloodmoon interrupted, "you say that she manipulated the portal to prevent any others from passing through, and you took this to mean that she wanted Dynamistress to enter."

I hesitated before nodding. "That was my interpretation," I said. "Although it could just as easily have been a situation where she somehow programmed the portal to allow only herself to go through. That our Dyna could also do so might have been an unavoidable consequence."

"Either way, that seems an aggressive action," she said.

"But it isn't!" Sinta insisted, and all eyes turned to her. "She needed to come here! She had research to do! And this was the only way she could come here without everyone freaking out and thinking we were having another 'incident' like last time."

"This is what she told you?" Invictus said.

Sinta nodded. "And she said she explained all this to our Dyna."

Nexus spoke for the first time, asking the obvious. "Then why couldn't she have had Dyna poke her head through first to explain that it was all hunky dory?"

Sinta's face fell and her ears seemed to flatten against her head as she shrugged. "I don't know," she mumbled.

"Well," I said, "the interface is more like a tunnel than a window. It's not possible to reach through to the other side, only to go through completely. Which, I imagine, the other Dyna would not have permitted ours to do."

There followed a period of awkward silence as we all looked at each other, concern on all our faces. Even Sinta's.

"And has the woman completed her research?" Invictus asked.

"I don't know," Sinta said. "She hasn't done any since the day after coming here."

"And she's not been taking her meds," I added. "So her mental state is even less stable than usual."

Nexus turned to me. "How unstable are we talking about, luv?"

"Well, she sort of detaches from reality. She hallucinates. Occasionally talks to fire hydrants, from what I understand."

"Schizophrenia?" Bloodmoon asked.

"No," I said. "All indications are that her brain has been affected by a disease similar to what Dyna contracted a few years ago." I paused, debating whether to volunteer the next bit of information. With a glance at Sinta, I said, "And Sinta believes this disease is killing her."

Invictus frowned. "How sure of this are you, Sinta?"

The girl spoke softly. "She hasn't come right out and said so, but things she has said make it sound like she expects to die if she can't find a cure. But she will. She will find a cure."

My heart truly ached when she said this. Sinta was so fond of the other-world Dyna that she couldn't accept the possibility of losing her. Which, I admit, was rather how I felt when Sinta brought up the possibility that our Dyna might also be dying.

After the meeting with the Gatekeepers ended, Sinta and I departed. It was beginning to get dark, but I desperately wanted to find Dyna. "Want to take one more stab at finding her?" I asked Sinta.

"Yes."

"Okay. Where's your instinct tell you to look?" I asked as we walked to my car.

She thought for a while, then said, "Kirby Cove. We went there, the first time she visited. And the bridge will be all lit up and pretty."

Visited. That's how Sinta regarded it. "I assume you've looked there."

"Twice. But third time's the charm, right?"

Kirby Cove is directly across the water from the Presidio. So we crossed the bridge, parked, and took the footpath down to the beachfront. It was chilly and breezy. The beach was deserted, save for a figure sitting cross-legged in the sand, staring out over the water.

"Hello, kitten. Jack," she said as we approached.

Sinta bounded over to her and gave her a hug. I stopped several feet away. "Dyna," I said.

"Are you okay?" Sinta asked.

"Not dead, yet."

"Don't talk like that!"

I stepped forward. "Have you finished your research?"

She turned her freakish eyes upon me. "You know research is never truly finished, Jack. I may be a while."

I frowned. "When are we going to see *our* Dyna again?"

She paused, as if in thought. "I could grow my hair long and smile more."

"That's not funny," I said.

She stood, walking over to stand in front of me. "No. No, it wasn't. I'm sorry." Then she smiled. "Now *this* is funny!" And she hooked her pinkies inside the corners of her mouth, pulled them wide, stuck out her tongue, and gobbled like a turkey. Abruptly, she stopped. "Or maybe it isn't," she said and turned her back to me.

Angry, I reached out and grabbed her shoulder, intending to spin her around. Only after I began to tug did I realize just how foolish an action it was. She whirled on me, energy surging from her eyes, one hand knocking mine from her shoulder, the other cocked back and radiating energy, ready to deliver a crushing blow.

I tensed up and prepared to drain whatever energy I could from her, knowing it was probably too late for that to make much difference. But no blow came.

"Look!" she said, moving her glowing fist through the night air in big, swooping arcs, her energy leaving a faint trail behind her hand. "I can write my name in the sky!"

Sinta and I looked at her with sympathy and irritation, respectively. Then Dyna looked at Sinta and said, "Race you home!" And she blasted into the sky.

We watched her soar across the water, then trudged back to my car. Unsurprisingly, when we got to the apartment, Dyna wasn't there.

FOUR

"When you have eliminated the impossible, whatever remains, however improbable, must be the truth."
~Sir Arthur Conan Doyle

No matter what the public sentiment toward metahumans is – good or bad – perhaps the most significant "gift" they've given the world is a deep and thorough re-examination of the laws of nature. As I've said before, if you can't show that something is fake, you have little choice but entertain the idea that it's real.

Even so, for me there's a big leap between the idea that a person can fly, which is something many creatures do naturally, and the idea that someone can, as if by magic, pull another being instantaneously from one point to another. And as I leaned against the wall, staring impotently at the closed blast door, I had to entertain the impossible idea that my double had, indeed, somehow teleported me.

I'd been walking ahead of her, nearly to the door, and then was behind her, a dozen feet away from it, with no apparent gap in awareness beyond the moment of disorientation and that feeling of being pulled in all directions at once. It was just like I'd felt when I'd been taken from my world to hers that very first time.

But more than wondering over this incredible ability of hers, I felt like a fool for believing she was different, for being taken in by her friendly demeanor, and by the fact that she and Sinta had their own mutual admiration society.

I stepped over and looked again at the control panel, confirming that it was beyond repair. The circuit boards weren't merely broken. Scorch marks indicated they were fried.

Then I remembered what my teammates had told me about my double's abilities, which was confirmed by my recent exposure to them. They weren't identical to my own. Rather than being solely a sort of concentrated plasma burst, like my own, hers included another form of plasma – a weak lightning. Her blasts were forceful and shocking, both. Turning away from the door, I decided to more thoroughly explore my new home, since there was no telling how long I'd be there.

Most of what I saw, I remembered from before. But there were some changes, obviously made by my counterpart. The biggest one was the laboratory. Most of the equipment there was familiar. But there were a couple machines completely foreign to me, including one that appeared to be a body scanner of some sort, but was like no MRI or CT scanner I'd ever seen.

I found a book, too. Her notes. I leafed through it quickly, but wasn't in the frame of mind to read it, yet. I continued my explorations, returning to the kitchen. Thankfully, the fridges and freezers were full, as were the cupboards. The coffee was mediocre, but at least it wasn't instant. I had no idea where to obtain food and didn't relish the idea of exploring her world to find a supermarket.

I checked out the sleeping quarters, finding that she'd chosen the one bunk in the large room that had a modicum of privacy. I assumed it had belonged to the leader of the paramilitary group that had previously occupied this place. I wondered why they hadn't reclaimed the facility. Perhaps my double had closed the other portal to anyone but herself, too.

A large footlocker sat next to the wall. It held a few changes of clothes and some books. A couple more books sat on the floor next to a standing lamp. She obviously liked to read before sleep.

And listen to music, too. On her pillow was what looked like a black digital music player and a pair of ear buds. Out of curiosity, I turned it on and scrolled through the contents on the tiny screen. I couldn't help but smile to see familiar names. Evidently, this world's music scene paralleled mine. Her player was like the library of a classic rock radio station, filled with The Beatles, Deep Purple, Led Zeppelin, The Doors, Jimi Hendrix, and much more. Strangely, none of the music on the machine was more recent than what would have been the late 70s in my world. I didn't know how time matched up, though. My double had said she was a few years older, but I'm not sure that even mattered. Maybe she just didn't like any music made after 1980. Or maybe it was around that time that her world went to hell and the music industry was one of the casualties.

I looked through her books. Sadly, they all appeared to be novels. Not that I have anything against fiction, but I was curious about the history of her world and had hoped for something that would have given me some perspective.

Eventually, I rediscovered the office back in the corner near the detention cells. I tried not to look at the cells as I walked by. I still had nightmares about finding Valora's lifeless body there in a pool of blood and piss. But, looking at them or not, my heart was heavy as I passed.

I sat at the desk and jiggled the computer mouse, bringing up the monitor's screen saver. It was the same one as on the other computer – a string of letters forming no discernible word: G O B A G. And naturally, the machine was password protected.

I tried a couple of the passwords I often use, on the off chance that she might use the same ones. But no luck. I even tried "GOBAG" itself in various iterations – in caps, lower case, with and without spaces, and so on. Nothing. I rubbed my forehead, suddenly exhausted.

Did she really mean to abandon me? I don't think I ever consciously believed that, but in the end, it didn't matter. She'd trapped me. And whether it was intended to be temporary or permanent, I didn't like it. And what if my teammates couldn't or wouldn't subdue her? I needed to be proactive about this, not just sit back and wait.

I had to get the door open. The computer almost certainly held a way to do that, despite the wall controls being destroyed. If not, the only way to get to the portal would be to blast through the solid rock walls. And I didn't even think that was within the scope of my abilities.

In my nightmare, I stand in front of a judge's bench, my hands cuffed in front of me. To my left, the jury box is filled with familiar faces – Scoutmaster, Invictus, Dana, Sinta, Valora, Rachel, and more. But as I look at them, all their faces change into mine. I look back and see the judge is also me.

"Dinah Geof-Craigs," the judge-me says, "you have been found guilty by a jury of yourselves of the murder of Philip Raymond Gray. You are hereby sentenced to life in a prison of your own making, with no chance of parole."

Two security officers take me by the arms. They are both me, as well. Suddenly, I'm behind bars, the prison guard (also me)smirking as she locks me in and walks away. I turn to look at my cell and see I'm not alone. I have a cellmate, who stares at me with intense disapproval.

My cellmate is Dr. Gray.

I jolted awake in a cold sweat, my heart pounding and my guts churning. I looked around, expecting to see the walls of my cell, until I realized it was just a dream. Not that the living reality was much better. I was still imprisoned, just in a much larger cell.

When I calmed down, I rolled onto my side and turned on the lamp near her bed. I pulled out her lab journal and, over the course of the day, read it through.

It was a strange mix of experimental data and personal diary. None of the entries were dated, but the earliest ones seemed to be during the days she was with Valora and company.

I found myself sympathetic when I read the accounts of her illness. Many of the scientific entries were her experiments in trying to eradicate the disease. Nothing was very surprising. I would have taken the same approaches she had.

The disturbing part of her journal was that many of the entries were clearly made when she wasn't in the most stable frame of mind. These entries rambled off on wild tangents, were repetitive, and sometimes degenerated into near incoherency. She wrote often of physical pain.

One unfamiliar word kept popping up in her entries – *Neukölln*. Aside from the name of a David Bowie song, I had no idea what that was. I couldn't even figure it out from the context. Sometimes she seemed to refer to it as a place, sometimes almost as a person. But always in the past tense, as though the person died or the location, I don't know, sank into the sea or something.

I read with interest her progress on pursuing a cure for her particular form of meningitis. The journal contained five or six different formulae for medicines. I thought it was strange that I could locate no hypodermics in the lab. Surely it wasn't taken orally.

Then I remembered the belt she wore and how she'd indicated it when talking about her illness. In a refrigerator in the lab, I found a box of the strange, metal ampules that had adorned the belt. Upon inspection, I noticed one end narrowed to a point and had a tiny hole in the tip. On two opposite sides of the cylinders were small indentations. I held one of them over the sink and squeezed it on these spots. There was a popping sound and a needle shot out the tip, extending about half an inch. The medicinal contents followed, coming out in steady drops. The ampules were obviously pressurized by the mixing of two substances that formed a gas. Vinegar and baking soda, maybe, or something more volatile. Pretty ingenious. I thought about taking one apart, but honestly wasn't that curious.

What did inflame my curiosity, though, was my other-self's apparent teleportation ability. It was occupying more and more of my thoughts. Her words came back to me, about how she saw things "differently." The ability to detect organic energy is a part of my abilities that I've never understood, and maybe never will. But I knew this had to be tied to her teleportation abilities, somehow.

When I detect the energy of another creature, it's more than just "seeing" it. It's a physical sensation, but I honestly can't describe it well. The closest analogy I can make is a stronger version of that feeling you get when you're certain someone is staring at you. And maybe that meant there was some sort of actual connection between all living things and I was able to detect it, to a limited degree.

So did that mean my other-self was not only able to detect this connection, but to latch onto it and somehow pull it toward her? What kind of freakish physics would even allow such a thing?

In the end, I decided, it didn't matter if I understood how she did it. The fact is, she did. I'd already determined that our abilities weren't identical, though, so there was no guarantee I could ever do it.

My counterpart might read or listen to music to fall asleep, but I tended to just think. The first few nights, I was preoccupied with getting home, and my brain was awhirl with all that business. Well, that and the nightmares I was having. I also thought about what I'd do when I got home, and those thoughts mainly involved Dana and K.T.

I decided I was a fool with regard to both of them. With Dana, I needed to stop being upset about not seeing him as often as I'd like. He'd taken more than a decade after his marriage ended before putting his heart out there again. He deserved a good relationship. He deserved to be happy.

And so did I. I hadn't truly been in a satisfying relationship since college, with Sharon and Jackie. Lee was a friend and shouldn't have become more than that. And Rachel was... I'm not sure. What we had was comfortable and pleasant, but not really romantic, and barely sexual. I always knew it wasn't what she was looking for.

So I was going to tell K.T. how I felt. My stomach got all fluttery when I thought about doing so. But she was amazing. And it was clear that she was into me. She called me just as often as I called her. And when she looked into my eyes, I just melted. How could I *not* take a chance again?

I took to listening to her music quite a lot. All my life, music had been so important to me, but over the past several years, I'd found less and less time in the day to listen to it. When I was young, I listened to Dana's collection, which was the same classic rock I saw on my other-self's little player. During college and after, though, those old favorites took a back seat to expanding tastes.

I smiled as I browsed the player's list, seeing so many albums by Alice Cooper. It took me back to my college years, working at Xeno's, reciting song lyrics with Brent behind the bar. And meeting Lee.

I saw one particular album in the list and immediately played it. *From the Inside*, Cooper's final album of the seventies. I remembered when I'd first heard it. I was seven or eight years old when Dana brought it home from the store. It was the first Cooper album he'd purchased.

We would often listen to his new acquisitions together. But not this time. "I don't think you'll like it," he said. Then, seeing my pout, he said, "Well, there's one song you might like." And he played for me a very pretty ballad from the album. I'd heard Dana sing it in the shower. But then, it was a love song, and he was fourteen or fifteen and hung up on some girl at school.

One night when he was out, I decided to listen to the whole album. I put the vinyl record on the stereo, pulled out the album sleeve with the lyrics, and plugged in the headphones. Our parents didn't approve of most of Dana's music, and I didn't want them to know I was listening to this.

It was much harder rock than I was used to hearing and, at first, I didn't care for it a bit. But I was curious about it. Dana had described it as a "concept album," where all the songs were based on the same theme, or about similar events or something. I didn't really understand, but as I listened, and read the lyrics, I got it. It was all about inmates at an asylum. That was kind of creepy, but even at that age, I found it fascinating.

My favorite song on the album was the final track. It had a chorus I found amusing the first time I heard it. "*We're all crazy... we're all crazy... we're all crazy.*" I knew it wasn't meant to be funny, though.

And as I lay there on my other-self's bunk, listening to that song, I found myself singing along. Then a shock ran through me. I sat bolt upright, my breath stuck in my throat. I jumped up and ran to the computer.

I sat and punched a button on the keyboard, bringing up the request for the password that had stumped me for so long. The letters scrolled across the screen, taunting me. It was a clue, I realized. She couldn't fully trust her own memory, so she needed a prompt. And I'd just figured it out. G O B A G.

"*Good old boys and girls,*" I sang quietly, "*congregating, waiting in some other world...*"

I typed in the song's title – INMATES. The screen saver disappeared, replaced by the desktop window. The background picture was the cover of the album. "We're all crazy," I said with a laugh, then shook my head. "Some of us more than others, though." My love for Alice Cooper increased tenfold that day.

It took a while to familiarize myself with the computer layout, but I soon found the system directory and began exploring. Shortly, I found the program that controlled the portal mechanism. There were many subfolders, one of which immediately jumped out at me. It was labeled "Tuning."

I clicked on it, to find a single file, a large document named "BRT." I opened it to find a several-hundred page book, which told me that BRT stood for Biometric Resonance Tuning. It didn't take long for me to realize that this was how she'd forced the portal to admit just me.

She'd said there were other portals. They must have known about them here for quite a while for there to be this massive book explaining how to control them. This, of course, raised a lot of questions. The main one in my head was if something this significant had been so well-studied, where was everyone? My other-self's letter to me had said the in-between was occupied by a paramilitary group, which they got rid of. But I found it hard to believe that such technology would have been abandoned. Surely they would have returned.

On the other hand, the letter also stated just how sorry a state this world was in. Perhaps this wasn't considered a high priority, any longer. Or maybe they'd gotten what they wanted out of our world. I didn't know whether to be scared or comforted by that thought.

The book revealed to me what the strange scanner was in her lab. There were a dozen body scans necessary to tune the portal to a single individual. Information from the scans was transformed by the computers into a unique electronic code, like a fingerprint, that the scanners in the portal's frame would read. And if the "print" of the body trying to come through didn't match, it would somehow prevent the person from passing. I had to assume that our bodies were similar enough, despite cosmetic differences, to allow me to pass when no one else could. And she evidently knew, or suspected, that would be the case.

In time, I figured out how to deactivate the BRT override on the portal. Then I found the controls for both blast doors. I opened the one she'd closed, then confirmed that the one at the other end of the complex was open. And then I changed the password on the computer.

The BRT document would have taken nearly a ream of paper to print, so I copied it to a USB drive I found in a drawer. It looked to have the same size connector as those used in my world, so I hoped it would work. I photocopied her notebook and snagged a couple ampules of her medication. Then I walked through the now open blast door, closing it behind me. Finally, standing before the portal, I smiled.

"Surprise, bitch."

And I stepped through into my own world.

FIVE

"Loneliness is being surrounded by love and feeling abandoned."
~ Shane Pendley

When I was thirteen, I ran away from home. I was tired of fighting with my mother, tired of my father's apathy, tired of Dana being away at college. I don't even remember what emboldened me to take such an action, but one Friday in the summer, while Dad was at work and Mom was at the grocery store, I packed a bag and headed out the door.

Naturally, I headed straight to my friend Rhonda's house. I took the back way, avoiding most roads by crossing the abandoned railroad trestle at the end of our street, over the creek and along the old tracks through the woods before coming out across town near Rhonda's neighborhood. Once on the roads again, I felt uncomfortable, walking around with an overnight bag in the open. Grown-ups driving by stared at me. I turned my head, not wanting to be recognized. I hoped they'd think only that I was headed to a sleepover. Which, I suppose, is what I really thought I was doing, too.

Rhonda's mother, I knew, would call mine immediately. And she did. I heard her make the call as soon as Rhonda and I went down to their family room in their split-level home. I didn't care. It's not like they could force me to go home.

But not long after, their doorbell rang. I expected my father and was prepared to give him an earful. But when we went upstairs at her mother's beckoning, Rhonda and I were shocked to find the town's Chief of Police standing there.

To this day, I'm not sure how he came to be there. Had her mother called the cops instead of my folks? Did my parents do it? And I don't think I ever really heard what he said to me there at Rhonda's house. I just remember being scared to death. Was running away a crime? Was I going up the river?

In the end, I agreed to be driven home, though I half-believed the Chief was going to take me to jail, instead. We did make one stop before going to my house, but it wasn't the police station. It was the convenience store. He went in and came out a minute later with two cups – a coffee for himself and a root beer for me. And then we sat there and talked.

I expected him to lecture me, but he only asked me why I ran off. So I told him. Everything. About how I never felt my mother really loved me. How my father was so distant. And all the while, he just sat there, nodding. And when he'd finished his coffee, he reached into his pocket and handed me his business card. "If things ever get bad again to the point of needing to run away, just call me."

I didn't ask why. I didn't ask what he'd do about it. I just took the card and thanked him. And then he drove me home, where he walked me up to the front door. I felt ashamed, but relieved at the same time. My father was home from work by now. He talked quietly with the Chief, then thanked him, and that was that. Neither he nor my mother mentioned the little escapade. Ever. I've never understood why.

But those mixed emotions were with me again when I came through the other side of the portal. I was still angry, of course, but mainly relieved to be back. I walked down the ramp and saw a DHS agent waiting for me. He nodded, then pulled a two-way radio from his belt and said into it, "She's back."

A moment later, a weary Captain Shepherd hurried into the room, a look of relief on his face that I'm sure was more profound than mine. "You don't know how glad I am to see you," he said.

"Why? Layla need help with her biology homework?"

He frowned at my feigned nonchalance. "Your double tried to convince us that you were okay with her being here."

And for a moment, I was like my parents, not wanting to discuss the truth of what had happened. So I nodded and said, "Yeah. It's fine."

"Fine?" he said, his frown intensifying.

"I'll explain on the way home," I said. "Think I could get a lift?" Just like thirteen.

On the helicopter back to San Francisco, Shepherd grilled me. For reasons not even clear to me, I deflected his questions. "Didn't she explain why she was here?" I said.

"Something about research."

I nodded. "Well, there you go."

"And what were you doing the whole time?"

"Mostly reading. Listening to music. Shooting a little pool. Catching up on my sleep."

Shepherd frowned at me. "That why you look exhausted?"

"I reset the system so you'll be able to get others through again. But make sure you close the blast door before you come back through," I said, giving him the password I'd created.

Shepherd stared at me for a long moment. I could practically hear him screaming in his head. Then he sighed and rubbed his eyes. "Why I trust you, I'll never know."

"It's my sparkly blue eyes."

"Yeah, that must be it."

I begged off on further conversation and fell asleep almost immediately.

I was famished by the time we got to the city. Shepherd had driven me from the air station and I had him drop me off at the pizza joint in my neighborhood that shares a name with that awful Kurt Russell movie, where I picked up two extra-large pies. Then I walked the couple blocks to my apartment. It was nearly midnight by the time I trudged up the stairs. I heard voices from inside as I reached the door. Sinta and Jack.

I unlocked the gate and went upstairs, where I knocked on my door. Jack answered. "Hi," I said. "That'll be fifty-one fifty." The look of shock on his face was priceless. "I know," I said. "Crazy, huh?"

Sinta almost knocked the pizzas from my hands as she tackle-hugged me. Not that it would have mattered. At those prices, I'd have eaten them off the floor before throwing them out.

We sat in the living room eating and talking until nearly two, bringing each other up to speed on what had gone on while I was away. I told them the truth about what had happened, but stressed that I'd been less than forthright with Shepherd.

"She's dying, isn't she?" Sinta asked.

I measured my words carefully. "She's very sick, sweetie. But she's working on a cure. I've read her notes, so I know how much effort she's putting into it."

She nodded, then said, "She thinks you're dying, too."

I shook my head. "I'm not."

"You're sure?"

"Positive. Last checkup was clean."

"Okay." She smiled, then yawned. "Gonna go to bed," she said, then gave both of us hugs and headed to her room.

Jack watched her head down the hallway, then motioned for me to follow him outside onto the fire escape, where we stood quietly for a minute in the darkness. "Look," he finally said, "I don't know why you're covering for her. I'm sure you have your reasons. But you'd better be dead serious about your story when you talk to Invictus. Your teammates are none too happy about this whole thing."

"I can imagine," I said. We stood looking at the city for a minute, then I said, "Thanks, Jack."

"For what?"

"For everything. For always believing in me, even when you don't believe me." I gave him a hug. He squeezed me tightly. I looked up at him and saw more in his eyes than I'd hoped. I knew how he felt about me. And though I hated having to do so, I needed to defuse it. "Ya big galoot," I said, and made an energy fist in mock threat.

He backed off in feigned terror, holding up his hands, palms out. I looked at my glowing hand as I poked at him. "Hey, look," I said, swinging my arms in big loops in the darkness, trails of energy following my fist. "I can write my name in the sky!"

Jack gave me a look I couldn't quite read, shaking his head. Then he kissed my forehead, wished me a good night, and left. I watched him go, then turned my gaze out over the city.

A cool breeze hit me and I thought of how different things were beginning to feel. The wind of change, maybe? I didn't know whether the coming change was good or bad, but I could definitely feel it.

I could also feel several days of grime on me. So I headed inside, where I took a luxuriously hot shower. Shampooing my hair had never been so delicious. And my night shirt felt so soft against my skin, after wearing the same clothes for days.

Back in the living room, I cleared up the pizza remains before going to bed. I took a step toward the window to the fire escape, but decided to leave it open.

For the breeze.

I slept late the following day, waking just before noon. I ate leftover pizza for breakfast while chatting on the phone with Dana. I briefed him on what had happened over the past week. He took it fairly well, but I know he worries a lot about me. He seemed distant, though, and that bothered me. It wasn't like him.

After that, I called K.T. and asked her if she was free for dinner. We made arrangements to meet at Allegro Romano, one of her favorite restaurants. Then I called and got a reservation for their best table. Being a Gatekeeper certainly had perks.

Then I suited up in the blue and whites and headed out. It felt good to be in the air. I felt full of purpose as I blasted through the sky, giddy with the promise of a new day and a happier life. I keyed my radio to my team's private band and announced my return. "Goooood morning, Gatekeepers!"

A moment later, amid the chorus of subdued greetings, Kimera's rasp broke through. "Your chrono's broken," she said. "It's almost two o'clock."

"Well, dip me in chocolate and throw me to the lesbians! So it is!" Laughter filled my ear, mixed with some shocked expressions.

"Welcome back, dear," came Bloodmoon's warm voice.

"Good to be back," I said.

"Dynamistress." The firm, deep voice belonged to Invictus. "Debrief. Now."

"Yes, sir," I said, changing my trajectory toward the Citadel as the radio chatter went silent.

I met Invictus in his private office. Bloodmoon, Kimera, and Nexus were with us as I told them about my experience and was informed of what had gone on in my absence. Then Invictus dismissed the others and asked me to remain.

I'd never been entirely sure what Invictus thought of me. He was a difficult man to read. His facial expression rarely changed from stern seriousness.

Finally, he cleared his throat. "From what you described, it sounds as though you did an adequate job of preventing this from happening again. Assuming she does not find a way to get around your password."

"Well, our knowledge bases seem to be similar," I said. "I have no idea how to do that, so I'm guessing she wouldn't, either."

"Let's hope," he said, and I knew that concluded the discussion of my other-self. "Now, then," he continued, "I think we need to have a talk." I nodded, not sure what to expect. He shifted in his chair, leaning forward to rest his arms on his massive desk. "I appreciate your exuberance," he said, "and your efforts to add levity to a job that is quite serious. But the Gatekeepers is a professional organization. Outbursts like yours on the comm today do not portray us in a good light." For a moment, I had no idea what he was talking about, and this must have shown on my face. "And along those lines," he continued, "your personal life is your own, and should be kept that way. I realize this is a liberal city with a large population of— "

"Wait a minute," I interrupted. "Are you seriously pulling a 'don't ask, don't tell' on me?"

Invictus leveled his heavy-browed eyes at me. "I prefer to think of it as keeping one's private life private."

"I see."

"It's nothing personal."

"Not to you," I said. "But then, there's nothing 'wrong' with you talking about you and Mrs. Invictus as a couple, is there?"

"There is no 'Mrs. Invictus,' but that's not relevant."

I frowned. "Missing the point."

"No, I understand your point perfectly," he said. "And I'm not judging you—"

"Please," I sneered. "I hate that expression. Of course you're judging me! We judge each other, all of us, every minute of the day. All interactions are based on judgments, one way or another. What you mean to say is that you don't judge me in a negative light because of my orientation. But the fact that this is even being discussed sort of undermines that claim, too."

I shut my mouth before I said something worse, taking a deep breath to calm myself. Invictus said nothing, but he wore a tiny frown. Finally, he sat back in his chair. "Thank you," he said. "I'm glad you understand where I'm coming from. Now if you'll excuse me, I've got a meeting with the mayor."

I hesitated a moment before standing and walking out without a word.

"Wow. That's so not cool," K.T. said over dinner when I told her about my little chat with Invictus.

"No," I said. "Truth is, there are several I know of in the group who don't agree with him and, in fact, a couple are in same-sex relationships. I assumed Invictus knew about them, but maybe he doesn't."

K.T. shrugged and sipped her wine. "None of his business, right?"

"Right." I glanced over the menu, my heart beginning to race. "So, speaking of relationships," I said, "I did a lot of thinking while I was away." K.T. nodded expectantly. "And I decided I've been being stupid."

"How so?"

"Well, mainly I've been scared. Afraid to get hurt again."

"I can understand that," she said, "after what you've told me about your previous relationships. But you know, they can't all be like that."

"I know," I said, and sipped my water to wet my suddenly dry mouth. I didn't know why I was nervous. I knew things were good and were about to get a lot better. "What I'm saying is that I'm not afraid, anymore. I'm ready for a relationship."

"Really?" she asked with a hint of excitement.

I nodded. "Really." And I felt my cheeks flush as I looked into her deep brown eyes.

She continued looking back, all smiles. "Have you met someone? Is it one of your teammates? Tell me!"

I blinked, then let out a tiny, awkward laugh, looking away self-consciously. When I looked back at her, there was comprehension on her face, and her eyes were wide.

"Oh, my god," she said.

The simple words felt like a gut punch. I couldn't breathe. This wasn't happening. It couldn't be. I looked away from her, not sure what to do.

K.T. was saying something, but it didn't register. In a panic, I stood, bumping the table and knocking over my ice water. I stared at it, but it never occurred to me to pick up the glass. Instead, I ran out of the restaurant.

My stomach felt like it was going to twist apart. My mind was numb. The unthinkable had happened.

I'd fallen for a straight girl.

Using public transit, it's about three and a half hours from my neighborhood in San Francisco to the Sacramento Amtrak station. It gives a lot of time to think. Not that I'd been doing much else since the aborted dinner with K.T. the night before.

She'd called me several times, both after the dinner and in the morning, but I didn't answer. I listened to the messages, which were mainly her apologizing and wanting to see me. But she had no reason to apologize. I was the one who'd made the mistake. We both knew that. She was just being nice, trying to make me feel better.

She said she didn't want this to ruin our friendship, that she really liked me and treasured our time together. But as I sat on the train, watching the landscape roll by, I couldn't see how that could be anything other than ridiculously painful for me.

I still couldn't believe it. I'd never before thought a straight girl was gay. Sure, I knew others who had made that mistake. I just never thought it would happen to me.

Then again, Rachel hadn't been gay. I'm not even sure she was bi. So maybe this was becoming a trend for me. I tried not to think about what that implied.

I stepped out of the station in Sacramento and immediately regretted wearing jeans. It was early June and, absurdly, the day was oppressively hot. In San Francisco, it had been a beautiful 70 degrees. But in the valley, three and a half hours later, it was in the high 90s. So I took a cab the one measly mile to my brother's apartment.

My decision to visit had been hastily made upon waking up that morning. I didn't even call him, first. But I got lucky. Not only was he home, he was alone. He was surprised to see me, of course. Aside from living with him briefly when I first moved out to California, I hadn't once been to Sacramento to see him. He'd always come to the city.

I sighed in relief as I felt the chill of his air conditioner. "So glad you have that thing blasting," I said.

"You kidding? I'm not Dad." I moved into the living room, where I collapsed onto his leather sofa. "You know," he said as he walked to the kitchen, "I offered to buy a central air system for the house. But he wouldn't have it."

"He loves the heat. Are you sure we're really his kids?"

Dana laughed as he pulled a couple bottles of his latest batch of home brewed beer from his fridge and poured them for us.

He handed me a glass and said, "Okay. What's wrong?"

As we lounged in the living room, I told him the full story of K.T., since I hadn't really told him much aside from her being the one who had interviewed me for *Supers*. He nodded as I talked, and looked at me with compassion when I related the details of the previous night. "I feel like such an idiot."

"For allowing emotion to affect your judgment?"

"Yes."

"So you feel like an idiot for being human."

I frowned. "It's not that simple."

"But it is," he said. "And you may not be the first person to make that assumption about her. Some people have a very intense, earnest interest in others that can easily be misinterpreted as going beyond friendship, as being flirtatious."

"I suppose."

"In fact, you're one of them."

I nearly choked on the last swallow of my beer. "What!"

"You don't even realize it, but it's true. And it makes sense."

I stared at him. "In what twisted, alternate reality does that make any kind of sense?"

"Dinah, come on," he said as he stood and picked up my empty glass. "What's your single most prevalent psychological issue?"

"Oooh, you know how it turns me on when you talk about my prevalent psychological issues."

"Just answer me," he said as he went to refill our drinks.

With a sigh, I muttered, "Abandonment and attachment issues."

"Right," he said from the kitchen.

"So?"

"You've got a brain. Figure it out."

He returned with refills. I glared at him, but understood what he was getting at. "Okay, so if I did have this flirtatious thing going on, it would be because I subconsciously need to be liked by everyone." He nodded, but then I said, "Except I don't have a flirtatious thing going on."

"You do."

"Bullshit."

"Think Jack would agree with you or me?"

I glared at him again. "If that's the case, why was K.T. so shocked? She should have seen it coming."

Dana just sipped his beer, a Spock eyebrow reaching for his non-existent hairline, waiting for me to figure it out. It bugs the crap out of me when he does that. I took a gulp of the cold beer, then frowned. I was starting to put it together. "Go ahead," Dana said.

"I kinda hate you, right now," I said, then gave a melodramatic sigh. "K.T. showed an obvious interest in me from the beginning," I said. "It was, as you said, intense. Earnest."

He nodded. "And?"

Now I looked away from him, staring into my glass. "Because she was interested, there was no need for my alleged flirtatious ways."

"And further than that?"

"I guess... my self-esteem issues make me think I don't deserve such attention." I put down my beer and stretched out on the sofa. "I have a need to be liked, but subconsciously think I'm unlikeable." I let out a small groan. "Holy shit, am I fucked up." To my surprise, and annoyance, Dana laughed. "It's not funny," I said.

"It sort of is," he said. "Dinah, everyone is fucked up. Every last one of us. You, me, everyone."

I glanced sidelong at him. "Well, that's nice, coming from a shrink. But you're just trying to make me feel better."

"Yes, but by telling you the truth, not by bullshitting you." He leaned forward. "Of course, there are all sorts of different ways to be fucked up, and some people are more fucked up than others. But you're not likely to meet anyone out there, not even those who seem the most 'together,' who hasn't got some personality-warping psychological issues. You'd be amazed at how many metas have self-esteem issues."

Now I turned to face him. "Seriously?"

"Seriously. I counsel several of them, online. What, you think just because someone has meta abilities, it automatically makes them want to go do heroic things?"

Obviously, the answer to that was a negative one, Dana himself being an example. And of course, some metas didn't have abilities that made them suitable for beating up bad guys. And then there was my own situation. I wanted meta abilities not so I could be a benefit to society, but because I wanted to be famous. Because I wanted the attention, the adulation. Which, perversely, I didn't feel I deserved.

"Point taken," I conceded. We were silent for a minute as I processed this. Then my curiosity got the better of me. "Okay, so how are *you* fucked up?"

To my surprise, Dana froze for a second, then shook his head faintly. "Let's not go there." I sat up, prepared to fulfill my little sister duty by pushing his buttons. "Please," he said seriously.

"Okay." After an awkward silence, I said, "So, how are things with... um..."

"Yeah, let's not go there, either."

"What? Why?" Avoiding my question, he swallowed some beer, a look of pain on his face. "Oh. Shit, I'm sorry," I said, understanding now why he'd sounded weird on the phone.

"Yeah, well..." he said, his voice catching in his throat.

"I know this therapist who says it helps to talk about things."

Dana doesn't often open up to me. I'd always assumed it was because he never had much he needed to talk about. To me, he'd always been one of those "together" people he'd just told me were nevertheless fucked up. But now he just chuckled ironically and nodded. "Okay," he said.

So I listened as he told me how his relationship had ended. I comforted him as best I could with platitudes that sounded just as empty to me as I'm sure they did to him. But it seemed to help.

We went out for sushi that night. I wanted to keep his mind off his breakup, so we spoke of other matters.

"Hey, you know how you once told me that you could teach me some defensive steps against... you know... your kind of abilities?"

Dana glanced around at the other diners nearest us. "Yeah."

"Think we could pursue that?"

He switched to his "inside voice." *I may not have properly described the nature of that. It's not just defensive steps for you to take. It's also that I'd mentally construct defenses in your mind for you to use.*

Sounds complicated, I replied in my head. *So, just how powerful of a telepath are you?*

I don't know how to answer that, he said. *Measuring such abilities isn't a straightforward process. There are different types of telepathic abilities and different telepaths will have different sets of them.*

Such as this procedure you're talking about?

Yes. In meta parlance, someone who can do that sort of thing is known as a "psychic architect," a term I don't like.

Because it makes you sound like you design homes for clairvoyants?

Exactly.

Well. Let's do it.

"Are you sure?" he asked aloud.

I reached over with my chopsticks to snag some pickled ginger from his plate. "Why wouldn't I be?"

"Well, because it's intrusive, for one thing."

I dismissed that with a wave of the chopsticks, sending the ginger into my glass of water. "I trust you," I said as I fished it out.

"That's not what I'm worried about," he said quietly.

I sat back in my chair. "Then what is?"

But he just shook his head.

It was still hot by the time we left the restaurant well after sundown. It reminded me of summers back home, minus the humidity.

"Want to watch a movie?" he asked as we climbed the stairs to his place.

"No, I want you to do that psychic thing."

He frowned at my phrasing of it. "Not now."

"Oh, come on. You're the one who keeps telling me I need to protect myself against telepaths," I reminded him as we entered the blissfully cool apartment. I badgered him until he consented.

"It'll take a while," he said. "A couple hours."

"Oh. Are you too tired?"

"No. I'm just saying you might want to get comfortable. The more relaxed you are, the easier it is to do."

So I changed into my nightshirt and stretched out on the sofa. He pulled a chair over and sat beside me. Once I was situated and comfy, he began the process.

I felt him enter my mind. He was right; it was more intrusive than when he spoke to me telepathically. I tried to relax. The problem was, I'd been drinking. And since I hadn't done anything to expend any of the energy my body created from the alcohol, I was fidgety, mentally as well as physically.

As Dana poked around in my head, doing whatever it was he was doing, I started to "see" flashes of things, things I eventually determined were from his mind, not my own. I understood, then, what he meant when he said trusting him wasn't the issue. It was that he was opening himself up to me, as well. He needed to trust me.

For a moment, I thought I should interrupt and let him know this was happening. But no, I was sure he knew about it. My interruption would only interfere with the process.

I tried not to pay attention, but failed. I was fascinated. And eventually, the flashes started to make a weird sort of sense. It's difficult to describe, but there were patterns to what I was seeing. Themes, almost. These weren't just images. They were thoughts. They were emotions.

But after a while, I started to feel like a voyeur. They had begun revolving around the women in his life, with the expected emotional surge for each. His ex-wife figured prominently. This made sense, I decided, since we'd been talking about her at dinner in relation to this process. Associated with her were the expected feelings of regret and sadness.

There was the woman I assumed to be the recent flame, whose name I still couldn't remember. The emotion here was raw and fresh. She was on his mind a lot.

There was his first love, who'd ripped his heart out in college. That pain was still there after all these years, though subdued.

And there was me – as a kid, as a teenager, and as an adult. The emotions attached to these memories startled me in their intensity. Almost immediately upon sensing these, there was a flash of panic. Not mine. Dana's.

The next thing I remember is his voice in my head. It was calm. Reassuring. And somehow I knew that time had passed, that I'd been unconscious. And I knew it had been his doing.

Okay, I heard him say in my head. *I'm going to give you a tour of what I've done.*

I was only semi-listening as Dana guided me through my mind, showing me the defenses he'd set up. I was amazed, seeing the visual interpretation of my mind as he saw it. It was a surreal landscape containing familiar physical representations of purely mental things. There were doors, passageways, even things that appeared to be vaults, all in an environment of swirling colors and textures.

But when he finished giving the tour, I didn't let him go. *What was that, earlier?* I asked. *Something panicked you.*

Even as I thought this, I felt it from him again, for just an instant, before he clamped down on it. *Nothing*, he said.

For being a telepath, he's a lousy liar.

K.T. and I sit at the restaurant. I work up the courage to tell her how I feel. "I love you," I say.

She laughs at me.

"I'm serious," I say. "I do love you."

"Of course you do!" she says. "But how could you think I'd love you?"

She laughs again, as do some of the other diners, who stare at me, judging me, pronouncing me ridiculous with their rolled eyes. K.T. stares at me. "I could never be with a murderer."

And now the other diners glare at me, accusing me, as I try to turn invisible or shrink under the table.

I woke with a start and an ache in my chest. I lay there, staring at the half-open window in my brother's guest room, waiting for my heart to slow to a normal pace. The beams from a streetlight shone through the slats of the mini-blinds, illuminating a corner of the bed.

It hurt so badly. Not the dream, but the loss. Knowing that I would never share my life with K.T. was like a great void inside me that couldn't be filled. It would only continue to grow.

I glanced at the clock on the night stand. Three o'clock. With a sigh, I got out of bed and shuffled to the bathroom. A couple minutes later, on my way back to the guest room, I paused in the hallway and glanced at Dana's bedroom door, remembering the pain I'd felt in his mind earlier. I wasn't the only one who was suffering.

Quietly, I opened his door and slipped inside. Trying not to disturb him, I crawled in beside him. But, since he's a light sleeper and I'm not a ninja, he woke.

"Bad dreams," I said, as though I was seven again, seeking solace from my big brother.

"Yeah," he said. "Me, too."

I curled up next to him and wrapped his arm around me. "Why do I suck at relationships?"

Dana chuckled sleepily. "Runs in the family."

I laughed, despite myself. "Love you."

"Love you, too. Now shut up and go to sleep."

"Seriously, though," I said, "maybe I'm just not cut out for relationships. I mean, it took me years to be ready to take a chance again, and look what happened." As soon as it was out of my mouth, I felt like an insensitive idiot. "I'm sorry. I know you did the same thing. And you waited even longer."

He squeezed me gently. "It's okay. And it'll *be* okay. Now go to sleep."

"Yeah," I said, knowing this wasn't likely.

Just before dawn, Dana finally fell asleep. Giving up on it, myself, I went to the bathroom, washed up, then found my nightshirt and stepped outside onto the balcony to watch the sunrise.

It was warm outside. Or at least, it was warm for that hour, from my perspective. Early morning should be chilly, like in San Francisco. I didn't know how Dana could tolerate Sacramento heat.

I stay inside, mostly, came his voice in my head, startling me.

I thought you didn't read peoples' thoughts without their permission, I shot back.

I don't! I was just...

The calm feeling in my mind disappeared, replaced by alarm. I went back inside and found him sitting up in bed with a stricken look on his face. I was about to ask him what the problem was when I suddenly understood. I hadn't just heard him in my head. I'd *felt* him.

"I knew we shouldn't have," Dana groaned. He hunched over in bed, his head in his hands. I sat in a chair in a corner of the large bedroom and drew my knees up under my chin, stretching out my shirt the way my mother always told me not to.

I felt stupid, because now I understood why he'd never had another relationship since his divorce, until just recently. He'd been terrified that this would happen with his next partner.

It made me almost feel guilty for being excited. I was fascinated with exploring this new connection we had. It was utterly different from when we were communicating telepathically, with Dana in active broadcast/receive mode and me being a mostly passive participant. I could literally feel his presence in my mind. There were flashes of his thoughts and emotions. Eventually, his anxiety snapped me out of my exploration.

It'll be okay, I mentally said to him.

The thought startled him. He hadn't been in active receiving mode, so the intrusion was unexpected. I felt him, then, blocking me. "No, it won't," he said. Then he threw off the blankets and got out of bed, pulling on a pair of jeans. "It might seem all new and cool for you right now, but believe me, that will change. And before long, you'll be hating it. Hating *me*." He sank onto the edge of the bed, staring at the floor. "Good god, Dinah. Why...?"

"Because you've never been able to turn down your little sister," I said with a teasing smile. His flashing eyes would have told me he didn't find it funny, even if his emotional surge in my head hadn't already done so. "Sorry," I said.

"We have to break it," he said flatly.

I frowned and thought back to when he'd explained this phenomenon to me. "As I recall," I said, "you described that as sort of like 'psychic surgery' when you told me how you broke the bond with Elizabeth."

"Essentially," he admitted.

I nodded, thinking about it for a moment. "Yeah. Not happening."

"What? Dinah, we have to!"

"No, we don't," I said. "Don't be absurd."

"Yes, we do!" he pleaded. Then, his voice breaking, "I can't lose you."

"Are you kidding? That's not happening, either!"

"You stopped speaking to me for almost fifteen years out of envy and resentment, so I think you can understand my concern."

"And that's all the more reason why it *won't* happen now," I said.

We went around and around on this, yelling at each other both verbally and mentally, until we were exhausted from arguing.

Finally, I said, "What about any natural restrictions on this? Things that interfere with it from the outside?"

Dana looked at me in confusion for a moment before his eyes widened. "Yes." He nodded cautiously. "Distance." He sighed with relief. "I'm sorry. I should have thought of that."

"Well, there you have it. We live, what, eighty miles from each other, as the meta flies. That's far enough, right?"

He shrugged. "Not sure. Definitely, fifteen years ago. Maybe not, now."

His abilities had grown stronger, over the years. Which meant, of course, that he very well might be able to perform this "psychic surgery" without it being as intrusive as it sounded. He might be able to break our newly-formed bond with little effort.

But the truth was, I didn't want him to.

SIX

"The real voyage of discovery consists not in seeking new landscapes, but in having new eyes."
~ Marcel Proust

I hated it when Dana went off to college. His school was far enough away that he rarely made the trip for a weekend visit. I went from having him as a constant presence in my daily life to seeing him mainly on holidays and summer break. I hated not seeing him every day. I hated the distance between us.

Later, of course, I would use that distance to my own ends when I pushed him out of my life. But since reuniting, I've never wanted to be far from him again. The distance from Sacramento to San Francisco wasn't much. Close enough to visit without notice. But far enough, evidently, to prevent us from "hearing" each other's thoughts. I couldn't help but appreciate the irony. Now that I wanted us to be close again, it was Dana pushing me away.

We monitored our progress as I rode the train. When I couldn't feel him in my mind any longer, I sent him a text message. We'd just reached Martinez, about fifty miles linearly from Sacramento. This put him more at ease, but made me sad. I couldn't help thinking that I'd be seeing a lot less of him, now. It was like college all over again.

I stuffed my phone back in my bag and stared out the window of the train. Now that I was returning to the city, my thoughts returned to K.T. Specifically, I thought about how much I'd come to care for her. I berated myself for keeping my feelings to myself for so long. If I'd only told her early on, all this could have been avoided, or at least minimized.

Maybe. Or maybe I would have still fallen in love with her, even though I knew she was straight. How was it, I wondered, that in all our months of hanging out, we'd never discussed her past relationships, only mine? How is it that I never knew she was straight? How had I missed the clues?

Or did I ignore them, rather than miss them? Did I subconsciously just not care? Was it denial? The more I pondered it, the more disturbed I became. Because I started to think that the truth of the matter was that I was selfish. I'd spoken freely and often about myself without asking much about her. I could tell you what her favorite pizza toppings were (ham and pineapple), but not where she grew up, or much at all about her family, or anything of real significance. She, of course, knew nearly everything about me.

I analyzed just why I'd fallen for her in the first place and had to laugh at the irony. What attracted me – the energy-wielder – to K.T. was, in fact, her energy. This dark-haired beauty was bursting with positive energy, while I, with my bright white locks, held so much darkness inside. We were a great example of opposites attracting. To a point, anyway.

For most of my life, I've never understood why so many couples are unable to remain friends after separating. It's never made any sense to me how so many seem to go so easily from loving to hating each other. I have my ideas on why it happens, but none of them paint human beings in a very good light.

Bloodmoon and Nexus sat in my living room for a meeting of the Gatekeeper Girls, an informal drinking and discussion group that met at my place. Attendance varied, but Jasmine and Vicky were regulars. This night, it was just the three of us. We sat on the floor around the coffee table and I related the K.T. story.

"Oh, honey," Jasmine said after I finished. "I'm so sorry."

Vicky nodded. "Yeah, that's a shame."

I smiled gratefully at them as I drained my drink and got up to make another round of cocktails.

"What can we do?" Jasmine asked.

"Get me drunk," I said, moving to the kitchen.

"Been ruddy well trying for the past couple months!" Vicky said. "Don't think it's possible."

"I've been meaning to ask you," Jasmine said, "why did Invictus want to talk to you in private after the debriefing?"

I rolled my eyes as I slurped my drink. "Got told to behave," I said. "No raunchy talk on the comm. And keep my sinful ways to myself."

"What?" Jasmine said, her jaw dropping. "He did not!"

I nodded. "More or less."

"Wanker," was Vicky's assessment.

I just shrugged. "Doesn't matter."

"It *does* matter!" Jasmine insisted and looked over at Vicky. "It's like Freddy all over again."

"Who's that?" I asked.

Vicky sighed. "He was with us about three or four years ago. Openly gay. Invictus gave him a hard time."

"Why?" I asked.

"To get him to quit," Vicky said. "See, if it were up to Invictus, the Gatekeepers would be made up of nothing but conservative, heterosexual, monogamous folks."

"Fortunately, it's not up to him," Jasmine said. "At least, not entirely."

"So what happened?" I asked.

"Well, he quit, of course," Vicky said with a shrug. "Was with us only about four months."

"Freddy was a good guy and well-liked," Jasmine said. "Last I heard, he'd moved to New Orleans."

The girls were introspective as they drank. For my part, I was becoming more and more appalled by Invictus. Was he trying to get me to quit? If so, he'd have to try a hell of a lot harder.

"Jasmine," I said, "I wanted to ask you something." Briefly, I explained to her about the telepathic link I now shared with Dana and about his fears. As I finished, I said, "I don't know how to put him at ease about this. I thought maybe your perspective would be helpful."

Jasmine frowned. "You say this link occurred when he was setting up defenses in your mind?" She gave me a funny look, as though she didn't believe me. Finally, she turned her attention back to her drink. "Well," she said, "I certainly can understand his concerns. I imagine I'd have the same ones."

"But how can I convince him that they're groundless?"

"Are you certain they are?"

Flustered, I said, "Yes!"

"But how can you be? You've never experienced this before. He has."

I sighed and polished off my drink. Truth is, I *couldn't* be certain. Jasmine knew that. So did Dana. And so did I. So I let the question die, unanswered.

After a minute, I said, "So I'm thinking of having my eggs harvested. In case I want to do the whole offspring thing someday."

"Wow," said Vicky. "That's an abrupt change of topic."

"What's involved in that?" Jasmine asked.

"First I have to be screened for candidacy. They test for infectious diseases. HIV, chlamydia, hepatitis, and so on. I believe there's a psych screening, too."

"Well, you're buggered, there," Vicky said.

I smacked her on the arm, then said, "There's a series of hormonal drugs to stimulate the ovaries, and finally the surgery to retrieve the eggs."

"Lovely," Vicky said flatly. "How long does all that take?"

"About a month, I think."

"You should be okay, then," Jasmine said.

"What do you mean?"

"Well, because of Proposition 8, of course."

Proposition 8 was the highly contentious ballot initiative that would amend the state's Constitution to make same-sex marriage illegal in California. The State Supreme Court had recently ruled that preventing same-sex couples from marrying was unconstitutional. Proposition 8 was the reaction to that. "What has a bigoted move against same-sex marriage got to do with harvesting my eggs?"

"The same-sex marriage aspect is, of course, the largest and most well-known segment of the initiative, but the proposition would also prevent metas from marrying other metas, from adopting, from being surrogates, and from donating sperm or eggs for in-vitro fertilization."

My stomach sank. "I didn't realize that."

"The press seems ignorant of it, as well. Or are ignoring it, for some reason."

"Because it's socially acceptable to discriminate against metas, even after all we've done," Vicky said.

I just shook my head. "Sometimes this country sickens me."

"Hey," Vicky said, "I know what'll cheer you up. Did you know you have an actual fan club?"

I nodded, forcing a smile. "Yeah."

"Well, geez. Don't be so excited about it."

"Oh, it's very cool," I said. "And Macy's sweet for putting it together. But it's not all wonderful."

"What do you mean?" Jasmine said.

"I get emails from people. Or rather, Macy gets them and forwards them to me. But there's one emailer who isn't what I'd call a fan."

"A detractor?" Jasmine asked.

I shook my head. "A stalker."

"Whoa," Vicky said. "What's he said?"

I shrugged. "First couple were flattering. Said how beautiful I was and he wanted me to email back, which I didn't, since I wasn't, you know, *here*. Had a whole slew of messages when I got back, the most recent of which was pissy, calling me a bitch and *insisting* I reply. This morning, I got another one. A threatening one."

"You forwarded it to the authorities, of course," Jasmine said.

"Well, not yet," I said. "Guess I should."

"Bloody right you should," Vicky agreed.

We chatted for another hour, until Sinta returned from her evening patrol. She sat with us for a few minutes before going to bed. We all bade her good night, then I cleared away the empty glassware.

I hugged both of them at the door. "Good night, Dyna," Jasmine said. "See you soon."

Vicky smiled. "Thanks for the drinks, luv."

"You're welcome."

She turned her gray-eyed gaze up to me. "So maybe we could do this just the two of us, sometime?"

"Sure," I said. "I'd like that."

She smiled. "Lovely. Ta!"

"She did *what*?" Jack said in disbelief.

"Teleported me," I said. "That's the only way I can describe it."

We sat in a break room at the robotics lab where he worked, drinking coffee from a single serve machine. "Wow," Jack said. "I didn't think teleportation was a known meta ability."

"I checked with the Office of Metahuman Affairs database, through the Gatekeepers," I said. "There are some metas who have abilities that seem like teleportation, but are not considered to be, by the government. In fact, one of them is a member of my team. I plan to talk to her about it, soon."

"Dammit, Jack," said a woman at the coffee machine. "Did you take the last Sumatra?"

"Guilty," Jack replied. The woman grumbled something as she made an alternate selection and began brewing her cup.

"You know," I said, "I struggled with this when we were all swapped with our other-selves. I remember something about that teleportation thing with photons, where when the spin of one photon is altered, it happens to its twin, too, at another location."

Before Jack could comment, the coffee woman spoke up. "That's not teleportation," she said, pulling her mug from the machine. "That's quantum entanglement."

Jack nodded as the woman stepped over to our table. "This is Dr. Paige Stephens, another physicist here. Paige, this is—"

"Dynamistress," she said. "Jack talks about you. A lot."

As Jack blushed, I shook her hand. "Nice to meet you," I said as she sat with us. She looked to be around Jack's age, with blondish hair that fell in a braid down the back of her lab coat. "So tell me about this," I said.

"Well," she said, sipping her coffee, "entanglement is where two particles – like the photons you mentioned – are linked together in such a way that they can almost be considered two pieces of a whole. So when you separate them by a distance, a change in one instantly changes the other to match. It's a basic element of quantum mechanics."

I frowned. "So it's not relocation of a photon, but instantaneous communication, with one photon 'telling' the other what to do."

She frowned. "Well, it appears to be more of a situation where, because of the entanglement, the second particle has no choice but to do the same thing as the first. Less like communication and more like programming. Either way, it's not teleportation."

"Right. It's not moving matter physically across distances."

"As far as we can tell, that's pretty much impossible. I mean, we've done something we're calling teleportation, but even it isn't what you're thinking of."

"What is it, then?"

"Again, it's been done with photons. It involves what you might call making a blueprint of the particle, breaking it into pieces, then sending the pieces and the blueprint through a fiber-optic cable. At the other end, the photon is rebuilt using the blueprint."

"And how is that not teleporting matter? You're sending the pieces and the instructions for putting them back together."

"Because what you have on the other end is a replica, not the original. It's like sending a fax, if your fax machine shredded your document during the sending. The original is gone. The very act of measuring a quantum particle destroys it."

I frowned. "Yeah, I keep hearing that, but it sounds like bullshit."

This caused her to raise an eyebrow. "Fundamental principles of physics aren't dependent on what you think of them."

"Right, like these fundamental principles haven't been called into question by the existence of meta abilities?"

"Well," Paige began, but Jack interrupted.

"I think she's right."

That took her both of us by surprise. "You're joking," Paige said.

Jack shook his head. "I think there are methods of detection that we just haven't tried."

"To pick up on the presence of a photon, that photon has to be absorbed. It's *light*, Jack!"

"Yes, but I still say there are other ways to 'see' a photon without coming in contact with it. We just haven't figured them out, yet."

Not wishing to witness a physicist pissing match, I said, "Let's get back on point. Whether or not destruction is unavoidable, if you end up with an exact duplicate, what's the difference?"

"Well, that's just it. If destruction happens, your duplicate will never be exact. No copy is ever exact, regardless of the method of reproduction. But that's the least of the problems."

"What's the biggest?"

"Destroying something releases energy. Break a photon to bits, you release energy. Not much, of course. Enough to kick an electron into a higher state. But destroying at the atomic level something with as much mass as, say, a human being? The amount of energy released would be... I don't know... equivalent to a thousand megaton bomb, probably."

"Well, then there's obviously another way to teleport without destroying the original or releasing that kind of energy."

She frowned at me. "Why do you say that?"

"Because about a year and a half ago, my teammates and I were teleported from our base into another world. And last I checked, San Francisco isn't a crater."

Paige stared silently into her coffee for a moment. Then she looked up at me. "The other possibility is that it was a relocation via some other method. After all, the portal itself is a gateway, as I've heard it described."

"Yes. Step through it and you come out the other side. But when my friends and I were taken, we were hundreds of miles from the portal."

"True," Jack said, "but Paige is right. There could have been something else at work."

I chuckled. "Well, you can call that 'something else' whatever you like, but the end result is what everyone would think of as teleportation." The pair chewed on that for a moment, but offered no response. I decided to change the subject. "Well, it is what it is... whatever it is. So what type of work do you do here, Paige?"

She looked up from her coffee and said, "I study ELF radiation."

I smirked. "Radioactive elves. Hot topic these days?"

"Extremely low frequency radiation," Jack said, while his colleague laughed.

"The sort of radiation generated by power lines, electrical wiring, certain appliances, and so on," Paige said. "And that would include the sort of electronics commonly found in robotics."

"I know what it is," I said. "Wasn't there some big concern years ago that it could cause cancer?"

"Yeah," she said. "But study after study showed no solid link. On the other hand, there was a meta-study released just recently that showed a connection between long-term exposure to ELF radiation and Alzheimer's disease. Not a conclusively causal connection, mind you, but it's something worth looking at closer, I suppose."

"That's not your focus, though, is it?"

She shook her head and drained her coffee. "No, I'm more interested in what could be done with it. But that's pretty much all I can say about it, I'm afraid."

"Fair enough," I said. "Well, thanks for the chat, both of you. I've used up enough of your work time." We all stood and I shook Paige's hand before Jack escorted me out.

The following day, while on routine patrol, my earphone beeped with a direct message from Transcendant, one of the Tribunes of the group, who was on monitor duty that day. "Dyna," he said, "we've got a hostage situation. Wells Fargo, corner of Fillmore and California. I ping you as being closest. Police are on site, but could maybe use you."

"Roger that," I said, turning to blast in that direction. "Four blocks away. Stay tuned."

"Notifying them of your imminent arrival. Thanks."

Seconds later, I touched down on the roof of the building. I stepped to the edge and looked down at the police, who were no doubt awaiting the arrival of a SWAT unit. I motioned to them that I was going in, then entered through one of the rooftop windows, quietly making my way down to the ground floor.

From my vantage point on the stairs, I could see the two would-be robbers. I've always wondered at the audacity of daytime bank robberies. Maybe they assume having hostages is their key to success, even though it's usually the key to getting shot. There were several patrons and tellers sitting on the floor, with one of the gunmen standing over them. The other kept his hostage with him, who appeared to be one of the bank managers. I described the scene to Transcendant. "Thankfully," I whispered, "he doesn't have a gun held to the man. Just seems to be using him as a shield."

"Do you have a shot?"

I ran the scenario in my head. A precise blast to take out the one holding the bank manager. Then, when the other turns to see me, I take him out. Quick and easy, no fatalities. Certainly better than letting the SWAT guys take them out permanently.

But then the fear hit. The fear, and the memory of killing Dr. Gray. What if this didn't play out how I pictured it? What if I missed? What if I hit the manager, instead? What if my blast didn't knock him out and he shot the guy? What if, in his panic, the other gunman shot another hostage? A cold chill filled my stomach.

"Dyna? Do you have a shot or not?"

I did. It was easy. Three seconds and all this would be over. "I'm... not sure."

"Don't take it unless you're certain."

I *was* sure. "Right."

Outside, I saw the SWAT van pull to a stop. Heavily armed officers piled out. Some, I knew, would be coming in the same way I had. I had to act soon.

Below, the man holding the manager moved further away from the street, deeper into the room. If anything, this made things easier for me. There was no way I'd miss him.

"I have the shot," I murmured.

"Excellent," Transcendant said.

I raised my arm, pulling a perfect line. I had the shot. I did. Seconds ticked by. Energy built up, ready to be set free. But the pounding of my heart was practically heavy enough to throw off my aim.

Footsteps behind me. Quiet. Slow. SWAT.

Take the shot, I told myself. Take it now!

A gun clicked behind me.

I'm startled by the click of a SWAT officer's gun. My blast erupts, thrown off by my surprise, and misses completely. Both robbers turn and begin firing on me, but are cut down by the SWAT team. Two dead, because of me.

I'm startled by the click of a SWAT officer's gun. My blast erupts, given more energy by the adrenaline rush of surprise, and the robber goes down, entrails spraying from a hole through his midsection. The other robber turns and fires on me, but hits a SWAT officer before he's cut down. Three dead, because of me.

I'm startled by the click of a SWAT officer's gun. My blast erupts, thrown off by my surprise and given more energy by the adrenaline rush, and the bank manager's head explodes. The officer fires upon the man holding the body and riddles him with bullets. The other gunman opens fire on me and the SWAT team. They return fire. A stray bullet strikes a hostage in the chest. The gunman takes out one of the officers before he's shot through the head. Five dead, because of me.

I met Invictus in his office. It felt like a visit to the principal. And for good reason. I sat in front of his imposing desk as he leaned forward, frowning.

"Transcendant says you told him you had a clear shot," he said.

I nodded. "That's correct."

"I have to assume you didn't take it due to the arrival of the SWAT team."

I was silent for a moment as I stared at nothing. "Well," I finally said, nearly under my breath, "you know what they say about assuming things."

The big man raised an eyebrow. "All right. So what was the real reason?"

There was no way around it. "I choked," I said. He waited for an elaboration, so I gave it to him, haltingly, avoiding eye contact as much as possible. I reminded him of how Dr. Gray had died. And I told him of the ongoing guilt that seemed only to be getting worse.

When I finished, he was quiet for a minute, frowning, and occasionally drumming his fingers on the desktop. Each second was an eternity. Just like in the principal's office.

Finally, he cleared his throat. "In this case, everything ended well, with no fatalities. But I don't think I need to point out that this is unacceptable."

My heart nearly stopped as he said it. But I nodded. "I know. It won't happen again."

"And how will you guarantee that?"

"I don't know. But it won't. You have my word."

"I don't want your word," he said. "I just want you to live up to your potential."

"Yes, sir."

"I hate to do this, but since this was a potentially lethal encounter, I can't risk putting you in another situation like that. Until further notice, I'm limiting you to Level Two assignments."

My heart sank. Level Two meant routine investigations not expected to be life-threatening. And for ones that were likely to be dangerous, I'd now be paired with another member, never acting solo. I wanted to protest, but knew it wasn't worth the effort. Plus, I'd look like a crybaby. "I understand."

"All right. That will be all."

We stood, Invictus gathering some paperwork as I headed toward the door. I felt like I was going to puke.

Exactly like a trip to the principal.

In the morning, I trudged, exhausted, into the kitchen where Sinta was making breakfast. I rooted around in the fridge for a drink and found something decidedly unappetizing.

"What the hell is this?" I said, pulling out a zippered sandwich bag of glass vials.

"Those are the samples the other Dyna collected when she was here," Sinta said. "From the cave where you got sick."

Despite myself, I cringed. "Oh," I said, gently placing the bag on the counter. "That's, um... nice."

"You're not throwing them out, are you?"

"Why? You want some on your French Toast?"

Sinta giggled. "No! But she wanted it for a reason."

"Right," I said, choosing not to state the obvious. Let her hold onto hope. "Tell you what. I'll take it to the lab at the Citadel later and store it there."

As we ate, I couldn't help but think about my double's situation. I read from her notes almost every day, trying to glean some insight into what she was doing, why she wanted these samples. Sinta was convinced the woman was trying to cure her disease, and the notes seemed to support this. I wasn't opposed to continuing her work. It was a challenge and intriguing. But until I figured out what Neukölln was, I was missing a critical piece of information.

After breakfast, I suited up and headed to the Citadel. We had a briefing later, but I wanted time to examine the samples. I took the proper precautions for someone prone to infection. I was gloved and masked, wearing goggles, and had a spray bottle of liquid death handy.

I thought back to the day Sinta and I had gone into that cave. I remembered the stench. The staggering number of mushrooms. The slime mold. The damn puffball spores that infected me.

What else was there? My memory told me there was something odd we'd seen as I was hacking up my lungs. Then I remembered. When I'd caught up with Sinta, she was stopped, looking straight ahead. I remembered how the beams of light from our lamps stretched out a ways in front of us, like car headlights in the fog. We left at that point and, considering what happened with my health immediately thereafter, I didn't really give that oddity any further thought.

I looked over the collection of vials, noting one filled with a colorless, gelatinous substance. I prepared several slides of this, using a variety of staining procedures. But after examining each, I still had no idea what the hell I was looking at. There was a distinct cellular morphology, but the cells themselves had traits common to both animals and fungi. I didn't understand that, nor why there was no natural pigmentation.

I took photos of all the slides and would contact someone more qualified than I to determine what it was. Then I packed everything back into the storage fridge.

As I did so, I noticed something odd about the chemical spoon I'd used to scoop out bits of the matter onto the slides. I lifted it for a closer look and verified that it was, indeed, corroded. The gelatinous matter was eating away at the metal at a rapid pace. Curious, I dipped a few other tools into it. A few different plastics, ceramic, even a polycarbonate. The plastics, both hard and soft, began to dissolve within seconds of contact. The polycarbonate lasted longer, but was definitely pitted before long. The ceramic seemed to stand up as well as the glass, however. I wasn't stupid enough to dip my finger in it.

A glance at the clock told me it was time to head to the briefing, so I packed up everything and headed down the elevator.

"Our latest assignment," Invictus said, standing at the front of our briefing room, "is to bring in this individual." As he spoke, the wall screen behind him brought up a black and white photograph of a girl who appeared to be in her late teens.

"Lily McKay," Invictus continued, "escaped from New Alcatraz last month. She is expected to be responsible for the recent string of minor explosions in the city."

I remembered reading about these in our private web forum. There were no obvious causes – no bomb fragments, no chemical residue. No witnesses so far had actually seen an explosion, though many heard the noise and saw the resulting damage.

"Do consider her dangerous," Invictus continued. "Details are uploaded, but I should stress the urgency of this. The girl's medical condition is extremely unstable. Her capture is literally a matter of life or death for her."

I frowned, then pulled up her dossier on my comm and read as Invictus gave details on the locations of the detonations. Lily McKay, the dossier stated, was born in 1990. At thirteen, she was orphaned when a mysterious explosion leveled her family's home. Her parents and two younger siblings were killed. Lily was unharmed. Physically, anyway.

Lily's living relatives refused to take her in because they were afraid of a similar "accident." No foster family would take her for the same reasons. So she was placed in the custody of the state, and it soon became clear that the girl was ill, and was eventually diagnosed with hypercalcaemia, a dangerous excess of calcium in the body.

She was hospitalized and treated to the point of stabilization, but the calcium continued to accumulate. It was all the hospital could do to maintain equilibrium.

When a blast destroyed the girl's hospital room and those adjacent to it, again with no harm to Lily, she was taken to New Alcatraz, where special facilities designed to hold dangerous metas could be used to analyze and perhaps nullify her strange ability. And she'd have the benefit of Pelican Hospital, the meta-oriented medical facility that was built on the southeast side of Alcatraz Island back in 2002, along with the billion-dollar revamp of the prison to accommodate metas. The dossier didn't explain how she'd gotten free of the facility.

I raised my hand and Invictus acknowledged me. "Two questions. First, how did she manage to escape from New Alcatraz?"

Invictus nodded. "It appears she had an outside accomplice. Since she was not actually a prisoner, she had freedom to walk the grounds. She communicated with this accomplice, who then effected her escape. Details are lacking on the method." He paused while we absorbed that. "Your second question?"

I looked over several additional photos of the girl. "Why are there no pictures of her in color?"

Invictus gave a slight smirk. "Those photos *are* in color. She has silvery-white hair and her skin is very pale."

"Might want to rethink her wardrobe choices, then," I said. "Put some color in her life."

He ignored my humor, as always. "Remember, everyone, the girl is not considered a criminal. We have no reason to believe the explosions are intentional, but an ability she cannot control. Please keep this in mind when you find her."

It didn't take long. It was Speed Freak who found her. We were able to predict roughly where she might be, based on the length of time between the explosions and the direction she appeared to be going.

As the name implies, Speed Freak can cover a lot of ground in short order. She has a top speed around a hundred miles per hour or so and can accelerate to half that in less than a second. Her reflexes are so fast that she can avoid obstacles the same as any street jogger.

She made circuits around the area we'd predicted, weaving between buildings, going in and out of them faster than any of us could. Within a matter of hours, Lily was taken back to Pelican Hospital for treatment.

I wasn't one of those who got to see her before she was taken back, but as I've mentioned a time or two, I've long been fascinated by meta abilities. And my curiosity was piqued by a girl who could ostensibly explode. So I made arrangements to pay her a visit.

I flew the few miles from my apartment to the island on a blustery Saturday morning, landing on the hospital's front steps, to the surprise of a gaggle of staff entering and exiting the building.

At reception, I was given a visitor pass and directions to her room. When I'd requested the visit, I made sure to do it during a time when her primary physician would be on hand.

Dr. Prashad met me outside Lily's room. She introduced herself and informed me that the girl was in pretty bad shape. She'd been away from treatment for more than a month and, as such, the accumulation of calcium in her system had approached crisis. Her urine output was low and she was lethargic. "Had your team not located her, she would have died before much longer," the woman said gravely.

We entered the room, where Lily lay asleep in her bed, a number of tubes leading into her arms, electrodes attached to her torso. "What are you doing for her?"

"We are using a variety of chelating agents that help to clear the excess calcium from her blood. We had also been administering calcitonin, which is an amino acid—"

"I'm familiar with it," I said. It would serve a similar function as chelation, but in a different manner.

"Well, we stopped it, as it wasn't helping. Frankly, we're getting desperate, trying therapies rarely used. Gallium nitrate, for example."

"What about removing the parathyroid?"

"Her levels of parathyroid hormone are quite low, so that's not responsible. The other strange thing is that she shows no signs of osteoporosis, so the calcium isn't being leached from her bones."

I moved to the girl's bedside, gazing at her pallid face. Even unconscious, she seemed to be in pain. My heart went out to her. Then I looked at her using my "other sight," as I'd gotten in the habit of doing, focusing on her energy patterns. And I gasped.

"What is it?" Dr. Prashad said.

I turned to face her. "I'm able to see organic energy patterns," I explained. "And hers is quite pronounced."

"Which means what?"

"I'm not certain. But she's got something going on in there that I rarely see even in metas." In truth, I'd only ever seen this level of energy in one other meta. And that was every time I looked in a mirror.

If the calcium wasn't being leached from her bones, where could it be coming from? I reached out and moved a lock of her hair away from her face, lingering a moment to study it. As someone with pure white hair, I'm always curious about unnatural coloration in others. To my surprise, her hair was coarser than it looked. Heavier, and on the stiff side. And as I inspected the strands, a slight beeping sound erupted from the comm unit on my wrist. I frowned. The only other time I'd heard that particular beep was in the comm's demo mode when I first got it.

It was the unit's Geiger counter. I activated the screen and saw that it was registering radioactivity from the girl, though in a very low level.

I frowned and canceled the alert, ignoring Dr. Prashad's inquisitive look. I was too busy mentally working on the puzzle. Calcium. Radioactivity. Then a thought struck me. "What about her potassium levels?"

"Interesting that you ask. They're high, but not anything that worries us."

"Have you done an isotope analysis on it?"

The doctor frowned. “Why?”

“One way calcium-40 is produced is by the decay of potassium-40, which is itself radioactive.”

“But potassium-40 in the blood is ridiculously trivial. It couldn’t account for the amount of calcium we’re detecting here.”

“What if the ratio of potassium isotopes is really out of whack? As I’m sure you know, when it comes to metas, the normal rules of chemistry don’t tend to work as we expect them to. I’m living proof of that.”

Dr. Prashad nodded and said she’d get the analysis done. I asked her to let me know the results.

“Where did you get these samples?” asked Dr. Boniface when he called. He was a well-known mycologist at UCSF, according to Google, which is why I’d sent him the digital photos as well as portions of each of the samples.

“Why?” I asked. “Have you figured out what they are?”

There was a pause before he responded. “Well, most of them are typical examples of fungi and slime molds. But this one—”

“The animal/fungus hybrid,” I said.

“Yes! This is astounding. Where did you get it?”

“I’m afraid I can’t reveal that,” I said. “I’m sorry.” As he expressed his disappointment, I said, “Can you tell me anything more about it? Is it dangerous?”

“Dangerous?” he said, seemingly surprised at the question. “Why would you think it’s dangerous?”

“Just trying to be cautious about it.”

“No, doesn’t appear to be. Other than being corrosive, as you warned.” His voice became excited again. “This is a spectacular discovery. It should be reported.”

“Right. Well, not just yet,” I said. “But I’ll let you know when we can do that.”

A week later, I met Dr. Prashad back at Pelican Hospital. She confirmed that my suspicion was correct, that Lily’s potassium-40 levels were absurdly higher than normal. Inside, we stood at the bedside of a wide awake Lily McKay. The girl was still attached to tubes, but looking much less like death.

“Lily, this is Dynamistress,” Dr. Prashad said. “She’s the one who figured out what was making you so sick.”

Lily looked up at me with grateful eyes. “Are you a doctor?”

"Not a medical doctor," I said.

"Your recollection of chemistry is obviously greater than mine," Dr. Prashad said. "And that made all the difference." She smiled at both of us. "I'll give you a few minutes."

After she'd left the room, Lily's grateful demeanor changed. Her face clouded and she avoided my gaze. "What's wrong?" I asked as I pulled a chair to her bedside and sat.

She was silent a moment, then said, "Ever occur to you that I didn't want to be back here?"

"You were dying," I said.

"That was the idea!" she snapped. "Thanks for screwing that up."

I'm not often at a loss for words, but I honestly didn't expect this reaction. I hate being thrown like that, so my mind whirled, analyzing everything I knew about her. And then I berated myself for being surprised.

"Sorry, hon. Saving lives is sort of in my contract."

Lily sighed, closed her eyes, and sank back into her pillows. "Fuck your contract."

There was such bitterness in her voice that it shocked me. I spoke softly. "If you were so set on dying, why didn't you? You had plenty of time to kill yourself. Why wait for your disease to do it slowly?"

Eyes still closed, she said, "Because it hurt."

"I see," I said. "The punishment you think you deserve."

Now she stirred, looking sidelong at me. "I *do* deserve it."

"Why? Because you weren't able to control a chemical reaction in your body? Might as well blame yourself for going through puberty."

"How about you get out of here and take your armchair psychology with you?"

"Mm. Should I just mention to Dr. Prashad what you've told me? Would you enjoy being on suicide watch?"

Lily glared at me. "Bitch."

I sighed. "Look, I know you don't know me and have no reason to listen to anything I have to say. But I know what it's like to feel guilty for the deaths of others." Lily's glare turned to a suspicious gaze, but at least had softened somewhat. "In fact, I struggle with it every day. And in my case, I have a lot more reason to feel guilty than you do."

The girl frowned. "Why?"

"Because in one instance, I missed the signs of someone being suicidal. And in another, I was negligent. A man died because of it."

"At least you didn't kill your family."

"No. But the suicide was... someone close to me. And the other was my college mentor."

She frowned. "Sucky. But not the same."

"No, it isn't. Especially because I didn't have the luxury of knowing it was all out of my control. If we're making comparisons, we might as well include that."

"Whatever," she sneered. "Why are you telling me this?"

I leaned closer to her. "I just want you to see that it's possible to get past the guilt. To function. Even to thrive, and be happy."

She rolled her eyes. "Yeah, you just reek of happiness and cheer."

Her words stunned me. I stared at her, amazed that she'd seen through my façade so casually. She was right, of course. I was being disingenuous. I wasn't happy. I wasn't thriving. And I certainly wasn't past the guilt.

Thankfully, Dr. Prashad returned at that moment, saving me from having to rebut her accusation. "Have a nice chat?" she asked.

"Yes, we did," I said, rising from the chair. "We learned we have some things in common. And I'm hoping we get the chance to talk more very soon." Lily remained silent, but her expression was softer. Whether it was because of my words or the doctor's presence, I didn't know. "Take care, Lily."

I stepped into the hallway and pulled the door closed behind me. Then I stood there, leaning against the wall, fighting off a wave of guilt-induced anxiety.

SEVEN

"I think the biggest disease the world suffers from in this day and age is the disease of people feeling unloved."
~ Diana, Princess of Wales

When I was in third grade, my school had an outbreak of chicken pox. More than a dozen kids were sick with it, including me. I was one of the lucky ones, though. My case was pretty mild. One of my classmates had it so bad that he had to be hospitalized. He had the blisters everywhere, even inside his mouth.

It had come on quickly and, it seemed, was just as quickly gone. At the time, I thought little of it. I was too busy being itchy and miserable. Even at that age, though, I knew that many disease outbreaks didn't just go away like that. I'd heard Dana talk about the "Black Death" in the 14th Century, which is estimated to have killed between 75 and 100 million people, worldwide.

Though it wasn't around when I was a kid, today we have a vaccine against chicken pox. We also have treatments for the Y. *pestis* infection that vastly improve someone's chances of surviving the plague, compared to those poor people in the 1300s.

As far as infections go, cryptococcal meningitis was more than enough for me. Fortunately, I'd had the benefit of modern antifungal drugs to get me through that unpleasant episode. And now it looked like a host of other people were going to benefit from them, too.

Practically overnight, hospitals were flooded with people complaining of flu-like symptoms – nausea, vomiting, and fever. But additionally, sensitivity to light, stiff necks, even hallucinations. Warnings were on the local news. Anyone with these symptoms was urged to get to the hospital right away to be tested for cryptococcal meningitis.

The warning sent a chill through me, as I remembered my own bout with the disease. But I told myself it was nothing to be worried about. My own case hadn't been diagnosed for quite a while, and I still pulled through. Just to be sure, I had another check-up.

"How bad is the outbreak?" I asked my physician as he removed the needle from my spine.

"Pretty bad. Especially over in Sausalito. The Department of Public Health is looking at trends, so I'm told."

"Are the cases just like mine?"

"Seem to be. Those infected generally have healthy immune systems. There's no obvious reason why these people should have contracted this. Fortunately, the treatments are working." He held up the vial of fluid he'd extracted. "I'll let you know how you fare."

"I admit I'm surprised you asked to see me," I said.

Lily and I sat in her cell in New Alcatraz. She'd been moved there against the wishes of just about everyone except the government. It was for "observation," they said. Just until they could determine how to prevent her from blowing up buildings.

As prison cells go, it was more like a hotel room. She could come and go as she pleased around the grounds. But that didn't change the fact that she was a prisoner.

"I wanted to tell you that you're wrong," Lily said. "I could have prevented my family from dying."

"Oh? How?" I asked.

She shifted uncomfortably in her chair and stared at her feet as she talked. "That explosion wasn't my first one. I had one a couple years earlier, when I was out in the woods behind our house, playing. It wasn't anywhere near as big, but it scared the hell out of me."

I nodded in understanding. "That's actually pretty common. Like regular puberty, 'meta puberty' tends to begin with a gentle display of what's to come, then subsides for a while before coming out full force, so to speak."

Lily shook her head as though to rid herself of the memory, her silvery hair falling in front of her face. She brushed it aside as she looked at me. "I should have told my mom and dad about it, but I didn't."

"Why not?"

"Because I was afraid of *this*," she said, gesturing around the cell. "I might have been just a kid, but I wasn't ignorant of what was going on in the world. I knew it meant I was a meta, and that meant I was bound to end up somewhere like this."

I nodded faintly. She was probably right. If she'd told her parents, they would have taken her to a hospital. And if the doctor felt she was any sort of threat – and "exploding" would sure qualify – then it would have become a government concern. I thought about saying that things were changing, that it wasn't like that, anymore. But the fact that we were sitting in a cell sort of undermined that claim.

Looking at Lily's face, I couldn't help but see how conflicted she was. On the one hand, she wanted to bitch slap me for implying that our situations were alike. On the other hand, she was scared and was hoping I could help. I had a hunch which one was the prevailing feeling.

"Okay. So you dragged me out here to tell me I was wrong. Fine. Not the first time. Won't be the last." I stood. "Anything else, or can I get back to work?"

Lily blinked in surprise as I stood. "Wait, seriously?"

I shrugged. "Yeah."

"What kind of hero are you?" she said, her voice rising.

I snorted. "Who told you I was a hero?"

In response, she got up, strode over to the tiny table beside her bed and grabbed something. She spun around, holding it out and pointing at it. "These guys!"

It was, of course, "my" issue of *Supers* magazine. I frowned. "Yeah, well, don't believe everything you read." Then my curiosity got the better of me. "Why do you have that, anyway?"

"The doc gave it to me after your first visit. Said I might want to know more about the hero who saved my life."

"Even if you didn't want to be saved." I folded my arms across my chest. "So you read it and...?"

"Well, what do you *think*? I read how you gave yourself abilities. So if you can give them, you can take them away!"

My jaw dropped. "What? Lily, no. It doesn't work like that."

"Why the hell not?"

I sighed, tired of having to explain this. "I'll tell you the same thing I've had to tell the government ever since that damned article came out. The only reason my experiment succeeded was that I already had the necessary mutations that would have made me a meta. They just hadn't been activated. But you're talking about removing something already there, something that's integrated into your DNA. It would almost certainly kill you. I wouldn't even try that with my own DNA, and I know it pretty intimately."

She stood there for a long time, just staring at me with a mix of disbelief, disappointment, and disgust. She threw the magazine into the corner. "Well, that's just great."

"I'm sorry," I said. "I had no idea that's what you thought I could do for you."

"What else would I *possibly* want you to do for me?" she said, collapsing onto her bed.

After a moment, I walked over and sat beside her. "Lily," I said softly, "removing your abilities wouldn't remove the guilt you're feeling. And isn't that what you really want?"

"I just don't want to be *here* anymore," she said. Then, more to herself than to me, "And I don't want to hurt anyone else."

I thought back to her dossier. "Don't you turn eighteen soon?"

"Yeah. Why?"

"Well, you haven't been charged with any crime. So when you're eighteen, you're legally an adult and can check yourself out of here."

"Yeah, except they're going to drag me back to the hospital every damn week for the treatments they're giving me. So I won't really be out. I'll just have a longer leash."

"So, you'd allow that? You'd come back for the treatments, rather than allow yourself to get sick again and die?"

Lily was quiet for a while, then nodded. "I guess." She shrugged. "Besides, I'd blow up some more and you'd just track me down again, anyway."

"Look, I can't promise anything. But let me do some research. Let me see just how long we can make that leash." Before getting up, I instinctively leaned over and gave her a hug. I'm not sure which of us was more surprised by it.

After leaving her room, I met with Dr. Prashad in her office. She gave me a complete rundown of how Lily was being treated. The "leash" she spoke of was essentially a dialysis-like treatment of chelating agents geared toward potassium, in addition to calcium, and then exclusively for potassium once her calcium levels were normal.

It was something I could work with.

Kimera and I sat at my dining table, sharing a pot of tea. We'd just returned from a routine patrol. With our combined meta abilities, we were successfully able to stop a purse-snatcher.

We spoke about the disease outbreak and my involvement with Lily's situation, and then the conversation turned where I knew it would. "Have you spoken with K.T.?," she asked.

I shook my head, a jolt of sadness stabbing me. "No," I said, hoping the pain didn't show.

"*Ahn top gam nae yo*," she said, and the compassion in her voice made me choke up. I nodded, accepting her sympathy. "You deserve to be happy, Dyna."

"Most people do," I said. "And what about you? Seeing anyone?"

Kim smiled ruefully. "No, I've given up on that."

"What? Why?"

She turned her large, serpentine eyes to mine. "Who could be attracted to someone who looks like I do?"

"Kim," I said seriously, "I think there are plenty who would be. I mean, yes, your looks are shocking, at first. But you're really quite beautiful."

"Oh, *jiral*. You're so full of it."

"I am not! Look," I said, taking her hand and stroking her arm, "your fur is gorgeous and soft. And where it tapers off and becomes scales," I said, indicating where her neck met her shoulders, "it's so fine. I mean, it's not like you have these enormous dragon scales. They're quite petite. And your horns are just damned impressive."

"Guys like hair. On heads. And I don't have any."

"You can't lump all men together like that. There are plenty of women who shave their heads and men still find them attractive."

"Easy for you to say."

"Besides, not having hair means it can't go gray. And scales don't wrinkle. There's no way to judge your age." I frowned. "I think I'm jealous."

Kim sighed. "Nice try."

"Seriously. If you were at all into girls, I'd go out with you."

"You would not."

"Would so," I said. "Don't argue with me." I poured more tea for us and changed the subject. "So, does the rest of the team know that I've been demoted?"

"You haven't been demoted," she said. "But no. Just the ten of us and whoever you've told. And the Prefects and Tribunes aren't gossips, so I don't think anyone else knows."

"Well, that's something, I guess."

"Dyna," Kim said, placing her hand on mine, "never think you're not an asset to this team. You are."

I smiled, appreciating her words. I just had a hard time not believing her statement was *jiral*.

I had the same result I'd had ever since my first infection. My CSF was still clear of *C. neoformans*. I called Dana to tell him. We discussed the outbreak. Some cases had been reported in Sacramento, as well.

Conversations with Dana were strained, now. When we spoke, there was always a tone in his voice that betrayed his feelings. He was still deeply disturbed by the fact that we had a telepathic link. Or I suppose the more accurate thing to say is that he was bothered by the fact that I didn't want him trying to break it.

I tried to engage him by bringing up the egg harvesting idea. "I've had my psych evaluation and medical screening," I told him. "And I have an appointment next week to begin the hormone treatments."

"That's a big step," he said.

"I don't know if I'll ever want to carry through with it," I told him. "If I don't, I guess I can always donate them to someone in need."

"Unless that initiative passes," he said.

Then he lapsed into silence. I gave up trying to get much out of him. And as I'd done every time we'd spoken since I last saw him, I invited him to come to the city for the weekend. "Come on," I said. "Friday is the Fourth. I bought us tickets for the fireworks cruise!"

"Sounds like fun," he said, "but I don't think so."

"Dana, come on. This is ridiculous. I want to see you!"

"We've gone a lot longer without seeing each other. It won't kill you."

His words were like a slap. I came very close to hanging up on him. Instead, I counted to ten, then said, "You know, you were so concerned about this mind link thing coming between us. But it's not. It's your *fear* of it that's driving us apart. Get it through your head, Dana. I'm not Elizabeth. This is not going to destroy our relationship. The only thing that's going to do that is *you*."

Then I hung up on him.

Twenty minutes later, I got a text. *See you Friday.*

He carried through with it, too, coming to the city on the Fourth. I sensed him as he drove in. He greeted me telepathically. *Figured I might as well get used to it if I'm spending the weekend with you*, he said.

Will it really take that much getting used to? I asked.

We'll see.

I know he didn't feel the same, but to me, our mind link was as comfortable as an old, favorite sweater. Oh, I could tell he was trying to restrict the free flow of information between us. He said it was so I wouldn't be overwhelmed. I think he just didn't want me to have run of the house, so to speak. To be fair, though, he also didn't poke around in my head, as far as I could tell.

We spent the day kicking around town, eating from street vendor carts and enjoying the cool weather. We talked a lot. Verbally, that is. And when six o'clock rolled around, we boarded the yacht for our cruise.

It lasted four hours, including a four-course meal and several cocktails. The several cocktails were mine. Dana wasn't drinking anything stronger than iced tea. I asked him why.

"You're not driving home tonight," I said.

"Might," he said. "But even if not, I just don't think it's a good idea for me to drink while around you."

"Afraid I'll take advantage of you?" I said with a smirk.

"You know why," he said, finishing his dessert.

"Mm hm. Because you're afraid."

"Dinah—"

"Well, that's it, isn't it?"

He wiped his mouth and dropped his napkin beside his plate. "I'm not having this conversation."

I thought about pushing it, but chose not to. Dana could be every bit as stubborn as I could. So instead, I changed the subject and told him about Lily and my approach to dealing with the girl's guilt.

"That's a tough one," he said. "Can't say I've ever had a client who accidentally killed her family. So what is it you think you can do for her?"

I leaned back in my chair. "I'm not sure. I just know, deep down, that she's able to control what's going on inside her. She just has to get past the blocks."

"Even if you're right," Dana said, "it wouldn't change the fact that her abilities are killing her."

"Yeah. Still working on that part."

We sat in silence a while before the fireworks began, then stepped onto the deck to watch. Dana zipped up his coat against the chill. My body temperature is such that I don't notice the cold until it approaches freezing. But I snuggled up next to him, anyway.

A few days later, I sat at an outdoor café. Against my better judgment, I'd agreed to meet "audiokit87," a mysterious emailer who wanted to talk about Lily. I'd received the email, sent through an anonymous proxy, requesting the rendezvous in a public setting.

I ordered a cappuccino and took a seat outside. Audiokit87 had requested we meet at the same café where I'd met Dr. Gray when he'd been in town for a conference. Because of course he did.

As if to reinforce that painful flashback, at the table next to mine was a familiar face. It was the same blond-haired meta who'd been on the phone then. And he was again, now.

"I don't *have* that power, Saul," he said into his phone. "No, I really don't. I'd know it if I did."

I smiled and suppressed a chuckle. This time, I knew who he was. "Chip" Tremaine, known to the public as my esteemed teammate, Transcendant. He looked in my direction. I gave a nod and a slight wave.

"Get a new agent," I said to him.

He grinned at me, somewhat shyly. "Even if I did, Saul, do you really think it's a good idea to sell kids an action figure that can spontaneously burst into flame?"

Just then, a man arrived and sat across from me. He wore a ball cap, sunglasses, and a ridiculous fake beard. I tried to hold back a laugh. "You didn't tell me you were in ZZ Top."

"Some of us actually care about keeping our identities secret." His voice was soft and unassuming, despite the reprimand. For some reason, it never occurred to me that the mystery emailer might be a meta.

"Quite right," I said. "So. Lily."

"How is she?"

"She was fine when I saw her last week," I said. "But who are you to her?"

"I guess I don't really know. I thought she liked me, but..."

"You were the one who took her from New Alcatraz."

He nodded, his bushy beard bunching up against his chest. "We met at Pelican Hospital before she was sent to New Alcatraz. I was a patient there for a few days."

"So you were smitten and arranged to 'rescue' her."

"Pretty much, yeah."

"And after you did, you dropped her off and never heard from her again." I thought about telling him the truth, that she'd used him in her suicide attempt. But the kid was clearly hurting enough. "How did you know she was back there? And how did you know to contact me?"

He was silent for a moment. "I'd rather not say."

I didn't like that answer, but I let it go. "You want me to get a message to her, don't you?"

"If it's not too much trouble."

I finished my cappuccino. "And if she has a return message?"

"She can use the email I sent from. Or you can."

I shook my head. "No more secret agent stuff."

He hesitated a moment, then nodded, before reaching inside his jacket and pulling out an envelope and a pen. He scribbled an email address on the back of the envelope before sliding it across the table to me. "I really appreciate this," he said as he stood.

"Sure," I said. "I'll be in touch." I slid the letter into my bag as he turned and walked off. I noticed Transcendant was also gone. I put my empty cup in the bus tub near the door, then headed home.

✧ ✧ ✧

I watched Lily as she sat on the edge of her bed, reading the mystery man's letter. I studied her face for any hint of emotion, but found none. She finished reading, folded up the pages, and tucked them back in the envelope. "Thanks," she muttered without looking at me.

"He really likes you, Lily."

"That's his bad judgment."

The tone of her voice didn't match her dismissal of him. "And you like him, too, don't you?"

"Doesn't matter," she mumbled.

The girl wasn't looking well. Dr. Prashad had told me that the treatment was working fine, at least for now. Her appearance, I suspected, was from the psychological distress of being kept here in New Alcatraz. She had hoped that, because her treatment was going well, she would be moved back to Pelican Hospital. But the powers-that-be weren't open to that idea. She'd stay in New Alcatraz until her eighteenth birthday.

My concern was that they'd find some way to keep her there beyond then, possibly by charging her with the crime of destroying property, endangerment of the public, and so on. But my actual fear was that the government would step in and "recruit" her for something. Despite the public sentiment slowly becoming less hostile toward metas, the government seemed more inclined than ever to exploit them.

"Listen," I said cautiously, "I've been giving a lot of thought to your situation. And I have some ideas."

"Do any of them involve you removing my tendency to blow up?"

"Um... yes and no."

She looked up at me from her bed. "What's that mean?"

I shifted in my chair and cleared my throat. "Well, if my idea works, it would remove your tendency to explode unintentionally."

"And why would I want to *intentionally* explode?"

"For the same reason I do? Lily, our abilities are not that dissimilar. We both generate a crazy amount of energy. If I don't vent my excess, which I do in a few different ways, it builds and builds until I 'explode' like you do. If you could learn to 'vent' your excess—"

"Yeah, well, it wouldn't change the fact that I killed my family."

I frowned. Getting her past this was going to be hard. "Nothing can do that," I said. "But you wouldn't have to worry about killing your boyfriend."

She glared at me. "He's not my boyfriend."

I shrugged. "Who said I meant *him*?"

"So how would I learn to do this?"

"We'll work on it together. But first, we need to get you out of here."

That got her attention. She stared at me with imploring eyes. "Can you do that?"

"I'm going to try," I said. "I can't promise anything, of course, but I'll do my best."

The first step in that process was to make sure no criminal charges were forthcoming. To determine that, I went to the one person I knew who could find that out in a hurry.

"I can – and will – find out for you," Invictus said. Then, with a tilt of his head, he said, "I admit I'm curious about your continued interest in the girl."

I considered my response carefully. "I suppose the primary reason is that she reminds me of myself. She's been through some terrible things and I want to help her. And I hate the idea of her being stuck in there."

"And the secondary reason?"

I smiled weakly. "I suppose I'm hoping that helping her deal with her guilt will help me with my own."

Invictus nodded in understanding, then said, "I'll let you know as soon as I hear anything." I thanked him and turned to leave. "Dyna," he said, and I turned back. "I'm impressed by your dedication to her."

"Kind of you to say," I said.

"But," he continued, "remember, we're not social workers."

I chuckled. "Had to go and ruin the moment, didn't you?"

To my surprise, he smiled faintly and shrugged. "It's my way."

The answer, it seemed, was no. There would be no charges against her. Invictus had gotten his answer within two days, showing again just how much pull the man had. If I'd made the inquiry, it would have been a month before I heard back, if ever.

My next step was to discuss my ideas with Dr. Prashad. We met privately, on her day off, at the Citadel. We sat in one of the smaller conference rooms, where I laid out my thoughts.

"I want you to stop Lily's treatment," I said.

The woman blinked in surprise. "What on earth for?"

"Because," I said, "I don't think it's actually necessary."

"Of course it's necessary! You were the one who pointed that out!"

"Well, no," I corrected. "I pointed out the likely cause of her excess calcium. I admit treatment was needed to get her stable, but going forward, I think there's a better approach."

"Which would be what?"

"For her to learn how to naturally vent the excess potassium."

The doctor narrowed her eyes at me. "Thereby avoiding its decay into calcium, so no risk of calcium build-up." She nodded. "And this is possible?"

"I have to assume so. There seems to be something about the meta mutations that allows our bodies to accommodate such things."

"Lily's body *wasn't* accommodating it. If it had been, she wouldn't have been near death."

"I think the trauma Lily experienced after the deaths of her parents and sisters prevented her from naturally adapting to her abilities. A psychological block."

"If so, it's pretty clear that block is still present."

With a sigh, I agreed. "We'll be working on that, too. My brother is a psychologist and I'm sure I can get him to work with her."

She nodded, considering this. Then she said, "I understand how the potassium causes her calcium accumulation. But what about the explosions?"

"Well, here's my thinking on that. Potassium-40 doesn't always decay to calcium-40," I said. "Other times, it decays to argon-40. Most of those conversions are by electron capture, and I suspect the bursts are caused by the remaining type of decay, which is positron emission. So the conversion of the metallic potassium to gaseous argon is what causes the bursts. The fact that the positron emission decay is rare is why her bursts aren't more common. I also suspect she'll be able to develop the ability to choose the types of conversions, too, making her explosions more common, if she wants."

Dr. Prashad focused her dark eyes on me. "And your education is in *biological* sciences?"

"Okay, I admit I've been brushing up on my chemistry since meeting Lily," I said with a grin. "You caught me."

"So have I," she said, "though not to that degree. My concern is that the isotopes you're talking about are all radioactive."

"Yeah," I said. "But it's really low-level stuff. Too low to be dangerous to anyone around her. Still, she'll be exposed to it perpetually, so we'll keep a close watch on her for signs of radiation poisoning, but again, I think her body has already adapted to that particular side effect."

"So what role do I play in all this?"

"Until she can learn to vent on her own, we'll still need treatment. But I don't want her to have to go to Pelican Hospital for it." Dr. Prashad frowned as I said this. "We have a medical facility here in the Citadel. Can you help make it possible for her treatments to be done here?"

Still frowning, she nodded. "Most likely, but I don't like it."

"Why not?"

"Call me a traditionalist, but I believe such things should be done in the proper environment, by the proper person."

"We have an excellent physician on staff. Kind of necessary."

With a sigh, Dr. Prashad assented. I showed her our medical bay and introduced her to the Gatekeepers' staff physician, Dr. Stone. She was young, only a few years out of medical school, and had been the team's doc for about a year and a half. The two of them talked shop, after which Dr. Prashad seemed okay with my idea. When Lily turned eighteen, she'd leave with me.

Now I just had to figure out how to get her off her leash completely.

Vicky and I sat in her living room, drinking martinis and sharing life stories. Martinis aren't my preferred cocktail, but Vicky made a good one, using Brecon gin, which she brings back from the U.K. when she visits. She's become my supplier, too. It's made in Wales, which makes it the perfect gin for the Welsh Dragon cocktail I invented for Dana.

I'd just finished telling her about the nasty relationship I had with my mother, including how she "killed" me for the people in my home town.

"That's awful," she said as she grabbed my empty glass and headed to the kitchen to make another round.

"Understatement," I said. "Ladies room?"

"Down that hall, second door on the left."

I admired her décor as I headed to the bathroom. It was overwhelmingly British. Union Jack-themed items abounded, as did Harry Potter and Doctor Who paraphernalia. A giant movie poster for Monty Python and the Holy Grail adorned the wall behind the sofa. I passed two other doors on my way to the potty. The Beatles peered at me from behind a glass frame on one door. On the other door was, to my shock, teen heartthrob Jesse McCartney.

I blinked, shook my head, and headed to the toilet. Minutes later, back in the living room, I said, "I couldn't help but notice that you have the wrong McCartney on one of those doors."

Vicky set down our drinks and rolled her eyes. "Bloody right. My cousin Bridget lives with me. She grew up here in the States. I haven't been able to educate her, musically, yet."

"What's she think about you being a meta?" I asked, returning to my seat.

Vicky chuckled. "Not much, since she's one, too. She's one of the reserve Gatekeepers. Bricky."

In fact, I had met her, briefly. The girl was probably fifteen or sixteen. Suddenly, I laughed. "Ha! Vicky and Bricky."

"Whatever, Dana and Dinah."

"Point," I said. "I didn't know we had reserve members."

"Well, it's not an official classification. Since she's a minor, Invictus uses her only in situations that aren't very dangerous."

"What about her parents?" I asked as she returned to the room.

Vicky sipped her drink. "They're good people. Live in L.A. Neither is a meta. When I moved to California, I contacted them and one thing led to another. So now she lives with me, under my protection, so to speak."

"Nice to have family around, isn't it?"

"Depends on the family member," she said.

I nodded. "Yeah. Glad my mother doesn't live nearby."

"My father and I have a somewhat antagonistic relationship," she said.

"Yeah?"

Vicky turned sideways on the sofa, facing me, her expression contemplative. "I haven't really shared this with many people, ever," she said, looking into my eyes. "But I think I can trust you."

I nodded, preparing myself for something shocking. "He didn't, um, molest you or anything, did he?"

"Oh, no. Nothing so simple." She drank again, then put her glass aside on the coffee table. "My father is a high mucky-muck in a secret society. A frightfully old one, in fact. I couldn't tell you how old, truly. But this group holds to the view that all things are connected in a sort of semi-mystical way. And I don't mean in some spiritual, 'Use the Force, Luke' kind of way. I'm talking about actual connections in space and time."

"Okay," I said, curious.

"Over the generations, the members have learnt to access other dimensions."

That got my attention. "What?"

Vicky nodded. "Not unlike the portal in the Nevada Incident, I understand."

"You're not saying this group is responsible for that rift, are you?"

"No, no. Not at all. But they can create similar ones, smaller ones, and use them in different ways. Instantaneous travel over short distances and the like. Well, you've seen my abilities, to a degree. Same thing."

"Your abilities?" I said, frowning. "You're saying that when you're tossing a fireball at someone—"

"I'm actually opening a tiny portal to a fire dimension and allowing it to spill out into our world."

"So when you sort of... you know... teleport..."

"Yeah, it's kind of like a tunnel through another dimension, rather than just a door into it. Not sure how to really explain it. When I open a portal, another one opens at the same time somewhere within my line of sight. Entering one tosses me out the other one, right off."

"That's what I was starting to put together," I said, wondering if that could be what my double had done. "Anyway, so this is a secret society of metas?"

"Well, yeah, I'd have to say so. But here's the thing. For many centuries, this group has been engaging in a selective breeding program."

"Not at all cliché."

"Right?" Vicky laughed. "Anyway, this program had one goal. You see, the different members of the society each have slightly different abilities, and each generation brings about a few who are more powerful than the generations before. Meaning they can access a wider variety of dimensions and so on. The ultimate goal, of course, being to bring about that one child who would be able to access *all* dimensions."

I shook my head. "Okay, ignoring for the moment the weirdness of that, just how would you know when you had *all* dimensions represented? How do you even know how many there are?"

"I know, yeah? It's absurd. But there's no talking sense to them. They're convinced they'll 'just know' when it happens. They're quite single-minded." She shrugged and retrieved her drink. After a sip, she said, "I guess they just expect this kid to have godlike powers or some such."

"And you're part of that breeding program."

She nodded. "I didn't learn about it until I turned thirteen. My mother was the one who told me, and she also told me just what their use for this tyke would be." Vicky finished her drink, her eyes avoiding mine. "A living conduit. An anchor for their ultimate rift, keeping it permanently open. They imagine it being the physical intersection of all dimensions, through which the others would channel and/or derive their abilities."

I frowned. "Anchor? What?"

Now she looked at me. "Like most secret societies, they have a meeting place. In this case, it's somewhere in the U.K. Not sure where. I've never seen it. But in that spot is a machine they've constructed. Their prize offspring would become part of that machine, bonded with it, powering it, becoming a physical amplifier, a living portal."

My head still couldn't wrap itself around this. But past "bonded with it," it didn't matter. I felt sick to my stomach. "And you're the one they've been breeding for?"

"Oh, I rather doubt it. But even if I'm not their Nexus Prime, as they call it, I would have become just another breeder toward it. I sure wasn't going to stick around for either of those scenarios. Mother smuggled me out of England and I've lived in California ever since."

"Wait. 'Nexus Prime,' you said."

Vicky grinned. "Yeah. The society itself is called The Nexus. So when I decided to do the meta thing, I named myself Nexus just to wind up Daddy."

I shook my head. "How could any father even consider allowing his child to become, um, whatever that is?"

"Such is the nature of zealotry."

"Has he ever tried to get you back?"

"Oh, sure. But catching me is easier said than done. I mean, I would probably have become much more in control of my abilities had I stayed there with them, to be trained by them, but I'm not too shabby."

"Hope I never meet this asshole."

Vicky chuckled. "You already have, love." Seeing my look of confusion, she said, "In Nevada, according to your report. My father is Dane Weatherford."

I gaped. "Son of a bitch."

"Could be. Never met his mother."

I frowned. "And a job in metahuman affairs would allow him to scout out metas who might be good additions to the group."

Vicky nodded. "That's my figuring, too."

We were quiet for a time, then I asked the question that had been on my mind for several minutes. "Vick, just how dangerous is this group? I mean, what you've described sounds pretty frightful."

With a frown, she said, "I dunno. On the one hand, yes, there's certainly potential for danger, there. But on the other hand, they've had that potential for at least a century and haven't done anything with it. They seem pretty self-contained, focused on their own thing. My father's an arsehole, no question. But I have no reason to think he – or the group – has any sort of evil, world-dominating inclinations."

I shook my head. "Either way, that's a hell of a history you've got."

"Suppose so," she said, looking at me with a slightly uncomfortable expression. "So are you okay with all that?"

I finished my drink and put the glass aside. "Why wouldn't I be?"

Vicky reached out and put her hand on my leg. "I dunno. I just don't want you to have any sort of worries about me. I really like you."

I looked down at her hand on my thigh, then back to her face. "Um..."

Then she leaned over and kissed me.

EIGHT

"If you wish a thing to be well done, you must do it yourself, you must not leave it to others."

~ Henry Wadsworth Longfellow

I graduated high school in 1988, making 2008 the twentieth anniversary of that event. Naturally, my class had a reunion. My friend Rhonda begged me to come home for it. I'd successfully avoided the previous three reunions and had no desire to break that streak, so I explained that Gatekeepers matters prevented me from making the trip (which was, in fact, true). But she guilted me into promising to be there for the twenty-fifth, in 2013. At least that would give me five years to come up with a legit excuse to miss it.

The team matter, oddly enough, was a very similar celebration. The Gatekeepers, which officially formed in 1978, was celebrating the thirtieth anniversary of the group with a big bash.

Like my high school, the Gatekeepers held these celebrations every five years. Initially, I thought that was a bit excessive. But then I realized just how much the composition of a team can change in five years.

We held the party in the main hall of the Citadel, of course. It was a lavishly catered affair, with wonderful food and drink, and a live chamber music ensemble. Almost all the Gatekeepers made an appearance at some point or other, as did many former members. Even having been a member for half a year, there were still some I hadn't met. But it wasn't just our team members. Members from other teams showed up. Solo agents, too. There were government folks, police officers, and of course, the press. As such, the metas were all in costume.

The Golden Bear was there. He wasn't in bear form, but the tattoo of California's state animal on his upper arm told everyone who he was. I hadn't seen Marcus in a long time. He brought his boyfriend, Wayne, who was delightfully entertaining. Marcus asked about Dana. "Saw him over the Fourth," I said. "But we haven't been communicating well, recently."

"That's a shame," Marcus said. "I'll have to talk some sense into him."

"Do you see him often?"

"No, but I think I know where to find him on weekends. A new café opened recently that has a great selection of Belgian beers."

"Good call. That's like a magnet to him. Hell, it's a magnet to *me*!"

"Then come on up!"

Just then, Captain Shepherd and his family found me. I introduced them to Marcus, who signed autographs for Layla and Sydney. The girls then bounced off in search of other signatures, mama Helena in tow. Marcus and Wayne bounced off in search of cocktails.

Before long, we were a little group off in a corner of the room, having been joined by Jack, Sinta, and Daniel. I was pleased to see that Daniel was walking with a cane and not using the wheelchair, though he spent most of his time sitting. It was like a mini-reunion of the Bay Scouts. Even Ping Song was there. We posed for a photo or two, then continued chatting until others interrupted us. Invictus came over especially to greet Daniel. Nexus arrived, along with her cousin, Bricky. With them was a girl of about eighteen or nineteen.

"Hey, love," Vicky said, giving me a quick hug and smooch on the cheek. I smiled and looked over the younger girl. She was thin and pretty, with deep red hair and a prominent scar across her left eye. She was dressed in black leather with purple accents, and had small, leathery wings.

"Hi, hon," I said. "I see you brought Bat Girl."

The girl sized me up. "Not the most original thinker, are ya?" she said with a slight Texas twang.

"This is Vesper," Vicky said.

I nodded. "I recognized you from the files."

"Nice to finally meet ya," she said, shaking my hand.

After introductions all around, Vicky said, "I'll drag her to the next Gatekeeper Girls meeting."

"Great," I said.

"Oh. Should I bring anything?" Vesper asked.

"Thanks for offering. How about chocolate chips?"

"Yay, cookies!" Sinta said.

"No," I said. "For melting."

Vesper frowned. "'kay. How much?"

"Well, it's not a very big hot tub," I said, laughing when her eyebrows shot upward. "Just a bag for fondue," I said.

"Oh," she said. "'Course. Sounds great."

Sinta and Bricky struck up a conversation, and Vicky put a hand on my arm. "Can I steal you away for a minute?"

"Sure," I said, and we headed for the nearest table of food.

"Thought I should apologize," she said.

I loaded a plate with fresh figs stuffed with goat cheese. "For what?" I asked.

"Well, after the way you nearly ran from my flat, I thought I'd upset you."

"Oh," I said, moving to lean against a vacant patch of wall. "I just wasn't expecting—"

"I know," she said. "Too bloody forward, that's me." She smiled faintly.

"It's okay," I said.

"So where does that put us?"

I looked up at the darkly painted granite next to me. "Next to a statue of Night Dove." Vicky narrowed her eyes and frowned at me. I let out a breath. "I don't know. Where do you want it to put us?"

"Wow. My snogging must be off if you weren't clear about that."

Despite myself, I felt my cheeks flush. "One can interpret a snog in a few ways."

"Fair to say," she said. "You don't know me well enough. But I don't go around locking lips with just anyone."

"I didn't think you did."

"Same time, I'm also not known for being coy or waiting for someone else to make the first move. Good thing, too, since I don't think you ever would have."

"I see."

She tilted her head and smirked. "Not sure you do," she said. "I find you fascinating, Dyna." I was uncomfortable before, but this pushed me near the edge. I started to protest, but she cut me off. "Don't question it. Just accept it."

I thought of the conversation I'd had with Dana about me not believing I'm worthy of others' attention. "Okay," I said. "Thank you. I'm flattered."

She reached over and snagged a fig from my plate. "Kinda curious whether there's any mutual feeling." I looked into her gray eyes and felt my heart race. I was flattered, it was true, but the main feeling I had was fear. The pain of the K.T. debacle was still there, lying atop the pain of all the others before her, deep and oppressive. I wanted to explain this to Vicky, but all I managed to do was nod stupidly, even as I wondered why I was nodding. "Brilliant," she said with a grin. "Now let's get back to the party."

One day during the summer, I learned that Bruce Edward Ivins was dead. Ivins was suspected of being the man behind the anthrax-laced letters that killed five people back in 2001, my distant, unmet cousin being one of them. Ivins had been found unconscious at his home a few days prior and had died in the hospital of acetaminophen poisoning. I remembered Dana telling me of a client who'd overdosed on it and his description of how agonizing such a death can be.

If Ivins was, in fact, the guilty party, I would feel no sympathy for his painful passing.

Still, I found no satisfaction in his death, either. I'm not sure it's even in me, anymore, to feel that way about anyone's death. Another result of having killed someone. The only positive result, I'd say.

I still thought frequently of the bloody death of the other-dimensional Valora. It took only a moment's thought to recall the feeling of her slick blood coating my hands as it flowed down the spear in her chest. I could still see the mad hatred in her eyes as the life slowly left them. I didn't hold any illusions about it. I knew that, as long as she lived, our world would never truly be safe from her. I'm not at all sorry she's dead. Maybe if it had been someone other than myself who'd killed her, I might even feel some satisfaction.

Of course, there was one death I thought of far more often than Valora's. I couldn't seem to stop thinking of Dr. Gray, much as I wanted to. I wondered if I ever could.

But Ivins' death also reminded me of my investment in Emergent Biosolutions, the company producing an anthrax vaccine. The economy wasn't doing too well and I didn't want to lose my investment, so I took a moment to check its value. I was pleased to see that it had increased since my purchase. I briefly considered selling at least some of it, but since I didn't need any funds at the moment, I decided to let it sit.

The rest of my savings was in CDs at Justice Federal Credit Union. My income from the Gatekeepers was pretty good. Even with rent in excess of two grand a month and the general high cost of living in the city, I was able to sock away a good bit.

I was also sending Dana a check each month, in some effort to repay him for all the times he'd helped me out. He kept saying it wasn't necessary, as he was doing fine. He reminded me that he'd never had much debt. Most of his education had been paid for by scholarships, and what few student loans he'd needed to take had been paid off years before. Every time he got a check, he'd call and tell me to stop. But I kept sending them. It was about the only way I could get him to call.

By the first week of August, the med-bay in the Citadel was outfitted with the necessary equipment to handle Lily's treatments. But that wasn't the only thing the girl would need when she left New Alcatraz. She'd need a place to live.

The answer to that came from her not-boyfriend, "audiokit87." I'd initially contacted him after delivering her letter and continued to keep him apprised of what I was doing for her. When I mentioned my concern about living accommodations, he offered space in his home. I learned that the kid had sold an invention to the military at the ripe old age of nineteen. He lived in a two-bedroom apartment, as it turned out, in the building right next to mine. The second bedroom was mainly storage, he said, but he could easily convert it into a sleeping room again, assuming Lily was open to the idea.

It was because we were neighbors that he'd known of my interactions with Lily. He'd recognized me and knew of my affiliation with the Gatekeepers. Knowing they'd been responsible for capturing Lily, he started keeping tabs on my activities, up to and including following me to the hospital on my first visit. I wasn't happy about having been tailed. Not because he did so, but because I hadn't been aware of it.

Eventually, I asked him about his non-civilian identity.

"I'm Resonator," he said.

"No shit?" I said. "That's very cool! I never would have guessed you to be so young!"

"I'm flattered that you've heard of me," he said.

Resonator was one of the "flying tanks" in the meta world. Though he was a newcomer to the meta world, he'd made quite an impression. He had a suit of armor that was capable of flight. His abilities were all sonically based. The armor was studded with tiny microphones that picked up ambient noises, which were then electronically amplified by the suit and turned into weapons. Sound cannons and the like. Now I knew what sort of invention he'd sold to the military.

I invited him over for pizza, and he accepted, showing up with a bottle of wine. I accepted the offering as I looked him over. Assuming the "87" in his email address was his year of birth, he'd be twenty-one this year.

Sinta stood with me as he entered the apartment. "Hi!" she said with a huge grin. "I'm Sinta."

The young man smiled and extended his hand. "I'm Kit," he said, brushing his shiny, black hair out of his eyes.

"Like Kit Carson?" Sinta asked.

"See," I said, "I was gonna ask if it was like the talking car in Knight Rider." Both of them looked at me without comprehension. I sighed and wallowed in my oldness.

"Actually," he said, "I was named after Kit Walker, the secret identity of The Phantom from the comics."

"How cool!" Sinta said as she dragged him into the living room while I poured soft drinks for us all. Over the next couple hours, we got to know one another. I found him to be friendly, earnest, and polite. By the time the pizza was devoured, any reservations I had about putting Lily in an apartment with him were gone.

Even so, Lily might have plenty of concerns, so when I told her later about Kit's offer, I made sure to offer to look into alternative housing situations for her. She thought it over for all of thirty seconds.

A week later, Lily turned eighteen and checked herself out of New Alcatraz. Kit and I were there to pick her up. Dr. Prashad was there to see us off and to wish her well.

We had a birthday party for her that night, then got her settled into the guest room at Kit's place.

I'd been on the hormone drugs for a few weeks, with frequent medical visits throughout, until I was ready for the egg harvesting procedure. I'd informed Invictus of what I was doing, and had requested to be taken off active duty during this period, so as to minimize any risk of physical harm. He was very understanding and kept it to himself, as well.

The day before the procedure, I was given an injection of human chorionic gonadotropin, which helps the eggs to detach from the follicles inside the ovary. Thirty-six hours later, I was anesthetized and had fifteen eggs removed, then taken to cryogenic storage. The process took half an hour. And once I woke, I went home.

The next day, I was quietly restored to active duty. As we hadn't had any assignments needing me during the time I was inactive, no one was any the wiser.

Ping Song and I sat at the Nefili Café in Berkeley, not far from the computer science building where she worked. We hadn't had much time to catch up at the Gatekeepers bash.

"It's great to see you," I said.

"You, too," she said with a smile. "I admit, I was surprised at the anniversary party. Made me quite nostalgic."

I nodded. "I agree. I never realized I'd miss the Scouts so much. I even miss the twins, believe it or not."

Song smirked. "I won't tell a soul."

"So," I said, pulling out a flash drive and sliding it across the table to her, "you might find that interesting." It contained the massive Biometric Resonance Tuning document I'd taken from the computer in the in-between.

"Very well," she said, pocketing the device.

I told her about my recent encounter with my other-self and her revelation that additional dimensions were known to them. "She said the Ping Song of her world had built a machine that could detect the rifts, and that she'd visited several such worlds, including ours."

Song nodded with a mysterious smile. "I have been using the data we took from the computer at Groom Lake for just that purpose," she said. "I was able to determine how the constructs worked, for the most part, in keeping the portals open. From there, it was not difficult to discover how to detect such anomalies."

"Wow."

"Jack was correct, by the way. Untethered, the rifts do, indeed, move. I have been tracking one for about a month."

"You're kidding."

She shook her head as she sipped her tea. "I'm not."

I was stunned. "And have you, you know, entered?"

"I don't particularly have such a desire, even if I had a way to do so. This one isn't as easily accessible as the one in Nevada."

"You thought a portal in Area 51 was easily accessible?"

"Yes, well, aside from that, it was easy. It was roughly at ground level. This one is approximately three miles above the Bay."

I don't know why it never occurred to me that such rifts would appear anywhere other than near the ground. "Wait," I said. "You've been tracking it for a month? The one in Nevada had nearly disappeared after a matter of hours, I heard."

"I'd heard the same," she said. "Makes you wonder, doesn't it, how they were able to develop machinery to hold it open in such a short period of time?"

I sighed. "Yeah." It was, indeed, something I'd wondered frequently. The clear implication is that our government had previously encountered portals. But that was a concern for another time, perhaps. "So you're saying this one is stable?"

"It seems to be," she said, finishing her tea. "Or stable enough, anyway. The readings I've been collecting from it indicate much less frequency variation than the one in Nevada."

"How long would you think it's been there?"

"No way to tell. But its movement is quite slow. In the month I've been tracking it, it has moved hardly at all. Very fortunate that it's so high, all things considered."

"Why?"

"We have several airports nearby. This rift is positioned above the arrival and departure flight paths."

"Right," I said. "So, in what direction is it moving? Can you tell?"

"It appears to be moving at an angle, away from the ground. Eventually, should it remain stable long enough, it seems as though it will leave our atmosphere altogether." She was quiet a moment, then said, "Do you have a desire to explore it?"

"No," I said. "Of course not!"

Song tilted her head, knowing as well as I did that I was full of shit.

"So tell me about stalkers," I said to Dana when he answered his phone.

"In what sense?"

"Well, how to tell if they're psychotically dangerous, for example. And why they, you know, stalk."

"Most aren't psychotic," he told me. "That being said, many of them do have some sort of mental health issue. Depression, the occasional personality disorder, substance abuse. As for why they do it, there are several common reasons. A few are just outright predators."

"Fantastic," I drawled.

"Some are looking for intimacy in all the wrong places. They feel 'close' to the victim for some reason, even if they've never met. They may have a fantasy relationship in their minds and want to make it a reality. In many cases, they're motivated by anger, stemming from some perceived slight or rejection. The victim not taking their calls or returning emails. That sort of thing."

"Oh."

"And if you have one, you should be talking to the police, not me."

"I'm not really afraid of this guy," I said.

"Stop thinking only about yourself!" he snapped. "Sure, he may not be able to hurt you, but what if you're not his only target? Or what if those close to you are in danger from him?"

Sometimes I feel stupid for not seeing the obvious.

I contacted Macy and had her set up a filter in her email. All messages from this guy would automatically be routed straight to me, taking her out of the loop completely.

Then I printed out the email history. Fortunately, though I'd deleted them, I only empty my trash folder a couple times a year. I took the printouts to the police.

The detective read over the emails as I waited. When he was finished, he said, "Well, it certainly does look like you've got yourself a stalker. This most recent email," he said, pointing to it, "is the clincher. By saying he knows where you live, there's an implication of potential danger."

"Well, maybe," I said. "But that seems a bit of an assumption."

He shrugged and said, "It's your call. As it is, this isn't enough to warrant an arrest, but it could certainly become so. At the very least, we'll trace this email to find out who he is. And who knows? He might be stalking others. I'll check the system for matches on his email address."

I nodded and agreed that I would forward any further emails to the detective. I left feeling a bit disturbed. Did I do the right thing? Should I have just responded to him, myself?

No matter. It was done. We'd see what happened next.

I followed the spread of cryptococcal meningitis, watching as the number of cases increased at an alarming rate. The CDC had become involved and were doing their best to pinpoint the origin of the outbreak. But if they knew anything, they weren't sharing it.

Lumen, one of the Gatekeepers' Tribunes, had come down with it. As expected, he responded well to treatment. Invictus urged all of us to be aware of the symptoms, and asked me to speak to the group about the disease, since I was more intimately familiar with it than anyone else, so I did.

A week later, when I began to exhibit symptoms, I immediately made an appointment with my doctor for another spinal tap. The symptoms weren't bad. A bit of nausea, some headaches, a touch of dizziness. But I definitely didn't want them to get worse.

Instead of receiving my test results via email the following day, I was called in for a follow-up appointment. "In all honesty, Dinah," my doctor said as we went over my results, "I'm not sure what's going on. *Something's* there. It's just not what you had before. Nor is it what's going around with everyone else."

"Weird. Any ideas at all?"

He frowned. "Under the microscope, it sure looks like your previous infection, but the labs don't back it up. I'd like to take another CSF sample. Urine and blood, too. And in the meantime, we'll start you on the anti-fungals again."

"Fine," I said. Then, as he prepared to do the spinal tap, I said, "Doc? How about you make it a double? I'll take an order of it to go."

The following weeks were busy ones. Sinta and I got to know our neighbors better. Sinta and Lily got along well. But then, everyone loves Sinta. The girls had in common the unfortunate fact that both were orphans. Lily had spent years in the custody of the state. Sinta spent her years on the streets after her final mistreatment in a foster home.

I found myself hoping that Lily would mellow a little from Sinta's general positive outlook and her belief that people are basically good. I wanted her to move past the guilt and enjoy life. She was too young to carry that weight around.

Her weekly treatments were going well. We kept a close eye on her for any sign that they might be inadequate. Lily wanted to know how we were going to train her to tap into the energies being produced. So we spent a lot of time talking about it.

There was a fundamental difference between us. When my powers manifested, I knew them for what they were and happily embraced them. Lily, though, because of her psychological issues, had developed a subconscious avoidance of the energy within her. In her head, it wasn't a power to use for good; it was the killer that robbed her of her family.

Naturally, I was of no use as a therapist for her, so I turned to Dana for help. It took a lot of convincing, but Lily eventually agreed to see him. Dana needed to be convinced, too, but agreed when I explained how Lily was open only to him as a therapist because of the modicum of trust she had in me. Any other therapist wouldn't have much chance with her.

Dana insisted on coming to the city for this, rather than having me take her to Sacramento. Probably so he could immediately leave when they were finished so as to not be in the same town with me any longer than he had to.

I won't pretend that the Gatekeepers' lab is the equal to a professional medical laboratory. But it has a lot of great equipment and I made the best use of it that I could. I prepared a slide of my cerebrospinal fluid, glad that my physician had done me the favor. It made the nearly forty-five minutes lying on my side, curled up almost in a fetal position, with a needle stuck between my vertebrae, worth it. It's not that I don't trust doctors. It's just that I believe no one is as dedicated to my welfare as I am.

As it did the last time, the amphotericin B had me puking my guts up on a regular basis, so I was prescribed something for that, too. A drug for my drugs.

Sinta was convinced that this illness was the same thing my other-self had, and that I was going to die. I assured her this wasn't the case, though in truth, I wasn't so sure. But her concerns reminded me to look more closely at my double's notes. And what I read in there wasn't encouraging.

I remembered her surprise when I told her the anti-fungal drugs had worked for me. Her notes revealed that they had no such effect on her, which was what drove her to develop her own treatment to begin with.

One day, I was studying my CSF in the microscope, comparing what I saw on the slide to pictures online of different sorts of fungi. It really did resemble *C. neoformans* more than anything else.

I watched, fascinated, as they floated in the fluid. And then I noticed something weird. Typically, each cell of *C. neoformans* is surrounded by a fairly large "shell" of gelatinous matter that prevents the actual cells themselves from touching each other.

Out of curiosity, I used my energy vision or whatever it is (I never know what to call it) to view the little buggers. I didn't expect much, because the smaller the organism, the less I can detect. Then again, I'd never tried it with a microscope.

What I saw startled me. The energy pattern was faint, but discernible due to the magnification. What took me by surprise was the fact that the pattern was familiar. It was identical to my own. And more alarming was the fact that there appeared to be something surrounding the shells. Like a second shell that didn't stand out in an ink stain, but that I could detect with my abilities.

I sat back, a sick feeling washing over me. Then I got up and fetched a hypodermic, then carefully squeezed a drop of the antifungal medicine onto the slide. And my breath caught in my throat as I watched the drug pool around the shells, which began glowing with a familiar bluish-white radiance. And in short order, the medicine was eradicated.

As incredible as it sounded, it seemed that the fungal cells had somehow adapted my own ability to fend off dangers with their own little energy shields.

The good news was that I could stop taking my puke-inducing drugs. The bad news was that it was because those drugs weren't going to kill the cells. In fact, it was highly likely that the cells would kill me.

Nine

"Nothing weighs on us so heavily as a secret."
~ Jean de La Fontaine

I've always been great at keeping secrets, even as a child. I understood how important it was, though for the life of me, I couldn't tell you where that came from. I guess I always thought that secrets were precious. Things that belonged only to you. Sharing them would diminish their intrinsic value.

Over the years, I carried a few. My brother's meta abilities, for example. And I learned the danger of sharing a secret, such as when my friend Rhonda told others about my attraction to girls.

But if I'm honest, I know that it's partially a family thing. My family tended to keep certain things... well, not secret, exactly, but on the down low. My grandfather's suicide, for example. Or the skin cancer discovered on my father's back. We were told his doctor visits were just checkups. I suppose the reasoning was that, since there was nothing Dana or I could do about Dad's melanoma, they chose not to worry us with the information.

This behavior always bothered me, so it's with no little amount of irony that I found myself doing the same thing. Since there was nothing to be done about it, the only person who knew about my condition was my physician. There was no sense in worrying my friends or teammates, I reasoned. My doctor and I would figure something out.

I'm not sure of the reason, but this incarnation of the disease progressed more slowly than my original infection. My symptoms remained steady, with very little change, for a long time. For a while, I thought perhaps this meant I wasn't really that sick, that whatever this was would fizzle out in time. But every time I'd settle into this attitude, I'd wake the next day feeling worse. My period of denial lasted about a month.

And it was an active month. Dana made the trip to the city twice a week for two-hour sessions with Lily. He wouldn't tell me the content of those talks, of course, but after their fourth session, he told me he was encouraged by her progress.

One way this progress was obvious to me was in the way she treated Kit. When she'd first moved in with him, she kept to herself, treating him like her landlord. After a couple weeks, though, they were acting more like roommates. To Kit's credit, he didn't push anything, even though it was clear how much he cared for her. By the end of September, they were together more often than not.

I kept myself busy with Gatekeepers matters. My symptoms didn't interfere much with our assignments, which weren't all that exciting at this particular time. I was easily able to hide my illness from them.

I focused on other matters, too. Like Song's discovery of the rift over the bay. I'd been thinking about it more and more ever since she told me about it. Truth is, I was dying to go in there and visit.

There were good reasons to go, beyond my own curiosity. This other world might pose a threat. There could be another Valora plotting to come through. And of course, there could be another me. Maybe one who had experienced this mutated disease I was facing. One who could cure me.

But the "me" from that world would pop into my world when I went through. What if she couldn't fly? It would be a hell of a fall.

I could pose all this to the Gatekeepers and get them to approve the trip, along with a contingency in the case of a flightless Dinah popping up three miles above the bay. But for some reason, I didn't do this. Instead, I went to someone else.

Kit's armor was heated, so the temperature at that altitude wouldn't pose a problem. I reasoned that he'd be capable of safely catching and lowering to earth anyone who came through. Besides, he owed me for hooking him up with Lily again.

"Okay," he said when I presented him with the idea. "I can grab anyone who comes through, but if I understand you right, when you come back, she'll return to her own world. Which could also be three miles in the sky."

I nodded. "That's right. But I figured in all your work creating your suit, you certainly must have something lying about – a jet pack or something – that she could learn to use."

Kit lifted an eyebrow. "In fact, I do. Let's just hope she's a quick study," he said. "But what about other differences? What if the other world doesn't have an oxygen atmosphere?"

"I've been led to believe that, for whatever reason, the overlaps are all earthlike, with regard to that sort of thing. Five out of five examples, in fact, so there seems to be some kind of cosmic kinship deal at play. I won't pretend to understand how."

"Great, but if this one is the exception to that..."

"Yeah," I said. "I'll sure feel stupid." In my head, I wondered if I was stupid for accepting my other-self's story. But I could think of no reason why she'd choose to lie about such a thing.

So one day in early October, I met with Ping Song again. "Okay," I said. "I'm curious."

She just smiled. "I knew you would be. I've got something for your trip." She pulled an item from a drawer in her desk. It was a portable monitor of some sort. "It's tuned to the rift," she said as I studied the phone-sized item. On its tiny screen was a radar-like scope, which Song said would allow me to reach the rift and even to orient myself for proper entrance. "Can't imagine why it wouldn't work from the other side, too."

"Thanks," I said. "I'll call you when I get back. If you haven't heard from me by this time tomorrow night, assume something unpleasant happened."

"You really should tell your teammates, don't you think?"

"Probably. But you know me."

"I do. Be careful."

I told Sinta it was a Gatekeepers thing, which was good enough for her. I hated lying, but I didn't want her to worry.

Just like my parents.

I dressed in dark clothing, including Capri jeans and a black jacket. Capris were my default legwear, anymore. They allowed me to blast into the sky without ruining my pants. I still had to do something about shoes, though. For this trip, they were stowed in my backpack, and my hair was in a ponytail under a knit beret. It was about four in the morning when I left my apartment. As arranged, Kit met me on the roof.

Flying to a height of three miles takes a lot of energy. I'd consumed a breakfast made up entirely of PowerPaste (a preview of the new Honey Nut flavor, thanks to my free allotment from the company) and carried several packets with me.

At this altitude, there wasn't enough ambient noise for Kit's armor to convert to energy. But there were internal converters, too. An MP3 player sat in a protective case on his belt, the music piped through to battery-powered speakers inside his helmet, where the mics picked it up and converted it to power. I think he was listening to Daft Punk during our flight.

Song's sensor did its job perfectly, directing me straight to it. The thing was about seven feet in diameter and shimmered faintly with pale rainbow colors.

"Pretty," Kit said.

I nodded, but shivered as I looked at it. According to the sensors on my comm, it was a balmy one degree Fahrenheit at that altitude, which I found a bit chilly. My heart raced in anticipation or fear; I'm not sure which.

"Once I go in," I said, "I'll see how big the in-between area is. If it's smallish, I'll be able to get out the other side quickly. If I think it'll take more than a couple minutes to do that, I'll pop back through and tell you."

"So either I'll see you or another you in a few minutes. Got it."

"And I'll be back in exactly five hours. So make sure, if she can't fly, that she's strapped into the jetpack at that point." Nodding to Kit, I maneuvered my way through.

The sensation was unlike going through the Nevada portal. There was no gelatin-like resistance, just a wash of warmth as I passed the barrier. To my great surprise, there was no in-between area. I emerged into open air, an instantly-recognizable San Francisco Bay far below me.

Panicked, I hoped Kit had quick reflexes, since my double would now be there in front of him. It was foolish to assume there would be an in-between zone. My double hadn't mentioned that part, either way. But she seemed to be right about the atmosphere. It was cold, but breathable.

I'd never been skydiving. Before gaining my abilities, the very idea of jumping out of an airplane held no appeal whatsoever. With abilities, who needed a plane? Or parachute? I cut my thrust.

My free fall lasted about a minute, by which point I was probably still a mile up. I ignited my jets, so to speak, slowed my descent and swooped in toward the city, pondering where to land. Did I want to go near where my apartment would be, way down on Page Street at the Panhandle? No. I didn't see much point to that. I wanted eventually to go to the library, but it seemed to be the same time of day here as it had been in my world. Most businesses wouldn't be open for hours, yet. Coffee shops, however, should be open soon.

On the corner of Octavia and Page is a small coffee shop, the Mercury Café. Assuming it existed here, I'd go there until the library opened. It wasn't far from the public library on Larkin (assuming it also existed), and was near enough to a residential neighborhood that I could land inconspicuously.

I landed a block from the café and semi-hid myself under one of the large trees that lined the street. I put on my shoes and made my way down the steep hill to the corner. And there it was, though still not open.

I peeked in the window, hoping they had a computer set up for internet use, but didn't see one. I was sure the library would have one, but then a thought struck me. This world seemed very much like my own, down to the same café with the same name. I wondered if our technologies might be compatible.

So I tapped my comm, pulling up the data connection screen. It immediately began to scan for multiple types of connections. It took a while, but eventually listed the café as a possible wireless connection. But it was password-protected. I'd have to come back when the place opened.

I roamed down the block, locating a trash can. Inside, I found a newspaper. I pulled it out, feeling like a stereotype in a time travel movie. I carried it with me back to the café, where I took a seat on a bench in the median across the street. I scanned the headlines, just to get a feel for what was going on in the world. To my surprise, the news wasn't all doom and gloom. There were stories about the upcoming summer Olympics in China and the election in November. But the main headline of the day had to do with the U.S. auto industry. Evidently, this fall would see the release of models by each of the major manufacturers that would feature the newest in green technologies, including hydrogen cells, high-capacity photovoltaic, and more. Analysts expected a banner year for the industry.

"Good morning!"

I looked up to see a uniformed man picking up trash with a long-handled, articulated grabber and dropping it into a large canvas bag over his shoulder. "Morning," I replied, noting that the sidewalks were remarkably free of refuse. "Have a great day," I said with a smile as he nodded and continued on his way.

I read the paper until the café opened. Even the ads, just to see what differences there might be. Very few, it turned out, except that prices seemed more reasonable than in my world. When the café opened, an employee brought out a few round tables and chairs, lining them near the outside walls. I put the paper aside and entered the tiny shop. I caught the cashier's attention. "Could I get your wireless password, please?"

"Sure," she said. "War of the Worlds. All lower case, no spaces." I thanked her and headed back outside to one of the tables, trying not to think of how ominous that was for a password, all things considered.

Using the comm for internet is little better than using a cell phone. Tiny screen, mediocre speed. But I only needed to look up a few things. I was pleased to find that my favorite search site existed here. I typed in "metahuman."

The results were plentiful. So metahumans existed in this world. Now for the second item. I typed in "Dynamistress." But I came up with nothing. It was a strange feeling. I was both relieved and disappointed to know that "I" wasn't an active meta in this world.

I searched for "Gatekeepers" and was mildly surprised to find the group existed, including many of the members I knew in my world. The Bay Scouts existed, too, and was still active.

Out of curiosity, I typed in "Dinah Geof-Craigs" and hit the search button. To my shock, there were several pages of results. I looked them over and, with a raised eyebrow, clicked the link to "my" very own Wikipedia entry.

There was a photo, of course. And it looked exactly like me – a younger me, that is. Aside from that, the biggest difference was the hair. Instead of pure white tresses, the Dinah in this world had lustrous, golden hair. I turned my attention to the entry. It confirmed that she was, in fact, younger by half a dozen years. She looked even younger, though, to me.

Dinah Geof-Craigs (born 12 February 1977) is an American singer-songwriter best known as the lead vocalist in the alternative symphonic rock band Dynasonic. She is also the sonic-powered metahuman known by the same name.

Holy crap, a rock band. I eagerly clicked down to the discography section, to find that the group had just released their fourth studio album, *In the Clear*. The other three had all been critically acclaimed, big-selling albums.

The band's webpage showed up on my comm display. They were wrapping up their latest tour in just a couple weeks with a single show at The Fillmore. I saved a copy of the website to the hard drive on my comm.

Wishing I'd thought to bring a set of earbuds with me, I located the music samples and clicked on the first file, the title tune of the new album. The sound quality from the comm's tiny speaker was poor, but I was mesmerized. The music was exactly the sort I loved to listen to, these days, reminding me of bands such as Enigma, Delerium, Massive Attack, and so on. The music was fantastic, but it was the voice that floored me.

"Man, she's great, isn't she?" I looked up to see a boy of about twenty, backpack slung over a shoulder and a steaming cup in his hand. "Is that from their new album?"

"Um," I said, "yeah. It is."

"I haven't picked it up, yet." Then he smiled and said, "Have a good one," before walking off.

I continued scouring the 'net for information about "myself" and, eventually, the world in general. When I got hungry, I dipped into my stash of PowerPaste, making sure to reserve enough for the return trip.

Time swept by as I sat there, the library forgotten, straining my eyes by reading on my comm. The history of the U.S. in that world was virtually identical to that of our world, up until the end of World War II, after which it began taking a hands-off approach to international relations. The U.S. in this world never got involved in the Korean War or Vietnam, let alone anything in the Middle East.

JFK served two terms and had passed away in early 1998, just shy of his eighty-first birthday, four years to the day after his wife Jackie died of cancer. His brother Bobby was his successor, also serving two terms. Then Ted, who left office in January of 1985. The ones who followed, I didn't know.

The nation, despite having no military actions whatsoever since 1945, nevertheless maintained its armed forces. But the enormous funds my own country funneled into the military-industrial complex were, here, invested in education, infrastructure, social services, and scientific research. Its economy was booming.

I thought of my own nation's economy, which was in the toilet. We'd just had major financial institutions tank, setting off a global crisis of bank failures in Europe and huge drops in stocks and commodities around the world. On a single day, the stock market had lost well over a trillion dollars. Nothing I read in this world indicated anything similar.

I read and read, taking breaks only to dash inside to pee. I briefly considered trying to pass off my money as theirs to give them some business, but thought better of it. Theirs might be blue, for all I knew. Or I'd end up getting some poor kid fired for accepting "counterfeit" currency.

When my battery was close to dying, I tucked my comm away, pulled my sunglasses from my backpack, and walked the neighborhood. I noted more mom and pop shops than in my city. There seemed to be a bookstore on every other block. All the streets were clean and not crowded. And people smiled and greeted me as they passed.

I felt like I'd entered the Twilight Zone.

When my five hours were nearly up, I sucked down some PowerPaste and blasted my way back to the portal. Soon, I was back in my own world, where I repeated my freefall before sailing in for a landing at my apartment. I found Kit waiting for me on the roof.

"Welcome back."

"Thanks," I said. "How did things go with the other me? Could she fly?"

Kit shook his head. "No one came through."

I frowned, not expecting that response at all. I knew "I" existed there. But then I realized I was operating entirely on assumptions. Just because there was an exchange of personalities with one world didn't mean it happened in all of them.

And that implied all sorts of interesting things.

TEN

"The secret to discovery is to never believe existing facts."
~ Bryant H. McGill

As I've mentioned a time or ten, my youthful exposure to music was mainly through my brother's record collection. And in recent years, we've enjoyed turning each other on to new artists. We didn't always love what the other offered up, but most of the time, we did. When we found a new disc that excited us, we'd share it online or occasionally call up the other and make a "music date." I now had one for him. But it would take a lot of explanation.

I waited until he came down for his next appointment with Lily. "Hey," I said to him as he was preparing to head back to Sacramento, "I know you're in a hurry to get away from me, but I've got something for you to listen to."

"I'm not trying to get away from you."

"Of course you are," I said as I plugged my earbuds into my comm and handed them to Dana. "I downloaded this from the band's website." I started the song and waited while he listened.

I could tell he was impressed. His eyebrows rose and he looked at me, nodding. While the music played, I fiddled with my comm, pulling up the saved copy of the band's website, complete with photos. When the song ended, he removed the earbuds and nodded again. "That was really good! Who is it?" I showed him the comm and tucked the tiny speakers back into their case. He squinted at the screen, swiping through different pages, reading, looking at the pictures, and giving me an odd glance now and then. Finally, he got to the close-up photo of Dynasonic herself. "What the hell?"

I know, right? I said in my mind. *No way that color is natural.*

He was so shocked by the photo that he didn't even seem to care about me thinking to him telepathically. His mind seemed to be just a ball of confusion. So I explained everything to him, from the conversation with Song to the trip itself.

When I finished, he stared at me. *You're going back!*

"What?" I said aloud. "No, I'm not!"

"Yes, you are! You're planning to go back to see the show at The Fillmore."

I blinked at him in exasperation. "Well, *now* I am!"

He shook his head. "You know, I should be freaked out by this, but it certainly seems less dangerous than the last alternate world you discovered."

"Hey, *they* discovered *us*."

He handed back my comm. "Dinah, I'm not trying to avoid you. I'm just trying to avoid... you know..."

"But you can only avoid 'you know' by avoiding *me*," I pointed out, rather unnecessarily, in my opinion. "I just don't understand what you're so afraid of. I don't live with you. I'm not married to you. What happened with Elizabeth is not, in any way, going to happen with me."

He was silent for a time, staring at his feet. Then he gave a curt nod. "Okay."

"Okay what?"

"Okay, I concede your point. I'm sorry."

"And?"

"And I'll come visit more often."

I grinned. "See? Was that so hard?"

"Yes, actually." Then he smiled slightly, leaned over, and kissed me on the cheek.

On a breezy Saturday afternoon in mid-October, I made an appearance at the "First Annual Dynamistress Fan Club Gathering" in Pioneer East Meadow in Golden Gate Park.

Macy was so excited to meet me in person for the first time, and I admit I was really looking forward to it, too. I met her and her parents there half an hour before the event began so we could talk. Macy was short, probably just under five feet, and on the thin side. She introduced me to her father as her "*caballero*." It was a bit of an oddity hearing an Asian-looking girl speak Spanish. Mr. Zhang, her "knight," was politely formal, but warm. His Spanish wife seemed very self-conscious, but was clearly very proud of the girl. Macy had always told me how close they were. And here was solid evidence to support her claim. I expect Macy had no idea how much I envied her.

Just before the event began, Macy removed her jacket. I stared in shock at the T-shirt she wore. "What the heck is *that*?"

Macy turned to face me. The blue shirt featured the same white double-helix design as on my website. And running up the side of the image was "TEAM DYNA" in a funky font. Underneath it all was my website address.

"This is the shirt you get when you join the fan club," Macy said with a casual shrug. "You didn't see it online?"

"I did not," I said, still a bit weirded out by it.

"You want one, D? I brought a bunch."

"No!" I said. "I mean, thanks, but I'm not really much for T-shirts." I made a mental note to send her more money.

The event itself was low-key. There were a couple dozen attendees, most of whom were around Macy's age, and virtually all of whom were wearing the Team Dyna shirts. I had a fan club of teenagers, apparently. There were a few adults, but I think they were just passing by and were curious to see what was going on.

Once everyone was gathered, Macy introduced me. I spoke for a few minutes, thanking them all for coming and for the emails many of them had sent me over the past few months. I apologized for not being able to answer all of them. And as I said this, I scanned the faces of the crowd, hoping to see a glimmer of resentment on someone's face, in case my stalker was present. But no one so much as flinched, that I could see. The rest of my "presentation" was answering questions from the group. It was kind of fun, actually.

After the speech, everyone helped themselves to the snacks and sodas Macy's family had brought. Then we sat at a picnic table and I signed publicity photos that Macy had printed up using some of the money I'd sent. A few people asked me to sign their shirts. Most wanted their picture taken with me.

I looked up at the next person in line, seeing the familiar face of an eleven-year old blonde girl. "Jenna?" I said.

The girl's eyes widened and her father chuckled. "See? I told you," my doctor said. I signed her photo, then we had our picture taken.

All told, I was there for about an hour and a half. But with each photo, I wondered if I was posing with my stalker. With each autograph, I wondered if I'd be followed home.

The meeting of the Gatekeeper Girls that week consisted of Jasmine, Vicky, Kim, Bridget, and Jennifer, in addition to myself. I'd invited Lily, but she declined, choosing to spend time with Kit. Sinta had gone to visit Daniel, something she did every week.

We sat around my dining room table, munching on pepperoni rolls and drinking wine. Well, my glass of wine looked a lot like beer, and Bridget's and Jennifer's looked a lot like soda, but the rest looked normal.

I noticed that the younger girls seemed to be feeling out of place. Jennifer's bat-like wings were folded neatly behind her back, but every so often they twitched and she adjusted them. "So, Jen," I said, "how long have you been with the team?"

She put down her glass. "Oh, 'bout nine months, I reckon."

"Eight months, two weeks," Kim said.

"Eight months an' two weeks, Dyna," Jennifer said, smirking at Kim.

"Bridget," I said, "it's hard to believe you're one of the toughest members of our team. You're so petite."

"Petite?" she said, flexing her puny biceps. "Look at that!"

Everyone laughed, but it was no joke that Bricky was tough. Bridget could turn her body into brick, of a sort. And while she lacked muscle, she had speed, which counted for a lot. "Guess I should pay more attention to the names we adopt."

"Oh, I've had that nickname since I was four."

"Really? Why?"

"I was always doing dangerous things. Climbing on book shelves, jumping out of trees, and so on. So my dad gave me the name. I guess 'bricky' is some old Brit term that means 'fearless' or something. Dad called me that more than he called me Bridget."

I nodded. "Good to know."

"So, yeah, the meta gods must have taken that to heart when they gave me powers. Just to be funny."

Vicky downed the last of her wine and got up for another bottle. "You sure keep a lot of wine on hand for someone who doesn't like it," she said, pulling out a cabernet.

"That's because you degenerates keep drinking it."

She circled the table, refilling glasses. "You love us degenerates."

"How are things going with Lily?" Jasmine asked.

"Quite well, actually," I said. "Dana has helped her a lot. We've started to talk about her abilities."

"Sorry," Jennifer said. "Who's Dana?"

"Dyna's hot brother," Kim said, and everyone turned to look at her. She looked back at us, eyes wide. "Did I say that out loud?"

"So you're into bald guys," Vicky said, placing the bottle on the table and heading toward the bathroom.

"Or psychologists," Jasmine offered.

"Or guys with excessive body hair," I suggested.

Jennifer wrinkled her nose. "Y'know, just sayin' he was Dyna's brother woulda been plenty."

"These pepperoni rolls are yummy," Kim said, trying to change the subject. "What's the recipe?"

"Pepperoni and cheese baked in pizza dough. Just like it looks."

Vicky returned from the bathroom and stood in the entryway. "Oh, Dyna," she drawled, "care to explain this?"

We turned to see her holding a blonde wig in her hand. And all eyes turned back to me.

"You didn't strike me as being the type to go for wigs," Jasmine said. "Especially since your white hair is so awesome."

"Well, thanks. But white hair also tends to stand out quite a bit."

"You're doing undercover work?" Kim asked.

I smiled faintly. "On occasion."

"Gotcha," Vicky said. "And what about the fuzzy handcuffs?"

"I don't have any handcuffs, fuzzy or otherwise," I said. "Those must be yours."

"Oh, right," she said. "So they are."

"Vicky!" Bridget sputtered.

"Oops. Forgot there were youngsters present."

"Just kidding," Bridget said. "I've seen them before."

As the others laughed, Vicky returned the wig to my bedroom. And I wondered again just what was going on between us. This was the first time we'd gotten together since the Gatekeepers party, so we hadn't had the chance to talk about it further. And to be honest, I wasn't sure I even wanted to.

Vicky was attractive, no question. I really liked her as a person, too. I enjoyed my time with her. But I just didn't think I was ready for anything, yet. Especially considering that little thing I was trying not to think about – my drug-resistant infection.

I berated myself for ignoring it. But in truth, I was hoping that the symptoms would never worsen, that the infection would go away on its own. Subconsciously, I knew that was a foolish hope.

"Earth to Dyna!"

Jasmine's voice made me jump. I blinked to see everyone staring at me, including Vicky, who was now seated back at the table. "Welcome back," she said.

"Are you all right?" Jasmine asked.

"Fine," I said. "Just distracted."

"Thinking about handcuffs," Vicky teased, but her eyes showed a hint of worry.

I didn't blame her. What had just happened? "Yes," I said, rolling my eyes. "That's exactly what it was." I finished the rest of my beer. "Actually, I was wondering how Jen manages to fly with such little wings," I lied.

"Poorly," Kim said with a grin.

Jennifer sulked. "They're growin'!"

My intercom buzzed and I got up to answer as Jennifer glared at those who were laughing. I hit the button to activate the video screen Jasmine had installed for us. It was Lily and Kit. I buzzed them in and opened the door. "No boys allowed!" I called down the stairs. Then I saw the worried looks on their faces.

"Sorry to interrupt," Kit said as they entered the apartment.

I made quick introductions, then asked what was up. Kit looked at Lily, prompting her. "Well, it's my hair," she said.

I looked it over. It appeared no different than usual. Perhaps a bit shinier. "What about it?"

"It, um, caught on fire. Sort of."

We all stared at her. "What do you mean 'sort of'?"

She looked up at me, her eyes holding a bit of fear. "Well, Kit said it looked like fire. But it didn't seem to put off any heat," she said. "And it was just a teensy bit, anyway."

Lily looked at Kit, who said, "It seemed to mainly be around her scalp. Oh, and it was like a pale purple color."

This caused some surprised looks with the girls, but to me, that made it make sense. "May I ask what you were doing when this happened? Were you, perhaps, sweaty?" Lily and Kit both blushed a bit. "Right." Then I turned and walked to the kitchen, returning with a small glass of water and a hand towel. As everyone watched, I dumped the glass over Lily's head. Her hair immediately burst into lilac flames, causing everyone to jump. Including me, because of the heat.

"*What the fuck?*" Lily screamed, though in panic, not pain. She'd backed up, arms spread wide, preventing anyone from getting near her.

I smiled and put the glass on the table. I looked around at my friends, who didn't know whether to comfort Lily or deck me, I imagine.

"I repeat," Lily said, face dripping and her hair still throwing off purple flames, "what the fuck?"

"Potassium," I said, handing her the towel.

"What about it?" she demanded, drying her face.

"Well, if you remember your high school chemistry classes – and I know you all do – potassium reacts with water," I explained. "In doing so, it gets pretty hot, enough to ignite the hydrogen that's emitted during the reaction. And it burns purplish. The reason your hair is silvery, I've been suspecting, is because it's laced with your body's excess potassium. I suspect the same of your skin. But your hair has evidently reached a point where it's got enough of it in there to react, when wet. Such as with sweat," I said, bringing it back around to their activities causing the first ignition.

"I definitely feel heat this time," Kit said, holding his hand near the dwindling flames.

"But you don't, do you, Lily?" I asked. The girl shook her head. "Right. Just like all the metas who can generate fire, you're immune to your own, at least." The flames were nearly out, now, since the fire had burned off the water.

Kit said, "We may need to fireproof the shower."

Lily was quiet a moment, drying the front of her shirt. "And I should probably be on top from now on," she said, bringing another blush to Kit's face and chuckles from the rest of us.

I looked around at my friends, who were still shocked by what had just happened. Jennifer stared at me. "You, woman, are bat shit crazy."

"Seriously?" I said, eyeing Fabian as I walked to his station, a towel around my just-washed hair. He was wearing a Team Dyna shirt.

"I joined your fan club!" he said.

"Obviously," I said, taking a seat.

"Oh, come on. It's adorable," he said as he began combing out my hair. "So what are we doing today?"

"I'm thinking maybe a shag."

"Aw, thanks for the thought, sugar, but you know I don't swing that way."

"Cute."

"But seriously. A *shag*, darling? That's so not your style."

"Well, as with everything, it'll just be for a month or so, right?"

Fabian shrugged, brandishing his scissors. "You're the boss lady. So dish. You and Vicky."

I sighed. "Nothing new. I still haven't talked with her."

"And what about the reporter babe?" he asked as he pulled my hair into a ponytail, securing it with a rubber band.

My heart stuttered. "No. Nothing."

"Surprised about that, luv. I really thought you'd have mended things by now."

"Yeah, well..." I fell silent as I watched Fabian in the mirror. He pulled out a tape measure and stretched it down the length of the ponytail.

"Thirteen inches," he said. "Locks of Love has got to be amazed at how often they get hair from you. I've lost track of how many times you've donated."

"Ten, I think." I smiled. "I just keep imagining a bunch of little white-haired girls running around out there. Little Dinahs."

“I don’t think many cancer patients are doing much ‘running around,’ hon.”

“Perhaps not, but most of the kids with hair loss have it due to alopecia, not chemo.”

Fabian shook his head and chuckled. “I learn something new every time I see you. You’re like a Dynapedia.”

I rolled my eyes. “Shut up and cut my hair.” We laughed as he carefully sliced the ponytail and took it away.

I’d had my hair cut so short because Dynasonic wore hers only to shoulder length. My scalp itched under the blonde wig, but it was worth it. Passing for her got me into The Fillmore hours before her show was to begin. I got a couple surprised looks from staff in the hallway, but figured that was because they weren’t expecting “me” this early.

But, in fact, it was because “I” was already there. The band was on stage doing sound checks. I froze in my tracks, then stepped back out into the hallway and headed for the stairs up to the balcony level, where I planted myself in one of the sitting alcoves, out of sight of the band.

This plunged me into another rush of doubt. Why was I doing this? It was supremely stupid. And risky. I’d found out enough from my first visit to satisfy my curiosity, hadn’t I? I’d already heard their music from their website, so I didn’t really need to be here, did I?

Dana would probably have some suitable psychoanalysis about my need to feel better about myself by having a positive “me” in another world to balance out the psycho bitch “me” now imprisoned back in her own world.

But Dana analyzes things too much. I was just here to enjoy seeing “myself” in a concert. Wasn’t I?

Just then, a piercing screech of feedback assaulted me. It was so strong, so loud, so painful that I plugged my ears with my fingers and huddled back into the corner, shoulders hunched, trying to block it out any way I could. It lasted for what seemed minutes, but was probably only a few seconds.

When it ceased, I slumped there, eyes shut, ears ringing, and head aching. “Okay,” I muttered, “you need a new sound guy.” My voice seemed distant to me.

I opened my eyes and was startled to see a leather-clad figure standing in front of me. It was Dynasonic herself. She was frowning, arms crossed, studying me. Panic rose inside me and I froze. I sat there, staring up at her. Eventually, I worked up the ability to speak. “Um, hi.”

To my surprise, she sat down at the table. “You’re not who I thought you were,” she said. Her voice sent a chill through me, just as I’d felt when hearing the other “me” speak for the first time.

She looked more like me than my spiky-haired other-self. We could be sisters. Of course, I'd need to look several years younger and a good deal less worn-out from years of abuse. Maybe I could pass as her older sister. Or cousin. "So who did you think I was?" I finally said, positioning myself across from her and rubbing my still-ringing ears.

She shook her head. "It's not important."

"Please," I said, "tell me." I had a sick feeling I knew what she was going to say.

Dynasonic shrugged slightly. "She calls herself Mistress Dyna. She's not exactly my biggest fan."

I would have laughed at the name if it weren't such a serious implication. And honestly, the idea that there was yet another "me" running around out there – and evidently not a nice one – depressed me.

"Let me guess," I said. "She's not from around here." She hesitated before shrugging noncommittally. "Well," I said, "neither am I." And I reached up and removed the blonde wig, revealing my own white hair.

She just sighed. "What do you want?"

Straight to the point. No question about where I'm from. No shock that I'm another Dinah. "Not to attack you," I said.

"Good thing. You seem to suck at it." Her arms were still crossed and she drummed her fingers against her biceps. "

"Look, if I were a threat, I wouldn't tell you about my abilities, would I?" As she frowned, I said, "You have sonic abilities. Quite painful ones, I might add. Mine are energy-based." I held up a fist and allowed power to surge into it, giving off a bluish-white glow. "Plasma-like energy blasts, enhanced physical abilities. That sort of thing. Oh, and a solid energy force field for protection. I'm known as Dynamistress. And I'm one of the good guys."

She uncrossed her arms. "Again, what do you want?"

To my embarrassment, I think I actually blushed. "Well, honestly, to see you perform." She snorted in disbelief. "No, it's true," I said. "I swear."

"Then why not wait until the doors opened? Why impersonate me in order to break in?"

"Because I couldn't buy a ticket," I said.

She stared at me for what seemed a solid minute. Then she leaned back in her seat. "You're telling the truth."

"You can tell?"

"I can hear your heartbeat. After it slowed down from the initial panic, it's stayed steady through everything you've said."

"Wow. Impressive." She shrugged, then I said, "How are you not overwhelmed by sound if your hearing is that acute?"

"It was like that at first, but I've become able to tune out the sounds, just like everyone does on a daily basis. It just took a lot of practice."

Before I could ask anything else, a man down on the stage yelled, "Dinah, come on!"

"Coming!," she yelled back, then addressed me again. "I have to get back." She studied me again with a tiny frown on her face. "Look, you can't stay up here. The balcony area is reserved."

I nodded dejectedly. "Yeah."

After a brief hesitation, she said, "If you want, though, you can watch from the wings."

"Are you serious?"

"If you're willing to go to this much effort to see a show, it's the least I can do. Especially since I nearly ruptured your eardrums."

And that's how I got to see a rock concert from the side stage on another world. It was a great show, lasting nearly three hours, not counting the opening act, a slight, Goth-like girl who played guitar and sang with a brooding, haunting voice.

We talked a little after the show, but kept the discussion to music. She gave me copies of all four of the band's CDs and a souvenir show poster as an additional apology for attacking me.

I had so many questions, but I'd have to save them for another time. I thanked her, wished her well, then made my way out into the San Francisco night and back to my own world.

Even with a protective energy shield, sometimes the occasional blow gets the better of me. Not long after returning from Dynasonic's world, I got into a tussle with a minor thug who got lucky, striking me in the mouth with the butt of his handgun when his clip was empty. He chipped two of my teeth. Angry with myself for allowing that, I was maybe a bit too harsh in my return punch. I think he was in the hospital for two days.

The other reason I was angry about this was because I hated going to the dentist. I was lucky to rarely need anything more than a cleaning, but when I did, it was like I was six again, terrified of needles and petrified of dentists in general.

But since I'm an adult, I dutifully went and had the teeth repaired. Afterward, I stepped out into the street, the entire right side of my face numb, including my tongue. I turned to walk home when I came face-to-face with one of the last people I wanted to see.

"Dyna!" K.T. said, coming to a halt in front of me. "Wow, how are you?"

I forced a smile that I'm sure looked like a grimace. "Okay," I drooled. "You?"

"I'm good," she said as I wiped my mouth in embarrassment. "It's great to see you." She looked fantastic. Her smile lit her entire face and I felt again the hollow ache of loss in my gut, while at the same time wondering why I was so self-conscious about how I came across, since she was straight. "Listen," she said, her smile fading, "I'd really like to talk sometime."

I felt another string of drool ooze out the side of my mouth. My lips felt like balloons "Gorramit," I said, wiping my chin.

"Can we?"

I nodded, despite my better judgment. "Subbozo," I managed to get out. I looked and sounded like a clown.

"Great," she said. "I'll call you."

"I goddago," I mumbled in my embarrassment. Instead of walking away, I blasted into the air. Straight into the power lines overhead.

The lines threw me off and the next thing I knew, I was blasting sideways, straight into the brick wall of my dentist's office, and falling in a heap to the sidewalk. K.T. saw the whole thing, of course, which only added to my embarrassment. I jumped up and ran off, before she could say anything.

I really hoped she wouldn't call.

In the ensuing weeks, I spent as much time with Lily as possible. I couldn't get over the change in her and knew I had Dana and Kit to thank for that. She was actually happy and excited to learn what else she could do.

She had learned to direct explosive blasts from her hands and, when need be, do a full-body blast like the ones she'd done unintentionally before. The first time she tried this and succeeded, I got a good chuckle out of it. "Don't worry," I told her, eyeing the remains of her clothing on the ground. "The secret is energy-transparent fabric. I know a guy."

She still needed a lot more practice to gain accuracy, but she was on her way. "So when do I get a cool name? If I'm gonna be out doing hero stuff with Resonator, I'll need one."

I smiled. "I've been thinking about that. Given the origin of your abilities and that your blasts are slightly radioactive, I was thinking a good name would be 'Half-Life.' I checked. No one else is using it."

She thought about it for a second or two. "I like it!"

And that's how a new meta is named.

ELEVEN

"We must accept finite disappointment, but never lose infinite hope."
~ Martin Luther King, Jr.

Life is full of surprises, they say. Quite a lot of the American population was surprised when, on November 4, we elected our first African-American President. Conservatives were beside themselves. Not to mention the multitude of American racists.

Metas were largely pleased by this development. Under the junior Bush, anti-meta sentiment had risen considerably since the days of Clinton. And while they'd improved slightly after the Nevada Incident, we hoped for a relaxation of the Meta Registration Act under Obama. Then again, Proposition 8 had passed in California, so things weren't all sunshine, lollipops, and rainbows.

Sinta and I decided to host a big Thanksgiving dinner. Vicky and Bridget helped us prepare everything. Dana came down from Sacramento. Kit and Lily came over, as did Kim, Jack, and Daniel. It was a great day and a historic one for me – it was the first time I was able to use all ten place settings of my china.

I felt Dana's presence in my head as soon as he was within range on his drive down. And at the end of the evening, when he drove home and his presence faded and disappeared, it felt like a part of me was missing. I wished he felt that way, too, but expected it was more of a relief to him.

However, in this instance, I was glad for him putting a barrier up against our thoughts mingling. It prevented him from discovering my illness. I wasn't ready to share that with him – or anyone – just yet.

And of course, K.T. did call, the day after Thanksgiving. I thought about letting it roll over to voicemail, but that would only delay the inevitable.

"I just wanted to say how sorry I am for how things went," she told me. "I really had no idea that you—"

"Yeah, I know," I said. "I'm sorry, too."

"I wasn't offended or anything, I hope you know."

"Mm."

"In fact, once I got over the initial shock, I was quite flattered."

"Well, good? I guess."

"I miss you," she said, making my heart ache. "But," she continued, "I understand why you stayed away."

"I'm sorry for not returning your calls. That was rude of me."

"It's okay." She was quiet for a while, then said, "I'm taking a new job after the first of the year."

"Really? I thought you liked working for *Supers*."

"Oh, I do," she said. "But this should be pretty exciting. I'm going to be an editor for a small publishing company. They've said they want to do biographies of metas."

"Right up your alley."

"Yeah. And I'd like to do a book about you, in fact."

"What?"

"Come on, you know how well your issue of *Supers* sold. People want to hear more about you. So would you consider writing it?"

"That's just crazy talk, woman."

"I think it's a sure sell. I mean, most meta books are, but I think yours would not only sell, but actually be good."

I was speechless. But then I remembered how my therapist had urged me to do some "deep journaling."

"Let me think about it," I said.

"Of course!" She was silent a moment, then said, "I won't be in San Francisco, anymore. So you don't have to worry about bumping into me on the street for much longer. Which means the power lines will be safer."

"That was so mortifying," I said, reliving the embarrassment.

"I'm glad you weren't hurt."

"I'm glad I didn't cause a blackout."

"So are we still friends?"

"Of course," I said after the briefest hesitation. "Always."

By the time we hung up, I was almost comfortable with that statement.

Gatekeepers activities were fairly constant, though assignments were given out on a rotating basis, so I had plenty of downtime. Kimera and I spent some of our off hours together and one day, over breakfast at the Presidio Café, I confessed to her that I wasn't feeling entirely at home in the group.

"It's such a huge team," I told her. "I still barely know half the members. And the rotating assignments make it almost seem as though it's more like several small groups that just happen to answer to the same boss."

To my surprise, Kimera agreed with me. "Don't misunderstand," she said. "The Gatekeepers has been very good to me. And good *for* me. I have the utmost respect for them. But you're correct. As a team, it does sometimes feel a bit disjointed. I suspect it may be unavoidable in any large group. And we've currently got forty-odd members."

"Yeah," I said. "The Bay Scouts felt more like a family, albeit a pretty dysfunctional one."

"To be fair," she continued, "you could make more of an effort to get to know other members. Spend more time at the Citadel when not on duty."

"I know," I said. "I'm not the most social person, I guess."

Kim nodded. "In my years with the team, I've considered it much like high school. There are certain cliques, as I'm sure you've noticed. New members – the freshmen – may be drawn to one or another little group and be accepted or not. As they go on, they either become entrenched in their little clique or move on to another one."

"And those of us who don't go for cliques?"

"Everyone has a clique. Even the freaks like me."

"So Invictus is what? The principal? And the Prefects and Tribunes are the faculty?"

Kim shook her head. "No. More like the senior class. They're the ones who don't pay attention to the petty matters." She was quiet a moment, then said, "You have more reason than most to be the target of jealousy. You have celebrity status due to the *Supers* feature and the Nevada Incident. But you're also one of the prettier members of the team."

"Oh, I am not," I said.

"You are," she said. "The only saving grace, there, is that you're into women, not men. So the jealousy of the other women is tempered." As I rolled my eyes, she said, "So. You and Vicky, eh?"

I felt my cheeks flush. "Um..."

"It surprises me, truthfully."

"It does?"

She nodded. "Vicky is wonderful, of course. But her personality is quite brash. Very unlike you. So how serious is it?"

"It's... well, it isn't serious," I said. "I mean, we haven't even... you know..."

There was an awkward silence before she said, "Why not?"

I took a deep breath. No need to tell her about my illness. But that wasn't the only reason, anyway. I let out the breath. "Fear, I guess." Seeing Kim's confusion, I said, "My relationships all tend to fail miserably."

"Then you're due for a success, yes?"

I forced a smile. "I don't think it works that way."

I spent a lot of time reading the copy of my other-self's journal, sometimes while listening to Dynasonic's music, while trying not to think about how bizarre that combination was.

My health had been deteriorating since Thanksgiving. I was having more frequent headaches and dizziness. I often felt weak. And I'd had another incident like the evening with the Gatekeeper Girls, where I'd zoned out for several minutes. I guess it could be called a waking blackout. I was hoping to find something in her notes that would help me.

Like my health, the economy continued to deteriorate, too. And since I feared that finding a cure for myself might be expensive, I decided to sell my stock in Emergent Biosolutions. I hadn't checked the price in a while and was quite surprised when it sold for twenty-five dollars a share. Since I'd bought it at five, this was a profit of a million dollars before all the fees and whatnot. I didn't really believe it until the deposit hit my bank account, at which point, I felt dizziness from shock, rather than my disease.

I kept my illness secret from nearly everyone. But there was one person I knew I had to tell. And that person wasn't my roommate. It wasn't my pseudo-girlfriend. It wasn't even my brother.

I was going to be utilizing the labs in the Citadel a good bit and Invictus was sure to notice. So I made an appointment to talk with him.

He was understanding, expressing concern for my well-being. I don't know why I found this surprising, but I did. I asked him to keep my illness private until such a point when I had to take medical leave. And I explained that I was working on a cure based on my other-self's notes, since there seemed nothing conventional medicine was able to do. Invictus shocked me further by telling me that I could order anything I needed and it would be covered by the Gatekeepers. He also gave me unlimited access to the labs, with only one caveat.

"Just don't burn it down," he said with a faint smile.

Despite myself, I laughed.

Christmas was difficult. Dana, as he did every year, went back to Pennsylvania to spend the holiday with our parents. It was really just Sinta and me. We exchanged gifts, had dinner, and then Sinta hit me with the observation that I was sick. It had finally begun to show, physically. Maybe not to people I saw infrequently, but it was clear to the person who shared an apartment with me.

"You look tired all the time," she said. "And you're always reading those notes of hers. You're trying to find a cure, like she was."

There was no sense in denying it, since soon it was going to be obvious to everyone. "Yes," I said.

After a long silence as she stared at me, she said, "What can I do to help?"

I smiled and hugged her. "Nothing, kitten. Other than being your wonderful self."

She didn't like that answer. Can't say I blame her.

By January, I'd manufactured three treatments that I hoped had a chance of getting through the weird barrier the *C. neoformans* had acquired. I based this hope solely on the fact that my other-self claimed they'd worked to some degree on her. But then, her abilities and mine weren't identical.

I needed a new sample of CSF, since the cells in the original sample had long since consumed all the available food in the fluid and had starved to death.

My regular physician, obviously, couldn't give me any medicine of my own creation, so I had him send my history to Dr. Stone, after explaining to him what I planned on doing. He wished me luck.

Dr. Stone was intrigued by my disease. "There's never any lack of challenges when it comes to caring for metas," she said. I got the full tour of our medical facility, since Dr. Stone insisted on scanning me with every machine we had. Eventually, she took a new sample of my CSF and together we applied my concoctions individually and in combinations. Unfortunately, none of them worked.

And in the meantime, I was getting sicker. My head hurt more often than not. I grew more and more lethargic. I had brief bouts of blurry vision, another blackout, and so on. By the middle of the month, when I began to exhibit signs of confusion, Invictus quietly put me on medical suspension.

Dana figured something was up when I didn't arrange for us to get together for his birthday, but he didn't push it. In February, I begged off having him come to the city for my own natal anniversary. When he showed up on my doorstep anyway, I glared at him. But he swore he was there for Sinta's birthday, not mine.

Kit and Lily came over, Sinta having invited them. Jack and Vicky showed up, too, so my plans for not celebrating my birthday went out the window. I put on my party face and ate cake and ice cream with everyone, all while Dana attempted to mentally grill me.

Just hang on. I'm gonna have to explain it as soon as one of them brings it up.

And I did. It was Vicky who took the initiative. “So,” she said, “I’d twigged you were sick even before I saw you were on medical suspension. But just how sick are you?”

“Well,” I said, putting my empty plate on the coffee table, “medically speaking, ‘pretty fucking sick.’”

“How long?” Jack asked.

“Since summer,” I said.

Vicky sank back into her seat. “So that’s why we haven’t really dated.” I smiled apologetically, deciding to let her think so. It was easier that way.

“So what will you try, next?” Dana said.

I sighed and shook my head. “No idea.” I hated how negative it sounded coming out of my mouth, but it was the truth. I looked around the room. Sinta had lowered her head the way she always did whenever she wasn’t happy with things. Kit and Lily looked at me with compassion. Vicky excused herself and headed toward the bathroom. Dana just frowned and gave me a look that said “no idea” was unacceptable. And Jack looked as though he’d been gut-kicked.

As I sat there looking at him, a thought tugged at the back of my mind. It wasn’t fully formed, though. More like it was my brain pointing out that there was an idea that wanted to be born, once I put some pieces together. I stared at Jack. What was it?

Either I blacked out again or I got lost in thought, because the next thing I knew, Vicky was back in the room and Dana was yelling in my head. I snapped out of my trance and looked around.

“Penny for your thoughts,” Jack said.

I smirked at him. “Cheapskate,” I said. As the others chuckled, I smiled. The idea had come to life.

A few days later, I sat in a massage chair in the medical unit of the Citadel. My upper body was arched forward, my face in a padded cradle. I’d had a lumbar puncture and a port was dangling from my spine, waiting for injections. I was hooked to every sort of monitor we had, it seemed. Electrodes were affixed to more locations than I thought necessary, but then, I was in no position to dictate.

Jack stood with me, looking more worried about what he was preparing to do than I felt about him doing it. “I’ve never done anything like this, before,” he said.

“So you’ve mentioned,” I mumbled through the cradle. “Repeatedly.”

“Sorry.”

I wanted to put him at ease, as much as possible. I turned my head so I could see him, motioning him closer with a finger. When he leaned nearer, I reached out and gripped his shirt, awkwardly dragging his head to me. “This will work," I whispered. And then, to our mutual surprise, I kissed him. After a moment, he kissed back.

I released his shirt and tried to keep from chuckling as he sat upright again. His eyes were big, but he no longer looked so worried.

I turned my head to the other side, toward Dr. Stone. Near her in a tray were hypodermics filled with the standard antifungals, as well as all the different iterations I'd manufactured. I wasn't about to trust just one of them to do the job. When she was satisfied with the setup, we began.

Jack held my hand and began draining the energy from me. He did it slowly, as gently as he could. All the while, Dr. Stone monitored my vitals. When we reached a point where body function was about to fail, she would inject the antifungals through the spinal port directly into my CSF. Jack would maintain that state for as long as possible, while Dr. Stone made sure I didn't die. The theory was that if I had no energy, neither would the little bastards making me sick. Once that was taken away, we could kill them.

I wish I could describe what it was like, but the truth is, it was much like falling asleep. Once Jack reduced my energy to a certain point, I passed out.

And then I woke up, Jack and Dr. Stone still at my sides. I was on my back in a bed, now. An I.V. was in my arm. I looked up at them, noting the looks of relief on their faces. Jack was squeezing my hand.

I managed a weak smile. "Wow. Do I feel like shit."

"You should see what you look like," Jack said, surprising me with the jab. I grinned at him.

"Hopefully better than you do." I said it jokingly, but the truth was that Jack looked like hell.

"Here," said Dr. Stone. "Eat this."

I snorted as she handed me a tube of PowerPaste in the white medical use packaging. "How long was I out?"

"About three hours," she said.

I looked at the tray next to her. Beside the empty syringes that had held my medications, there was an additional plastic syringe. The imprint on the barrel identified it as atropine sulfate. It had been used.

I felt my heart skip a beat, as if to confirm the success of the drug. "So... Any problems with the procedure?"

Jack forced a small smile and shook his head. "Nope." He's such a poor liar.

"Oh, good," I said. "I'll just pretend that whole tunnel of light thing didn't happen."

Jack paled and his mouth hung open. "Dyna—"

I shook my head. "You look beat. You should go get some rest."

He hesitated, then nodded. He squeezed my hand again, then leaned in and kissed me. He smiled awkwardly, then left.

When he was gone, Dr. Stone confirmed what that atropine syringe had already told me. "You went into cardiac arrest," she said. She explained that Jack used his freaky ability to stimulate my own adrenaline production, but that was insufficient, so the atropine was used. She looked at me with concern.

"I was kidding about the tunnel of light thing," I said. "Just wanted to get a rise out of Jack."

"Good," she said, relieved. "I'd hoped it hadn't lasted long, but in the excitement, I sometimes lose track of time."

I ended up staying overnight under her watchful eye, even though I felt fine.

A few days later, we did another spinal tap. I waited with no patience whatsoever for the results until Dr. Stone brought me the news.

"I'm sorry," she said.

TWELVE

"Desperation is the raw material of drastic change. Only those who can leave behind everything they have ever believed in can hope to escape."
~ William S. Burroughs

I've always been somewhat pessimistic, thanks to being raised by a man who constantly warned me not to get my hopes up too high. I've decided his attitude is why he ended up with my mother. He settled for what he could get, rather than setting his sights higher. Unlike him, I did tend to set my hopes pretty high, in certain areas. Nevertheless, I've almost always needed a kick in the pants to really follow through with trying to make them reality.

It had been Lee who finally convinced me to go through with my experiment. Without her prompt, I probably would have continued to fiddle with it on paper for years, until I was too old for it to matter, anymore. And today, I'd probably be teaching biology at Penn State. Or in alcoholic rehab.

My move to San Francisco had been mostly in order to get away from the pain of Pennsylvania. Even though I knew California was a better place for a meta, I probably wouldn't have uprooted myself, had things back home been better. And today, I'd probably be the Penn State meta mascot. At least my costume is the right colors.

It was this sort of desperation I was feeling now. Everything had failed. All my great ideas, including nearly dying, were for naught. That procedure had slowed my illness for a while, but now I was back to getting sicker and sicker.

Dr. Stone tested my intracranial pressure regularly. My latest test showed it to be 22 mmHg, so she drained some of my CSF to reduce it.

Normal pressure for an adult is between ten and fifteen. Twenty-two was alarming, but it would be at 25 that I'd really get worried. Prolonged levels between 25 and 30 mmHg can be fatal. Even a brief spike to 40 could be severely damaging. The higher the pressure, the more likely that blood flow in the brain will be restricted. And at some point, it's goodbye oxygen, hello ischemic cascade.

This is probably the most common cause of death for those with cryptococcal meningitis. And the spinal taps are only so useful, since they carry their own risks. Frequent taps are thought to raise the risk of brain herniation. Of course, without lowering the pressure, herniation is pretty likely. Damned if you do...

I obviously needed to avoid all that, so I spent almost every waking minute studying my other-self's notes, feeling I was overlooking something. But there was only one thing that kept glaring at me, one item that I knew for certain held the key to the answer.

"*Blood from the heart of Neukölln,*" her notes said. But I had no idea what the hell it was. I'd gone through the notes, highlighting every mention of it. The pages were riddled with yellow splotches when I was done.

There was no way around it. The only way I was ever going to find out was to ask her.

I don't know whether it was my diseased confusion or just my general nature, but I decided I had to do this alone. I reasoned that this wasn't a DHS matter, so I couldn't talk to Shepherd about it. And it wasn't a Gatekeepers matter, so I could leave Invictus and the others out of it. No, this was entirely a personal matter.

I did tell Sinta. She'd not left my side since the failed treatment. It would be simple, I told her. Book a flight to Las Vegas. Rent a car. Drive to Groom Lake. Gain access with the DHS pass I still had. Ooze inside, find out what Neukölln was, get out, come home, and whip up some Neukölln-inspired cure.

Easy peasy.

The drive from Las Vegas to Groom lake is about three hours. Twice as long as the flight from San Francisco to Vegas. That's going the shortest route, up 95 to Mercury, then Mercury Highway through the Nevada Test Site to Groom Lake Road into Area 51. I made the entire trip without incident, though I had a headache and nausea the whole way.

I got a lot of strange looks when flashing my DHS badge. I wasn't sure why. I'm used to stares at the white hair, but this was different. I got the feeling the Air Force still wasn't keen on DHS co-opting their space.

But I finally arrived, pulling up to the familiar building housing the dreaded portal. Another round of security questions (since I obviously wasn't bringing in one of the displaced people), but I finally reached the portal. A minute later, I was through to the in-between zone.

The blast door was still closed. This didn't surprise me. If she'd gotten it open, I'd probably be stranded on the other side, myself. I stood before the panel in the wall and stared at the numbered keypad, suddenly realizing I couldn't remember the pass code I'd set.

I vaguely remembered, in my illness-addled mind, spending a good bit of time trying to come up with a code she wouldn't think of. It certainly couldn't be something I often used, like my ATM PIN. Nothing that could possibly be common to both of us. But now I couldn't remember it. For that matter, I couldn't even remember how many numbers it was. Was it four or five? Six or more?

I could go to the computer and get to the override, but I couldn't remember what I changed that password to, either.

I leaned my forehead against the panel. My head was pounding, my thoughts spinning. I forced myself to focus, as much as was possible.

The drive had taken a lot out of me. And I hadn't even thought to buy a bottle of water for the drive. I was dehydrated, which wasn't helping matters any.

I kept thinking that a birthday was the clue. But using my birthday would be the same as using her birthday, and that would be stupid. Even though she was, as she pointed out, a couple years older than I was, she would get it in only a few tries. Even using Dana's birthday wouldn't be good, as she'd figure that out just as easily.

Then I blinked. Not *my* birthday. *Sinta's* birthday. Easy for me to remember, but my other-self wasn't likely to know we shared a birthday. I knew the two were close, but I doubted they'd discussed birthdays. I hoped not, anyway.

I punched five numbers onto the keypad: 2-1-2-9-1. I held my breath as I hit the Enter key. And then sighed as the door cranked open.

Okay, I thought. First things first. I was parched. I made my way to the kitchen and found a pitcher of water in one of the refrigerators. I chugged a glass, then poured another to carry with me as I searched for my double.

To my dismay, she was nowhere to be found. I checked every room, every hallway, every bathroom stall. I even used my energy sight. But she wasn't there. I admit I panicked a little. Then I told myself that she'd be back. Certainly she wasn't living anywhere else. She was just out somewhere. Perhaps getting supplies at the town not far away. All I had to do was wait.

There was plenty for me to do while waiting. I read through her lab notes. No new entries, unfortunately. I shot a lot of pool. Badly. I couldn't seem to focus, so my aim was off.

I availed myself of her music collection again. I even started one of the novels on her shelf. And then I was famished, so it was back to the kitchen for a sandwich.

Back in her lab, I looked in the refrigerated storage, finding a stash of those ampules she wore on her belt. Out of curiosity, I decided to use one. Probably wouldn't help much, but it wasn't likely to hurt, either. I held the point of the ampule against my skin and squeezed the depressions on the sides. With a pop, the needle shot out and into my flesh. I felt the medicine follow. It was an unpleasant sensation. I guess that's the price paid for convenience.

Not long after the injection, though, my stomach started to churn. I dashed to the toilets, where I upchucked the sandwich. After cleaning myself up, I returned to the open area of the huge room. Memories flooded into me.

To my right were the holding cells. I remembered first waking up there, a prisoner, and my unexpected method of escape. I could still feel the pain of the blisters covering my body.

My heart ached as I recalled finding Valora's impaled corpse in one of the other cells, and the grief when we took her body home to her family.

And I remembered the battle with the other Valora, where I fully expected to die, but ended up killing her, instead. I would never forget the look of hatred she gave me before succumbing to death.

All these thoughts swirled inside my head. They were dizzying.

Why wasn't she back?

A thought sent a jolt through me. Maybe she *couldn't* come back. Maybe she was stuck out there. Maybe something had gone wrong with the portal into her world.

Heart pounding, I made my way down the narrow corridor, past the other blast door, to the thrumming machine. I stood before it, my skin clammy, panic rising. I stumbled up to the interface and looked over the monitors. From what I could remember of how they worked – and in my mental state, that wasn't much – it seemed as though everything was in order. All the needles pointed to green, which seemed right.

I tried to relax. The machine was fine. I just needed to be patient. I'd go lie down and wait. But just as I made that decision, a wave of dizziness and disorientation swept over me. I stumbled and reached out toward the machine for support. But I missed the frame, my hand plunging into the swirling portal interface instead. I pitched forward. And sank through.

One thing I'd forgotten was that this portal didn't have a floor and a ramp leading up to it, leaving it several feet above the ground on the side of my double's world. As I came through, I fell hard.

I had to get up. Had to get back in. Had to bring her back to this world. But my body had other ideas.

It decided it was time for a full-blown seizure.

THIRTEEN

"You can't connect the dots looking forward; you can only connect them looking backwards. So you have to trust that the dots will somehow connect in your future. You have to trust in something - your gut, destiny, life, karma, whatever. This approach has never let me down, and it has made all the difference in my life."

~Steve Jobs

I hate having to keep secrets, though I have a lot of them. The first one I ever had to keep was after the first time I was beaten by a foster parent. I was warned never to tell anyone or something worse would happen to me. I was really young, so I believed it and never said a word. Besides, I couldn't prove anything. Bruises don't show through my fur. Even most cuts are pretty well hidden. You have to really look for them.

So I kept secret all the abuse, from family to family. I always appreciated the good people, but somehow ended up with the bad ones far more often. I held it all inside until it became more than I could take. And then I lashed back. And it wasn't just at the man who'd whipped me with a flail made from a chainsaw blade. I was getting revenge on all of them. All the ones who'd ridiculed me, thrown rocks at me, spit on me, hit me. Everyone. Even the nice ones who just found caring for a catlike girl too hard.

With that last one, it was my turn to give the warning. This time, the abuse was clear to see. It was a deep, bloody line across my chest. He could keep secret the wounds I'd given him, for a change.

He didn't, of course. He went to the police. They were never able to catch me, though. And eventually, I was taken in by Daniel. And I found that

I couldn't keep secrets from him. I told him about the attack. I showed him the scar. I told him I was wanted by the police.

It was Daniel's reputation that cleared me. The police and Child Protective Services listened to him and, because of that, they listened to me. Self-defense, they agreed. They eventually arrested my foster parent. And I was allowed to stay with Daniel.

Worse than my own secrets, though, are secrets others need me to keep. "Don't tell anyone," Dyna had said. "I don't want anyone to worry." Anyone but me, apparently. She'd been gone for four days, when she'd said it should only be two, at most. She wasn't replying to texts. So, yeah. I was worried.

I wanted to confide in someone. Daniel was the obvious choice, but he was out of town doing speeches at high schools on the East Coast. I couldn't tell Jack. He'd flip out.

As it turned out, I didn't need to tell anyone. Because on the fifth day, Dyna came home.

Sort of.

The intercom buzzed in our apartment. I went to the view screen and was shocked to see the "other" Dyna standing there. I unlocked the door and she came up. I let her inside. Then I stood there, just staring at her. I didn't know what to think.

"It's good to see you, kitten," she said.

I forced a smile. "You, too. But, um, I wasn't expecting you."

She frowned. "You weren't?"

"Well, no. Why would I?" I said, but this only seemed to confuse her. "How did you get here?"

"I don't know."

"I mean, my Dyna must have gone through to bring you here."

"Oh." She nodded. "That makes sense."

"Are you okay?"

"Yes!" Her face lit up as she smiled at me, flashes of energy coming from her eyes. Then she frowned. "Aren't I?"

I asked her to sit down and went to the kitchen to make some tea. My head was spinning as I boiled the water. "How did you get here from Nevada?" I asked.

"I flew, of course."

"Wow. How long did that take?"

"Dunno. Wasn't timing myself."

I returned with the tea and handed her a cup.

"Ow! Hot!" she said at the first sip.

"Careful," I said, somewhat late. She put the tea aside and sank into the sofa. "Did you see her?" I asked.

"Who?"

"Who do you think?" I demanded, losing my temper a little.

"Oh." She shook her head. "No. One minute I was standing in the middle of the store, looking at oranges. The next minute, I was in that building in your world where the portal is." She shrugged. "And now I'm here." She frowned. "Do you have any oranges?"

"Listen," I said, "Dyna went to find you."

"Why?"

"She's sick. Dying."

"Ha! I knew it!" Seeing my expression, she said, "Sorry."

"She said there was something in your notes that she didn't understand. Something she thinks will be the answer for her."

She looked at me for a long while, then shrugged again. "I'm sorry. I don't know what to tell you."

I stood and went to Dyna's room and grabbed the photocopied notes. I slapped them on the coffee table in front of her. "See here? She spends hours just reading and re-reading these. She's highlighted something. That's what she doesn't understand."

Dyna tilted her head and leaned forward, looking at the yellow marks. She nodded slightly, then sighed. "Right. Neukölln."

"What is it? And can it help her?"

"It possibly could," she said. "If it still existed. But it doesn't."

My heart sank. "What?"

She seemed perfectly normal when she said, "Yes. If I'm correct, it's the missing piece of the puzzle. To cure me. And maybe her. Assuming her illness is the same as mine. Though there's no reason to assume that."

"But—"

"But Neukölln is no more," she said. "So..." She shrugged.

Just then, my phone rang, startling me. It was Jack. "Sinta," he said, "I've been trying to call Dyna for a couple days, but it just goes straight to voicemail. Is she around?"

I sighed. "Not exactly," I said. "You should come over."

I don't think I can put into words what I felt when I entered their apartment to see Sinta and the other-world Dyna sitting on the sofa eating sardine sandwiches. My stomach twisted. And not just because sardines are super gross.

"Hi, Jack," the other-worlder said, as casually as may be.

As Sinta brought me up to speed, explaining how she'd arrived and what our Dyna was doing, I observed the woman. She paid no attention to Sinta, instead seeming to stare with her freaky eyes at the sandwich in her hand, which she ate by tearing off and nibbling small pieces of bread, then dropping whole sardines into her mouth. When she (mercifully) finished, she took a damp teabag from a cup on the coffee table, placed it on her empty plate, and cut it open with a fingernail. Then she began scooping the wet leaf particles onto the plate in tiny piles, studying each scoop intently before deciding onto which pile to dump it.

When Sinta finished explaining, I tore my gaze from the teabag surgery. I didn't know if I was mad at Dyna for not telling me she was going or at Sinta for allowing her to do it. Not that there's much chance of talking Dyna out of something, once she sets her mind to it.

"Dyna," I said. Then I said it again, since she didn't acknowledge me the first time. When she finally looked up, I said, "Will you tell us what Neuköln is?"

Returning her attention to the teabag, she said, "A neighborhood in Berlin, I think." Sinta and I looked at each other, puzzled. "And a David Bowie tune," Dyna said with a nod.

"Okay, but, in your notes—"

"Oh, that," she said. "Yeah, that's different."

We waited for her to elaborate. When she didn't, Sinta uncharacteristically lost her patience. "Tell us!"

Now Dyna looked up at the girl. She blinked, as though genuinely surprised. "I'm sorry, kitten. What did you want?"

"Neuköln."

"Oh. Yes. I told you. It's gone."

"But what was it?" I asked.

At this, she frowned. "Not sure I can really explain it. It was unusual. Quite large. And deadly." She stopped, turning her attention back to the teabag, apparently considering this to be enough of an explanation.

"A quite large and deadly *what*?" Sinta asked.

She looked up again and shook her head. "I don't know."

"Come on!" I said. "Give us a clue! Animal? Vegetable? Mineral?"

"Yes!" she said. "That's a good way to describe it."

Sinta and I exchanged looks again as Dyna put aside the teabag and began inspecting her tea-stained fingernail. We were both at a loss. As for me, I was torn. I wanted our Dyna back. But she needed to know what Neuköln was. Returning this Dyna to her own dimension without that knowledge would put us right back where we were, no closer to a cure. I was still devastated that our energy-draining procedure hadn't worked, so I believed this was our last hope. But trying to pull information from this woman was so difficult. And I didn't know that we could trust anything she said.

"Dyna," I said in as soothing a manner as I could manage, "can you tell us anything else about Neuköln? Anything at all?"

She pulled her attention away from her fingernail and sucked tea residue from it, then leaned back into the sofa cushions. "Pizza often helps me think," she said with a nod.

"Of course. Great idea," I said. Sinta picked up the phone and stepped into the kitchen to make the order. "So," I said, "Neukölln?"

The woman rubbed her forehead, frowning. She closed her eyes, causing the energy leaks to vanish. When she spoke again, it was with more clarity. "We first encountered it about six years ago. Maybe seven. Back then, Valora's group was larger than when she came to your world. She had a team of scientists and one of them made the discovery and then the whole bunch of them were examining it. Including me, briefly. Until I became ill for the first time."

I thought about Dyna's illness. She believed her infection came from when she and Sinta were exploring the cave over in Marin, when she inhaled spores from a type of mushroom. "How did you get sick?" I asked.

"While working with samples of Neukölln," she said with a shrug. "At least, that's always what I assumed."

"It wasn't from inhaling spores?"

She shook her head. "No."

"So, again, can you describe it?" I asked as Sinta returned to the room. "Explain what you meant by the animal, vegetable, mineral comment."

"Best we understood was that it was a colony creature that had traits of all of those things. Parts of it were fungal in nature – the sample that got me sick, for example. Other parts seemed almost mineral in content, like an exoskeleton, almost. Not made of chitin, but rock."

"And other parts were animal in nature?"

"Seemed so, yes."

"How is that possible?"

"No idea. Maybe they figured it out eventually, but after my illness, I stopped working on that project. Valora wanted me to concentrate on my own field. She had other scientists who continued to work with it. They, of course, were fascinated with trying to understand how it could even exist." She looked me in the eye. "Personally, I think it must have been alien in origin. Nothing else like that existed on Earth." She nodded decisively, as though there were no room for debate. "Valora, however, was only interested in finding out how we could use it as a weapon."

I frowned. "Weapon?" Then I listened as she described the many defenses the creature had. Growths filled with poisonous gas. Stinging barbs on the rocky growths. Energy-draining organelles suspended within a gelatinous body, which itself was highly corrosive. With every word, my head spun. When she finished, I was stunned. "And how large was this thing?" I was afraid she was going to say it was the size of a football field. That would be unimaginable.

"Difficult to say, since we never really saw the entire organism all at once. Our best estimates were maybe twelve to fifteen square miles."

"My God!"

"Yeah, but keep in mind, Jack, that much of it was fairly innocuous and underground. It was toward the heart of the creature that these defenses were concentrated."

"Heart?" Sinta said. "It had a heart?"

"Sorry, kitten. Not an actual, beating organ of muscle. But I don't know how to accurately describe it. Nothing is quite right. It's not a nucleus, though it serves a similar function. It's the control center, so to speak. But not a brain, exactly, either."

"In your notes," Sinta continued, "you wrote *'blood from the heart of Neukölln.'* What did you mean?"

"This central area was a large structure. I never had the chance to examine it, but it was the true 'heart' of the creature. I was referring to the genetic material within." She smiled with a shrug. "My prose becomes a bit picturesque, sometimes."

My mind was still reeling. Fifteen square miles. I couldn't get over that figure. I knew of some colony creatures that covered vast areas. Certain groves of aspens were technically one plant, with a shared root system. And there was a mushroom colony that was believed to be the single largest organism alive. But it was "only" about four square miles.

"And how did it come to disappear from your world?"

"It was destroyed."

"How? How do you destroy something that large without laying waste to so much landscape?"

The woman tilted her head slightly. "You haven't seen my world, Jack. Destroying landscape isn't much of a concern."

"Do you think a version of it exists in this world? Is that why you and Sinta collected samples?"

"It's possible. But I can't say. I never did anything with those samples. Kitten, are they still here?"

Sinta shook her head. "Dyna took them to the Gatekeepers' building and stored them there." She paused, then said, "If it does exist here, do you think you could cure yourself with a sample from it?"

Dyna hesitated a moment, then said, "Your version of Neukölln could be very different. Or just different enough to make it not work."

"But it would be worth trying, wouldn't it?" Sinta said hopefully.

With a gentle smile and nod, Dyna said, "Sure. Worth a try."

I confess my heart swelled when she said that. The affection the two had for each other was palpable.

The pizza soon arrived. I wasn't hungry, so I left the girls to chat while I stepped outside. I called Kimera and briefly explained what was going on. "We need those samples," I said. "They could hold the cure for Dyna."

"I'll see if I can locate them," she said. "But can we trust this woman?"

I sighed. I understood why Kimera, especially, would ask this, remembering well the unprovoked attack on her outside the restaurant. "Not fully," I said. "Her illness makes her unreliable. But I don't think she would intentionally do anything against us."

"I'll need to tell Invictus of this development."

"Of course," I said. "And that girls club you have."

Kimera hesitated for a second. "I didn't realize you were familiar with that."

"Dyna told me the meetings involve pillow fights in underwear."

"She said *what*?"

"Or perhaps that's just what I heard in my head."

Kimera laughed. "You're funny, Jack. I can see why Dyna likes you."

Now it was my turn to pause. And like a teenager, I wondered what sort of "like" she meant. My brain had been replaying over and over the kiss we'd shared in the Gatekeepers' medical bay. I'd been trying not to read too much into it, but what if she'd meant it like I felt it?

"Thanks," I said. "I'll be in touch."

There were all kinds of similarities between the two Dynas. They both loved New York style pizza, for one. They both had the same favorite toppings – black olives and mushrooms. Or as they both called it, fruit and fungus.

I'd ordered an extra-large pizza, since there were three of us. But Jack didn't want any. And even though I only had one slice, Dyna finished the rest. I can't imagine eating that much. For that matter, I couldn't imagine eating mushrooms if I had an infection caused by a fungus. Unless it was out of revenge.

We didn't talk much more after eating. Dyna claimed to be tired, though I couldn't see how, after having eaten so much. Anyway, Jack went home and I offered my room for Dyna. But she insisted on sleeping on the couch. I don't know why, but I had a weird feeling as I went to bed. I guess that's why, when I got up the next morning, I wasn't too surprised to see that she was gone.

I called Jack, of course, who said many bad words when I told him. When we hung up, I said a few bad words of my own. But they were aimed at myself, for promising my Dyna that I wouldn't tell others of her plans. It might not have changed anything. But then again, it might have.

Jack said he'd ask Kimera to get the Gatekeepers involved. Meanwhile, I told Kit and Lily, who offered to help in the search. As for me, I planted myself on stakeout at Kirby Cove, but I didn't really think she'd turn up there, this time.

After several hours, I called Jack to see who all was involved. He sounded upset. "Not as many as you'd think," he said. "I don't know why the Gatekeepers don't treat this as more important."

After we hung up, I made another call, this time to the one person I should have called first.

FOURTEEN

"The bigger confrontation is the one an individual has with itself."
~ Asghar Farhadi

I never pursued the "hero" career for a number of reasons, but high among them is the fact that my telepathic abilities frighten me, possibly every bit as much as they frighten the public.

"Meta puberty" for me was horrifying. I was eleven. I was in school at the time, in the middle of a social studies class, when I was suddenly assaulted by voices in my head. I remember holding my hands up to cover my ears, and looking up in alarm at the teacher. I must have made some sort of anguished noise, because she stopped class and rushed over to me. I knew she was talking to me, asking me what was wrong, but I couldn't discern her voice from the cacophony in my head. She took me to the nurse, who decided I was having a migraine and gave me some painkillers, which didn't help at all, of course. By the time my mother came to pick me up, I was lying in a fetal position on the couch in the nurse's office, rocking back and forth and whimpering.

Mother wasn't keen on going to the doctor unless blood was spurting. I have no idea what she considered worthy of a trip to the E.R., but a "migraine" certainly didn't cut it. So she took me home and tucked me in bed. Mercifully, I was so exhausted from the ordeal that it didn't take long to fall asleep.

I woke the next day to the voices again. Evidently, two days of a "migraine" was enough for Mother, so she took me to the doctor, who asked many more questions than the nurse had. Being eleven, I didn't understand what a medical professional might think upon being told that I was "hearing voices." But I saw the shock on my mother's face when I said it.

"Are you hearing them now?" the doctor asked. When I nodded, he said, "What are they saying? Are they talking directly *to* you, or are they just voices in general?"

"Well," I said, a little afraid, "mostly just voices, but some seem to be talking to me. Or about me."

He nodded, then told me to wait in the room as he escorted my mother out. And in my head, I heard him clearly. "Schizophrenia" was the word I didn't understand. But I understood well enough the words "psychiatrist" and "mental illness."

We rode home in silence, my mother obviously distraught, not realizing that I knew what they feared. "Honey," she said, "the doctor thinks you should see a specialist."

"Okay," I said, already determining what I was going to say to the psychiatrist.

And a few days later, I gave my speech to this new doctor. "Well, it *seemed* like I was hearing voices the first couple days," I said. "But once the headache went away, so did the voices." I shrugged. "I dunno. It was all kinda fuzzy. Maybe it wasn't voices at all." And that's how I was able to keep my telepathy secret for a few more years.

In the months following this, I experimented. What kid wouldn't? At first, I was excited at being able to hear what others were thinking. It allowed me to misbehave and never get caught. It allowed me to cheat on tests, which I didn't actually need to do, but found thrilling nonetheless. Had I been at all interested in girls at the time, I'm sure it would have allowed me to know which ones might be interested in me.

Sometimes, though, I would hear things I wished I hadn't. I was shocked at the horrible things some people thought of others, in complete opposition to the things they said about the same people. I saw just how two-faced many people are at an age when kids should still believe people said what they meant and meant what they said.

There were the strange sexual desires, some of them quite disturbing. There was racism, which didn't surprise me much in my small town in which people of color were pretty much non-existent. But there was outright misogyny, too, which truly shocked me.

Worst of all were the things I picked up from the minds of my parents. Not because the thoughts themselves were so bad, but because they came from my own mother and father. *Oh, my god, just shut up, woman.* This from my father when my mother was telling him about her day, all as he smiled and nodded. Most of the time, I came to realize, he couldn't stand her. Years later, he'd have an affair. When he was found out, he ended it. And things did improve between them. But it was never a healthy, happy marriage.

Mother was, in some ways, worse. Her thoughts weren't aimed at her husband, but about people she didn't even know. Homosexuals. Non-Christians. Liberals. And worst of all, metas. And one day, her mind turned back to that day with the psychiatrist. *Thank God he isn't sick in the head*, she thought. But I probed deeper, as I'd learned to do. *Lord, please don't let him be a meta freak. I can handle anything but that.*

I understood the word "freak" well enough, too.

I have to confess that I would need to figuratively "wash" my mind after hearing the horrible thoughts of others. I'd do that by listening to the thoughts of someone who wouldn't have such stuff going on. That particular someone was my little sister, whose thoughts at that age were about Saturday morning cartoons, ice cream, ponies, and what color nail polish she next wanted to use to humiliate our dog. But most significantly, her mind was the only one that reflected unconditional love for me.

I knew what Mother thought of metas, and I wasn't so naïve that I didn't realize that's what I was. Father was ambivalent about everything other than sports and how much he couldn't stand his life. But Dinah thought I was the most awesome person in the world. And after my experiences hearing other peoples' thoughts, that feeling was very much mutual.

I spent a lot of time in her mind. It's fair to say that I knew it intimately, certainly better than she knew it, herself. And definitely better than I knew my own.

By the time I turned twelve, I decided I would never listen to someone's thoughts without their permission. At first, it was because I just didn't like what I was hearing. But then I came to understand just how much of an invasion of privacy it was. I wouldn't want someone hearing my thoughts, either. Not even Dinah.

It would be a while, of course, before I learned to prevent myself from accidentally hearing others' thoughts. And in fact, every so often, I have to reinforce those walls, since my abilities have become stronger over time.

Aside from a few select incidents, I've never engaged in any telepathic behavior without permission since that time. And, with the exception of my ex-wife, it was always distasteful.

After Sinta's call, I knew I was going to be in exactly the sort of situation I most dreaded. To my shame, my concern about this overshadowed my worry for my sister. I'm not sure if that's because I was so fearful of what might happen with me or because I couldn't accept the idea of Dinah not being okay. Either way, I thought about nothing else for the entire drive to San Francisco.

✧ ✧ ✧

The truth of the matter is that I'm intimidated by Dana. I've always had the feeling that he didn't approve of me. That he knew I had feelings for his sister and that he didn't believe I was good enough for her or something. It feels embarrassing to admit that, as a grown man, but it's the truth.

So when he arrived at the apartment, I felt uncomfortable. Bloodmoon was there, too, as she said she had something to tell all of us. Sinta invited Dana inside and brought him some iced tea as he greeted the rest of us. Sinta and I explained to him everything that had led up to this point, much of which she'd already told him on the phone.

We turned to Bloodmoon at this point. She half-smiled, but I could see in her eyes that she was distressed. "It's true," she said, "but only to a point." She frowned and let out a breath. "A small number of us are actively searching for her. But it is not an official Gatekeepers matter."

"Why not?" Dana asked, his voice holding the same degree of astonishment that I was feeling.

The woman took her time before answering. "It's political, I suppose." She looked up at us all. "First of all, I have to reiterate that the Gatekeepers is, when it comes right down to it, a government organization. The majority of our work is assigned to us; we do not choose the tasks. That being said, in many cases, the disappearance of a teammate would certainly qualify as an elective 'official' assignment. Other times, it would not." She hesitated, frowning again. "It pains me to say this, but the reason that this is purely a voluntary effort is because there is a faction within the Gatekeepers that believes Dyna should be removed from the group."

"That's not fair!" Sinta said. And in my head, I agreed. "Invictus doesn't like Dyna," Sinta announced.

"Invictus?" Bloodmoon shook her head. "No, dear. He isn't in favor of removing her from the group."

"He's not?" I asked.

"No. In fact, he called the movement for her eviction 'shameful.' Which it is. Still," she said, "if those calling for her dismissal can sway enough of the others, Invictus may have no choice."

"How does that all work in your group?" I asked.

"Well," Bloodmoon said, "the voting membership consists of the six Tribunes, two Prefects, and the Legate, Invictus. There are a total of thirteen votes, with each Tribune having one vote, Prefects two, and the Legate, three. So if the Legate and both Prefects agree, they have a total of seven votes, enough to hold majority over all six Tribunes, if it comes to that. In this case, we appear to have the majority. Invictus is on Dyna's side, as am I. That's five votes. Blockbuster, the other Prefect, is uncertain. If he's on Dyna's side, that would give us the majority. And if he's not, they'd still need to have five Tribune votes. Not likely, in my opinion, but stranger things have happened."

"Okay," Sinta said, "but *why* do they want Dyna gone?"

Bloodmoon smiled sadly. “Well, because of things like this, for one. They believe Dyna’s other-self is dangerous and that Dyna brought her here intentionally.”

“But she’s *not* dangerous!”

“I believe you,” Bloodmoon said. “But some others do not. Also, they seem to resent Dyna’s recent fame, feeling she’s done nothing to deserve it. Some have called her a grandstander, using her own words against her in quoting her *Supers* interview.”

“In other words,” Dana said suddenly, “the Gatekeepers are no different than most any other group of humans, subject to the same pettiness, despite being regarded as heroes.”

Bloodmoon smirked. “Exactly.”

“So,” Dana said, “how do we find this other-worlder?”

To my surprise, everyone turned to me. It appeared I’d been elected to speak for the group, so I looked at Dana and said, “I guess we’re hoping that you’ll be able to pick up on her thoughts or something. You and Dyna have some sort of telepathic link, isn’t that right?”

He seemed surprised that I knew about that, but nodded. “Yes, but not with this one.”

“Right, but wouldn’t her thoughts be of a similar sound or feeling or something?”

“It doesn’t work like that, Jack,” he said. And to my ear, he sounded annoyed.

“I’m sorry,” I said. Then, after a pause, “Do you have any ideas?”

Dana took a deep breath and let it out. “One or two. But I don’t like them a bit.”

The reality is that I was less concerned with how to locate this woman than I was about what we’d do once we’d found her. Convincing her to return willingly to her own world would be difficult, if not impossible.

Collective fear is that telepaths have the ability to force others to do their bidding. In reality, only a small percentage can command an outright domination of another person’s mind, literally making them do something with no say in the matter. Far more, however, lack that level of influence but are nevertheless capable of persuading others to do something by continually putting the thoughts in their heads. The majority, however, are unable to do either of those things, their abilities limited to shared thought conversations, “mind reading,” and such, to different degrees.

I’d always let Dinah believe my abilities were in that third group. But they’re not. Another thing I’d never told her was that setting up the psychic defenses in her mind was surprisingly easy. She had some natural defensive abilities, as some do, and they were quite strong. I was surprised by this, but didn't dwell on it at the time. But now I was forced to consider that, should it come to it, this other-worlder's mind might not be at all easy to control. She wouldn't willingly let me in, as my sister did.

Dinah told me that the reason her self-experimentation worked is because she already had the meta-mutation, which for some reason had never naturally expressed itself. That seems to be the case with her other-self, too, as she also engaged in self-experimentation. And if she is correct, her other-self is stronger than she is, which implies that her psychic defenses may be pronounced, as well. Trying to force her to go home could end disastrously.

At any rate, the first step was finding her. I knew a fair amount about Dinah's friends. Bloodmoon, for example, was another telepath. But Dinah said the woman also had empathic abilities. Detecting another person's emotions is something telepaths can do, but it's not easy, as the myriad thoughts don't always give an accurate indication of what's being felt. Empaths, though, can sift through them quite easily, pinpointing emotions among all the other clutter.

I believed we might get lucky by searching for our target using a combination of thoughts and feelings. Even so, San Francisco's a big place. So we worked together. I telekinetically floated us far enough above the ground to be able to criss-cross the city without worrying about pedestrians, street traffic, or most buildings. As I focused on keeping us aloft and moving, Bloodmoon allowed the emotions of the populace to flood over her. Whenever she felt something akin to confusion, she would focus on the thoughts of that person, who invariably turned out to be a homeless person seeming to be in need of psych meds.

I can't begin to convey the intricacy of this. San Francisco has a population density of more than 17,000 people per square mile, and an area of almost fifty square miles. We were able to scan for about an hour at a time before we needed to rest. All the while, of course, the others were looking for my sister's double in a more traditional manner.

After twelve hours, Bloodmoon and I had covered perhaps a quarter of the city. We slept a few hours, then began again. Six hours later, Bloodmoon's communicator beeped. She looked at the tiny screen. "They found her," she said. "City Hall."

By the time we made it to the building, Sinta, Vesper, and Speed Freak were already there. Our target was hovering in the air, admiring the building's dome. Bloodmoon and I landed quietly several yards away from the girls as Sinta called up to her.

The woman pulled her attention from the building and looked down. "Hello, kitten," she said. "Who are your friends?"

"This is Vesper," Sinta said, "and Speed Freak."

The other-worlder descended, landing in front of Vesper. She reached out and gently touched one of Vesper's small, bat-like wings. "Little Wing," she said.

"Um... Fair 'nough," said Vesper.

Then she looked to Speed Freak, with a frown. "Drugs are bad."

The speedster blinked. "That's not..." She left her sentence unfinished as the other-Dyna turned her back.

At this point, she noticed our presence. She turned, but did not approach. "Hello, Jasmine," she said, causing Bloodmoon to blink.

"Um, hello." In my head, Bloodmoon said, *I had no idea she knew who I was!*

Then she glanced at me. "I don't know you," she said dismissively.

"I'll introduce you," Sinta said.

The woman looked at me with her crackling eyes. "I'm not sure I trust him."

"Well," Vesper said, grasping, "ya should. Always trust bald people."

"Really?"

Vesper and Sinta both nodded, which was evidently all the convincing she needed. As she slowly crossed the rooftop, Jack, Kimera, and Nexus arrived in a flash of light and kept their distance, watching.

Sinta escorted the woman over to me, as I tried to decide what approach to take. My instinct told me not to use telepathy. At least, not yet. To my surprise, she walked right up to me, stopping only a pace away, and frowned. "You remind me," she said, "of my father. Before he died."

I wasn't expecting that. "I see," I said. "How... how did he die?"

"Heart attack," she said casually. "Your voice reminds me of someone, too. Not my father."

I nodded. "I'm not surprised, Dinah."

The others had formed a half-circle around us, which I didn't like. It was intimidating. But she didn't seem to notice, so I let it be.

Then she took a step back. *She's afraid, Dana*, Bloodmoon's mental voice said.

Can you calm her? I asked.

No, I can only sense emotions, not manipulate them.

Just then, the woman's eyes seemed to widen. The flickering energy surged and her mouth opened. She retreated a step. "No. No, it can't be. You're..."

I nodded slowly, my mouth suddenly dry, wondering what was she going to do. My emotions were surging, and I needed to get them under control. I needed to treat this encounter no differently than I would a session with a client.

She turned, then, looking toward the girls. "Kitten? Little Wing?" she pleaded. "This isn't... I can't..."

"Please," I said, while wondering what she'd do if she didn't calm down. Attack us? Fly away?

"It's okay," Sinta said. "He's my friend."

"But he's *dead*!" she screamed, her face contorted in distress. "I watched him *die*!"

"No, not this one," Bloodmoon said soothingly. "Remember where you are."

She spun toward me again. "I saw your brains sprayed against a wall!" she wailed, eyes flashing. I heard sizzling noises. Tears vaporizing from the energy leaking around her eyes, I assumed.

"I'm sorry," I said, as gently as I could.

"For *what*? Why are *you* sorry?"

I licked my dry lips. "I'm sorry you've had to endure the things you've lived through. For the pain you still carry." I waited for some sort of reaction, but she just stood there, fidgeting. "Sinta has told me much about you," I said, marveling at how her expression softened at just the mention of Sinta's name. She glanced over at the girl, who nodded.

"I... I like Sinta," she said, her voice cracking. She glanced awkwardly between us.

"I know you do," I said, "and I know Sinta's right to think highly of you, too." This caused her to look at me almost shyly. "Please," I said, "My sister is missing. I don't know if she brought you here intentionally or what, but we need her back."

She shuffled her feet, staring at the ground. "I... don't..." Then she shook her head violently. "No! You're not here!" She put her hands to her head. "*Not* here. Not *here!*"

Seconds passed as she continued to deny my presence. Just as I was considering intruding on her mind, Sinta stepped over to her, put her hand on the woman's back, and leaned against her. The others looked around at each other, at me, all of them hesitant to speak or take action. The woman looked down at her and fell silent, putting her hand atop Sinta's head and stroking her.

"Dinah," I said. "I *am* here." She shook her head again, still avoiding looking at me. "And I..." I hesitated, second-guessing myself. Treating this as a client encounter was difficult. She was too like my sister. When I heard the pain in her voice, I could think only of the years when Dinah and I were alienated. As painful as that was for me, it was nothing like if she'd died. That would have destroyed me. And Dinah's death is something I feared every day, due to her meta activities. She looked up at me, waiting for me to finish my sentence. I tapped into that long alienation and said, "I've missed you"

She looked up, her face hard to read. Was her gaze accusing? I hated that I was playing on her delusions, but she was looking at me, and that was a start. Then she surprised me by taking a step forward. She looked me in the face and spoke quietly. "I'm... I'm sorry... Dana," she said, struggling to get the name out.

I kept my voice as calm as I could. "For what, Dinah?"

Another step forward. "For the way I treated you."

I smiled gently. "Thank you," I said. Then I decided to try to bring it back to reality, to be the counselor again. "But you know, that wasn't me."

"*I know that!*" she yelled, her eyes surging, energy crackling around her fists. My heart raced, and I berated myself. She wasn't *that* detached from reality. Fortunately, she calmed quickly. "I know that," she said softly. "But I want... I *need* to say it." She shook her head. "I'm not like her, you know," she said, looking me in the eye. "I really hated you. Him." She paused and took a breath. "I know you two went through some estrangement. But I..." She shrugged. "I never got over it. Not even when you – when *he* – was killed."

I hated that I was about to ask, but my curiosity got the better of me. "How, exactly, did you witness that?"

"On TV," she mumbled. "They showed all the executions of the telepaths." She looked up at me with welling eyes. "I was nineteen. *Nineteen!*" she yelled. "And you left me! *Forever!*"

My stomach was a bundle of knots from her words. I wanted to soothe this woman. But I couldn't bring myself to put a hand on her shoulder, or even say anything of consequence. So I just nodded and said, "I'm sorry," again. I couldn't have meant it more, but it still felt empty.

I looked back at this woman in front of me. I stepped forward, closing the gap between us, and reached out a hand toward her. She looked at it, unsure. Then she lifted her hand toward mine. A spark of electricity snapped between us as our fingers touched. Then she gripped my hand, bringing it up to her face, examining it.

Time stood still. I knew this was likely the best time to touch her mind, but I couldn't bring myself to do it. Forget the disease-induced confusion. Ignore the embedded circuitry in her flesh. Overlook the energy surging from her eyes. In all ways that mattered, this was my sister.

"Dinah," I whispered.

In response, she yanked me forward and crushed me in a hug. I heard the sizzling of her tears as she wept.

My own just wet my cheeks.

After that, it didn't take a lot for Dana and Sinta to convince the other Dyna to go back to her own world. I stayed out of that particular negotiation, since I'm not her favorite person.

Jasmine was able to commandeer the Gatekeeper's jet. I tagged along for the ride, since I still had clearance to Area 51. Sinta came along, of course, and the other Dyna insisted that Dana come, as well. The two of them chatted the entire trip. It was almost as though she were trying to catch up on her lost years with her own deceased brother. I admit I found it uncomfortable to observe.

Also hard to watch was the good-bye between Sinta and the woman. I've known Sinta for several years. Like most people, she's a bundle of contradictions. In a fight, she's a relentless explosion of flying claws and kicks. But she's also probably the kindest person I've ever known, always willing to give the benefit of the doubt and the first to forgive an offense. Seeing the effect she had on this other-worlder, I couldn't help but wish the world had many more like her.

Finally, the moment came when the woman stepped through the portal. The four of us stood impatiently, waiting for our Dyna to appear. It seemed to take forever and I became convinced that her other-self had decided to remain in the in-between, rather than go into her own world to bring ours back.

Eventually, there was a flash of light and our Dyna appeared on the platform in front of the interface. My breath caught in my throat. She was lying motionless in a crumpled heap. All of us dashed forward, but I was the first to reach her side.

Fifteen

"A static hero is a public liability. Progress grows out of motion."
~ Richard E. Byrd

My senior year of high school was particularly bad for me. It was the year I decided on my academic path (for my own selfish reasons), but it was also a year of alienation. Not only had my resentment of Dana truly blossomed, but I withdrew from all my school friends. My relationship with my mother deteriorated badly. And, though I didn't realize it at the time, all of this deeply hurt me, emotionally.

Despite the academic goal, I felt aimless. I'd lost any anchor in real life and lived only with my goal of being a metahuman. It's not that I sacrificed my social and familial life for my goal. Sacrifice is giving up something one considers important. I regarded these things as inconsequential. I didn't give them up; I ignored them.

One might think that, because of this focus, my grades would have been superb. But they were never exceptional. Good, but not great. At that point, I was fixated on the idea as a concept, rather than on something I needed to make a reality.

But there were times, usually when I was alone in my room, tired of schoolwork, when I'd find myself overcome with loneliness. I'd miss Dana, but would push away the feeling the same way I'd pushed him away in the first place. I'd miss Rhonda, but only until I reminded myself of what she'd done. I'd even miss my mother, until I remembered how much of a bitch she was.

I should have just admitted how lonely I was, how much of a failure I was. But no one I missed took the time to reach out to me, so I told myself they were just fine not having me as an important part of their lives. Often, I would use that as an excuse to continue resenting all of them. But on those lonely occasions, it just made me feel worthless and unloved.

And as I lay in my hospital bed, yet again sidelined by illness, I felt the same way. Jack had told me about the controversy I'd somehow created within the Gatekeepers. And suddenly, I was seventeen again, feeling just as worthless, just as unloved.

But I wasn't seventeen. I was thirty-eight. I was mature enough (I kept telling myself) to understand the reasons behind things. I understood now that my situation as a teen was almost entirely my doing, just as my situation today was almost entirely not. Still, here I was, in the hospital again. Not being part of the team. Being useless. I had to face the possibility that the faction in the group wanting me gone might be right. It might be better for the team if I left.

As it was, I was in pretty bad shape. I was dehydrated. For the first couple days, I couldn't keep any food down, my nausea was so bad. I was also having trouble thinking clearly. These were common symptoms of my disease, which Jack and Dana thankfully explained to the doctors there at my "second home" in Las Vegas, the University Medical Center of Southern Nevada. The doctors did a spinal tap to drain some fluid, reducing my intracranial pressure.

My brother hardly left my side while I was there. And, perhaps because he was so worried about me, he wasn't concentrating on blocking our mind link. I didn't exploit it, but his presence in my head was comforting. It was about the only thing that was.

Once I was stabilized, I was flown back to San Francisco to take up residence in the medical bay at the Citadel, where Dr. Stone could keep close watch over me. In catching her up, I told her about my seizure. "It was like my whole body just locked up," I said. "I had no control over anything. And then I passed out."

She nodded. "That's the tonic phase of the seizure. From the way you described how you felt after waking, it's pretty certain you also had a clonic phase, involving convulsions. So a full-scale tonic-clonic seizure."

"Tonic-clonic," I said. "That sounds like a cocktail."

With a frown, she said, "I dunno. Sounds too much like 'tonic colonic.'" As I wrinkled my nose, she said, "And that would be one shitty drink." And with that, Dr. Stone became the only physician ever to make me laugh out loud. Any doctor who appreciated potty humor was okay in my book.

After the spinal tap in Nevada, I developed a pretty nasty headache. This is common after the procedure, and it wasn't the first one I'd gotten, so I didn't think much of it. But when it was still around after a few days, Dr. Stone determined it was the result of a leak of cerebrospinal fluid from the puncture. "Bound to happen eventually," she said, "with as many of these as you're doing. You're lucky you haven't experienced worse." I knew she was talking about the risk of brain stem herniation. "You do seem to heal exceedingly quickly, though," she said. "Anyway, we need to stop the bleeding."

She described a procedure called a blood patch. This would be done by injecting some of my own blood into the site of the leak. The blood would coagulate and seal the leak. It sounded like a simple procedure, but she said it isn't. It required absolute sterility and had to be done quickly, before the extracted blood had a chance to coagulate.

When the procedure was performed, Alexis, our staff nurse, drew out a syringe of blood and then a second one as Dr. Stone injected the first into me. It didn't take long, thankfully.

Alexis was the one who pampered me in the days to come, during which I improved quickly. The headache cleared up, my nausea was gone, and my thinking grew clearer. Dana and my friends visited regularly. Even Invictus dropped in once. I was hardly ever alone. Strangely, this made me feel worse. I felt like a burden. A liability.

Sinta's visits primarily focused on her worry about me. She told me about the conversation with my double, in which she revealed what the "heart of Neuköln" actually was.

Naturally, the bit about Neuköln being animal, vegetable, and mineral made me think of the animal-fungus hybrid thing I'd sent to the mycologist. And the description of the enormous size of the creature in the other world made my head spin.

Jack verified all this when he visited. But there was an air about him that I can only describe as expectant. I'd felt a different vibe coming from him ever since I somewhat foolishly kissed him in this very room, before the failed attempt to weaken and destroy my infection. As he wrapped up his visit, he leaned down to kiss me. And I let him. It was a bit perfunctory on my part, but he didn't seem to mind.

Then there was Vicky, who visited the next day. The awkwardness here was noticeable to both of us, and since she didn't bring it up, I felt I had to.

"It was wrong of me to let you think something was happening between us," I said with no little amount of guilt. "I'm sorry."

Vicky blinked in surprise, then frowned. "Are you saying that because you're really not attracted to me, or because of this silly illness?"

"This 'silly illness' may well kill me!"

"Oh, rubbish. You just don't think I'm pretty," she said with a mock pout.

"Of course I do!"

"Then you don't think I'm smart enough for you."

"Vicky! Get real."

"Then I'm too – I dunno – coarse."

Now I just laughed. "One of your more appealing qualities, actually."

"Then I'm not a good kisser." Before I could deny this, she said, "Maybe I was having an off night." Then she leaned over me and planted a serious one on me. I couldn't *not* respond to it. Vicky is a kissing artist. When she withdrew, I lay there, a bit breathless. She smirked at me. "Guess that wasn't it, either."

I caught a flash of movement out of the corner of my eye and looked in time to see Jack retreating out the door. I closed my eyes and sank back into my pillow with a sigh.

Vicky, too, had seen Jack's quick about-face. Noticing my reaction, she said, "Ah. I have competition."

"Oh, this isn't happening," I sighed.

"I'm sorry, luv. I mean, I know how Jack feels about you. I just didn't realize it was mutual. I didn't think you were into guys."

"In general, I'm not."

Vicky was quiet for a bit. Then she said, "I don't mind sharing." I looked up at her, my mind bringing up happy memories of my days with Sharon and Jackie. "Just don't ask me into a *ménage à trois* with him."

"He'll be so disappointed," I said.

Vicky tilted her head. "So where does that put us?"

"I don't think I can answer that."

"Because you don't want to?"

"Because I don't know what I want," I said, looking her in the eye. Then I looked away. "I mean, you have no idea how much..." I shook my head, not even sure what I was trying to say. "I really miss... closeness. Just being *with* someone, you know? Simple, physical touch."

"You don't need to miss that."

"But I don't know what I really want out of a relationship. Or even if I should have a relationship. I just feel adrift."

She frowned and squeezed my hand. "How so?"

I shook my head in frustration. "Vicky, it's not Jack. I like Jack. A lot. He's not like most guys. But, as fond of him as I am, I don't want a romantic relationship with him."

"And the same goes for me, I take it."

I looked up at her, my cheeks flushing. "You know I'm attracted to you, and I'm flattered that you're interested. It's just that I'm..."

After a moment, Vicky said, "What?"

"I'm *afraid*, okay?" I snapped, startling Vicky. "I'm sorry. I'm upset with myself, not with you." I let out a deep breath and said, "I just don't have a good track record. I'm afraid of being hurt again."

"I see."

"Of course, right now I'm more afraid of dying than of heartbreak."

Vicky nodded. "Tell you what," she said. "How about this? Let's not worry about 'us' until you get rid of this bug completely, all right?"

I looked into her beautiful, gray eyes and nodded. "All right."

"However," she said, "that doesn't mean I won't try to snog you every chance I get." I blushed again and laughed. Then she said, "So. What about Jack?"

I shrugged. "I'll figure something out."

As luck would have it, I didn't have long to figure it out. He returned later that day. I began to have the same conversation with him that I'd had with Vicky, but he cut me short.

"It's okay," he said. "You don't owe me any explanation."

"But I do."

He shook his head. "I read too much into things."

I lost my patience. "Would you stop being so fucking stoic for five minutes?" Jack blinked at me in surprise. "Look," I said with a sigh, "I don't care whether you think it's necessary. I just want to say I'm sorry. I didn't mean to lead you on, though I know I did. I led Vicky on, too."

"Led? Past tense?"

"Sorry you had to see that," I said.

"Oh, don't be," he said with a smirk. "High point of my day." We laughed and then he said, "So when are you getting out of here?"

"Tomorrow," I said. "Wish it could be today. I'm sick of lying around."

"The operative word there being 'sick,' you know."

"Whatever. It's not like lying here is helping."

Jack apparently didn't have a response to that. We talked a bit longer, then he left me to dwell on my own predicament.

The outbreak of cryptococcal meningitis was growing. Though there wasn't a specific vaccine against it, the CDC had been administering a general P13-protein conjugated vaccine that seemed to be helping, if only a little. But dozens of people had died, already. We had to find the source.

I knew the outbreak was heaviest in Sausalito. And Sinta and I had encountered it on the opposite side of the peninsula from there, if that's indeed what we'd seen. Based on the description of it we'd gotten, we had to assume that the creature's extremities, which consisted of the fungi and molds and whatnot, had infiltrated an area in Sausalito. And probably all through Golden Gate Park, which would explain how people in other cities had contracted the disease, taking it back with them after visiting.

My hope was that I could somehow detect the energy signature of this creature. In order for that to happen, the assumed center of its life-force

– the pseudo-nucleus my other-self had described – would need to be away from centers of high population for me to detect it. It would also have to be strong enough for me to detect from a decent altitude.

So it was that I sat in the open doorway of a Gatekeepers helicopter hovering over the Marin headlands, Bloodmoon at the controls. It was equipped with significant noise reduction, and I wore noise-cancelling earplugs, allowing me to concentrate as much as possible.

After about an hour, I'd sensed nothing, so I took a break, climbing up to sit with Jasmine. I was weak. It was an effort to maintain even my fairly passive energy-sensing. Jasmine noticed this and expressed her concern. "You look tired," she said. "Do you need to stop?"

"No," I said, looking vacantly out at the bay. "I have to find it." I stared at the sunlight glinting off the waves and sighed. "I have to."

I closed my eyes and cradled my aching forehead in my hands. All I really wanted to do was sleep. But I rubbed my eyes and prepared to return to the doorway. I smiled at Jasmine. "Okay. One more try." As she nodded back, the sunlight on the waves caught my eye again. And then it occurred to me that I might have better luck scanning the water than land.

So I returned to the doorway and focused on the bay itself. I asked Jasmine to reduce our altitude. The closer to the water we became, the more I could detect. There was a good bit to see. I knew from Daniel, who enjoyed the occasional fishing trip, that the Bay had plenty of fish, including salmon, sturgeon, halibut, shark, and more. The larger fish would show as individual blips, most likely, while many of the smaller fish would travel in schools, and would probably show as moving splotches. What I was hoping to see was something big, but stationary.

I tried my best to ignore anything that was moving. And that's when I saw it – a long "arm" of energy that extended out into Rodeo Cove for about a quarter mile before fading. I traced it back toward land. It led straight toward Rodeo Lagoon, disappearing about a hundred yards before the beach. Across the beach, in the lagoon itself, another energy signature appeared, or the same one reappeared, I assumed. It was fainter than I'd expected. Then I realized what I was seeing could actually be an energy signature under several feet of water and a shell made of rock, which meant it was a pretty serious amount of energy.

At my urging, Jasmine took us out over the lagoon. Normal vision showed nothing, predictably. I looked again at the energy signature of what I decided was Neuköln's main body.

I actually gasped as I took in the enormity of it. It covered nearly the entire lagoon, reaching from the beach on the west to just shy of Bunker Road on the east. My stomach dropped, but it had nothing to do with nausea.

I had a private meeting with Invictus, explaining everything I knew about the creature and how it was responsible for the meningitis outbreak. He seemed skeptical. "Do you really think we can take your double's word as gospel?" he asked.

"Why would she lie?" I asked, amazed that he'd imply such a thing.

"I didn't mean that she was lying. Just that, as you've said, her mental state isn't exactly trustworthy."

"God damn it, Invictus! You are the most insufferable, stubborn..." I trailed off, suddenly realizing what I was saying.

"Your own behavior has been affected by your illness, too," he said, ignoring my rant.

I let out a heavy breath. "I know. I'm sorry."

"Not your fault," he said casually. "Now, is there any sort of evidence you have that will back up what you're saying?"

It took me a minute, but then I realized there was. "Dr. Boniface," I said. "He's at UCSF, a mycologist. He has a sample of what my double took from the cave over in Marin. Call him."

A week later, the Gatekeepers gathered in our conference room. I sat in the front row, as Invictus had asked me, since I might be called upon to speak. Invictus himself stood at the podium and got everyone's attention. He began by giving a brief background on the situation, going back to describing my first encounter with what I believed to be part of the creature, in my early days with the Bay Scouts. He detailed my illness at the time, stressing its similarity to the current outbreak. He needed to do this in order to convince the rest of the team. My word alone wasn't going to carry much weight.

"Dynamistress believes she has detected the creature's center mass in Rodeo Lagoon," Invictus said, indicating the aerial photo showing on the main presentation screen. "Here to tell us about the lagoon is someone I'm sure many of you will remember."

I smiled as the man sitting next to me rose and went to stand next to Invictus. He had a mane of golden hair and a beard to match. His neck had the scarred remains of gills. Jasen Rey. Sea Lion. Former Gatekeeper, now a fine costumer, and still an expert on matters involving the waters around San Francisco.

"Good afternoon," Jasen said. "Rodeo Lagoon is about thirty-seven acres," he said, circling it on the screen with a laser pointer. "The current water depth is about eight feet, thanks to the fairly wet winter we had. Under that is a thick layer of dense mud, mostly organic in nature." Here he switched slides, showing a series of black and white photographs, each of which showed a circular structure of varying diameters. "These," Jasen said, "are images from ground penetrating radar. They were taken aerially by the U.S.G.S. and what they're showing is a rock-like structure underneath the lagoon. As you can see, it is vaguely round and dome-shaped. The top appears to be about fifteen feet below the surface of the water, and the bottom edges roughly forty feet below. The diameter, in case you were wondering, is nearly eight hundred feet." A few members made shocked exclamations at this.

"How do we know this is the alleged creature and not a natural rock formation?" asked one of the Gatekeepers. I didn't see which one.

Invictus spoke up, switching to the next slide. "Dynamistress also detected one of the 'arms' of the creature, stretching out from the lagoon. Divers using thermal photography took these," he said, indicating a slide with a few dark photos showing bands of violet. "The 'arm' evidently tunnels under the earth until it emerges into the open water at a depth of about forty feet." He indicated the heat signature in the photo. "As she described, it is translucent, making it virtually invisible under the water. We've measured it as being approximately two thousand feet in length, from tip to the edge of the shell, with about one third of it being underground."

Invictus turned off the screen and the lights came up. "Since the detection of the creature," he said, "government scientists have been working to figure out what's causing the disease. I wish I could say it was encouraging, but it isn't. If anything, it's the opposite, since the parts of the creature spreading the disease seem to be, as Dynamistress first described to me, very similar in appearance to common fungi. And the area covered could conceivably stretch for many square miles, from Rodeo Lagoon over to Sausalito, even stretching underwater. It's possible we could even have the foreign fungi here in the Presidio." Murmuring erupted in the audience at this. "Dynamistress also believes that the source for a cure to the disease will not be found in the arms, such as the one underwater, or the fungal extremities. Rather, she believes it will be found inside the main body of the creature."

"And how is it that she's an expert?" came another question.

In response, Invictus nodded to me. I rose and stepped up to the podium. "As most of you know," I began, "at the time I first encountered the creature, I was a member of the Bay Scouts. Later, I would be one of several members of that team 'replaced' by versions of ourselves from another world. The government labeled this 'Project Echo,' but most everyone calls it 'the Nevada Incident.'"

I scanned the crowd and was relieved to see most people just listening attentively, but there were a few scowls on the faces of those who weren't terribly fond of me.

"A version of this creature also existed in that world," I told them. "My double was working to find a cure for the disease that had infected her. Her notes indicate that material from the creature's central body were vital to the cure."

"So she found a cure?" Blockbuster asked.

"I'm afraid not," I said. "The creature in that world had been destroyed, so she had no such material to work with."

Invictus stepped over to the podium again and I took my seat. "I have successfully lobbied for the opportunity to obtain material from the creature, in the hopes of finding a cure."

"Why don't we just kill the goddamn thing?" came a voice from behind me.

"Language," said Invictus with a quick glance. Then he cleared his throat. "The main reason is the ethical dilemma. Do we have the right to destroy this creature? Consider that it is the only such life form we know of, and could, in fact, be unique. For all we know, it could be sentient."

"So you're saying PETA would be all up in our faces?" one person in the crowd yelled.

"To my knowledge, PETA isn't even aware of the creature's existence," Invictus said. "But we don't need animal rights organizations to point out that killing the only known representative of a species is essentially genocide."

There was a moment of silence as the group considered this. Then, the original questioner said, "People are *dying*, Invictus! The death count is up to, what, more than thirty at this point, right? A dozen of them were children! If killing it will stop the disease, I say we do it!"

The big man frowned. "First, there is no guarantee that killing the creature will immediately stop the spread of the disease. It may, in fact, have no effect at all. The fungi at the creature's extremities could continue to thrive apart from the main body. That would pose an enormous problem, of course, which I'm not prepared to address, today. However, the fact remains, the decision to kill the creature is not one we are entitled to make." He shifted his stance, clasping his hands behind his back. "That being said, we have been offered the opportunity to propose a method of extracting a sample of the creature's interior for the purpose of finding a cure. But even that will be exceedingly difficult. Jasen?"

Sea Lion stepped up to the microphone again. "The problem is that Rodeo Lagoon is off-limits. Living there is a protected species of fish, the Tidewater Goby. Anything done will need to be carried out without disrupting the ecosystem."

"Well, how the hell do we do that?" asked the same individual.

Invictus nodded to the Prefects and Tribunes. "We've been having discussions, and are of course open to suggestions from you all."

Through the murmuring of the crowd, Transcendant spoke up. "Do we have any idea how it came to be there?"

Invictus nodded. "Scientists consulted seem to agree that it most likely grew there. The rocky carapace appears to be integral to the support of the lagoon, suggesting that it is quite old." He then nodded to someone else in the audience.

"What I'm wondering," she said, "is why now? I mean, if this creature is as old as you're saying, why has this outbreak not happened before?"

"Impossible to say," Invictus replied. "We know nothing about the creature's life cycle. It could be that it has only recently reached its version of puberty."

"So there could possibly be worse to come?" the person asked.

"Possibly," he said. More hands raised in the audience, but Invictus waved them off. "I know you have many more questions," he cautioned, "but we simply don't have answers. Our role is quite limited, in fact, and we're not the only ones proposing ideas. Again, all ideas are welcome. Thank you," he said and left the podium, leaving the rest of us to absorb everything.

Eventually, the group dispersed and filed out of the meeting room. More than a few pointedly ignored me on their way out the door. Most of the rest had pensive or shocked looks on their faces.

The expression on Dr. Stone's face was one of concern as I lay on a bed in our medical bay, having yet another spinal tap to relieve the pressure on my brain. "That bad?" I said.

She looked at me and frowned. "Yes, in fact."

I wasn't honestly expecting that reply, so I just said, "Oh."

"Do you know what the mortality rate is for this disease, untreated?"

"Um—"

"One hundred percent," she said, with both exasperation and annoyance. "Dyna, it's just a matter of time, unless we figure out how to attack this fungus. And you don't seem to be taking it seriously."

I was silent for a moment, then said, "It's not that I'm not taking it seriously. It's just that I don't know how to get past the energy barrier. So I guess I'm just hoping for inspiration." I didn't tell her about my double's notes, how she believed a cure could be manufactured using something from Neukölln. But I did find myself wishing I knew exactly what that something was.

At home, Sinta and I sat having dinner. I'd just finished telling her about the creature in the lagoon and the summary we'd gotten from Invictus and Jasen.

"So what do you think will happen?" she asked.

"I really don't know," I said. "Invictus raised a good point regarding the ethics of the situation. Even if we do get the okay, it's anyone's guess what approach we'll take."

Sinta frowned. "But if they don't give the okay, how will you get what you need from it?"

I looked at her, noticing now that she'd hardly eaten a thing, and had just been pushing her food around on her plate. She was so worried about me. It was touching, but painful at the same time. "That's the big question," I said.

"So figure it out!" she yelled, then stood and ran to her room.

SIXTEEN

"You don't have love without sacrifice; you can't have sacrifice without love."

~ Karen Kingsbury

In college, I knew people who seemed preoccupied with death. Angsty girls would quote Sylvia Plath and pretentious guys would pontificate on the rationality of suicide.

I never liked to think about mortality. I suppose I viewed death as something that happened only to other people. Ridiculous, but it seems a not uncommon mentality for teens. It was Lee's suicide that forced me to be more than passingly aware of death.

It's ironic. During the days when I was still working on my genetic goals, I worked into my programming a way to enhance my body's natural healing abilities, all the while drinking myself to death. It's as though I've always believed myself invincible, but have needed to test it.

Dr. Stone had accused me of not taking my disease seriously enough. Sinta certainly held that opinion, too. I had to wonder if they were right. Was I just in perpetual denial of my mortality? I was convinced I'd beat this, even if I currently had no idea how that was going to happen. So, yes. I probably was.

It was another week before Invictus gathered us together for an update. In the end, it came down to the plan that would have the least amount of disruption to the Lagoon. And that happened to be our plan.

Sinta was glad we'd finally made a decision, but was still upset that I didn't know exactly what we were looking for, within the creature. She didn't seem to care that we'd have several government scientists on site.

When the day finally came, we gathered on the south side of the lagoon, as far from buildings as possible. The beach and trails around the lagoon had been closed to the public, but that was the extent of clearing the area. Cars still came and went. This was an immobile creature, after all. Its threat was passive.

Because of this, our team was fairly small, for a Gatekeepers assignment, and included a few non-Gatekeepers. I'd been a bit surprised when Invictus asked me to recruit my brother. He explained that we'd need several telekinetics, and one who was also a telepath would be useful.

"Are you kidding?" he said when I expressed my surprise that he'd agreed. "To be up close to a possibly alien creature? Try to keep me away!"

The plan was beautiful in its simplicity. At least, in concept. From an operational perspective, it was going to be tricky. As we prepared, Dana stood talking with the other six telekinetics. Two of these – Booster and Newton – were Gatekeepers; the other four were recruited from other teams. I never did meet them. I made sure not to intrude on Dana's mind. He was going to need his full concentration with this and couldn't afford any distractions.

Jack was there to provide adrenaline boosts to the telekinetics. Jasmine would be empathically monitoring them and would telepathically alert Jack when they began to tire. The two of them were chatting with Lumen, who was there to illuminate the interior of the creature, once the shell was penetrated.

The government scientists were off to one side, awaiting their turn. Their role – and this included me – was to assess the creature, once the innards were exposed, and to grab samples before it was closed up, again. This wouldn't come for a while, yet, so I trudged up the embankment to the trail, looking back down on the others. A pair of pelicans swooped in and landed on the water, gazing at the group of strangely-clad visitors.

I frowned impatiently. We'd been there almost an hour, already. How long were they going to talk about it before actually doing something?

It was a struggle to keep my mind on the mission at hand. I was preoccupied by the fact that Sinta hadn't been in her room when I got up. It wasn't like her to go off without leaving a note on the board on the door. I guess she was madder at me than I'd thought.

I couldn't blame her. The reality was, my life pretty much depended on this mission. And I still wasn't sure exactly what I was looking to get from the creature. I felt sure I'd know it when I saw it, but Sinta didn't think that was enough. She said I needed to be certain.

If only.

Finally, it seemed like they were ready to begin. Invictus was walking over to Dana's group, so I headed back down the trail.

But I never made it.

When Invictus gave the word, we began. The first step was for me to carry the other six telekinetics out over the water, arranging them in a circle. As they hung there, they focused their considerable abilities to clear the area. I began by plunging a telekinetic marker in the center, pushing aside a circular area of water and mud perhaps six inches across. Then each of the others formed a telekinetic "scoop" and carefully pulled back a section. It was a fascinating sight, seeing the water move out away from the center of the circle, as though being held back by a cylinder of glass. Eventually, a twenty foot wide area of the rocky carapace was revealed.

At this point, I lowered the six to stand inside the cleared area, where they would hold back the water and mud while the rest did their thing. I carried Jack over, and Lumen.

Finally, I brought over the ones who'd be cutting it open. These were professionals who cut concrete and asphalt for a living. There were two of them, with their saws. In less than fifteen minutes, they'd cut out a square of the "shell" about six feet per side. We knew the fissures had gone through the whole way by the stench that erupted from them. At this point, their work was done. I lifted them back to shore.

Then I turned my attention to the carapace itself, carefully pulling out the huge piece of cut rock and placing it aside. Lumen knelt by the edge of the hole, extending his hands outward, fingers spread. Powerful beams of light shot forth into the creature. At first, only a shimmery effect indicated the presence of anything at all, just as Dinah had described it from her encounter in the cave. But Lumen moved his hands around and in a few moments, the interior was lit by a dull glow all around. I could make out globular shapes inside.

Now it was time for Dinah and the other scientists. I glanced toward the shore, preparing to lift them over to the hole, but Dinah wasn't there. I opened my mind to hers.

And felt nothing.

"*Are you fucking kidding me?*" I screamed into the air, standing in the desert of my other-self's world. The familiar stomach-churning sensation I'd felt as I tromped down the bank toward the others was fading as my anger was growing. The timing of this could not possibly have been worse.

I found the hidden portal, having pretty much memorized its location by now, and oozed through to the in-between. Then I rocketed down the hallway, into the main area, then over to the passage leading to the room containing the way back to my world. I didn't question why the blast door was open. I was just thankful it was. I shot past and into the portal room – where I came to a dead stop in surprise.

"What the hell?" I said. Sinta stood there in front of the portal. "What are you doing here?"

She looked up at me with an expression both apologetic and resolute. "I'm sorry, Dyna. But you can't go back."

I stood there in shock for a moment before I remembered how to speak. "Kitten, we were just starting! I've *got* to get back!"

"But you don't even know what you're looking for!"

"Damn it, we've been over this!"

"Admit that you don't."

"I don't have time for this," I said, and began walking past her. But Sinta blocked my way. "Move," I said flatly.

"No."

I walked up to her and reached out to lift her small body out of the way. But her arms were up in a flash, knocking mine away. And then, to my surprise, Sinta dropped into a fighting stance, claws extended, her face taking on the same fierce expression I knew so well from our days fighting together. I stepped back and frowned. Sinta stood firm. And I quickly put aside any thought that I could get past, in my weakened state. Not that I wanted to fight her, anyway.

"Explain yourself," I said.

"I told you. Because *you* don't know what you're looking for. But *she* does."

I stared at her. "You can't be serious." But she was, of course. I shook my head and sighed. "Kitten, I know your heart is in the right place, but this is... this is bad."

She shook her head. "Please. You have to trust me."

I let out an ironic laugh. "It's *her* I don't trust!"

"But I do," she said simply. "And if you trust *me*, you have to trust me *about* her."

A sudden sinking feeling in my chest made me swallow my reply. I shook my head and turned away from her. She was young. And she was allowing her feelings for my other-self to get in the way of her reasoning. The woman was crazy. She didn't deserve Sinta's trust or...

Or what? Didn't deserve Sinta's friendship? Her love? I mentally berated myself for even considering such a thing.

I had to remind myself that this was a girl who had every reason to be suspicious of others, yet put total trust in this woman. And I, who had every reason to trust Sinta, was showing that I really didn't.

Even so... this was my *life* we were debating. If Sinta's trust proved to be misplaced, I would die. I had no doubt of that. And yet, she was right. I really didn't know what I was looking for. This mission was really about finding a way to halt the spread of the illness, not to save my life. That part was incidental.

"You're right," I said quietly.

After a second, Sinta said, "What?"

I turned to face her. "I said you're right. If you really trust someone, that means you trust their judgment." My adrenaline rush had worn off, now, and I was exhausted. I pulled out the chair at the computer desk and sat. "So, okay."

Sinta grinned and jumped on me, hugging me tight. I hugged back, but couldn't help wondering if I'd just condemned myself to death.

As word spread that Dinah was missing, a quick search began. Those who could fly took to the air and searched the immediate area. I knew there were only two reasons why I wouldn't be able to detect her. One would be if she were dead. But I'd have felt that, were it true. The other would be if she were too far away. My stomach knotted. I could only think of one way that could be the case.

Either way, while they did the search, I carried the other scientists over. They stood around the hole, wearing protective gear, and extended long rods into the creature's soft insides. The rods had clamshell tips, which they closed with levers, pulling back small samples of the material. They emptied these into glass jars.

"Whoa," Lumen said from his vantage point near the opening. "Something's moving." I lowered myself to stand next to him and peered in. Four of the globular forms were moving toward the opening. They were bluish in color and appeared to be of varying sizes, so it was difficult to judge their distance.

I gave Invictus a telepathic update as Jack went from one telekinetic to the next, giving them little boosts that would keep them going for a while longer.

Dana!

Bloodmoon's warning tore my attention from the hole. I rose above the water and looked out into the bay at her command and saw what looked like the wake of a boat rushing quickly toward the beach, with a swell of water in front of it. But as I looked closer, I realized it for what it was. The enormous underwater "arm" was mobile! And it was rising from the bay, a huge, translucent tentacle, water dripping along its massive form, and rushing toward us.

This was incredible, I thought as I lifted the startled scientists from the hole and quickly planted them back on the shore. Nothing had given any indication that these arms had any sort of musculature. As two of the Gatekeepers – Miss Fire and Starburst – took to the air, Bloodmoon told me to grab Icecap and take him with me.

The four of us moved toward the beach. Miss Fire and Starburst reached it first. Fortunately, the arm refracted enough sunlight to be detected. Miss Fire immediately shot flame blasts at it. Icecap sent a fusillade of sharp icicles toward it. And Starburst... well, I'm not sure what the hell his blasts are, but they penetrated deeply, leaving a trail of sparkles behind.

Preparing to test the limits of my telekinetic abilities, I reached out with my mind and gripped the arm, slowing it, and eventually holding it mostly still in the air. But I couldn't do it for long. It was simply too massive.

I lowered myself to stand on the beach, as this was taking all my strength. The others were doing their best, while I was fading fast. Then Icecap succeeded in freezing a small cross-section of it about twenty feet above the water, which Starburst then hit with a blast. The section shattered, leaving me holding the rest of the arm. With great effort, I managed to push away from the lagoon as it fell with an enormous splash, missing the beach by mere yards. This took almost every bit of strength I had remaining. They were on their own to battle the remaining stump of the arm.

I made it back to the hole before collapsing to my knees, spent. Jack was on the opposite side from me and began walking over, intending to give me a boost. But then Lumen yelled, "Look out!"

One of the inner globules had reached the opening and was shooting out dark filaments. One struck Lumen in the chest while another snaked its way around his body. To my shock, it began dragging him toward the opening.

Sinta explained how this had all come about. Frustrated with my evident aimlessness and indecision, she'd gone to Nexus and Kimera with her own plan. Kim commandeered the Gatekeepers' jet and the three of them flew out to Nevada. Kim still had access to Area 51, just as I did and Sinta knew the pass code to the blast door, since I'd told her about it. The plan had initially been to just ask my other-self what I should be looking for.

"But when I told her that we'd found the creature and what you all were doing, she got this wild look in her eyes," Sinta said.

"How can you see her eyes to tell?"

Sinta frowned at me. "You just have to look, Dyna." She shrugged, then continued. "Anyway, she convinced me that she should be the one to go through with it, not you."

"Why?"

"Because she knew what to look for. And because..."

"What?" I prompted after a moment.

"Because she said it might kill you."

I frowned. "Yeah, right."

"She said because of your disease, being so near the creature could make it much worse."

I shook my head. "We were all inoculated before we started. Besides, she's sick, too."

"Yeah, but as she said, this creature is probably different from the one that got her sick."

"So they flew her back."

"No," Sinta said. "Vicky took her. With her portal thingies."

I let out a long sigh and rubbed my forehead, thinking about it all. It didn't seem right.

"What's wrong?" Sinta asked.

"Nothing," I said.

She didn't believe me, of course. "You're thinking I'm putting my trust in the wrong Dyna."

My heart skipped a beat. Was I that transparent? Or was Sinta that perceptive? I shrugged and said, "I just feel—"

"Scared," she finished for me.

I nodded. "And guilty."

"Guilty? Why?"

I shifted uncomfortably in the computer chair. "Because I'm just sitting here, maybe?"

"But you can't do everything," Sinta said. "Especially as weak as you are. You have friends – *good* friends – who would do anything for you. Let them."

"Yeah, well, I'm not used to that," I admitted. "All my life, I've relied on myself. No one else. To sit idly by while others are fighting my battle for me? That's something I can't feel good about, no matter how ill and weak I might be."

"I know what it's like to rely only on yourself."

"It's satisfying. It gives me a sense of accomplishment," I said.

Sinta tilted her head. "But it's lonely." We were quiet for a time, then she said, "I've often wondered why you joined the Gatekeepers."

"Are you kidding?" I said. "They're the most prestigious group on the west coast. Why would I *not* join them?"

"Well, like you said, you're used to doing things on your own. You're not exactly a team player."

I admit I was a little offended by the statement. "Did you feel that way when we were in the Scouts?"

"Yeah. But that was different. You were there to learn. Daniel always regarded the Bay Scouts as a sort of training ground, anyway. That's why the team had such a high turnover rate."

"I didn't know that," I said.

"He said that's what scouting does for kids. Prepares them for life. So the Bay Scouts was meant to do the same thing, but for metas."

"Between you and me, I think Daniel's a bit over-obsessed with scouting."

Sinta giggled. "I won't tell him you said that."

Lumen tried to brace himself against the rock, his flood of light vanishing, and looked at me in alarm. I reached out with my mind, having regained enough strength to snap the filament around him. I also ripped the remainder away from his body, and he quickly removed his jacket, which still had residue of the creature's corrosive goo. Jack reached him, then, and pulled him back from the edge.

I knew everyone else's attention was on the arm. The action near the hole couldn't be seen by the others, due to the depth of the water around us. I updated Invictus and urged Jack to continue aiding the other telekinetics. I needed to replace the chunk of its shell, but didn't have the strength, yet.

The creature extended more tendrils, somewhat randomly, but none came near us. "They drain your strength," Lumen warned.

Just then, there was a flash of light from above. I looked up and saw, to only a little surprise, Dinah's other-self plummeting from the sky toward the hole. But she wasn't falling. She was blasting full-tilt toward it, her arms outstretched in front of her, energy crackling around her fists. Instinctively, I put up a telekinetic shield to protect us. Lumen, Jack, and I watched as she blasted straight into the creature. The extended tendrils vanished into the hole with her, while small drops of goo splattered against my shield and fell harmlessly to the carapace.

Jack looked at me in shock. Then we both stared into the creature as flashes lit up the interior, one after the other. Lumen rushed forward and illuminated the interior again. The flashes continued for a few seconds, then stopped. Seconds later, we saw the woman moving toward the surface.

But she didn't make it. She slowed and came to a halt not far below. I tried to mentally drag her out, but simply didn't have the energy. The goo was too thick and I was too drained. Jack saw me struggling and, realizing I couldn't help her, plunged his arm deep into the creature. His face contorted, whether from the effort, pain, or both, I didn't know. But, with a strength I wouldn't have expected from him, he somehow hauled the woman from the muck and dragged her onto the surface.

Two things happened simultaneously, then. One was that Nexus appeared in a flash of light, scooped the other-Dinah up in what appeared to be a fire blanket, then disappeared with her into a hole that opened up next to them in the air.

The other was that Jack started screaming.

The portal glowed suddenly and, as Sinta and I turned our attention to it, Vicky stepped through, looking exhausted. She was carrying a big, silver bundle, which she lowered quickly to the floor and unrolled.

My other-self tumbled out onto the floor. She wore goggles and was dripping with what appeared to be Neukölln goo. Her breathing was labored.

Sinta broke out of her shock. "Dyna!" She knelt next to the woman and reached out to her.

But my other-self held up a hand, stopping Sinta from touching her. Then she smiled faintly. "Kitten," she rasped.

"What happened?" Sinta asked, though it was obvious what the woman had done. I looked at the fire blanket that hung from Vicky's hand and saw that it was dissolving in spots.

"Went... diving," she said. Then she looked up at me and held out her other hand, revealing two glass vials, one filled with a dark purple substance, the other with a bluish fluid. "Might want... to rinse those off," she said, gasping.

"Is this—" I began, only to have her nod.

"Fight fire... with fire," she said.

I grabbed a stack of papers from the desk and used them to carry the vials. Then I hurried out of the room to the lab, where I rinsed them. The corrosive goo came off easily enough, but there was a film left over that made me curious. I tentatively touched it with a fingertip and rubbed it. It seemed to be petroleum jelly.

Ingenious. She'd slathered the stuff all over herself before her "dive," which explained why she wasn't currently a writhing mass of pulpy flesh. I wiped off the vials with a towel and tucked them into my pocket. Before returning to the portal room, I gathered up the remainder of the ampules filled with her drug cocktail.

Vicky caught my eye as I returned and motioned that she'd be waiting for us on the other side. Then she stepped through the portal, giving us some privacy.

I knelt next to an increasingly distressed Sinta. "We have to get her to a hospital!" she said, looking between the two of us.

My other-self had removed her goggles. No energy leaked around her blue eyes, which were severely bloodshot. Dark blood was trickling from her nose. "No... point," she said to Sinta. And then her head lolled backward.

One at a time, I took the ampules and held them against her body. I squeezed the sides, breaking the interior walls, and let the medicine flow into her.

"What's wrong with her?" Sinta demanded.

"What she said would happen to me," I said as I continued injecting her. "Going inside the creature caused her infection to spread rapidly. And she's right. There's nothing a hospital could do for her." Sinta looked at me, her eyes pleading with me to do something.

The woman roused a little. "H'lo, kitten," she mumbled. "What're you doing here?" She coughed and blood sprayed her chest.

"You can't die!" she screamed at her.

The woman chuckled faintly. "Bet I can," she rasped. "Overdue."

I hated to do it, but I had to ask her. I leaned in and said, "What's the final step?" She focused on me, as though not comprehending the question. Or not knowing who I was. So I fished the vials from my pocket and held them up. "Your notes," I said, "are unclear." That was putting it nicely. They were incoherent.

Recognition seemed to hit her and she struggled to speak. "In... noc'late."

"Inoculate with what?"

She coughed again and blood shot from her nose, dark and ugly. "Chrys... ryso..." She closed her eyes for a moment. She opened them a moment later and seemed to have difficulty focusing. She noticed Sinta. "H'lo... kitten."

"Hi," Sinta said in a low, choked voice. Then she turned to me, tears soaking the fur on her cheeks. "Do something!"

I looked at the pile of spent ampules. "I don't know what else I can do," I said.

"My... time..." the woman croaked.

"No! It can't be!" Sinta insisted. Then, her voice cracking, "I... I still need you."

My eyes burned as I looked at her, only now realizing just how much my double meant to her. I put my hand on her shoulder in a way I hoped was comforting.

"No, kitten," my other-self said. "You don't." The woman laid her head back on the floor.

Sinta sobbed openly, now. "I love you," she choked out. She wanted so badly to embrace her friend, but the goo prevented that.

"Love you, too. So much." Then, to my surprise, she looked up at me. She fixed me with a gaze that was at once pleading and accusatory. "Not... alone," she said. "Like me."

Sinta shook her head. "You're *not* alone."

She looked back at Sinta, her face relaxing into a smile and her eyes closing. "Goodbye... kitten."

Through her tears, Sinta whispered her farewell, then clung tightly to me. Together, we watched the woman's chest rise and fall more and more shallowly until, finally, all breathing stopped.

SEVENTEEN

"Healing yourself is connected with healing others."
~ Yoko Ono

If I'm honest with myself, I have to admit that I never really healed after Lee's suicide. I suppose that's because I didn't consider at the time that I had any healing to do. I felt guilt over her death and dealt with that, eventually. But the healing from her loss took a back seat to a much larger recovery that I went through following her death, which was the mending of the rift between my brother and me. The happiness that brought me was great enough to minimize my sadness.

The root of my guilt is that Lee and I weren't on good terms when she died. Had we been, would she have made that plunge to the pavement? I try not to think along those lines, but sometimes it's hard not to. It's easier to believe that her actions were beyond my ability to influence, which may or may not have been true.

Sinta, however, was in full self-blame mode after the death of my other-self, believing she was directly responsible for it, since she was the one who thought to go to her for help in the first place. Sinta had merely wanted the woman to explain what needed to be done. Taking my place was her own idea, but she never told Sinta her full plan.

We brought her body back to our world, where we had her cremated. Sinta and I spread some of her ashes into the waters of Kirby Cove. Some of them, we buried at the western end of the beach where it meets the hillside. An exposed rock there served as her headstone. Sinta used her claws to scratch "Dinah" into its surface. The tiny bit of cremains left, Sinta kept in a little white urn in her bedroom.

Sinta wasn't the only one who needed healing. After Jack pulled my double from the creature's body, Dana got him over to the shore where the medic tried to tend to him, while Dana did his best to telekinetically remove the goo from Jack's arm. But as it turned out, this stuff ate through flesh far more rapidly than anything else. Once all the skin was gone from Jack's arm, there wasn't much Dana or the medic could do.

It seems this is how the creature fed itself. Organic material would be captured by the thing's "arms" and dissolved, the nutrients then being absorbed. By the time Jack arrived at the hospital, there was so much muscle tissue missing that they couldn't save the arm. It had to be amputated, but for a few inches below the shoulder. He had a very long recovery ahead of him.

Speaking of recovery, I'd given half the recovered samples of Neuköln's fluids to the government, which was working hard to develop a vaccine for the disease.

As for Neuköln itself, we were pretty sure it was dying. Whatever my double had done inside there, aside from stealing a piece of its "heart," seemed to have done it in. The "tips" of its arms, meaning the fungi that were causing the breakout of crypto, began to disappear. The monitoring of the remainder of the arm in the bay indicated it was slowly shrinking.

And the Tidewater Goby's habitat was preserved. After Dana lifted Jack out of the area, Dana maneuvered the removed piece of rocky shell back into place. Others stuffed quick-setting cement into and around the cracks, and the mud and waters were replaced. Though dead, the creature's shell would continue to act as an integral part of the bed of the lagoon for the foreseeable future.

The portal in Nevada was gone. Shepherd himself saw to it, destroying the mechanism in the other world with the judicious application of C-4. The one in our world was unplugged and dismantled. The end.

There were, however, two puzzling things in the aftermath of the event. The first was that we didn't know where Vicky was. Kim said she'd come through the portal from the in-between, then vanished into one of her own portals. She wasn't answering her communicator or cell phone. I left voice messages and sent texts, but she didn't return them.

The second puzzle was that I still wasn't sure what I was doing with the rest of the goop sitting in the fridge in the Gatekeepers medical bay.

"'Chryso?' That's all she said?" Dana asked as he prepared breakfast for us.

"Yeah. She wasn't very coherent. I didn't want to push it any further."

Dana scooped some scrambled eggs onto my plate. "Because?"

"Because she was dying."

"And you're not?"

I shrugged. "Not as rapidly. Besides, Sinta was a wreck. It just seemed wrong, somehow, to – I dunno – intrude, I guess."

"I see." Dana put the skillet in the sink and came to sit at the table with me, setting down glasses of orange juice beside our plates. "So does it mean anything to you?"

I scooped some eggs onto a piece of toast. "Well, the term 'chryso' means 'gold.' Lots of minerals have 'chryso' as a prefix. As does a family of beetles. But we're talking about inoculation, so I doubt those apply. There's an algae, too, but, I dunno. That doesn't make a lot of sense to me, either."

"What about chrysotherapy?" Dana said, surprising me. I often forget he knows a fair bit about medicine.

"Gold salts. Yeah. That would be fine, if I had arthritis, but I've never heard of it being used for a fungal infection." I sighed and turned my attention back to my breakfast. "Thanks for cooking."

"Sure."

"And for sticking around."

He nodded. "Of course."

"No, I mean it. I know this whole mind link thing still bothers you."

Dana spread marmalade on his toast. "It's okay," he said. "I... may have overreacted to the whole thing. You're right. You're not Elizabeth. There's no reason other than my own fear that I should think things will go the same way with you."

I smiled, then mentally said, *Does that mean I don't have to work so hard to keep my guard up?*

Dana chuckled. *I suppose not.*

"Good," I said. "It's a pain."

"Perish the thought that we inconvenience you," he said, taking a drink of his orange juice. He said something else, but I didn't hear it. I was too busy staring at his glass, an idea forming in my head.

"That *wasn't* all she said!" I lifted my own glass and held it up, the idea firming into a plan. "She also said, 'fight fire with fire,' just as she gave me the vials."

Dana looked at me, not comprehending. "You're going to juice it to death?"

"*Penicillium chrysogenum.*"

Dana frowned. "Penicillin?"

I put the glass down. "Penicillin is made from the same mold. It's a mold that produces glucose oxidase, one of the uses of which is as a preservative in fruit juice!"

"So..."

"It's a mold that kills other molds!"

He frowned. "Okay, I see where you're going with this, but wouldn't you then just end up with an infection of a different fungus?"

"The problem isn't that I have a fungal infection. The problem is that the creature's infection somehow co-opted my abilities, allowing it to generate its own little defensive barrier. And the fact that it was a resurgence of my previous infection, not a new one, indicates that it's developed a resistance to the antifungals used on me last time. This new mold wouldn't be able to put up shields, and would respond to regular antifungal treatment."

Dana frowned. "Okay, but how will you get it past that barrier?"

"She gave me two vials," I said. "Remember the blue organelles you said drained energy from Lumen? Well, I assume the second vial's fluid is from one of those. So it will theoretically be able to nullify the shields."

"Seems logical. But I'd still get the opinion of your doctor."

I did, of course. And she additionally consulted with one or two other physicians. A few days later, we had a plan.

Before we implemented the procedure, I visited Jack in the hospital. It had been about a week since the amputation, but it was only my second visit to see him, and the first during which he'd been conscious.

He looked surprisingly well, aside from missing an arm. After our initial greeting, he looked at me with compassion in his eyes. "How's Sinta?"

I pulled a chair over to his bedside. "Morose," I said. "She spends most of the day in her room. Then she goes out at night and I don't see her again until the following day."

"Poor kid." He shook his head. "She came to see me yesterday and thanked me for pulling your twin from the muck. I've never seen her so broken up."

"I want to get her into grief counseling, but she's resistant to the idea. I may ask Dana to talk to her, since she seems to trust him."

"And how are you taking it?"

"Me? I'm fine." Jack raised an eyebrow, clearly not believing me. "I'll be fine," I amended. Then I asked him the question that had been eating at me ever since that day. "Why did you do it?"

"Do what?"

"Why did you pull her out? You knew the danger."

Jack snorted. "No, I didn't. You said the stuff was corrosive, but I didn't think that meant it would go through my arm like you going through a pizza." He smiled as I chuckled. "But she was trapped. What other choice did I have? Let her die in there?"

"Right," I said. "Don't know why I asked." I looked again at his stump, covered by a strange, bubble-type wrap. "I'm so sorry, Jack. It's all my fault."

"What is?"

"It's my fault this happened! You were there because of me, because I needed to find a cure."

Jack frowned and stared at me for a moment. "Dyna, we were there, all of us, because the creature was spreading death in the area."

"But if I hadn't been sick, I never would have looked for the creature in the first place."

"So then it's a good thing you got sick," he said. "Who knows how many more people might have died?"

After an uncomfortable silence, I changed the topic by nodding at his stump. "So what's it like?"

"It's kind of surreal, honestly. I mean, I'd always heard about phantom limb sensations. But it's so weird to experience them. It feels like my arm is still there, sometimes."

"Freaky," I said. "But what is that thing? It's not a bandage. Some weird sort of compression sock?"

"No. I forget what they called it, exactly, but it's necessary for what's to come. Get this," he said with a hint of excitement. "My company is footing the bill entirely for my prosthesis."

"Your insurance, you mean. Yeah, it typically would."

"No, not the insurance. I mean, yeah, insurance would cover a normal device, but I'm talking about a fully robotic arm."

"Robotic."

"Well, I do work for a robotics company, after all."

"Right."

"You wouldn't believe some of the advanced things they're working on. I'll be one of their prototype guinea pigs. The limb will have loads of microprocessors, myoelectric tactile sensors, and even targeted muscle reinnervation."

"Reinnervation? Is that what it sounds like?"

He nodded. "Controlling it with my own nerves, my own thoughts, just like a real arm."

"You're kidding."

"Nope. We're way ahead of anyone else with developing these sorts of things. It's part of what drew me to the company in the first place. Anyway, we'll start on that pretty soon."

I started to say that surely he needed more time for recovery from the amputation, but then remembered his own healing abilities. Undoubtedly, his recovery was faster than a normal person's. "Pretty cool. But I think having your real arm back would be better."

"Obviously. But I'm trying to stay on the positive side."

"I'd say you're succeeding. Better than I would, anyway."

"Oh, that's because I'm so drugged up," he said with a nod.

"Ah."

We were quiet a moment, then he said, "And what about you? If you don't mind me saying, you look awful."

I shrugged. "I'm weak. I can't be on my feet for very long without needing to sit down. And yeah, I know I look like shit." I ran a hand through the tangle of my ponytail. "I don't even look in the mirror, anymore."

"Have you figured out how to use the goo she collected?"

I briefed him on the plans. "We do it on Monday," I said.

"Wow. That's complicated."

"You're talking about controlling a robotic arm with your mind and you think *this* is complicated?" I smiled as he laughed.

We chatted about mundane matters until a nurse came in to bathe him, then said our farewells and I headed home.

Jack wasn't wrong, though. It *was* complicated. We had to minimize the amount of inoculated goo that needed to be fed into my body. Too much and it might have all sorts of unintended consequences. Too little, though, and I wouldn't be any better off. So in order to be as precise as possible, Dr. Stone wanted to do a targeted treatment. The first step was to find where the alien fungus was living in my CSF. A modified PET scan was able to detect the energy emissions from the fungus, based on an analysis of my own energy shield. Fortunately, the stuff tended to grow in fixed colonies, rather than just floating around on a grand tour of my cerebrospinal system.

Once we nailed down the locations of the infections, the actual treatment was sent in via microfilaments. The medical term for this type of surgery is "extended endonasal," because they access the brain by going in through the nose.

More disturbing than the idea of having these things threaded up through my nose was the fact that I was awake for the procedure. Thankfully, it wasn't painful. Some discomfort as the filaments made their way up through the nose and into my CSF by way of the top of my spine, but that was about it. Everything was monitored carefully, the filaments guided gently toward the areas where the fungus was concentrated, and the first part of the treatment released. This was the bluish fluid, which we hoped would eradicate the barriers.

The PET scanners showed the surgical team when the energy signature of the fungus disappeared. Then the second step, which was to release the inoculated "heart of Neuköln." I still wasn't sure what this stuff was supposed to do. The best guess I had was that it would be "familiar" and not arouse any defenses in the fungal invaders, allowing for a surer delivery of the *P. chrysogenum*. The process took hours. But by the time we finished, Dr. Stone was encouraged that it had worked.

A second PET scan a week later revealed no traces of the signature emission in my CSF. At this point, I began the treatment of standard antifungal drugs. By the first of May, I was pronounced cured. My CSF was free of any infection of either fungus.

Physically, I was on the mend, feeling stronger every day. Emotionally, though, I wasn't so great. Vicky responded to one of my texts, finally, apologizing for her absence and saying she'd explain later, but that she would be incommunicado for a while for personal reasons. And that was all she said. It was cryptic and disappointing, but better than having no idea where she was.

Sinta, though, was more withdrawn than ever. I'd suggested she talk to Dana, but she wasn't interested. She continued to spend very little time with me and I began to wonder if she blamed me for my other-self's death.

One evening, I caught her on her way out the door. "We need to talk," I told her.

"About what?" she said, not removing her hand from the doorknob.

"About us. About our living situation."

She hesitated for a moment before taking a seat in the armchair, from where she fairly glared at me. "What about it? Do you not want me around, anymore?"

I was shocked by her directness. "Why would you think that?"

She shrugged. "I guess because you've been so distant."

I blinked. "*Me*? You're the one who stays in her room all day and is out all night."

"But you never want to spend time with me."

"That's not true! I've been a bit preoccupied with getting rid of this disease, you know." Sinta tilted her head at me, saying nothing. My heart sank. "Which," I said slowly, "I never could have done without you."

"You mean without *her*."

"Without both of you," I said. "If you hadn't gone there—"

"It's just that you've never expressed any gratitude toward her!" she spat. "She gave her life to save you, and you don't care!"

"Of course I care!"

"You've never said it!"

I looked at her for a bit before responding. She was so angry. It was an emotion I hardly ever saw from her. And never aimed at me. "You know," I said softly, hating that we had to be talking about this, "she loved you very much. If things were different, I know she would have wanted to be with you all the time. But that wasn't possible for more than one reason." Sinta lowered her head and stared at her lap as I spoke. "You're right," I continued. "I do owe her my life. And more than that. I owe her for showing me how wonderful you are. We wouldn't be living together if it weren't for her." Sinta still didn't react, just continued avoiding my gaze. "What I'm getting at is that she didn't die for me. She died for *you*." Now she looked up at me. "She knew she couldn't be with you. So she wanted *me* to be with you. She saved me so you wouldn't be without both of us."

Sinta shifted in her seat, her eyes glistening. "You're certain you're cured, this time?"

"There are few guarantees in life, kitten, but it seems so. My doctor is pretty thorough."

She sniffed and wiped away a tear. Then she got up and joined me on the sofa. She wrapped her arms around me and laid her head against my shoulder. "Love you, Dyna."

I squeezed her tightly. "Love you, too."

"But you're wrong," she said, sitting upright. "She didn't want you to be without me, either. She loved you, too."

My first urge was to refute that idea, but I didn't. Because what my other-self said suddenly came back to me. *Not alone, like me.* In everything that had gone on since, those words had slipped my mind. I didn't know if this qualified as her having "love" for me, but I wasn't going to quibble.

"You're right," I said, looking down at Sinta and stroking her fur. "I really do owe her a lot."

As Sinta hugged me again, a slow and painful realization grew inside me. A truth I could no longer ignore, as much as I wanted to.

"So. What's bothering you?" Invictus said, pushing aside Dr. Stone's final medical assessment.

"What do you mean?"

"You're hesitant about returning to active duty." When I looked surprised, he said, "Dyna, you can't be an effective leader of a team without having insights into your members. And you don't exactly have a poker face."

I nodded, acknowledging his point. "I just feel as though I haven't been pulling my weight as part of the team."

"How so?"

"Well, come on. I've been on medical leave almost longer than I've been active. I just don't feel like I've contributed."

"You mean aside from discovering the source of an illness that's killed fifty-three people and sickened thousands?"

I cringed when he mentioned the deaths. Most had been young children and the elderly. Several were in the same nursing home and died when someone there brought the infection in. "Well that wasn't exactly heroic."

The big man frowned at me. "I think you'd benefit from removing that word from your vocabulary, regarding what we do."

"What? Why?"

"Because it's a media buzz word. It's not how we see ourselves. Or at least, it's not how we *should* see ourselves."

"Of all people, I never expected to hear *you* say that."

"Why? Because I've been with the group forever and leader for so long? Because I'm serious about what we do? Or because the media often refers to me that way?" He shook his head. "Sure, what we do is dangerous, much of the time. As is the work of the police or firefighters."

"Whose actions are often heroic," I pointed out.

"Indeed," he said. "But you're unlikely to hear any of them referring to themselves that way. It's just part of the job." When I remained silent, he said, "So what's really bothering you?"

This wasn't something I should be talking about with Invictus, I told myself. But it came spilling out, anyway. "My other-self gave her life to save me," I said.

"You're feeling guilt over that?"

I frowned. "I think 'shame' is the more accurate word."

"My goodness, why?"

I avoided looking at him as I said, "Because, had the situation been reversed, I wouldn't have done the same thing."

Invictus shook his head. "Dyna—"

"I wouldn't even have done what Jack did. I wouldn't have pulled her out of the creature."

"You say that now, being distanced from the situation. But we all do things in the heat of the moment that we would be unlikely to do if we had time to think about it."

"You can maybe say that about Jack," I said, "but she put time into planning her actions. She knew very well that it would kill her. And believe me, I wouldn't have taken those actions."

Invictus stared at me for a while. Then he nodded faintly and gathered up my papers. "Let's keep you on leave for a bit longer. We can revisit this when you feel ready."

I agreed, understanding his reasoning. Having self-doubt made me an unreliable member of the team. I could put my teammates in danger. I could be a liability to the team. Or, more accurately, I'd continue to be the liability I'd always been to them.

I left the Citadel more conflicted than I'd been in a long time. It was a beautiful day, so I removed my shoes and tucked them into my bag, then launched myself into the sky. Sometimes being up high helped, as though physically distancing myself from the ground helped me take a more objective look at my problems.

I flew home by a circuitous route, first along Baker Beach on the South Bay. Some of the people on the beach saw me and looked, almost certainly not knowing who I was. Around the horn and along Ocean Beach and down to the west end of Golden Gate Park.

I really tried to see things as Invictus suggested, but the simple truth was that I couldn't stop thinking of metas and their teams as anything other than heroic. Maybe it really was nothing more than normal media sensationalism. And maybe my reasons for wanting to be a meta had nothing to do with actually being a hero. But after spending time around the likes of Invictus, Scoutmaster, the Maltese Falcon, the Golden Bear, and so many others, I'd developed a pretty clear set of expectations of metas. Expectations I applied to myself, and clearly wasn't living up to.

I flew over the golf course and North Lake, the polo field, and Stow Lake. Some ducks buzzed me on their way in for a swim. The thing was, when I thought of myself in comparison to those other metas, I really did find myself lacking. I tried to rationalize this. I told myself that the reason I wouldn't have done what Jack did, and the reason I wouldn't have sacrificed myself to save my other-self, was specifically because it *was* my other-self. I had negative emotions attached to her and the entire Nevada Incident.

Finally, I flew up the Panhandle of the park, halfway, then crossed over Oak Street and landed on the back side of my roof. As I entered the building, I told myself that, had it been someone else stuck in that muck, I would have pulled them out. If it had been Jack. Or Sinta. Or any of my teammates, really.

But what about a total stranger? What about one of the "bad guys"? Would I go out of my way to save them, at an almost certain chance of major physical harm? An affirmative answer wasn't one I could give with any certainty.

And that, I told myself, was why I wasn't a hero.

That night, unable to sleep, I turned on my bedside lamp and pulled a stack of folded pages from the nightstand's drawer. I opened the letter, dog-eared from many readings, and once more lost myself in the words of my other-self.

I read again of her history and that of her society. I read of her disease and her involvement with her world's Valora. And finally, I read the words that had haunted me ever since I first read them, years before.

I know that, on my world, you are probably suffering. Ten days ago, I'd have cared little. Today, I feel remorse. But if it's any consolation (and I feel it may be), please know that, by exchanging places with me for this short time, you have saved me. You and your friends.

Because I've seen, now, what I came here to see. In you, I've seen the heroic force I could have been.

Thank you.

I folded the pages again and tucked them back into the drawer, then turned off the light. I lay back on my pillow and stared into the darkness and whispered to the past, "You, too."

EIGHTEEN

"Guilt is feeling bad about what you have done; shame is feeling bad about who you are – all it is, is muddling up things you have done with who you are."

~ Marcus Brigstocke

Like everybody else, there are things I've done in my life that I'm not proud of. I don't think I need to make a list of them. And of course, there are things I didn't do that I wish I had, and these inactions bring their own kind of guilt.

I don't often allow myself to think about this, and hesitate to even put it in writing, but I'm not as uncaring about my relationship with my mother as I let on. It's actually a subject of considerable conflict for me. Generally speaking, I think my responses to her actions are perfectly understandable. But sometimes I do feel guilty. I look at the idiotic grudge I held against my brother for so long and wonder if I'm doing something similar with my mother. Would things between us be okay if I weren't so hard-headed about it? Am I a bad person for having done these things with my family members? I struggle with these questions. But the anxiety they bring is nothing compared to what I was feeling now, because of my dead double.

I think my therapist was surprised to see me. It had been a long time, and I hadn't exactly been making great progress before I stopped going. And here I was with a whole new flavor of self-hatred.

"The last time we talked," she said, "you'd been having some problems dealing with guilt. How's that coming along?"

"Not well," I said. "I still have nightmares about it." I explained how I not only didn't feel any differently about Dr. Gray's death, but now I was afraid something similar could happen again. I told her about the incident with the bank robbery. "Even if Dr. Gray maybe deserved what he got, due to allying himself with Valora, the point remains that I was negligent. What if there had been someone else there?" I shook my head. "But that's not why I came to you, today."

I told her about my recent conversation with Invictus about my work with the Gatekeepers. After I'd laid everything out for her, she said, "What did you think of what Invictus said? About you finding the solution to the outbreak?"

I shrugged. "I dunno. I guess that it was no big deal."

"If it had been someone else who'd discovered the cause of the outbreak – let's say Invictus himself – how would you feel?" I didn't answer. I didn't need to. She knew how I'd have viewed it. "Remember, we look for patterns in our behavior. What pattern does this fit?"

I sighed. "The pattern of never finding myself good enough."

She nodded. "And you even said that in a self-deprecating way."

"Okay!" I snapped. "I understand *why* I'm this way. But how does that help me *stop* the behavior?"

"You have the ability to change how you see things. Like that energy-sensing vision you told me about. It takes a deliberate act for you to make that switch, right? It's no different with your mental perceptions. Look, you're able to see the good parts of your other-self, right? You've told me you like Invictus, despite his apparent homophobia. We do this all the time, choosing to focus on a person's good traits. You can do the same with yourself. Focus on your good qualities; forgive yourself for your mistakes."

I rolled my eyes. "Self-forgiveness is an asinine concept. If I hurt someone, the only one capable of forgiving me is the person I hurt. And of course, if that person is dead, then I'm fucked on the forgiveness front."

"What about when your actions hurt yourself?" I just frowned and looked away. Then she said, "What about forgiving your mother?"

Now I stared at her. "You must be kidding. She thinks I'm an abomination, in a couple ways. I can't forgive her for that."

"Why do you think she holds such views?"

"Because she's a religious nut," I said, stating the obvious.

"And why is she a religious nut?"

"I dunno. Mental illness?"

"Do you really believe that?"

I frowned. "No."

"Then what is it? What drives her fanaticism?"

I opened my mouth to reply, but suddenly realized I had no answer to give. I'd honestly never given it much thought. But once I did, it was fairly obvious. "Fear," I said softly.

"Go on."

"She's irrationally afraid of things that are different, like a lot of people are. And, like most people, she believes her fears are sensible. She's been afraid of my brother's telepathic abilities ever since she found out about them, even though he'd never in a million years do anything to harm her. She should know that, but allows the fear to dominate her thinking. To dominate her life, I suppose." I shook my head. "All her fears are groundless. Paranoid."

"But as you said, that's not how she perceives them." I nodded in agreement. "So, do you think she could get over her fears if she could change how she looks at these things?" I started to agree, then frowned, glaring at the woman. "Dinah, you and your mother aren't so different."

"I don't let fear rule my life," I said.

"No? How many times have you told me you're afraid of being hurt again, and that's why you've not pursued a romantic relationship?"

I stared at her, hating the fact that she was right. Then I hung my head in defeat.

One of the questions my therapist had asked me was whether I was still doing the "deep journaling," which caused me to mention K.T.'s suggestion of doing a book. She thought it was a great idea. So the following day, I phoned K.T. and told her I was interested.

"But," I said, "I don't really know the first thing about writing a book, nor do I have the time."

"Right," she said. "Well, how would you feel about a ghost writer?"

"I don't believe in ghosts," I said.

She laughed. "Are you comfortable with turning copies of your journals over to me? I'll find a writer suitable for turning them into something readable."

I hesitated. There was an awful lot of personal stuff in my journals, obviously. "Well..."

"If there's anything I think might be too private, I'll talk to you about it, first."

I had to admit that I could trust K.T. to pick what to give the writer and what not to. "Okay," I said. "Let me start putting some things together for you."

K.T. was excited, but I still had doubts about the whole thing.

After the call, I went online. I'm pretty bad about regularly checking my personal email and hadn't done so in ages. There were quite a few from visitors to the website that Macy had forwarded for me to answer, but only two from the stalker, both of which were sent during the height of my sickness. Neither were threatening, exactly, though it was obvious he was still angry that I hadn't replied. After that, nothing. I really hoped that was a good sign, though I knew it wasn't uncommon for long stretches without contact.

There was also an email from the detective on the case, also from months ago. He said they'd learned the identity of the stalker. He was, as expected, a teenager. He lived in the city, which made me think I probably had seen him that day in the park.

There was, however, nothing linking him to any other stalking cases. I was glad to hear this. I replied to the detective, thanking him for his message and apologizing for the delay. I attached the two "new" emails from the kid, and said that, since it had been several months without contact, maybe we'd heard the last of him. But I didn't really believe it.

Then I called Macy. I thanked her again for screening the emails and for maintaining the site. I updated her on the stalker situation. Even though she was out of the loop, I knew she was still curious.

I told her the kid's name. "Holy crap," she said. "I go to school with him! Man, I'm gonna let him have it!"

"No," I said. "That's not a good idea. Please don't give him any reason to suspect that you know. No telling how he could react to that."

Macy agreed, reluctantly.

Later that day, Sinta and I went to visit Jack at his home. He greeted us warmly and invited us in. "I just made coffee," he said as we walked to the kitchen. Sinta and I both offered to help him, but he declined. As he pulled down extra cups for us, we both stared at the prosthetic arm he wore.

"Pretty cool, huh?" he said, propping it on the counter for us to inspect. And cool it was. Very life-like in appearance, even down to hair on the synthetic skin of its forearm that matched his other arm. "This is my 'civilian' arm," he said. "It's one of two I'm currently testing for them."

"What's the other one?" I asked as he filled our cups.

"Let's just say it's one more appropriate for dangerous work." He poured the coffee with the new arm and I was surprised at how well it gripped the handle of the carafe. "Not great for delicate work, though."

"I didn't think you'd be using one this soon," Sinta said.

"Honestly, neither did I. But the physical therapy has been going really well."

"That's great," I said.

"Check this out," he said. He rolled up the short sleeve of his shirt and depressed a hidden button under his artificial triceps. He held it for a couple seconds, then there was a click and the arm came loose in his hand. He pulled it free, revealing the stump of his arm. Except it wasn't flesh that we saw, but a metal "base" that appeared to be permanently attached. Jack pointed out its massive array of electrodes. "These are wired to my own nerves and connect inside the prosthetics, carrying the electrical impulses to the motors inside them. In theory, I could have dozens of different arms for different uses."

"Wow," Sinta said.

"Impressive," I agreed.

Jack snapped his arm back in place and wiggled his new fingers. We moved from the kitchen to his living room. As Jack queried Sinta on her well-being, I studied his face. He was smiling. At first, I assumed it was just because he was glad to see us. I couldn't imagine someone being truly happy, having lost a limb so recently, no matter how well the recuperation was going. There seemed to be more to it, so I asked.

Jack nodded as he spoke. "Well, from a scientific perspective, this is new territory for me, and there's something both exciting and satisfying about being the test subject for brand new tech."

I knew what he meant. I remembered how I felt back in the U.K., when I realized my self-experimentation was beginning to work. It was tremendous, even without the level of success that came later. "Still," I said, "I don't think it's just excitement I sense."

To my surprise, Jack's cheeks reddened slightly. With a shrug, he said, "Well, I may or may not have met someone."

"Yay!" Sinta said. "Who?"

Still embarrassed, Jack said, "Her name's Aimee. She's the primary engineer for arms and the main person I've been dealing with. And she's the daughter of the founder of Wonderland Robotics."

"Is she cute?" Sinta asked, grinning.

"Very. But she's also brilliant, which is just as attractive."

He looked at me with an expression that seemed almost apologetic. I smiled in return. "Have you asked her out, yet?" I asked.

"Oh, no. No, of course not."

"Why not?" Sinta asked.

"Because he's too chicken," I said.

"Because we have a professional relationship," he said. "I don't want to make that awkward."

I tilted my head. "I suggest you get over that."

It was odd. I was hopeful that something would come of it that would bring him happiness. But at the same time, there was a small part of me that was disappointed.

We visited with him for another hour before making our way home. I don't remember much of the conversation, honestly. It wasn't that I was jealous. I really did hope Jack would find the right person for him, whether it was Aimee or someone else. I knew, deep down, that the right person for him wasn't me. But that only reminded me of my own loneliness. And of all the doubts I was having. Including my role as a meta.

A few days later, I sat in an isolated corner booth at a bar in a San Francisco that wasn't my own. Dynasonic sat across from me, dressed in black motorcycle leathers with yellow-gold accents, a nearly empty glass of white wine in front of her. I'd been able to contact her through her band's website. I was just glad she was in town and not on tour, and of course that she'd actually been online to receive the message.

I'd decided to tell her the story of my *other* other-self, including showing her the letter and relating her recent death. But as soon as I got to the part of the story where my teammates and I confirmed that we'd been taken to another world, replaced by that world's versions of ourselves, Dynasonic stopped me.

"*What?*" she gasped.

I paused. "Um... what?" I repeated. "Are you okay?"

She stared at me as though I'd just asked the stupidest question possible. "*Okay?* How could I possibly be okay?"

I shook my head, confused. "I don't understand."

"Seriously?" Lowering her voice, she said, "You tell me that there are other worlds – other *universes* – and you're wondering what's *wrong*?" She ran a hand through her hair, staring vacantly toward the table.

"But... you *knew* that. You met *me*. And that other one you told me about. I don't understand."

Again, she looked at me like I was a lunatic. "You said you weren't from around here. I figured you meant L.A. or something. I thought both of you were just doing some sort of obsessive cosplay or something."

"You're kidding."

She shrugged. "Seemed likely. Cosplay is pretty popular, and some of those guys aren't exactly playing with tuned instruments. Besides, it's not like either of you look *exactly* like me. You're both older. Different color hair. Why would I possibly think..." She sighed heavily. "This... this is a lot to take in."

"I'm sorry." I remembered how the realization had first hit me and regretted that I was the one to inflict that truth upon her. She was clearly rocked by the information and sat quietly for several minutes. I didn't speak, knowing she needed to assimilate.

Finally, she said, "Look, just go on with your story while I try not to freak out, okay?"

"Sure," I said, and told her the rest of the tale, including showing her the letter my other-self left me and her recent selfless sacrifice.

When I was done, she said, "So, for all I know, my world could be flooded with alternate versions of our people."

"I suppose that's possible," I said. "But the silver lining in that cloud is that there seems to be no displacement in this world. You didn't disappear when Mistress Dyna came here, or when I did."

"True. Still doesn't seem right, though."

"Concerned about illegal aliens coming to steal your jobs?"

She chuckled. "I guess."

"Well," I said, "I can suggest a way to find out if there are others who've come here." And I told her of how we'd used telepaths to find the imposters on my world after the events in Nevada. "I'm assuming some of your metas are telepaths," I concluded.

But this made her seem uncomfortable. "That would be problematic, here." I prompted her to elaborate, and she said, "We do have telepaths. But they're not exactly—"

"They're mostly distrusted on my world, too," I said, assuming what she meant. "But we found that their assistance in finding the imposters helped raise them in the eyes of the public. Not much. But a little."

"Here, it isn't so much lack of trust as..." She shook her head. "Look. You didn't come here just to tell me about what happened and to show me that letter. Why are you really here?"

I looked up at her, a bit self-consciously. I knew she'd ask this, but I still hadn't figured out how to put it. "You and I pursued different paths," I said, "and we've both achieved our goals, it seems. But you appear happy with your life, while I'm... not."

She frowned. "Okay."

I looked down at my beer, dragging my finger through the condensation on the glass. "I guess you could say I'm going through a bit of a crisis of confidence. I'm questioning myself. All my past decisions. All my future plans." I shrugged. "Everything."

"I'm sorry to hear that. But I'm not sure how I can help."

"I'd like to know more about you. I'm curious to know how similar our lives are."

She hesitated a moment. "I'll need another drink for that."

I watched as she approached the bar. After ordering the drinks, she surveyed the room. She seemed worried, but relaxed when she finished looking about the room.

She returned with a glass of wine for her and a beer for me, then settled back into the booth. "All right. Fire away."

I thanked her for the beer and, because it had been on my mind, lately, I said, "Tell me about your parents."

She sipped her wine and shrugged. "Not a lot to tell. Dad worked an office job until he retired. Corporate sales. Boring. Mom was a hairdresser in town."

"You get along with them?"

"My mother passed away about five years ago, but we were close. It was hard, losing her. Dad and I talk every weekend."

A good home life. Major difference, already. And one that explained why she wasn't as messed up as I was. "Any siblings?"

She paused. "Yes."

I had to prompt her. "Brother? Sister? More than one?"

"One brother," she said. "But I don't feel comfortable talking about him."

"Don't get along? My brother and I went through that."

"No, it's not that," she said. She took another drink, somewhat nervously, it seemed. "I can't. Not here, anyway."

"Oh. All right." I was insanely curious, but I'd have to wait to find out the deal on that one. "Okay, pardon me for being so direct, but are you straight?"

She laughed. "Have to admit, I wasn't expecting that." She nodded. "I am, yes. I take it you're not?"

"Not very," I said, embarrassed that I'd even brought it up. "So what about relationships? Have a boyfriend?"

She smiled, but it was pained. "I did. Until about eight months ago. We'd been together for almost ten years."

"What happened?"

"He kept asking me to marry him. I kept declining. Not because I didn't love him," she was quick to say, "but because I knew he wanted to settle down, raise a family, and whatnot. And I've never been in a hurry to do that. I want to continue recording and touring as much as possible. That's not fair to a family."

"So he broke it off?" She nodded. "Wow. I'm sorry."

"It's for the best, I suppose." Then she said, "So how are we faring, similarity-wise?"

I gave a slight snort. "My mother and I can't stand each other. Dad lives in his own little world of sports and cable news channels and goes to great lengths to stay out of my mother's way. My brother and I were alienated for a while. My fault. But now we're really close."

"Interesting. And what about relationships?"

I briefly told her about my triad with Sharon and Jackie. And the unfortunate relationship with Lee and her suicide.

She looked at me in sorrow. "I'm so sorry," she said. I nodded my appreciation. She was quiet a moment, then said, "My boyfriend's name was Lee."

"Of course it was," I said, shaking my head, then switched subjects to something less painful. "The first time I was here, I read a newspaper. There are a lot of differences in our worlds. We've got an economy in the toilet, right now. Yours is booming. Your city is clean. I mean, ridiculously clean. Cities in my world are dirty. Trash in the streets, and so on." I shook my head in wonder. "What's the secret, here?"

She hesitated before shrugging and saying, "It's been this way my whole life."

"What about other countries? Are they as well off as the U.S.?"

"Well, no. We probably lead the world in prosperity. Our crime rates are quite low. We're consistently in the top five in rankings of things like education, healthcare, equal rights, and so on."

"I can't even imagine what that's like. In my world, you've got to live in one of the Scandinavian countries to rank that highly with any consistency. The U.S. is rather abysmal, honestly."

"We're not without our problems," she said, with a strange tone and a faraway look in her eye. "Some of which are pretty big." She cleared her throat and looked at me. "But for the most part, it's quite good." She sipped her wine, then said, "So how is this helpful?"

Good question, I thought as I took another drink. "I believe one's environment has a huge effect on development. My other-self who died – you read how awful her world was. She saw my world, my friends, and so on. And she seemed to believe this caused her to become a better person." I paused before coming to my conclusion, averting my gaze from hers. "I guess, in some twisted way, I was hoping the same thing would happen to me."

She was quiet for a bit. "You want to be a better person," she said flatly. I nodded. "Then what's stopping you?" When I hesitated, she said, "You're right. Environment has a big effect. But you can't let yourself be trapped by that. Look, as great as I got along with my parents, they weren't at all supportive of me pursuing a career in music. They never dreamed I'd be successful, even a little bit, and didn't want to see me devastated when I ended up having to wait tables the rest of my life. All through high school, I was encouraged to go to college, to become something safer, more traditional, purely because it was more likely to lead to a more stable life and so on."

"So you didn't go to college at all?"

"Nope. I moved to San Francisco right out of high school. I couldn't resist, y'know? The Bay Area. Home of so many classic bands. I ended up sharing a shitty little house with three roommates while I got to know the music scene. Did the whole starving artist thing for a while, and then it all just started to fall into place. Gained a loyal following on the bar circuit, and so on." She shrugged. "I'm convinced it's because I made my own environment. I surrounded myself with other motivated people who shared my goals. I hung out with musicians who were talented and driven, and that's how I put together the band. In my mind, success was never in doubt. Granted, I didn't think we'd be *this* successful, but I never thought for a minute that we'd wash out."

I smirked. "You should write self-help books."

She laughed. "Yeah, no."

"Think you'd ever be interested in seeing my world?"

She frowned. "If our two worlds had the swapping thing, like you had with the other, I would have done that without any warning."

I felt a pang of guilt. "Yeah. Sorry. I admit I was surprised when it didn't happen. If you ever do want to visit, I'd be happy to take you. The portal is actually way up in the air over the Bay. I'm guessing you can't fly."

"Hell, no. Can you?"

"Oh, yeah," I said. "One of the cooler aspects of being me."

"Wait a minute," she said, frowning. "I would have fallen to my death!"

"No. I had a friend waiting for your arrival, just outside the portal. He would have caught you. And for your return here, he had a jetpack he was going to teach you to use." She took a long drink, draining her glass, as she stared skeptically at me. My smile vanished and I suddenly felt horrible. "I guess it was pretty irresponsible of me to come here that first time."

"Ya *think*?"

"I'll admit I wasn't thinking clearly. The disease I had affected my judgment in a lot of ways. You're right. I never should have done it. I'm sorry."

She didn't acknowledge the apology. After an awkward few moments, she looked at her watch. "I need to be in the studio soon."

"Right," I said, feeling as though I'd just irrevocably harmed our budding friendship. I stared at the table, berating myself.

"Right," she repeated, and started to get out of the booth.

"Wait," I said. "Please."

She hesitated, then settled back in her seat. "What?"

"There's another reason I came." I couldn't look her in the eye, so I stared at the table. And with no small amount of shame, I said, "I never allowed for the possibility of friendship with my other-self. I wrote her off, for a number of reasons, none of which were particularly good ones." Now I looked at her. "I don't want to make that mistake twice. I don't want to pretend you don't exist. I want us to be friends."

She frowned slightly, then said, "I dunno. You've really laid a lot on me."

"I know. And I'm sorry I didn't realize you didn't know. And I don't want my actions to drive you away."

She studied my face for several seconds. I don't know what she saw there, but eventually she cleared her throat and said, "Jetpack, huh?"

I offered an apologetic smile. "Yeah."

She smirked. "That would be pretty cool."

"Yeah, it would." I smiled hopefully. "So, are *we* cool?"

Dynasonic snorted. "The coolest. And don't you forget it."

The sudden relief made me realize how tense I'd been. "Good." I smiled and shifted in my seat. "I guess you have to go to the studio."

"Soon," she said. "Want to come watch?"

"Seriously?"

"Sure. We're not recording today, just working on some stuff. The guys won't mind."

"That would be amazing!" I said. "Where's your studio?"

"In the basement of my house, actually," she said.

We headed out into the street toward her sport bike, black and yellow-gold. But then she said, "We should probably make it easier for you to contact me when you visit. Come on."

She led me down the block to a convenience store, where she first accessed the ATM. She withdrew five hundred dollars and handed it to me. "You may need that at some point."

"Thanks," I said.

Then she purchased a pay-as-you-go smartphone. She loaded it up with minutes and data, then programmed her phone number into it for me, and that phone's number into her own.

"Again, thanks." I smiled. "I'll do the same when you visit."

"You're welcome," she said.

We walked back to her bike. She mounted, grabbed a matching helmet, and pressed the starter. The dashboard lit up, though the bike itself remained almost totally silent. It was electric, I realized. With a smile, she lowered the helmet over her golden hair and motioned for me to hop on behind her.

I'd never actually been on a motorcycle, before, but figured I was unlikely to get hurt if I fell off. So I climbed on and we zipped quietly away.

One short ride later, we pulled up to a gated cul-de-sac off Post Street. She parked the bike on the street, then entered through the pedestrian door in the gate. We stepped through, then walked to a brick building a few doors down.

"That goes to the main home," she said, pointing to an ornate wooden door with inlaid stained glass. Several feet away was a second door, this one plain. "This goes straight to the studio," she said, unlocking it.

We descended a flight of stairs and emerged into the refinished basement. Instruments were segregated. Drums in one corner, guitars in another, keyboards on the opposite wall, an isolation booth for the vocals, I assumed. The other band members weren't there, yet.

"Wow. This is sweet."

"Used to be the kitchen when I bought the place."

As I wandered around, exploring, I said, "Can you tell me about the problems here that you so cryptically alluded to?"

"I suppose so." She plopped into one of the leather armchairs that sat around the studio. I did the same. "You asked me how it is that things are so nice, here." She took a deep breath. "Truth is, it's because of what many people refer to as the 'Thought Police.'"

I frowned. "Like Orwell?"

"Sort of, but this is more literal. Orwell's Big Brother was a ubiquitous surveillance network. Ours is, too, but it's not technological in nature. You might say we're a cross between *1984* and 'The Minority Report.' Here, the government employs a cadre of telepaths to literally monitor the thoughts of the populace."

"Wow. That's disturbing." The irony of this statement wasn't lost on me. I remembered back two years earlier, to my interview for *Supers*, in which I defended the use of telepaths by the police. This society was evidence of what K.T. had said could happen.

"I agree. But most people here just see a very low crime rate and a government that seems to know what the public wants and responds to, accordingly."

"Like what?" I asked.

She shrugged. "Clean streets, free parking, lots of public space, a ton of free programs and services for everyone."

"Okay," I said cautiously.

"That's the apparent difference between our world and Orwell's. His surveillance of society was a totalitarian system, designed to control everything the populace did or thought. Here, the goal is to make society a more peaceful thing, a more productive thing. A happier thing."

I nodded. "Yeah, I'd rather live here than in Orwell's society, though I can see why it makes you nervous."

"Here's the thing," she said. "All telepaths are part of this network. You won't find any super teams with a telepath. They're all in surveillance."

"Really? All of them?"

"It's a requirement," she said. "And the government knows when one is born. The other telepaths can sense it. And as soon as the abilities surface, they're taken into service and plugged into the network."

I frowned. "As kids?"

She nodded. "Yup. And the families have no say in the matter. And they never see them again, from what I've heard."

"You're not serious!"

"I am. Most families don't talk about it. Those who do will always say they're 'honored' to have their daughter serving."

"You think they're telepathically coerced into thinking that?"

"That's easier than believing everyone is happy about losing their daughters that way."

"Or sons," I added.

"Well, no," she said. "All telepaths are female. So they say."

I stared at her. "How odd." That was putting it mildly. How could that be the case? It made no sense. "So, here's a question," I said. "Assuming the incidence of metas in your world is similar to mine, there really couldn't be all that many telepaths out there. How is it that such a small number of them can monitor the entire population? Or is this a localized thing?"

"No, it's national in scope. When I used the term 'network,' I meant it literally. The telepaths work together as a unit. The more of them there are, the greater the reach, and the stronger their combined abilities."

"So aren't you concerned that our conversation is being monitored right now?"

She shook her head. "No, we're safe, here. The walls, floors, and ceilings in this basement are lined with thick sheets of tungsten."

"Because tungsten is to telepaths like garlic is to vampires?"

"Yes. That. Exactly." Dynasonic laughed. "No, it's because telepaths have trouble with dense materials. Tungsten is one of the densest metals. The denser ones are either far too expensive or far too radioactive for my liking."

"Is this common knowledge?"

"Well, no."

"And would I be off-target if I said your brother has something to do with this?"

A brief hesitation, then, "No, that'd be a bullseye."

"Okay, what's the story with him?"

Before she could reply, her bandmates arrived and came tromping down the stairs into the studio. As they entered, I was introduced as her cousin, "Dee."

Our conversation was over, I knew. It upset me, because it was so interesting. But sitting in as they worked on new songs was awesome enough to make me forget about my disappointment.

NINETEEN

"It doesn't take a majority to make a rebellion; it takes only a few determined leaders and a sound cause."
~ H. L. Mencken

I've always found it a bit surprising when people refer to me as rebellious. I've never really thought of myself that way. My rejection of religion wasn't "rebellion against God," as my mother called it, but simply a matter of logic. And my preference for women over men was simply a matter of biology, not a rebellion against conformity, as my father viewed it.

I pursued a career in science. Hardly rebellious. But what I chose to do with that education has been called a rebellion against nature. And I continued to throw it in nature's face over the years.

Months earlier, I'd finalized my latest tweak of my DNA. But I'd waited to implement it until I was certain I was cured of my illness. Now that I was, it was time to perform the enhancement.

The idea now was to cause my body to become more efficient in its conversion of food to energy. Yes, part of the reason for doing this was so that I didn't have to consume so many calories every day, but also to minimize the chances of running out of juice in a bad situation.

So in late May, Nurse Alexis assisted me with the transfusions. It would, of course, take several months for it to insinuate itself and bring about the results I'd planned. In the meantime, there was no lack of things to keep myself occupied.

Sinta and I were spending more time together and our friendship was solid, again. She wasn't her normal, upbeat self, though. Part of me suspected she'd never fully be that way again.

We visited Jack regularly, impressed at his recovery. Daniel joined us on one occasion. As always happened when I saw him, I found myself missing our days in the Bay Scouts. And yes, I found this highly ironic, since all I'd ever wanted to do was be a member of the Gatekeepers.

During one visit, as we sat in Jack's living room admiring his "battle" prosthesis, Jack asked Daniel if he'd ever consider some sort of mechanical enhancement to help him walk better. "You might even be able to return to being Scoutmaster again," he said.

Daniel just shook his head. "Those days are over. Even if that were possible, I'm not a young man, anymore."

I snorted. "You're thirty-two!"

"Exactly," he said. "In this business, that's getting up there."

"I'm thirty-eight," I reminded him. "What's that make me?" Both men looked at my white hair and made non-committal noises. I narrowed my eyes at them. "Fuck both of you," I said, causing Sinta to giggle.

Daniel smirked and said, "So what all can this monster do, Jack?"

And we listened as Jack laid out the technical specs of the arm. First and foremost, it was strong. It was durable, with titanium construction. Not as strong as the best steel, but non-magnetic, anti-corrosive, and could tolerate temperature extremes better. It had an extremely powerful grip and enhanced servos, allowing him to lift well beyond a normal person's ability. It had two built-in Tasers, one for distance, and one for direct contact. And "a couple other goodies" were in the works.

"Wait a sec," I said. "It takes more than a strong arm to do heavy lifting. You're still limited by the strength of your whole shoulder region, upper back, and so on."

Jack nodded. "Yeah, well..." He smiled sheepishly. "I'm having some work done. Reinforcements to help with exactly that"

My first instinct was to call him crazy. Why would someone undergo surgery for mechanical implants to supplement a mechanical arm? But then I realized I was the last person in the world who should question someone else about body modification for meta purposes. So I just nodded. "Cool."

Transcendant and I sat outside at his favorite coffee shop. I'd met him there at his request, out of uniform.

After the initial pleasantries, I said, "You come here every day? I mean, this is the third time I've been here, and you've been here each time."

"Well, not *every* day," he said. "But it's close to my apartment."

I nodded and sipped my caramel hazelnut latte. "Yum."

He cleared his throat and said, "You've made quite an impression on the team, Dyna."

I snorted. "Not all of it good, I understand."

"To those who really matter, it has been."

"Well, thanks," I said, not really believing him, and suspecting that Invictus had put him up to this, as a morale-booster.

"I mean it," he said. "That business with the creature under the lagoon? That was impressive. No one else would have discovered it."

"Thanks for being part of it," I said.

"Of course." He sipped from his mocha, then said, "So, you're cured, now?"

I nodded. "Seems so. Feeling better every day."

"That's good." He smiled awkwardly and fidgeted in his seat.

"So what was it you wanted to talk to me about? You sounded – I dunno – a bit odd on the phone."

To my surprise, his cheeks flushed slightly. "Nothing in particular," he said. "I was just hoping to get to know you, y'know?"

"Oh," I said. "Considering nominating me for a Tribune slot?"

"What? No. I mean, sure, I could, but..." He held his mug in front of his mouth, but didn't drink.

I frowned and stared at him, noticing how nicely he was dressed. And he was acting weird, almost nervous. "Wait," I said, shocked. "Is this a *date*?"

He continued to avoid looking at me, his face quite red, now. "Well, I mean, if you want it to be." He glanced up at me and saw my surprise. "God. I'm sorry. Stupid of me."

My surprise, however, was mostly at how awkward he was being. This was a guy who could lift a truck and laugh at shotgun blasts. A man with a huge fan base, who'd been featured in every meta publication you could name. And here he was, shy as an awkward kid talking to his grade school crush. "Why stupid? And why sorry?"

He shrugged again. "I don't know. I figured I wouldn't be your type."

"I'm really flattered," I said. "Honest. But I'm kind of seeing someone."

He nodded. "I wasn't sure. That Jack guy, right?"

I shook my head. "No. Jack's just a friend. A very good friend."

"How is he?"

"Doing well," I said. "Thanks for asking."

He smiled weakly, then shook his head. "I'm sorry. I never should have—"

"Chip." He looked up at me and I smiled. "Stop apologizing. Anyone would be flattered to be asked out by you, including me. And while I'm not really on the market, I am here with you now. So let's enjoy each other's company, okay?"

He smiled shyly and nodded. And we did exactly that.

On my walk home, I was preoccupied with many thoughts. First and foremost was the question of why I hadn't been trying to get to know more of my teammates. Chip was a lot of fun, once he got past his nervousness. He had a quirky sense of humor. And that day, we established what I knew was going to be a solid friendship. Who knew how many others on my team might be friends as well as allies?

I did wonder, however, why I didn't tell him that my interests lay primarily in women. I guess because I wasn't sure if that would make him feel more relieved at my non-interest, or make him feel bad for not knowing that about me.

The coffee shop was on Market Street. For old times' sake, I walked through my old neighborhood, including past my old apartment on Turk Street. I looked around, struck by how awful the area was. Had it been this bad when I'd lived there?

Homelessness in San Francisco is rampant and the Tenderloin was one of the most densely populated areas for them. I'd seen my share when I'd lived there. I'd seen people walk by, pretending they didn't exist. I'd see others grimace, as though offended that they *did* exist. What I never saw, though, was what I was about to witness.

Four teenagers surrounded a homeless man in the gated doorway of a closed business. They took turns kicking him. The man's groans of pain were faint. They'd been at this a while.

I was beyond angry, ready to give them a kicking of their own. But then a flash of movement caught my eye. Before the punks knew what was happening, the Maltese Falcon was on them.

It was over in seconds. The four never had a chance. Falcon laid them all out, one by one. And then he zip-tied their wrists and ankles, pulled a cell phone from one of their pockets, and called 9-1-1. When he ended the call, he dropped the phone on the guy's chest.

I stepped forward as Falcon gave the homeless man a once-over. "An ambulance will be here, soon," he said. Then he turned to me. "You'll talk to the authorities, Dyna." It was a statement, not a question. He knew I'd witnessed everything.

"Of course. Good to see you."

He nodded, then shot his grappling gun to the top of a fire escape and zoomed out of sight. It was, as always, a thrill to watch him work. Just as it was frustrating trying to talk to him.

The homeless man struggled to sit up. "He shouldn'a done that," he said, blood dripping from a split lip.

"Why not?" I said, kneeling beside him.

"Next time... will be worse."

My anger returned. "How often do they do this to you?"

The man shrugged, rubbing gingerly at his torso. "Whenever they see me. Prolly two, three times a month."

"Well, the Falcon called the cops. They'll be in jail, soon."

"Won't stay. Prolly kill me when they get out."

I knew he was right. And it made me sick to my stomach.

The police and the ambulance arrived at virtually the same time. One of the officers questioned me; another talked with the homeless man, while two more loaded the perpetrators into the squad cars. As I answered the questions, I couldn't help but notice that the other cop's demeanor was dismissive. He wasn't writing anything down. He just stood there, arms crossed, paying scant attention as the medics tended to the man.

I offered the cop my card. He didn't even look at it as he tucked it away. I wanted to say, "Hey! I'm one of the Gatekeepers! Pay attention to what I'm telling you!" But I didn't. He wouldn't have cared. This was just another faceless, homeless man. He didn't really exist. He didn't *matter.*

I watched as the man was loaded into the ambulance and the police drove away. I stood there, the crowd now gone. Then I kicked off my sandals, tucked them in my bag, and took to the sky.

But instead of flying home, I followed the ambulance to the emergency department at St. Francis. I landed near the bus stop in front of the hospital, then followed the medics as they wheeled him inside. They seemed surprised when I stepped up to help with the paperwork, but shrugged and left us there.

"I'm covering his bill," I said to the intake nurse. He nodded and took my information, while the homeless man – whose name I learned was Jeremy – looked at me in confusion. Or perhaps suspicion. I wasn't sure.

And then we waited. And talked. The first thing he said, of course, was, "Why?"

I didn't have a great answer to that, so I just said, "Because."

Jeremy shrugged and looked away. I asked questions, but only got the shortest of replies, delivered in a near monotone. He didn't make eye contact. Jeremy was my age, but looked much older. An only child, he lost his parents in a boating accident the summer after he graduated high school. Their life insurance policy was modest, but allowed him to handle their final affairs and make the mortgage payments until he could sell the house. The profit from that sale was barely enough to pay a few months of living expenses, including rent on a studio apartment.

He scrapped college plans and looked for work. But for a kid just out of high school, options were limited. He did manual labor and odd jobs for a couple years, until a workplace accident broke his left hand quite badly.

I looked down at his hand, noticing now that it seemed to be stuck in a semi-open position. "Never did heal right," he said. "Can't hardly grip anything with it."

After that, it was fast-food work. The money was enough to keep him from starving, but not enough to pay rent. He began living on the street at twenty-six. And that was all I could get out of him. I asked about shelters, work programs, and so on. But he was done talking.

After about half an hour, Jeremy was able to see a doctor, while I waited. And as I waited, I wondered about what I was seeing. The Falcon did good by saving Jeremy from a further beating, just as I would have done if Falcon hadn't been there. But then, after calling for aid, he just took off.

Just as I would have done. Just as I *had* done, on many occasions. Just as we all did, every day. Because the homeless were faceless, even to "heroes."

And suddenly, I felt embarrassed. Sinta had been homeless. And she didn't regard the homeless as non-existent. It occurred to me now that, whenever I was with her and we encountered homeless people, Sinta always evaluated them. Some, she spoke to. Most, she didn't. "Some of them see any sort of contact from non-homeless as an act of pity," she'd once told me. "And they don't want pity."

Was that what I was giving Jeremy? I thought of it as sympathy, rather than pity. But truthfully, I just wasn't sure.

Before long, he was back. A doctor escorted him over to me and confirmed that I was the one who brought him in. Jeremy wandered over to sit down. "Our only concern is that there may be internal bleeding," the doctor said, "but for now, there are no indications of it. I've explained that if he starts feeling cold and clammy, or sweaty, or confused, he should come back in." As I acknowledged this, he said, "We don't generally see people bringing in transients, let alone offering to pay their bills."

I thanked him, then returned to Jeremy. We went through the discharge process, I gave my billing information, and we left.

Once in the street, I asked if I could take him anywhere. He just shook his head. "Is there anything you need?"

He looked at me as though that was the stupidest question he'd ever heard. "Got any jobs for a guy with a gimp hand who drinks too much?" And untreated depression, I added mentally. But Jeremy didn't wait for a reply, just shook his head and said, "Thanks, but no."

"Here," I said, holding out the forty bucks or so I had on me. "It's not much, but you're welcome to it."

Jeremy stared at it for a moment, but then accepted it. "Thanks." And then he limped away, head lowered, trying his best to be invisible. I watched him go, until he turned a corner and was out of sight.

We gathered in my apartment for the first Gatekeeper Girls meeting in months, Kim, Jasmine, Jennifer, and me. I was the one to bring up Vicky's absence, it being the first meeting she'd missed. None of us had heard from her since I received the text message, weeks before. Bridget hadn't heard from her, either. The entire thing just seemed odd to me, and I said as much.

"Why is no one else as bothered by this as I am?" I said as I scooped spinach dip onto a cracker. "Invictus basically brushed it off when I brought it up."

"Maybe she's hidin' from him," Jennifer said as she poked ice cubes in her soda with a straw. When we all looked at her, she said, "Well, maybe she doesn't want to have him yell at her like he yelled at Kim."

I tore my attention away from the dip bowl and blinked in surprise at Kimera. "He *yelled* at you?"

She shrugged. "We did take the jet without clearance."

"You've got to be kidding."

"We have a procedure. Exceptions only in emergency situations, which this wasn't, as far as Invictus is concerned."

"So what happened? You get detention? Have to write 'I won't take the jet without clearance' five hundred times on the blackboard?"

Kim chuckled. "Something like that."

"I hate bureaucracy," I muttered, turning back to the dip.

Jasmine spoke up. "Dyna, this isn't the first time Vicky has pulled a vanishing act. We all have personal things we sometimes need to tend to. It's pretty much understood." She was silent a moment, then said, "Though, I admit, her method of departure wasn't one I'd expect of her."

"I just don't get it," I said. "Kim gets read the Riot Act for not following protocol, but no one bats an eye when a member takes an unannounced leave of absence? How does that make any kind of sense at all?"

"We don't know she didn't clear it with Invictus," Kim said.

"He says he has no idea where she is," I countered.

"We're not required to give reasons or say where we'll be when we take a leave. Nor would he be required to tell you, even if he knew."

"Jesus, Kim! Come on!" I waved my arm in emphasis, tossing dip onto the sofa.

Kim frowned at me for a moment, then sighed and put down her wine glass. "Fine. You're right. It's odd, even for her."

"Thank you!" I said as I mopped up my mess, glad it was leather and relieved that I'd finally gotten her to agree. "So, what do we do?"

Kim shook her head. "Not sure there's anything we really *can* or even should do. She did send you a text message."

Jasmine spoke up again. "Dyna has doubts about the legitimacy of the text." I looked over at her. "No mind-reading necessary, dear. It's pretty obvious."

"You're right. I do have doubts. I don't know, maybe I'm just being paranoid. I guess I just figured she'd give me more information."

"Because you're lovers," Jasmine said.

I felt blood rush to my cheeks. "Because we're close." We were quiet for a while. The others sipped their wine. I picked at the uneaten cheese ball on the coffee table. "I just feel something's missing. People don't just disappear without a clue, these days."

Jennifer finished the Italian soda I'd made her and set the empty glass on the table with a clunk. "Well, maybe she didn't." When we all turned to her, she said, "Y'all just need to look closer."

A moment later, Jasmine nodded. "Right," she said. And then I understood. If there was anything more to see, it would be in Kim's head.

Jasmine looked at Kim, who nodded and said, "Okay."

For the next few minutes, Jennifer and I sat quietly while Jasmine went into Kim's subconscious memory. When she finally came out of it, she frowned.

"What did you see?" I asked.

Jasmine looked at all of us. "It's strange. When the portal opened in front of Vicky, it almost seemed as though she wasn't expecting it."

A shiver ran down my spine. "Oh, shit." The others looked at me curiously. I hesitated, not knowing how much of her past our colleagues knew, nor how much I should share. Then I figured that holding anything back might be a mistake. "Vicky told me of a group that has made attempts to abduct her in the past. And they use the same sort of portal thingies that she does."

I proceeded to tell them about The Nexus and their ultimate goal of creating a "Nexus Prime," an individual who would be the focal point of all dimensions and having access to same. As expected, my friends stared at me in semi-disbelief.

"Vicky doesn't believe herself to be their 'Nexus Prime,' but she is nevertheless important to them for some reason," I concluded. "I'd bet anything that they're the ones who intercepted her after she came through."

The others were quiet. Finally, Jennifer said, "So what do we do?"

"We get her back, of course," I said.

"Well, yeah. But how?"

Jasmine spoke up. "We'll need to find out all we can about this organization. And of course, we'll present all this to Invictus. Get the full team involved."

Kim cleared her throat. "Yeah, I don't think I'll be part of presenting that to him. I'm still on his shit list."

"I'll do that," I said. "The research, though—"

"Probe?" Kim asked.

Jasmine nodded. "Probe."

I was in Invictus's office so often, it almost felt like my own. And he had become so accustomed to my visits that we would often sit casually at a small table, rather than at his desk, drinking tea.

"All right," he said as he poured. "You have a memory that Bloodmoon pulled from Kimera. You have the information Nexus gave you about her father's organization. What else? Convince me."

I toyed with my cup. "I'm not sure I can," I said. "Jasmine is contacting Probe, to see what he knows about The Nexus. Beyond that, I have what I've told you, as well as what I consider the most significant thing."

"Which is?"

"My gut," I said. "This just feels wrong. Vicky wouldn't do this."

Invictus frowned. "Dynamistress—"

"Just 'Dyna,' please," I reminded him for the hundredth time.

He nodded. "I understand that you think you know Nexus. But she has never been the most reliable of members. This is not entirely outside the realm of known behavior for her."

I sighed. "Yeah, so I've been told."

"Still," Invictus said after a moment, "trusting my gut has rarely done me wrong. I'm willing to put it to a vote of the Prefects and Tribunes. I'll withhold my own vote unless there is a tie among the others. But Dyna, I must remind you that even if the team votes to pursue this, I'd still have to get the green light from the DOJ to allocate personnel to the task."

"Right," I said. "I appreciate you listening to me."

"That's my job," he said, smiling.

Probe was, like Bricky, a sort of reserve member of the Gatekeepers. I'd never met him. He was an expert researcher, with an appetite for information that crossed the border into obsession. He also had a memory capable of retaining and accessing ridiculous amounts of knowledge. Probe was not an active member because his abilities came with a price. External stimuli quickly became overwhelming to him. Thus, he spent the majority of his time alone in a dark apartment near the public library, surrounded only by the most basic necessities, a kick ass computer network, and a massive tank of tropical fish. I guess that's what he watched instead of television.

"He's working on it," Jasmine told me one day. "He said he had only a passing familiarity and knew it only as having some sort of connection to some secret society in England. What sort of connection, he wasn't certain."

"Okay. You'll let me know as soon as he has more info?"

"Of course," Jasmine said.

"Also, I have a secondary request of Probe. Can you have him find out everything he can on Dane Weatherford?"

Jasmine frowned. "The former Director of Metahuman Affairs?"

I nodded. "That's the one."

"I'll ask." She was quiet for a moment. "Dyna, what if the vote fails?"

I just snorted. "It won't."

"I'm sorry," Invictus told me, leaning forward on his desk. "The vote failed."

I clenched my jaw in anger, wondering who voted against the plan. I glared at him. "This is not right."

He met my gaze as though studying me. After a few moments, he cleared his throat. "I should point out that you're still on medical leave."

"So what?" I spat.

"Maybe you should take a vacation somewhere. For your health." As I contemplated how best to tell him to stuff his suggestion, he lifted a clipboard off the wall near his desk and clicked his ballpoint pen. Scanning the papers on it, he made a couple marks, then said, "That's interesting. Looks like Bloodmoon and Kimera are on personal leave."

I frowned. "No, they're not."

"Vesper, too, it seems," he said, jotting on the paper again. Then he looked up at me. "Anyone else?"

I stared back at him, not sure I was understanding his meaning. Then I blinked, astounded. "Not... um... not that I know of. Unless you're due a break."

He smiled and hung the clipboard on the wall again. "Afraid not."

"Transcendant?"

He shook his head. "Sorry."

"Worth a shot. Thank you."

"For what?" Before I could speak, he said, "Anything else on your mind, Dyna?"

I chuckled. "Just trying to figure you out." I shook my head. "I can never quite decide if you're awesome or a bit of a jerk."

"The two attributes are not mutually exclusive," he said. "Which particular actions have seemed jerk-like?"

I thought about mentioning his admonishment of me for the "throw me to the lesbians" comment on the comm, but instead said, "I guess mainly the deal with Freddy."

Invictus frowned. "That was before your time. What's the rumor mill saying about it?"

"That he was kicked from the group because he was gay."

Invictus raised an eyebrow. "No."

I shrugged. "That's the common perception. You have a reputation of being not exactly friendly toward... you know..."

"Dyna," he interrupted. "*I'm* gay."

My mouth hung open, I'm sure. I don't think there was anything else he could have said that would have surprised me more. When I finally found my words again, I said simply, "Bullshit."

He nodded at a photo on his desk of himself sitting at an outdoor table at a café, mugging for the camera with another man. "Everyone seems to believe that's my brother." He shrugged. "Few people know otherwise because I don't talk about my personal life. It has no bearing whatsoever on what I do."

"Well, no," I said. "But—"

"Years ago, we had a female member who was, in all honesty, stunningly beautiful. She viewed herself as God's gift to men and constantly let everyone know it. We let her go, too. Freddy's sexual preference wasn't the issue. His incessant focus on it was. It became a distraction, making him, and the rest of the team, less effective."

"Wow. I'll have to correct the misunderstanding, then."

"That's not your responsibility."

"Maybe not, but it's not right that people hold an inaccurate view of you because of it."

"They can think what they like, so long as they do their jobs." He rose from his chair. "Anything else?"

I shook my head and stood. At the door, I looked back and thanked him again for what he was doing. It was an action that might get him into trouble, if it were to be found out.

I never would have figured Invictus to be a rebel.

Twenty

"No one gossips about other people's secret virtues."
~ Bertrand Russell

The life of anyone in the public eye is grist for the rumor mill. Metas are no exception. Most of us try to ignore rumors, of course, but it's impossible to avoid them entirely. Trashy shows such as most of the ones on *MetaTV* and the supermarket tabloids like *Super Star* titillate far more than inform.

Though I've been fortunate enough to have avoided intense scrutiny, I've certainly been mentioned a few times. I think my favorite was when one of the rags proclaimed that I was pregnant and Invictus was my baby daddy.

The common assumption is that the "reporters" who churn out these headlines (and little else) just sit around making stuff up. But in fact, there is sometimes a smidgeon of research involved. And every so often, the rumors turn out to be at least partly true.

But then, that's the nature of gossip in general. There's often a kernel of truth hidden in the rumor. And sometimes, rumor is the only information you have.

"Probe has emailed me the results of his research," Jasmine said at the next Gatekeeper Girls meeting, "which I have forwarded to you all. He has agreed to this call in order to give us an overview as well as answer questions. I have to stress, though, that too many voices will disturb him. If you have a question, just get my attention. I'll pick it up telepathically and relay it to him." We all nodded in agreement. Jasmine then took her phone off mute and activated the speaker, placing the phone in the center of the dining table. "Probe," she said, "we're all gathered and ready."

Without preamble, Probe began to relate his findings, his dry voice sounding very fragile and thin with age. "In 1781," he said, "an organization was founded in London called the Ancient Order of Druids. The specifics of its origins are unclear, but it was not a religious organization, despite the fact that neo-pagan groups regard druidism as a religion. Nor was it political in nature. It was primarily a social organization, devoted to taking care of its members during difficult times.

"As in many organizations, different views on how it should be run led to a schism. Ultimately, in 1833, about half the membership split off, forming the *United* Ancient Order of Druids.

"It seems, however, that there was a third group that split off at the same time. There are no actual documents I was able to locate to verify this, but my various sources do agree that it happened.

"The Nexus, as the group is known, is much smaller than either of its sister organizations. And it is not actually a druid organization, having its own agenda that is unrelated to those of the AOD or UAOD."

His recitation was interrupted by a coughing fit followed by silence. We looked around the table at each other. Then he resumed. "Further investigation led to corroboration of the information initially provided by our missing teammate. The group does appear to be populated by metahumans exclusively."

I frowned and indicated to Jasmine that I had a question. She lifted it from my thoughts and relayed it. "Probe, a question. Vicky indicated that this group was much older than the AOD."

"One source did imply that The Nexus was already in existence at the time the AOD formed," Probe replied, "and that key figures joined the group upon its formation, possibly for the purpose of finding new recruits. Given that you were told this by a former member of The Nexus, I'm inclined to believe it.

"My sources disagree on exactly where the group carries out its activities, which are purportedly of an arcane nature, but the most convincing argument favors the area around Abergavenny, a town of about fourteen thousand in the Monmouth region of Wales.

"Now," he said, "regarding your other inquiry. Dane Weatherford was Director of Metahuman Affairs during the presidency of George W. Bush. He has a dual citizenship, American and English. He maintains a residence in London, as well as in Arlington, Virginia. And he is, indeed, a member of The Nexus. Records indicate he was born in 1940 in Cornwall, England."

"No way!" I blurted before I could stop myself. "Not a chance he's nearly seventy years old."

Probe was silent, and I muttered an apology under my breath for speaking. Eventually, he spoke again. "In fact, he could be significantly older. His birth certificate lists the informant as 'Dane Gregory Weatherford' and states, 'as per declaration dated 15 April 1940.' Weatherford's middle name is Arthur, which would imply that the informant was his father. It would also indicate that the registration of birth was done at an office somewhere other than where the birth took place, which was not uncommon during the war.

"What's unusual is that I was unable to locate any information on the elder Weatherford's death. No death certificate. No obituary. Nothing. I did, however, locate his birth certificate, which dates back to 1861. And it contains even less information than the 1940 certificate."

Probe fell silent and Jasmine voiced the question that was forming in my head. "Are you insinuating that Dane Gregory Weatherford and Dane Arthur Weatherford may be the same person?"

"Either that or he sired a child at the age of almost eighty years. And given the nature of metahumans, either is possible."

"Probe, are there records of metas having such incredibly prolonged lives?" Jasmine asked.

"Not to that degree, no. But consider that we've only been collecting data on metas for a relatively short time."

Any other questions? Jasmine asked us telepathically. When no one indicated any, she thanked Probe and ended the call.

We sat around the table, mulling over what we'd learned and what it could possibly mean. I looked at my friends. "So. Who's up for a long plane ride?"

I had no idea what we might be in store for if and when we met up with Weatherford or anyone else in his little secret society. I'd made the mistake of not being well-prepared in the past. This time, I wanted as good a team as I could put together.

There's no question that Kimera was a powerful ally. Bloodmoon, too, with her telepathic abilities. Vesper certainly had some good things to offer, too. But I wanted more.

Problem was, Kit, Lily, Sinta, and Bridget didn't have passports, and we didn't have time to wait even for the rush processing on them. I remembered Vicky talking about some sort of machine that the group had, so I thought Ping Song would be a good addition, but she was obligated to some things at the university. Jack was certainly not ready for any missions, yet. And I didn't feel right in asking my other former teammates to take breaks from their current teams. I briefly considered Golden Bear or The Maltese Falcon, but quickly abandoned that line of thinking.

So that night, I called Dana and asked him if he felt like blowing the dust off his passport.

"To go where?" he asked.

"Back to the U.K."

"Tempting. What's the occasion?"

I filled him in on the essential details of the situation. "I don't really know what to expect."

"Dinah, you know I don't—"

"I know, I know," I said. "You don't do 'the hero thing.' But Vicky's in big trouble. I'm sure of it. Just like Rachel was."

He let out a long breath. "Nice use of the guilt trip."

"I'm sorry." I found myself wishing I'd been able to ask him in person. Our mental link would convey my desperation more than my words could.

"When are you leaving and how long do you expect to be gone?"

I smiled in relief. "We'll leave Monday. And I'm expecting a couple weeks."

"Okay. I'll get coverage for my clients. I'll see you Sunday night."

One of the things many metas take for granted – including me – is how little our daily lives are disrupted by our abilities. Most of us cannot be identified as metas by our looks. And some with obviously meta features, such as Jennifer, can often hide them under a jacket or other article of clothing. But some, like Kim, are unable to do more than partially hide or obscure their features.

Any disguise for her would be quite involved. She could tuck her tail into her pants and wear gloves on her hands. Heavy makeup could hide the scales on her face and dark glasses could cover the serpentine eyes. But then there were the horns. A turban? It would have to be a big one, and that would draw attention to her, making the whole illusion unlikely to succeed. At any rate, Kim felt this was too much effort. Besides, she didn't especially care, so she did none of these things. I admired the hell out of her for that.

As we were going through security, Dana expressed his displeasure. *When you convinced me to come*, he mentally said to me, *I assumed it was because you needed a telepath. But you've got Jasmine. I find it unlikely that you needed a telekinetic. So why am I here?*

Because of this, I replied. *Our link.*

He sighed and frowned at me. *I don't know what use you think that will be.*

Neither do I. But I wanted you here because it comforts me. And honestly, there are scenarios here that could result in me needing a good bit of comforting.

And that seemed to be enough for him.

I'd saved Probe's impressive amount of detailed information on my comm's drive and studied it for hours on the flight. I know others did the same. Our total flight time was something less than sixteen hours, landing us at Bristol Airport around nine-forty-five Tuesday morning, local time. From there, we took the train to Abergavenny, then walked from the station to the Kings Head Hotel, where I'd booked rooms for us.

The first thing Jasmine did when we arrived was to try to telepathically contact Vicky. Her broadcast/receive range was greater than Dana's, plus she'd had telepathic contact with Vicky in the past, so she understood what her mind "felt" like. But she got nothing.

Once we were settled into our rooms, it was nearly one in the afternoon, so we decided to grab some food. Kim hadn't slept much on the flight and decided not to freak the locals by going out in public in the town, where metas were uncommon. So she stayed at the hotel while the rest of us went out.

The Kings Head Hotel is next to the Abergavenny Market. And as luck would have it, Tuesday is their big market day. There were well over a hundred stalls, like a cross between a flea market, an arts and crafts fair, and a food festival.

Of the five of us, only Dana and I had been to the U.K. before. I laughed at Jennifer's reaction to some of the foods for sale. She spied a steak and kidney pie from one vendor. "Okay, that's just gross," she said.

"I agree," I said.

"No, that's delicious," Dana said.

I purchased a loaf of *bara brith*, one of the native foods I'd fallen in love with the last time I'd been there. It's a sweet and spicy bread, made with tea, and filled with raisins, dried currants, and candied fruit peel.

We picked up a variety of foods, including Welsh cakes, Glamorgan sausages, Caerphilly cheese, and so on. Then we headed back to the hotel, where we grabbed Kim and gathered in my room. We discussed our strategy as we nibbled and sipped tea.

"Okay," I said. "I know we've all read Probe's report. Thoughts? Insights?"

Jasmine was the first to speak. "I think it's clear that the town itself is not where Vicky is being held. Though not necessarily true druids, The Nexus does seem to favor settings in nature."

"That doesn't exactly narrow it down," Jennifer said.

I nodded. "From the way Vicky described things, it would need to be well hidden."

"Could it possibly be mobile?" Kim asked.

"I don't think so," I said. "Vicky mentioned a machine. I got the feeling it wasn't a small one, so I doubt it can be carted around. She also said the location itself was 'ancient.' But that's about all she said."

"Again, doesn't narrow it much," Jennifer said.

"A machine needs power. And protection from weather," Kim said. "So how could this be something right out in nature? Wouldn't it need to be in a building?" The rest of us exchanged glances. "Maybe Probe is wrong," she continued. "Maybe everything is in London, with Weatherford."

After a few moments, I said, "Maybe. But since we're here, we should start here and hope Probe is right. If it's a wash, then we go to London."

Jasmine turned to Dana. "Shall we try sweeping the area, as we did in San Francisco?"

Dana nodded. "We could. Wait until dark, go outside of town and sweep areas where no people should be congregating, see if we can pick up stray thoughts or emotions."

Kim spoke up again. "How do we know, though, that this place is populated at all? I mean, are we assuming that people live there full-time?"

"If that's where they're keeping Vicky," I said, "then someone will be there with her."

"The more people there with her," Jasmine said, "the easier they'll be to detect, but the harder it will be for us to extract her."

"So where to begin the search?" I asked.

"*Ysgyryd Fawr*," Dana said.

"Y'all need to speak English, dude," said Jennifer, twitching her wings.

"The Skirrid. It's a mountain about four miles northeast of here. Sometimes referred to as the holy mountain or the sacred hill." He shrugged. "Kind of cliché, but it seems like a possibility."

"As good as any place to start," I said. "I suggest we all get some sleep. Let's meet downstairs at the restaurant at seven for dinner."

Sleeping is all well and good, when you can manage it. As it happened, I couldn't. And neither could Dana. So we decided to go exploring the pubs in town, first heading left from our hotel, going around the block.

We had a beer at each of the four or five we came across, becoming chummy with the bartenders. We'd ask somewhat vague questions aimed at determining whether they knew of The Nexus. Unsurprisingly, we were met with shrugs and blank stares.

As we were on the last corner of the trip, we stopped in at the Hen & Chickens, across the intersection on Flannel Street, literally within line of sight of our hotel. We entered and stepped up to the bar to order, and when the bartender turned to us, I heard Dana's thoughts, something along the lines of "holy shit." And it wasn't hard to understand why. The woman was probably around my age, with gorgeous features, and long, obscenely red hair. Dana has always had a thing for redheads. More recently, he'd developed a thing for pink hair, too, but that was entirely the fault of Gwen Stefani.

Dana ordered us a couple of cask ales and soon we began in with our questions. "Hi," Dana said. "I'm Dana and this is my sister, Dinah." I had to suppress a chuckle. Dana hadn't introduced me as his sister to any of the others. He was making sure she knew we weren't a couple.

"Bronwyn," she said, shaking our hands. "Americans. On holiday?"

"Not exactly," Dana said. "We're doing research on secret societies in Britain and we've heard that one of them often has meetings here in Abergavenny."

This was the point where everyone else told us they had no idea and apologized for not being able to help us. But Bronwyn just narrowed her eyes. "And what's the reason for your research?"

"It's for my book," he said. "I'm a psychologist and secret societies have always been an interest for me. The personalities that are drawn to them."

Bronwyn nodded. "I have a degree in psychology, myself," she said. "You know, to prepare for being a bartender." She smiled as Dana chuckled. "Sounds like an interesting book. Excuse me a moment." She turned to serve other guests.

Interesting, Dana thought to me.

Is it?

She hasn't brushed us off, yet.

True, I conceded. *And she's beautiful.*

Dinah, come on.

Which is why you've dominated the conversation. Don't bother denying it.

Bronwyn returned to us with a wary smile. "So which society allegedly meets here?"

Dana smiled awkwardly as I sipped my beer. "It's called The Nexus," he said.

With a gentle nod, Bronwyn said, "I've heard the name."

This startled me, but I tried not to show it. "Great," Dana said. "Would you be able to share any information about it?"

She was quiet for a bit and I could see the conflict on her face. She indicated the several patrons of the pub. "A bit busy, now. Stop by tomorrow morning around nine-thirty. We open at ten-thirty, so we'll be able to chat a bit."

"Wonderful," Dana said.

She smiled faintly, nodded at me, then turned to other customers. We finished our beers and headed back to the Kings Head.

"Don't be orderin' anythin' with organs or whatnot," Jennifer said to Dana as we were seated.

"You have no sense of adventure," he said.

After we ordered our meals, we briefly told the others about our visit to the Hen & Chickens.

"Nice place," Dana said. "And they have Brains in casks!"

The others stared at him in shock and disgust. "What'd I just say about organs?" Jennifer said, sticking her tongue out in a gag.

"It's a brand of beer," I said. "But given that it's Dana, I can understand how you might assume otherwise."

We told the others about Bronwyn as a potential information source, then worked out our general plan. Jasmine would cover the summit, trying to detect whatever she could. I'd do the same, using my energy-sensing sight. Kim would try to detect heat signatures. And Dana would try to pick up thoughts.

"An' I'll do what, exactly?" Jennifer said.

"You," I said, "have the most important job."

"Which is what?" she asked.

"You fly around me and eat all the mosquitoes."

"Dyna!" Jasmine said, unable to contain a laugh.

"So insensitive," Kim added. "You know she can't fly, yet."

Jennifer narrowed her eyes and said, "People keep tellin' me you're funny, but I still haven't seen it."

"Honestly, Jen," I said, "I think your skills will be more appropriate for when we find her, rather than in the finding."

"Suits me," she said. "Guess I'll just go hang upside-down somewhere until I hear from y'all."

After sunset, we made our way to the mountain. It was a popular hiking area, but after dark, we were safe to take to the air unnoticed.

Well after midnight, we'd finished a more or less full sweep of the mountain, but none of us had detected anything. We met on the summit and vented our frustration.

"I felt so sure about this," I said. The others nodded and shrugged.

"Just because we didn't detect anything doesn't mean this is the wrong spot," Dana said. "They could have powerful shielding against telepaths. I'd expect that from a secret society."

Kim spoke up. "And the heat sources could simply be too faint to reach the surface." I nodded in understanding, since that's pretty much what I was thinking about energy signatures within the mountain.

"Truth is," Dana said, "the entrance could be hidden almost anywhere. There are several buildings around the base of the mountain. An entrance could be in one of them, owned by a member of the group."

I shook my head. "I thought of that, but my gut tells me that such a meeting place would have existed probably long before those structures were built."

"They could have been built over an existing entrance," he said.

"True," I said. No one had anything further to add, so we made our way down the mountain and trudged back to town in frustrated silence.

At nine-thirty the next morning, Dana and I arrived at the Hen & Chickens and knocked on the locked door. Shortly, Bronwyn opened it. "*Hi-ya*," she said with a small smile. "Come in."

Inside, she indicated a table already set with tea and a plate of Welsh cakes. We sat, thanking her as she poured the tea. I looked around at the décor of the wall near us, my attention caught by a pair of framed photos. They were old, black and white, clearly from the very early 1900s. In one, a man held a large barbell over his head with one hand. In the other, a woman held a full-grown man above herself, also with one hand. Both were dressed in dark and light leotards with sashes around their waists. "Who are they?" I asked.

With a quick glance at the photos, Bronwyn said, "Atlas and Vulcana. The originals, obviously."

"Originals?"

She nodded. "Performers from early last century. Strongman and strongwoman from here. From Abergavenny. Lovers, but like you two, pretended to be brother and sister to preserve their performing act."

"But we *are* brother and sister!" Dana said.

I tried to contain a smirk. *You're so cute when you're smitten*, I mentally said.

Shut up.

"But you said 'originals' as though there are others," I said.

"Aye, of course." She turned and pointed to another pair of photos further down the wall, these obviously recent. They echoed the first pair, except that in these, the man and woman were lifting a truck and car over their heads. Again, one-handed. And dressed in sleek black and white bodysuits with sash-style belts. "They'd be the current pair."

"Metas," I said.

"Obviously," she drawled.

"And are they from here, too?"

"Indeed they are. Vulcana's a fair regular here, in fact." She turned to Dana. "So shall we discuss your book?"

"The Nexus, specifically," Dana said with a nod.

"Most of what I know is just hearsay," she said, lifting her cup, "from my father and his cronies. I always thought they were all jaw, but maybe not. One of 'em claimed to once been a big noise in the Druids of Cardigan."

I remembered the nickname I'd given Dana, the same night he dubbed me Dynamistress. *Sage of Cardigan.* I elbowed him. "Didn't know you had your own order."

Bronwyn sipped her tea and looked at us curiously. "Never mind," Dana said, frowning at me. "Please continue."

"They used to go on about all manner of things, and that's how I heard of The Nexus." She stopped, looking at me. "You seem awful attentive, but you're not taking notes?"

"Oh," I said. "Well—"

"I think it would be better for you to tell me why you really want to know. You're not writing a book, are you?"

Dana deferred to me, and I decided to put all the cards on the table. Or most of them, anyway. "No, we're not," I said. "We're investigating an abduction. In an unofficial capacity," I said, noting her skeptical expression.

"You think The Nexus abducted someone? Why?"

She asked the question of Dana, but I answered. "There's a history," I said, turning Bronwyn's attention to me again. "And the evidence is pretty strong."

She frowned and sat back in her chair, arms crossed. "I'm listening."

I sighed and mentally said to Dana, *Your girlfriend doesn't like me.*

She thinks you're *my girlfriend.*

You mean I'm not? That hurts.

I nodded to Bronwyn. "The Nexus is entirely made up of metas."

She raised a red eyebrow. "For someone asking about this group, you sure seem to know a lot about it."

"Our friend who was abducted – her father is a member."

"Then why'nt you ask him about it?"

"Because he's the one who abducted her."

Bronwyn frowned and looked between us. Then she pulled out a cell phone and dialed a number. Dana and I sat quietly as she spoke.

"*S'mae, tad,*" she said into the phone. Her conversation was in Welsh. I could only pick out a few words, among them being "*Americanwyr*" and "Nexus." The conversation was short. When she disconnected the call, she looked at us both. "My father will speak with you," she said as she stood. "He'll be here in a minute." She strode to the bar and brought back a pair of menus before heading to the kitchen.

"In a minute" evidently meant shortly after eleven o'clock, by which point Dana and I had finished our brunch. When he arrived, Bronwyn escorted her father over, setting down a pint of dark beer in front of him.

"*Iechyd da*," he said, raising the glass in a toast to us. He drank deeply before setting it down and extending his hand. "Daffyd Couch-Jones," he said. "A pleasure."

"Nice to meet you," I said, shaking his hand. Dana did the same and we introduced ourselves. "Thanks for coming to meet with us."

The man nodded his white-haired head and took another gulp of beer. "*Bron fach* says you're asking about The Nexus."

I nodded and quickly filled him in on what we'd already told his daughter, and then some. "So now we're trying to find them," I finished.

Mr. Couch-Jones studied us for a long minute. "An' when ya do locate 'em?"

"Get her back," I said firmly. "By any means necessary."

The man frowned and let out a long sigh. "*Rydych yn dawnsio ar y dibyn,*" he muttered.

Dana and I exchanged glances at that. The smattering of Welsh we knew wasn't much help. Bronwyn set down another beer for her father, along with a bowl of what I knew from the menu was *cawl*, a sort of stew loaded with chunky vegetables and lamb. "Means yer dancing on the edge of the cliff. Dangerous," she said, then walked back to the bar.

"We're used to that," I said quietly. "And we're not without our own resources."

"*Na?*"

"No. Nor are we alone. There are three others with us."

He shook his head and chuckled. "Need an army, you will."

"This is a rescue mission, not an assault," I reminded him. Then, after a pause, "Sir, we're at a loss for where their stronghold might be. We'd thought they might have an underground area inside The Skirrid, but were unable to find it. Do you have any knowledge about that?"

"Afraid not," he said. "What I know of the group came from my old *cyfaill*, Owen, rest his soul." He ate some of his stew, then leaned forward in his seat. "Back in the day, before metas became well-known, The Nexus was regarded as a gathering of wizards. Powerful wizards," he emphasized. He looked each of us in the eye as he said this. "Elementalists. Able to control fire, water, wind, and the very earth itself."

"Control in what way?" I asked.

"To summon fire or wind, and the like. To part seas. Move mountains."

I frowned. "Move mountains."

Mr. Couch-Jones shrugged. "Owen tended to embellish. Even so, there were enough rumors to put the fear into a man. Now, mind, this was fifty-odd years ago. I've heard nothing of them for decades."

I mulled over this information as our informant finished his lunch. Someone able to "move mountains" could certainly develop a system of tunnels and space within a mountain for clandestine operations. And that meant finding the entrance was going to be immeasurably more difficult.

"Sorry I've not more to tell," Mr. Couch-Jones said, wiping his mouth. "An' I'm afraid I need to get on, now. Pleasure to meet you both."

We all stood. "Thank you for meeting with us," I said.

"*Diolch yn fawr*," Dana said.

"*Rydych yn croesawu*," he replied with a smile at Dana.

"One last question," I said to him. "Based on what you know of the group and how they might be inclined to do things, do you think we're right to consider The Skirrid as the place to look for them?"

He thought about it for a moment, then gave a slight shrug-nod. "Aye. Seems likely." We thanked him as he headed to the door, waving to his daughter. He opened the door, but paused before stepping out, looking back to us. "Of course, there's more than one Skirrid. *Hwyl!*" He waved and stepped out the door.

What he meant was *Ysgygyd fach*. The Little Skirrid. Dana pointed it out on a map as we sat gathered in my room. It wasn't a mountain, but a hill, less than two miles east of town.

"I say we explore around it, looking for an entrance," Kim said.

"Thing is," I said, "There might not even be an entrance." Everyone turned to look at me. "Look, we know Vicky has the ability to go from place to place using her little portals. And if Kim's memory is correct, she's clearly not the only one who has that ability. Maybe all of them do. Remember, these abilities are things they've been breeding for. So, for all we know, the members can just pop right in."

The others were silent for a time. "You may well be right," Dana said. "But I still think it's likely that a physical entrance exists, even if it's no longer used."

"Which puts us right back to having a huge area to search," I said.

"Then we oughtta get started," Jennifer said.

This time, we didn't wait for dark. We hiked out, reaching the hill in early afternoon. Little Skirrid, though nowhere near the elevation of its big brother, was more heavily wooded and surrounded by farmland. There were two footpaths, one of which went over the summit and one that skirted the bottom edge of the hill for a ways. There was also a dirt road for vehicles.

We started with the lower path, then made our way to the other. Kim was our point person, always staying fifty yards or so in front of us, so as not to be distracted by us. We all looked for anything that might indicate a little-used side path, knowing full well that our chances of finding such a thing were virtually impossible.

We encountered many hikers and greeted them with polite nods and hellos. But we got a lot of odd looks from them. It was obvious to them that we weren't out for a pleasant walk.

After a time, we stopped to rest and discuss options. The sun was beginning its descent in the sky and my hopes dropped along with it. Jasmine stood next to me, removing her heavy pack and dropping it beside me. "Don't fret," she said, adjusting her bandolier of enormous ammo as she sat next to me in the grass.

I nodded, staring off into the grove of trees before me. "Trying not to," I said. We rested quietly for a moment. Then a thought struck me.

"Druids," I said, drawing the attention of the group. "Pretty much the original tree-huggers, right?" Getting shrugs and nods from the others, I said, "So, while The Nexus might not really be druids, I think it's safe to assume that they still had a nature affinity. I'd like to focus our attention on the trees."

"Because that narrows it down oh so much," Jennifer drawled.

"Miss Sarcasm has a point," Kim said.

I pulled out my comm and pulled up the satellite photo maps. I located Little Skirrid and zoomed in, noting that there were, indeed, a crazy amount of trees. But, judging from the canopy, there were areas where the trees were much larger than others. On a hunch, I chose an area on the north side that seemed to have the largest trees, expecting them to be the oldest. Then I activated the GPS and set the coordinates. I handed the phone to Kim. "That's where we're going."

With a shrug, Kim took the phone and used it to guide us to the grove in question. The path didn't lead through it, so we stepped off the trail and into the woods. Before long, the tree trunk sizes were larger than those near the trail.

"So what are we looking for?" Jasmine asked.

I frowned. "I'm not certain," I said. "Just look for anything unusual."

I turned to Jennifer, who held up a hand. "Lemme guess. Mosquito duty."

"Your time will come," I said with a grin.

And so we searched. For hours. The daylight was dimming, but as none of us were relying on light for our searches, we barely noticed. The other thing we didn't notice was that we weren't alone.

TWENTY-ONE

"The greatest mistake you can make in life is to be continually fearing you will make one."
~ Elbert Hubbard

When I was fourteen or fifteen, I was a fairly typical girl. I was obsessed with being popular in school. I wanted to have the coolest clothes, the best hair, and so on.

Trouble was, I wasn't popular. I wore whatever clothes we could afford. If Dana had been a girl, I would have been wearing hand-me-downs. As for my hair, it was the mid-eighties, so I had what was often called "mall hair," with the bangs all poufed up with lots of hair spray, the rest often crimped or spiral-curled. Some girls seemed in competition to see just how high they could build it.

Most girls with mall hair looked ridiculous, and I was no exception. We thought we looked great in a mirror, not realizing (or caring) how silly the style looked from the sides or back.

I suppose I should consider myself lucky. When it came time to have class pictures taken, my mother flatly refused to allow me to wear that style. This prevented me from having to burn those pictures out of sheer embarrassment.

I am embarrassed about my younger self, but for far bigger reasons than ridiculous hair. That embarrassment covers a far longer period of time than just the teenage years, of course. It goes right through my twenties and into my thirties.

I know it's not wise to dwell on past mistakes, but sometimes I can't help it. I've tried to learn from them, but am not sure how good a student of self I am. I continue to make mistakes, some of which are pretty big. My biggest fear is that one of them will be the death of me. Or someone I love.

A deep, male voice rang out from behind us. "Dynamistress!" It sent a surge of alarm through me. Was it Weatherford? Had we been discovered?

Dana and I spun to see two figures stepping quietly toward us from the direction of the path. I recognized them immediately. Atlas and Vulcana.

I let out a relieved breath. "Hi," I said, stepping forward with an outstretched hand.

"Bronwyn thought you might need a hand," Vulcana said. Then, noticing the rest of my team coming in from their scattered points, she shrugged. "Or perhaps not."

"All hands are welcome," I said. As everyone introduced themselves, I wondered how they knew my identity. Dana had introduced himself by his full name to Mr. Couch-Jones. Bronwyn must have overheard and looked us up online. Too simple.

The two were dressed as I'd seen them in the photo, masks and all. "How did you know we were here, though?" I asked.

"It's a small town," Vulcana said. "With a decided lack of white-haired women."

"That, and Bronwyn also *told* us," Atlas said.

I nodded. She'd obviously overheard our parting words with her dad. "And the hikers here pointed you in our direction," I said. Then I brought them up to speed, including why we were searching in this particular location. "I don't suppose you'd have any input, being locals?"

"We used to come out here as kids," Vulcana said. "Explored all around. So if you're asking if we ever saw anything unusual, the answer is yes."

"I don't think I could remember how to find it, though," Atlas said.

"I can," Vulcana said. "It's this way." We all followed as she led us to the southeast, slightly up the hillside. After several minutes, we stopped. "There," she said, pointing to an area overgrown with brush, no different than many other such areas we'd passed.

Jasmine produced a flashlight and aimed the beam at our target. Dana telekinetically cleared the brush away, roots and dirt flying, to reveal what appeared to be nothing more than a roughly square slab of rock about six feet across.

"We discovered this when we were kids," Atlas said. "It struck us as strange, since was so obviously out of place."

"We couldn't move it," Vulcana said, "even with our combined strength. We have to consider it could be magically locked."

I rolled my eyes. "Magic, my ass. Dana, clear it out around the edges."

"Yes, mistress," he drawled.

"Please," I added with an apologetic grin.

I'm not one of your teammates, you know, he said in my head as we watched as rotting leaves and other detritus were propelled away from the stone.

Well, maybe you should be.

When more of the rock was exposed, I got down on my hands and knees and felt around the perimeter. Halfway around, my fingers encountered an indentation caked with dirt. I dug out the soil with my finger, revealing what felt like a stone button. I pushed with all my strength, to no avail.

"Let me try," Atlas said and knelt next to me. He shoved his finger into the indentation and we all heard a grinding sound, then a loud click. The stone then shuddered and moved, the side with the button lowering into the ground.

"Ah, yes. The magic of physics," I said over the noise of squeaking pulleys.

It took several seconds for it to swing the full way down, revealing a drop of about a dozen feet. One by one, Dana lowered us into the pit. Flashlights showed a tunnel, but not heading south into the hill, as we'd expected. Rather, it ran north.

"I detect no one," Jasmine said.

"Me, neither," Dana said.

"No heat," Kim added.

My energy vision revealed nothing, either. I turned and scanned the elaborate counterweight system. The pulleys were rusted, as was the steel cable running through it. "I guess we're going for a walk, then."

The air in the tunnel was dank and thin. Roots from the trees above punctured the walls and extended into the floor, nearly blocking it entirely in some spots. The occasional rodent scurried away from our light. Spider webs were everywhere.

Fungi grew along the roof of the tunnel in spots, which caused me more than a little concern. None were puffball. Still, I breathed as shallowly as possible.

We walked slowly, eyes carefully looking for booby trap tripwires, the telepaths scanning for the presence of others, and Kim leading the way, trying to pick up heat signatures.

The compass in my comm unit told me we were on a constant northeast track. After we'd been walking for half an hour, I said, "You all realize where we're headed, right?"

"The senior Skirrid?" Jennifer offered.

"Sure looks that way," I said. "Guess we had the right idea from the start." I figured we were about halfway there, since it was about two and a half miles between the opening of the tunnel to the center of *Ysgyryd Fawr*.

What's troubling you?

Dana's thought startled me. *I'm just surprised we haven't been accosted, yet. I find it hard to believe that this tunnel isn't being monitored.*

I've been looking for cameras, he replied. *Haven't seen one, though our flashlights aren't hitting every nook and cranny. This tunnel could be quite old. Its last use could predate electronic surveillance.*

We continued on, my anxiety growing with each passing minute. I couldn't help but remember the hunt for Rachel after Hellion snatched her from her apartment. As nerve-wracking as that had been, this was worse. As I continually told Rachel, Hellion was a punk. Despite his abilities, he'd never amount to anything.

Weatherford, though, was a different story. I knew virtually nothing of his abilities. From our one encounter in Nevada, I knew he was quite strong. And he was smart. Shrewd. If Probe's suspicions were correct, he was also really, really old. And if I understood the implications of Vicky's description, he could easily defeat me. Maybe all of us.

Well, that's a joyful thought.

I sighed, upset with myself for not actively shielding the thought. *Guess I should have told you the real risks involved, huh?*

Yeah, try to do that next time.

"Guys," I said, "I need to reiterate that this is just a grab and go situation. We find Vicky and we get her out. We're not here to take on this group. We don't know enough about them."

"Tell us again 'bout that whole 'movin' mountains' thing," Jennifer said. "I totally wanna fight someone who can do that."

"Let's not talk about that," I said.

"How about we just not talk at all?" Jasmine said. "It's distracting. And unproductive." She swung her backpack around and pulled out a weapon. It was vaguely gun-shaped, but with a barrel maybe three inches across.

"Oh, thank god," Jennifer said. "You brought the blow dryer. I was worried."

"What the hell is that?" Dana asked.

"Specialty weapon," Jas explained. "Fires non-lethal rounds. Flash-bang, electroshock, a variety of compressed chemicals, explosive. That sort of thing."

"Maybe it's just me," Kimera said, "but 'non-lethal explosive' sounds like an oxymoron."

"I don't use those on people," she said. "But they come in handy for other things. Now hush."

I'd brought several tubes of PowerPaste on the trip. But the truth was, I didn't think I'd need any of it. Not because I didn't expect to be fighting anyone, but because for the past few weeks, I'd been feeling pretty amped up. It hadn't been very long since the last tweak of my DNA. I was surprised that it seemed to be incorporating so soon, but wasn't going to complain. I felt brimming with energy. And in truth, I was looking to unleash some of it on the son of a bitch who'd taken Vicky.

Eventually, we reached the end of the line. Our flashlights revealed that the tunnel came to an abrupt end in a wall of brick. I looked at Jasmine, who was much more of a tactician than I. She made a motion to Jennifer, who nodded. At Jasmine's urging, we doused the flashlights, then hugged the walls. I heard her load a cartridge into her "blow dryer," then the *choof* of the gun, followed almost immediately by a concussive blast that practically split my eardrums in the close quarters. And then, warm light flooded the tunnel.

When the dust settled, I saw four men beyond the doorway, dressed in what seemed like ceremonial robes, staring into the tunnel. But none of them seemed about to attack us. In fact, they seemed puzzled. That was when I realized that, despite the light coming in from the room, I couldn't see my companions. Jennifer had cloaked us in shadow.

And then the shadow moved in to blanket the room. Smart girl. I could still "see" them and immediately targeted the one furthest away. But before I could blast him, bright light filled the room, driving away Jennifer's shadows. I was so surprised by this that my blast missed my target.

"What the hell?" Jennifer gasped.

Jasmine fired another round and one of the men dropped, his body in spasm from the electric charge going through him. Then we rushed into the room.

Immediately, we were hit with what felt like a hurricane. I tumbled backward and fetched up against a wall, noting that three of us were still standing. Atlas and Vulcana, somehow, were still on their feet. As was Dana, holding himself in place telekinetically. Our Welsh friends slowly advanced upon the man who clearly was controlling the winds. But before they could reach him, the man shot upward, smacking his head against the ceiling. The wind stopped, then, and as the rest of us got to our feet, I watched Dana fling the unconscious man into one of the two remaining, knocking him over. Before he could rise, Kimera had sprinted across the room and knocked him out.

And then, as I looked at Dana, the floor literally spiraled open beneath his feet. A blast of heat engulfed the room. In the opening, all I could see was fire. I gasped as Dana fell and the hole began to close. A wave of searing pain tore through my mind. Dana was burning.

The pain in my head was crippling, but no more so than the panic and abject horror. I was frozen, unable even to scream.

I'd just killed my brother.

Then, just before the hole snapped shut, Dana soared up through the hole, his arms clamped over his face and head. He bounced off the ceiling and fell to the floor, unconscious.

The distracting agony vanished and relief flooded me – followed abruptly by anger. I immediately spun and took out the flame controller with a heavy blast. Then I dashed to my brother's side, my heart pounding. His clothing hung in smoking tatters and his flesh was reddening.

I knelt there, not knowing what to do, worry and guilt rendering me stupid. Then Jasmine appeared by my side, dropping her pack, from which she pulled a tactical field kit.

She removed several packets of burn dressing, ripped them open, and applied them to the worst areas. This was mainly the parts of his head that he hadn't managed to cover with his arms, and his hands, as they were the only areas of totally exposed flesh. His clothing had protected him fairly well, it seemed, for the second or two he'd been inside the hole. But if he'd breathed at all in there, I realized, his lungs could be damaged.

I could only sit there and watch, numbly. "Kimera," Jasmine said as she zipped up her pack, "Dana needs a hospital." Kimera nodded and scooped him in her powerful arms. A moment later, she was speeding down the tunnel. "Atlas, Vulcana, we need you as sentry on those two doors." The pair nodded and complied.

Then Jasmine found one of the men who was regaining consciousness and hauled him to his feet. But she said nothing, merely stared at him. His mouth contorted and twitched. His eyes rolled upward. I'd never seen her mentally interrogate someone like this, before. It was disturbing.

"We must hurry," she said as she dropped him, unconscious again, to the floor. "More are coming." I heard her, but couldn't seem to translate that into action. She strode over and shook me by the shoulders. "Dyna!"

I took a deep breath and nodded. "Right. Do you know where they're keeping her?" In response, I felt her mind in mine, planting an image of the floor plan of this huge base, including the room where Vicky was being held. "Okay," I said. "Let's go."

"No," Jasmine said as she loaded another explosive round into her gun. "You get Vicky. We'll be your distraction."

I nodded, heading toward the western door as the others took their positions. As I stepped through, I heard the explosion of Jasmine's weapon.

I moved as quickly and quietly as I could, relying on my energy sensing vision to alert me to the approach of others. I could sense them through walls and was able to take them out as soon as they came into view. It took about five minutes to reach Vicky.

As expected, she wasn't conscious. She lay on a cot, held down with leather straps. I unbuckled her arms and legs, then tried to rouse her. When that failed, I threw her over my shoulder.

All told, I encountered six members of The Nexus. None of them had a chance in the hallways, as I picked them off as soon as I detected them. I hoped my friends had as much luck.

Back in the first room, I found them waiting for me, a pile of incapacitated figures littering the floor around the doorways.

"Okay, time to go," I said.

Just then, a flash of light erupted near one end of the room. We turned to see a bear of a man standing there. "I think not," Weatherford said.

Time seemed to stop as fear ripped through me. I remembered how lucky we'd been last time I met him. Only Jack's ability to drain energy from him prevented our easy defeat. But my anger displaced the fear. I clenched my fists, ready to take him on. A quick glance told me the others were prepared to do the same.

Weatherford, too, was sizing up his enemies, and he must have realized how outnumbered he was, because he ignored everyone but me. I didn't have time to lower Vicky to the floor as he sprang forward. So I put most of my energy into my shield, bracing for the impact.

Atlas and Vulcana ran forward. Jasmine got off a shot. There was a flash as the round struck him, and he roared in pain.

I clasped Vicky to me as he slammed into us. I had a moment of odd vertigo, then we hit the floor. I let go of Vicky and sprang to my feet, only to realize we were no longer in the underground. Weatherford had 'ported us outside.

He was standing, but unsteady, gasping for breath, his eyes puffy and watering, thanks to Jas hitting him in the face with one of her chemical rounds. He stretched his arm out toward me and I saw what appeared to be a rip in the air open in front of him, just before a glowing glob of magma shot toward me, followed by another.

I was able to dodge both and, luckily, they missed Vicky. Weatherford was having difficulty tracking me as I moved, so blurred was his vision.

I dashed forward, gritted my teeth, and put everything I had into a punch that knocked him to his knees. But he grabbed my ankle with a crushing grip and yanked. I dropped, my head bouncing off the ground.

Then he snagged my other ankle and, before I could react, he was on his feet and swinging me like an Olympic hammer. He let go, and I sailed up and away from him.

I stabilized myself in the air using just my hands. No sense in ruining a good pair of hiking boots. Then I saw him heading for Vicky. I dropped to the ground, hitting him with as heavy a blast as I could manage. Again, he staggered, but recovered quickly. I saw his face was now flushed red and his eyes had nearly swollen shut. He ignored me and went for Vicky.

This time, I was the one to hit him like a linebacker. Or more like a plow. He flew onto his back and slid across the grass as I came to a stop next to Vicky and scooped her into my arms. Seeing this, Weatherford hesitated briefly, then abandoned his quest. He opened a portal and vanished into thin air.

I stood there for a minute, looking all around until I was sure he hadn't just moved to a better location of attack. I had no idea where we were. The sun was just above the horizon, red and hazy. There were no buildings anywhere I could see, just a broad expanse of open countryside.

Satisfied that Weatherford was in full retreat until he could see again, I sat next to Vicky and rubbed my forehead, thinking of how lucky we'd gotten. I pulled out my comm unit, selected the private channel we'd assigned for this mission, and keyed the mic. "Dyna here. Weatherford's gone. I've got Vicky. Your status?"

I waited for a reply. And kept waiting. I repeated the request and waited some more. My stomach knotted. I switched to the GPS to get an idea of where we were. But it wouldn't connect. Our team channels were satellite-based, just like GPS. And I had access to neither, nor any phone connection. I frowned. Had I damaged my comm, somehow, or was it something else?

It seemed clear that Weatherford had opened a portal behind us just before he tackled us. But evidently, he hadn't just popped us outside the mountain. How far away were we?

I sighed and removed my jacket, laying it over Vicky. "C'mon, Vick. Time to wake up."

Being stuck in the middle of nowhere with an unconscious teammate and no way to contact anyone gives a person a lot of time to think. And for me, that's something of a dangerous way to pass the time.

There were so many thoughts bouncing around in my head. First and foremost was worry about Vicky. A close second was worry about my brother. And, of course, feeling guilty about his injury, since I had persuaded him to come along.

I had no doubt that my team would get back to Abergavenny safely. And I'm sure Kimera would get Dana the medical care he needed. But none of that was thanks to me. Jasmine's quick actions probably would save him from needing skin grafts.

In fact, when I thought about it, Jasmine had been the most indispensable member on this mission. If she hadn't shot Weatherford, I very well might be dead and Vicky back as his captive. I owed her a lot.

I glanced at my friend. Still no signs of coming out of it. And Weatherford could be healing by now. It would be prudent to move from our location. But where to go? There were no areas of cover as far as I could see. Still, anywhere else was better than where he'd left us. So I stood, hoisted Vicky over my shoulder again, and started walking.

Maybe I should be more open to something serious with Vicky, I thought. That would make my therapist happy. For that matter, maybe I should go home for the holidays. Give one more chance to heal things between me and my mother. That would make my therapist happy, too. Not to mention Dana. He regularly urged me to do so, claiming that it would be better, this time. I told him he was probably right, since it could hardly be worse than my last visit.

But would these things make *me* happy? I guess that was the real question. Did I want a good relationship with my mother? Or at least a *civil* relationship? Yeah. I did. I just didn't think it was possible.

I was tired of being lonely. Living with Sinta certainly helped, since I always had her to talk to. I loved my friends and felt genuinely lucky to have them. But something was still missing.

And that reminded me of something else my therapist had once asked me. "Will any relationship ever meet your expectations?" I couldn't answer her. The truth is, I automatically compare any potential relationship to Sharon and Jackie. Nothing seems to be its equal. Though, if I'm honest, I have to admit that I've probably built up that relationship in my memory. That's probably why I've never really made an effort to track down either of them. As for why neither of them had tried to contact me, I had to assume it was because I hadn't been as important to them as they'd been to me.

But if I'm even more honest, I have to admit that even that relationship lacked something. I just didn't know it at the time because I didn't even know the thing missing even existed. And that thing was the kind of mental bond that Dana and I shared. As much as he feared it, I loved it. I understood his reasons for fearing it, but I couldn't imagine ever reacting to it the way his ex-wife had. Nor could I really imagine being satisfied with a romantic relationship that didn't have that.

Or maybe that was a perfect example of setting my expectations too high. I was never going to have a mental bond with anyone other than Dana. I knew that.

I stopped walking and looked around, realizing I hadn't even been aware of my trek. How long had I been walking? Still nothing around me but rolling, grassy plains.

It was dark, now. I gently lowered Vicky to the grass and draped my jacket over her again. I should rest, I told myself. Except I wasn't tired. I felt like I could have kept walking for hours. I should expend some of this excess energy, I told myself. But if Weatherford had returned, that would be like shooting up a flare to alert him of our location.

I looked up at the stars, summing up my thoughts. And what they were telling me was that, all things considered, I wasn't very happy with my life. Not with my familial and romantic relationships (or lack thereof). Not even with my membership in the Gatekeepers, even though it was something I'd dreamed of for decades. The question now was, what was I going to do about it?

Suddenly, I had a deep sense that something was wrong. I scanned the sky, realizing with a sinking feeling that I couldn't pick out a single constellation. No Big Dipper. No Cassiopeia. A chill hit me as I realized Weatherford had taken us away from Earth altogether.

But before I could even begin to fathom this, I heard Vicky stirring. I turned to see her lying on the ground, propped up on an elbow, squinting bleary-eyed at me. “Aren’t you... a li’l short... fer a storm trooper?”

I laughed and knelt next to her. “Hey, you.”

“Oh,” she mumbled as she saw my face. “Tha’s hair... not a helmet.” I reached out and caressed her cheek. She grinned lopsidedly. “H’lo, luv. What’cha doin’ here?”

“Rescuing you, of course.”

“Oh.” She rubbed her eyes and blinked at me. “Brilliant.” She moved to a sitting position, wrapping my jacket around her. “So where are we?”

“Ah, now that was going to be my question for you. Your dad shoved us here through one of his little gateways. And I don’t think we’re on Earth.”

“Well. That’s no good.” She looked around groggily, then frowned. “Wait. You went up against him?”

I sat down and spent a few minutes filling her in on everything, from how we realized she’d been abducted to how we came to be here. She took it in with the occasional nod and more than a couple questioning looks. And I couldn’t blame her. In reciting it all back to her, I saw just how lucky we’d been throughout the entire affair.

This was apparent to Vicky, as well. “I should have told you more about my father and The Nexus. Especially about what he can do.”

I shrugged. “You told me plenty, I think. So does he still think you’re the Nexus Prime?”

Vicky stiffened slightly and stared at the grass in front of her. “I don’t think so. I mean, I was drugged the entire time, so I can’t be certain of anything that made it into my head. But I *think* he’s realized I’m not the Nexus Prime. But it seems I’m his opposite number.”

“Pardon?”

Vicky rubbed her head, still feeling the effects of being drugged. “You’re familiar with the concept of planes, right?”

“How do you think we crossed the Atlantic?” I smirked as she glared at me. “Sorry. Can’t help myself.”

“You could at least try.”

“Elemental planes,” I said. “Air, earth, fire, water. That sort of thing. You explained this to me before.”

Vicky nodded. “And I compared it to the portal in Nevada.”

“Right,” I said.

“And like that overlap between our world and the other one, the elemental planes also overlap, creating hybrid zones.”

“Like what?”

“Well, what do you get when you combine earth and water?”

“Mud? Swamp? Quicksand? There’s a plane of mudswampsand?”

"More or less."

"He shot what seemed like balls of lava at me."

"Fire and earth," Vicky said. "There are also planes of energy. Positive energy. Negative energy. And these can combine with others, as well."

"Making what?"

"Positive energy combined with fire creates light, for example."

"And with negative energy, darkness?"

"Exactly," she said.

"What about your, um, whatchacallit? Teleportal?"

Vicky snickered. "Because only two of the primal planes ever overlap, it takes something extra to combine three of them. Doing so creates a fold in space, as best we've been able to figure, and that's what creates them."

"What about all four together?"

She nodded. "That would be how we got here. Another world. It's somewhat random. Adding the energy plane allows choice of destination."

"I see," I said quietly.

"But no one can tap into *all* of these planes. Meaning all four, plus both energy planes. That would be the Nexus Prime's talent."

"And what do you suppose that combination would do?"

"Yeah, that's the question, isn't it?" Vicky said. "There's no consensus among the group, but the prevailing idea is time travel."

"Whoa. Seriously?"

Vicky shrugged. "I dunno. I have a hard time taking thoughts of time travel seriously, but yeah, that's what some of them think. Including Pops."

"So he seems to be the head honcho. I'm guessing he can access the four basics, negative energy, and the combinations of them. And of course, the location jumping, like you."

"Yup."

"So when you say you're his 'opposite number,' you mean that you can do what he does, except you access the plane of positive energy."

"Exactly."

I frowned. "So if you're not the Nexus Prime, why was he keeping..." My voice trailed off as I suddenly understood. My stomach fell.

"Yeah," Vicky said softly. "When we get back, I think I need to pee on a stick."

"Jesus Christ."

"No, I'm pretty sure Jesus was conceived without roofies and rape." She shook her head, knowing my next question. "And no, I'm not certain. But it wouldn't surprise me. Daddy dear is the only one with access to all the planes plus negative energy; I'm the only known one with access to all plus positive energy. Theoretically, a child from the two of us could be the Nexus Prime."

I just shook my head, trying not to voice what I was truly thinking. "Wow. That's... that's not okay." We sat silently for a minute, until I said, "Can you get us home before he comes back?"

"Sure," she said. "Once my head clears." She looked around again. "I may have been here, before. Or at least somewhere much like this."

"Really?"

She nodded. "Some people go to the beach or the mountains when they need to 'get away from it all.' I go world-hopping."

"Not as touristy, I suppose."

Vicky smiled faintly. Then I wrapped my arms around her as she rested.

Vicky kept a flat in London. We arrived there around ten a.m. The effort took a lot out of her, so I urged her to rest while I tended to business. She agreed and flopped on her bed as I pulled out my comm.

Jasmine responded immediately and I explained what happened to us. She told me Dana was going to be fine. The emergency department doctors said his burns weren't too bad, largely thanks to her quick actions. And while his breathing was a bit ragged, they didn't think any damage to his lungs was bad.

I told her we'd return as soon as possible, once Vicky was back to herself. I signed off, then considered joining Vicky for a nap, but I still wasn't tired. So I tapped out an email to Invictus on my comm, giving him the rundown of what had happened. Then I hit the streets.

Vicky's flat was in Islington, a neighborhood I knew nothing about. I kept it simple, just walking out and going to the first pub I stumbled across. I ordered a couple pasties and a beer and sat in a corner booth, thinking.

My mind, of course, was on Weatherford and what he'd done to Vicky. I tried not to think about that part, actually, but instead tried to determine what threat, if any, The Nexus posed to the world at large. Truth was, this was a group that had existed for an awful long time, without taking any aggressive actions. At least, none that we knew about. Certainly, what had just happened with Vicky was such an action. It would be up to Vicky to decide what, if anything, to do about it. But we had no jurisdiction in the U.K., so it was doubtful that anything would come of it.

After eating, I found a clothing store and purchased a new outfit. Then I returned to the flat, where I slid in bed with Vicky. I watched her sleep for a while and eventually dozed off. We woke around the same time, then shared a shower. She offered me an outfit of hers to wear, including an old costume of hers that had red slacks with a flame pattern from the bottoms to the knees. I thanked her, but showed her my purchase, which was utterly lacking in flames.

She was starving, so we grabbed some food on our way to the train station. We arrived in Abergavenny just before six, by which time Dana and I had been "talking" for an hour.

Dana had been discharged. His doctor said his wounds would heal and, thanks to the application of the burn dressing, he would have almost no cosmetic damage.

Our rescue of Vicky having been successful, we made our arrangements to return to California. Or rather, most of us did. Dana chose to stay for a while, saying he wanted to treat it as a mini vacation. What that meant was that he wanted to see Bronwyn again. I wanted to make sure Dana tended to his injuries, but I also wanted to spend some alone time with Vicky. So we stayed, too.

The night before the others flew back, we held a debriefing of the team in my room at the hotel. I began by saying, "I need to apologize to all of you. I had no idea of the extent of the dangers awaiting us here." Jasmine and Kim began to protest, but I cut them short. "Listen, when the Gatekeepers have an assignment, we have as complete an understanding of the situation as we can get. We know who to send in and who not to. There are rarely any surprises. But in this case, our advance knowledge was far too slim."

Jennifer chuckled. "Hence, *secret* society."

Jasmine said, "Dyna, with enough advance time, we would have learned more. But we needed to find Vicky as quickly as possible."

"Which I appreciate, by the way," Vicky said. "But look, if this was any bit of a cock-up, that's my fault. I never shared enough about The Nexus. Never saw need to."

"True enough, both of you," I said. "But it doesn't change the fact that my brother nearly died. Only his own quick thinking and telekinetic ability saved him."

"Those are usually the only things that save any of us," Kim said.

"Stop bein' so hard on yourself," Jennifer added.

"I'm not being hard on myself," I insisted.

Yes, you are, came Dana's thought in my mind. I blocked him out.

"Dyna," Jasmine said in her soothing voice, "I don't see that we have anything significant to discuss, here. All things considered, I think we fared quite well. And now we have a good bit of information on this organization, too."

It was pointless, I realized. They weren't going to agree with me. So I just nodded. "Fine," I said. "I guess unless anyone else has something to say, we're done."

No one did. So I wished them a safe flight back to the States as they filed out of my room.

Vicky and I strolled through the Abergavenny Market. It was a Friday. Not the big day at the market hall, but there were still maybe fifty stalls in the indoor area.

"What's on your mind?" I said, since Vicky seemed distant.

"Bought a pregnancy test," she said, "but it's probably too early for me to take it."

I nodded. "When's your period due?"

"Not for another week."

"Hope you actually have it."

"You and me both."

We idly scanned the tables in silence for a few more minutes before I noticed that she'd been watching me. "What?" I said.

"So what's on *your* mind?"

I let out a long sigh and said, "Far more than I'd like."

"So talk."

"Wouldn't know where to start."

"Well," she said, "let's skip the conversation about us, since I know you're not quite ready for that. What else is bothering you?"

I shrugged. "Dana's injuries."

"He'll be fine, luv. Doctors said so."

"I mean that he got them at all," I said, glancing over a display of Welsh love spoons. "He's not like us, Vick. He's a counselor, not a combat meta. He only came along because I asked him to. I never should have done that."

"Y'know, he's a grown man. As much as you like to think he can't say 'no' to you, he bloody well can."

"Even so," I said. "The fact remains—"

"The fact remains that I'm right and you need to let it go."

I scowled at her. "Okay. Fine. But his injuries aren't the only thing I blame myself for."

Vicky stopped in her tracks, staring at me. "Don't tell me you're gonna mention that Dr. Gray guy again." My face must have betrayed that I was. "Dyna, why do you cling to things for so long?"

I shrugged and hung my head. "I don't know."

"Besides, he deserved what he got!"

I looked up at her. "I don't think his actions warranted his death."

"Look. Dr. Gray is no different from Dana."

"Huh?"

"Dana willingly chose to join you. So any dangers he faced were entirely on him. Not on you. And Gray allied himself with the bad guy. So anything that happened as a result of that was his own damn fault. Not yours."

I was quiet for some time, looking at the wares on the table in front of me without really seeing them. "I know what you say is technically true," I finally said.

"But you don't *feel* it." I shook my head and she continued. "So let's turn this around. If it had been me in that situation, exactly as you were, and my actions resulted in his death, what would you say to me?"

I frowned, "That's—"

"Just answer me. Would you think it was okay for me to carry that guilt with me for the rest of my life?"

"Well, no, but—"

"But this is *you* we're talking about. You hold yourself to a higher standard than me? Dyna, you can't do that. You're no less human than I am. Or anyone else. Quit holding yourself apart from us all."

I frowned. "What do you mean by that?"

"Well, it's what you do," she said, moving on to the next table. "It's like you have this wall around yourself. I know you've had some hard knocks, but you've got to stop being so frightened of being hurt again."

Her words cut right to the center of things. I averted my gaze and let out a breath. "I know," I whispered.

"Well, good," she said. "Okay, we're buying these." She held up a pair of knitted slippers that looked like the Beatles' Yellow Submarine.

I laughed. "Yes. Yes, we are."

The following morning, Vicky and I joined Dana for brunch at the Hen & Chickens. Atlas and Vulcana were there, too, and waved at us from their table. I went over to say hello and to thank them for helping us out.

"It was our pleasure," Atlas said.

"How is your brother?" Vulcana asked.

I glanced over at him. "At the moment, I think he's just upset that Bronwyn doesn't seem to be working." I turned back to the pair. "He's got a crush, I think."

"Is that right?" Vulcana said and immediately pulled out her cell.

"Other than that, he'll be fine."

"When do you return to the States?" Atlas asked.

"The rest of my team left this morning. Not sure how much longer the three of us will be here. Do you guys ever make it over there?"

"We've been there once," he said.

"Well, if you ever manage another trip, I'd love to see you." I fished out my cards and handed one to each of them, interrupting Vulcana's texting. Then I smiled and nodded. "Take care," I said.

I returned to my table and sat. "I want all the desserts," Vicky said. "Every last one."

"I'm down for that," I said.

Dana just shook his head and sighed. "It's like I'm out with six year-olds."

"I know who you *wish* you were out with," I teased. Like a six year-old. "Dana and Bronwyn, sittin' in a tree—"

"Are you kidding me right now?" he said.

Vicky laughed. "Oh, how much I miss by being an only child."

Dana nodded. "Yes. Be very thankful."

Vicky laughed. "Please. I'd be like Dyna."

"It really is one of the joys of my life," I said. "But to be fair, he gives as good as he gets."

"Me?" Dana said in mock offense. "I never do anything."

"Not true," I said. "You do what I tell you to do." Vicky frowned and glared at me.

Dana shrugged in defeat. "Pretty much."

We ordered our meals and sat talking for a while. A few minutes later, Bronwyn walked through the door. She spied us immediately and came directly to our table.

"Hi," Dana said in surprise, getting to his feet.

Seriously? You're standing?

It's reserved for ladies. You don't qualify.

"Hello," she said, and sat with us. I glanced over at Vulcana, who winked back at me. The little matchmaker.

"Nice to see you," I said, then introduced Vicky.

"Ah, the rescued one," Bronwyn said.

"Guilty," Vicky replied. "And I understand you're among those I have to thank."

Bronwyn waved it off. "Not a bit. And very nice to meet you."

Our food arrived, including a meal for Bronwyn. We chatted as we ate, but my thoughts revolved around only two things. The first was that Dana really was smitten with Bronwyn. I could sense it through our bond. I began to question why, since he barely knew her. Then I stopped. There's no sense in questioning chemical attraction.

The other thing on my mind was the conversation I'd had with Vicky at the market, and the things she'd said about me. There was truth in all of it. What I'd been slowly realizing was that my general unhappiness was because I didn't know what I wanted.

But that wasn't entirely accurate. There were some things I did want. I wanted the Gatekeepers to feel more like a family than it did. I wanted to feel like I was doing something good with my abilities, rather than just whatever the government told me to do. And I wanted to stop being so overprotective of my heart.

But the Gatekeepers would never be like a family. It just wasn't possible with a group that large and diverse. And because they were a government affiliate, we would never have a lot of say in what we did on "company time."

And what about my heart? I knew I was keeping out the potential for happiness by avoiding the possibility of getting hurt. That had to change. But why was it so hard?

I was jolted out of my reverie by a call on my private comm channel. I glanced at the screen. It was Invictus. "Excuse me," I said and quickly left the table, answering the call as I headed for the door.

"Dyna," Invictus said. "I got your report. Happy to hear everything went well."

"I don't know if that's the right word," I said, stepping outside.

"I trust your brother is on the mend?"

"He is," I said. Then, when Invictus remained silent, I said, "So why are you really calling?"

"I'm letting certain members know personally before sending out the general announcement," he said in a voice uncharacteristically soft for him. "Transcendant is dead."

TWENTY-TWO

"Our desires always disappoint us; for though we meet with something that gives us satisfaction, yet it never thoroughly answers our expectations..."
~ François de La Rochefoucauld

All my life, I've been disappointed with how reality lived up to the way I thought things should be, even though my father had always cautioned me about it. I guess I never expected he meant it about mundane things.

In second grade, I joined the Brownies, imagining that my life would suddenly be full of camping trips, singing around fires, and eating s'mores until I was sick. But those events were rare, during my short stint with the group. In retrospect, maybe I shouldn't have joined in winter.

Obviously, my genetic self-experimentation didn't go precisely as planned, though that had more to do with sabotage than my own failings or unreasonable expectations.

My relationships, both romantic and familial, were grand disappointments, even though I felt my expectations were perfectly reasonable. But in truth, it wasn't difficult to see where the failings were.

It always came down to people. Sometimes myself. Sometimes others. I had to be careful with the expectations I had of others. Even metas. Because, as it turned out, some metas weren't as nice as I expected. Some weren't as intelligent or as noble.

And some weren't as invulnerable.

The memorial for Transcendant was a private service for metas and invited guests, held at the Golden Gate Club a week after his actual funeral, which had been private, just for his family and closest friends, as is common with meta funerals.

Transcendant hadn't been killed in the line of duty, or in an accident. It was a brain aneurysm that took him from us. It had happened while he was on the phone with his agent, while sitting at his coffee shop where we'd had our "date." Another patron called for an ambulance. From what Invictus told us, he died en route to the emergency room. The doctors never had the opportunity to open his skull with their high-powered lasers, never had the chance to fix a burst blood vessel in one of the most powerful men around, never had the possibility of keeping my friend among the living.

At the memorial, the entire team was obviously still in shock. A few wept openly. Others, it was clear, barely held back their tears. The rest of us, I suspect, were just numb.

Metas came in from all over the state. It was incredible, really. So many heroes. Yes, I knew Invictus thought I shouldn't use that word, but it was the only one that applied to so many of these people. Some of them, many times over. Or at least, so I believed. Under other circumstances, I'd have loved the opportunity to meet them. But this wasn't the time for that. So after the service, I stuck to chatting with those I knew.

It was nice to see some old friends. El Martillo came up from San Diego. Ping Song was there. The retired Sea Lion. Golden Bear. Even the Maltese Falcon made a brief appearance. I don't know why, but I was surprised to see him sporting the black armband that everyone else wore. I was more surprised when he expressed his condolences and, to my shock, gave me a brief hug.

I watched him depart, still stunned, when there was a tap on my shoulder. I turned to see a dark-skinned woman with long, brown hair. But it was the huge wings that made her memorable. "Dynamistress," she said, with a French lilt to her voice.

I smiled softly. "Caracara," I said. "Nice to see you. Thank you for coming."

"*Bien sûr*," she said. "How have you been?"

"Mostly good," I lied. "And you?"

She gave a slight shrug. "Well enough."

"Still doing the solo thing?"

"*Oui*." Another shrug. "No team seems to suit me."

Her simple words struck an uncomfortable nerve. "I understand that," I said.

Jack walked over to us. He had modified his black jumpsuit to be sleeveless, since a sleeve wouldn't work with his "battle arm." Today, however, he wore his civilian version.

With him was a woman dressed in black cargo pants tucked into shiny, calf-high, combat boots that were oddly stylish. Her purple shirt was made of heavy mesh, a black, leather jacket over it. Her blondish hair was pulled back in a ponytail, and a purple, full domino mask completed her outfit. I had no idea who she was.

"Jack," I said, "you remember Caracara."

"Of course," he said, and extended his robotic arm to shake her hand. "Nice to see you."

"*Bonjour*," she said. But as she gripped his hand, the entire arm detached. Caracara gasped in alarm and stood there staring at the limb hanging from her grasp.

Jack hung his head and sighed. "It was funny *once*," he said to his companion.

"On the contrary," the woman said. "It's funny every time." Her voice, sounded familiar. "And I'm going to continue doing it until you get some electromagnetic shielding put in there."

"Okay, okay!" Jack retrieved his arm from Caracara and snapped it back into place. "Dyna, you remember my colleague, Paige."

"Or Quanta, when I'm in what passes for a uniform," Paige said.

"I'm sorry, Cara," Jack said. "Quanta can control certain types of radiation, which apparently gives her the ability to break the electromagnetic field that holds this thing in place." He glowered at Quanta. "Which she promised not to do again."

Quanta gave him an innocent look. "Did I?"

"Well," Caracara said, "it was nice to meet you. But I should be going."

We said goodbye to her, but as she was about to wander off, I said, "Hey, let's grab coffee sometime."

She smiled. "I would like that."

I got her number and told her I'd be in touch.

That night, Sinta made spaghetti and we had Kit and Lily join us for dinner. Though I'd already told Sinta everything that had happened in the U.K., I repeated it for the others. When I was finished, Sinta remarked on what was obviously the most significant point to her. "Dyna thinks Bronwyn likes Dana, too!"

"Doesn't make for the easiest of relationships, though, being on different continents and with an eight-hour time difference," Kit pointed out.

"Suppose not," Sinta said, nibbling on garlic bread.

I turned to Lily. "So how have you guys been doing? I feel like I haven't seen you in forever."

"We're good," she said.

"No visits from the guys with the funny hats and hoses?"

Lily laughed. "No. I'm pretty careful about that, now."

"How do you wash your hair?" Sinta asked.

With a grin, Lily said, "Truth is, I don't have to. I just get it wet and it burns off all the crud I'd normally wash out with shampoo."

"Cool," Sinta said.

"And you've got control of your abilities?" I asked.

She nodded. "Yeah. Pretty much. I talked to that Jasen guy about energy-transparent clothes. And Kit's designing some armor pieces for me!"

"That's great," I said. "So then what?"

"We're still discussing that," Kit said.

I nodded. "I might have some ideas."

"Okay," Fabian said. "So now that you've got Vicky back from the bad guys, you're gonna get serious, right?"

I frowned, watching him in the mirror. "I dunno."

Fabian stopped snipping and turned the chair so I was facing him. "What is *wrong* with you, girl?"

"Nothing!" I said. "I mean, lots of things, but—"

"What are you afraid of? Being happy?"

I shrugged and looked down at my feet. "It's crossed my mind."

"Love bug, look. You've got to get over that. You're a total sweetheart and you deserve to be happy. So get your ass out there and talk to her! Just *man up*, bitch!"

I snorted. "I'd say that was sexist if anyone but you said it."

"I just say it to make people laugh," he said, spinning me back around and continuing with the cut. "But the sentiment remains. Face your fears and all that."

I just smiled politely. If only it were that simple.

As it would for many people, Transcendant's death made me do a lot of thinking about mortality. Not just my own, but those of my loved ones. For some reason, Lee's suicide never had this effect on me. Nor had Valora's murder. But now I was thinking not just of those who'd died, but the close calls. I'd almost lost Dana just a few weeks before. If we hadn't found Vicky, I have no doubt she'd have ended up dead sooner or later by the collective hand of The Nexus.

Life is short, and you never know when it's going to end. When we're younger, we think we're invincible and we'll live forever. But, pushing forty, I wasn't young, anymore. I couldn't think that way. Obviously. Even the toughest of us could be taken down by a bad blood vessel.

But I wasn't focusing just on mortality. I was also thinking about relationships. I wished I'd gotten to know Transcendant better. I wanted to know my current friends better. I decided to take Fabian's advice and start with Vicky.

Ever since we rescued her, I think she had been clinging to the hope that she'd only imagined being raped by her father. But the pregnancy test destroyed that hope.

Dr. Stone had gotten her mifepristone and misoprostol. I tried to be there for her, in the days following her chemical abortion, but she'd become distant. I couldn't imagine how traumatic it must have been for her, even though the actual memory of it was hazy, at best. But until she opened up, there wasn't much I could do for her.

As for her father, I was certain we hadn't heard the last from him. And that thought gave me no small amount of satisfaction. I couldn't wait to take that bastard down.

But now it was time to try again. I wasn't going to let her crawl inside a shell. In truth, I didn't think she'd stay in one for long, because that's just not the kind of person she is. But I wanted to give her a reason to climb out sooner than later.

I showed up unannounced at her apartment door. Bridget answered the door with a smile and a hug. "I'll go get her," she said.

I waited in the living room and soon Vicky trudged out. I heard Bridget's door close down the hall. "Hi," I said.

Vicky smiled, but kept her distance. "Hi," she said, passing by and entering the kitchen. "Drink?"

"Sure," I said, following her. I pulled out a bar stool and sat as she poured glasses of iced tea for us. "How are you doing?"

"Ducky," she said, forcing a smile. "You?"

"Good, thanks." I accepted the tea, but clasped Vicky's hand before she could pull it back. "Listen, there's something we need to talk about."

She gently removed her hand from mine. "All right."

"Look," I said, "I wanted to apologize to you."

"What on earth for?" Vicky's earnest gaze pleased me. At least now she was looking people in the eye.

"For keeping so much from you. My illness and whatnot."

"You've already apologized for that. I told you not to worry about it." She stepped toward the living room.

"I know," I said, following her. "But I also kept myself from you."

Vicky frowned. "What?"

"You know what I mean," I said.

She slumped into the sofa, then said, "All right. So what are you saying now?"

I fought down butterflies as I sat next to her and put my hand on hers. "I'm saying that, if you're still interested, so am I."

Vicky was quiet a moment, looking at me as though trying to determine my degree of sincerity. "Dyna, I don't know."

My heart sank. But before I could say anything, Bridget's muffled voice came from her room. "Don't be stupid!"

I laughed as Vicky dropped her face into her hand. "I will box your ears!" she yelled back.

"You can try," Bridget replied, now standing in the hall entry.

Vicky looked up at me, a wry smile on her lips. "Well. Seems I'd be 'stupid' not to be interested." She shrugged. "What can I say? When the kid's right, she's right."

"I'm *always* right," Bridget said, then spun on her heel and headed back to her room.

I grinned. "Awesome. Now get some shoes on. I'm buying lunch."

The next relationship I wanted to address was one that gave me much more anxiety than talking to Vicky. And it involved a long flight.

This time, I wanted to avoid the 4th of July in my home town, with the throngs of tourists coming in for the festivities. So I waited until the Sunday of the holiday weekend and hopped on a redeye flight to Pittsburgh.

As I had three years before, I rented a car and drove the hundred miles up Route 28, through the rolling hills of Western Pennsylvania. I was pleased that the weather was unseasonably cool for the area. It was in the low 70s as I drove.

I called Rhonda during the drive, telling her I was expecting to be in town for about a week. She invited me to dinner, saying the kids would be excited to see me.

I still had no idea what I was going to say to my mother. My last visit had ended about as badly as possible. Her communication since then had been virtually non-existent, and had gotten less frequent with each year. In fact, I hadn't heard from her at all since Christmas.

I pulled up in front of my parents' home around two in the afternoon. I got out and just stood there for a minute, staring at this house I'd grown up in. It looked much the same. They'd installed vinyl siding since my last visit, and planted yellow forsythia at the corners of the flower beds in the front.

The curtains of the living room window shifted, and I saw a face peering out at me. A moment later, the door opened and my father stepped outside. "Well," he said. "Look what the wind blew in."

I strolled up the sidewalk. "Yeah. And I brought some San Francisco weather with me."

"Too cool for July," he said.

"You're insane," I said with a laugh, climbing the porch steps and giving him a hug.

He hugged back. "Good to see you, sweetheart. Come on in."

Inside, I heard rustling in the kitchen and looked to see my mother poking her head out to see who'd come in. I smiled faintly. "Hi, Mom."

She glanced at my father for a second before coming into the room. "Dinah," she said, and I couldn't blame her for the trepidation in her voice. She embraced me in a hug with no hesitation, though. "What a surprise," she said, stepping back and looking me over.

"Sort of a spontaneous decision," I said.

"Must have been an expensive flight," my father said, moving over to his recliner.

Mother and I followed and sat in the love seat and rocking chair, respectively, the two seats in the room farthest from one another. "I suppose," I said. "But money isn't really an issue for me, these days."

"Even so," he said, "no sense in wasting it. Could have bought a ticket for later in the month."

"Dad. Let it go."

"I didn't think we'd ever see you back here again," my mother said, "after last time."

And there it was. Good to bring it up quickly, I thought. So I nodded and said, "Neither did I, honestly." I hesitated, still not certain how I wanted to phrase things. "A friend of mine died, recently," I told them. "Another one, I should say. And I guess it got me to thinking about other friends and family and how I'd feel if I lost any of them, especially if things between us had been left... unpleasant. Don't get me wrong," I quickly added, "I'm still hurt by what you did. But I'm trying to look past it, now."

Mother nodded slightly. "That's... that's good," she said. "Are you hungry? We just had lunch. Still some left."

I shook my head. "Thanks, but I ate on the drive up."

"How about a beer?" my father asked.

"Oh? Have you started drinking beer?" I replied. "Or are you still drinking that fizzy, yellow water?"

Dad frowned and shook his head. "You and your brother..."

"...know what real beer is," I finished. "Which reminds me, I brought you a bottle of his latest homebrew in my luggage."

"Dana told us you were sick," Mother said.

"Oh?" I said, surprised he'd done so. "Well, yes. I was. But I'm fine, now. Fully recovered."

I caught a glance between my parents, then Dad said, "He told us we almost lost you."

Dana never told me how much information he passed on to our parents. It was obviously more than I'd believed. "It was pretty rough," I said. "But we have a very good doctor for our team."

Mentioning the team caused a brief stiffening of Mother's posture, but she smiled and said, "I'm glad to hear that. But didn't that make you reconsider what you're doing? Always putting your life on the line with your... with what you do?"

She was showing remarkable self-control with her words. Was it possible she'd actually changed her views? "No," I said. "It hasn't. But I appreciate your concern." I hesitated a moment and, in an act rare for me, actually took credit for something. "In fact, Mom, I was the one who discovered what caused the outbreak of the disease, and therefore how to stop it."

"How did your friend die?" she asked, surprising me yet again. "Was she – you know – on your team?"

I nodded. "He was. And a very respected member. But he died of a brain aneurysm, not because of his job."

"We sure hear a lot more about metas now," Dad said, "ever since that thing in Nevada." As Invictus has said, I don't exactly have a poker face. Dad saw the shock reflected there. And probably a lot of other emotions, too. "What is it?" he asked.

Had Dana told them about my involvement with that, too? I doubted it. "I... lost a friend in that, too." After an awkward silence, I redirected the conversation. "You know, telepaths like Dana were vital in finding the ones who'd replaced our people."

"Yes," Mother said tersely. "So they said."

I felt anger rising, but I fought it down. I took a deep breath and said, "Look, I've been wanting to say this to you for years. I know you both have always been afraid of Dana's abilities. Mom, you always said they were a curse. And sometimes, honestly, I suspect he agrees with you. But what you and Dad need to understand is that Dana would never in a million years use his abilities on you. Please stop worrying about that."

As Mother looked away, Dad said, "We have. And you're right. It was a fear we had for a long time." He was silent a moment, his face showing what appeared to be shame. "I guess we've grown up a little."

I glanced between my parents. Mother still said nothing and wouldn't look at me. I suspected she was waiting for me to say something mean. Instead, I just nodded. "Been doing a bit of that, myself, lately."

They asked me a few questions, then. I got the feeling they were asking only as a courtesy, to demonstrate that they no longer felt I was a demon-spawn. Dad did laugh, though, when he told me how his buddies were impressed that his daughter had been involved in something so Top Secret that the world needed to think she'd been dead for several years.

We talked for hours, until it was time for dinner. We went out to their favorite steakhouse, my treat. Over dinner, they filled me in on the little things. Dad spoke excitedly about his new riding mower. Mom gossiped about people in town. I barely remembered any of them, but listened, anyway.

"So are you seeing anyone?" Mother asked, causing me to nearly choke on my ribeye.

"Sort of," I said.

"What's her name?" she asked.

I narrowed my eyes and stared at her. "Who are you, and what have you done with my mother?" She shrugged faintly. "No, seriously," I said. "This has now become creepy."

She cleared her throat and was quiet a moment before saying, "You remember Stephanie Lynn, don't you?"

I nodded. "Yeah, of course. Your friend Marjorie's daughter. Went to Yale." She was about four years older, so I didn't really know her well at all.

"Yes. Well, she got married in February. Your dad and I were invited to the wedding, up in Connecticut." She smiled slightly. "Marjorie had talked about Quinn a few times, and she was so excited that they were getting married." She was quiet a moment. "But in all that time, she'd never indicated that Quinn wasn't a man."

"Wow. No kidding? The invitation didn't give it away?"

She shook her head. "Quinn's middle name is Cameron."

"Unisex all the way," I said.

"We didn't know until we saw two brides walking up the aisle."

"Did that anger you?" I asked. "That she hadn't told you?"

"At that moment, it did," she admitted.

"Did Marjorie not know how you felt about... you know..."

"Truly, Dinah, I don't know. I'd thought so, but..." She looked down at her plate and fell silent.

I glanced at Dad, who seemed content just to eat and let his wife do all the talking. After a moment, I prompted her. "But what?"

Now she looked up at me. Her eyes were wet. "I've known Stephanie Lynn since she was a baby," she said. "I couldn't have loved her more if she'd been my own daughter." She smiled and I tried not to think that she would have preferred Stephanie Lynn to me as a daughter. "When they were little, I always imagined she and Dana would grow up to get married."

A part of me tried to imagine this woman, who had always been so bitter and judgmental, fawning over babies. I reminded myself that all this was before she learned of Dana's abilities and that I really had no idea what she'd been like before that.

"So what happened?"

"They exchanged vows. Everyone else clapped. And they walked back down the aisle, holding hands. When they passed our row, I looked at

Stephanie Lynn's face." She was quiet a moment, staring vacantly. "And all I saw was my own. She had the same joyful smile as I'd had when I married your father." She pulled a tissue from her purse and dabbed at her eyes. "We saw Marjorie and Steve at the reception, and they were so happy. It was like nothing was unusual about it. And then, Stephanie Lynn brought Quinn around to our table." She stopped talking again and her eyes welled.

I glanced at Dad, who looked at her with compassion. This was huge for Mother, so I sat patiently until she was ready to talk again.

"Quinn," she said with a little pause, "is lovely. Very polite. They stood talking to us for probably ten minutes. Never stopped smiling."

"I wouldn't call that smiling," Dad said.

"What would you call it?" I asked.

"Beaming. Glowing. Something flowery like that."

I looked back at my mother, who was nodding. "And they held hands the entire time," she said. "The entire time."

I wanted to say they sounded like any married couple should look on their wedding day. But I didn't. "Sounds like they're really in love," I said.

To my surprise, Mother nodded vigorously and tears spilled down her face. I was too stunned to say anything. She excused herself and headed to the ladies' room.

When she was gone, I looked at my father, "Wow."

He nodded soberly. "It's been a hard road. I appreciate you taking it easy on her."

"Dana always urges me to come home, or to call. He's even told me it would be better. But he never said why."

"She still has her moments," he said.

"Is she still a Bible-thumper?"

"She's stopped with the guys on TV," Dad said. "And she's started going to a new church. One that's more focused on the New Testament than the Old, if you know what I mean. They even have a gay minister." Dad shook his head. "You know, they say homophobic people get over it when they realize their child is gay. In this case, it took seeing her best friend being *happy* about her daughter marrying another woman."

"And if Marjorie hadn't been accepting of it?"

"Then your mother probably wouldn't be, either."

Mother soon returned and the rest of the meal passed without incident. I told them a little about Vicky. Dad told me about his plans for landscaping the back yard. Mother said she wanted to expand her flower garden.

Afterward, we drove home mostly in silence. When we got there, Dad settled in with his newspaper. "I'll get your room fixed up," Mom said, and went upstairs before I could even reply.

I watched her go, then turned to Dad. "I'm gonna go for a walk," I said. "Don't wait up."

I stepped outside into the cool air and headed up the street. I pulled out my phone and called Dana. "You won't believe where I am," I said when he answered.

The rest of my visit was quite nice. I spent time walking (and occasionally flying) around town. I had a great time with Rhonda and her family. Her kids had grown so much. And her husband welcomed the opportunity to show off his grill skills.

I had more slightly surreal conversations with my parents. It was never as overwhelming as that first night, but they did want to know about my work with the Gatekeepers. They asked about some of the things I'd done, and I told them about some of the less dangerous activities.

"So you've saved lives," Dad said.

I nodded. "But you know, as far as that goes, the one that sticks with me is one that resulted from my education, not my abilities." And I told them about Lily, whose undeveloped abilities had been killing her.

"Sounds like your mother isn't the only one who's changed," Dad observed. And I certainly couldn't deny it.

The folks were impressed with my stories. But I didn't tell them about my failures and the crippling guilt that resulted from them. I wanted to let them think well of me for a change.

On Friday, with mixed emotions, I said farewell to my parents before driving to Pittsburgh. On the one hand, I actually did regret leaving. On the other, I needed some separation to process this new dynamic.

I returned my rental car and checked my luggage at the airport before settling in to wait for my flight. I'd picked up the latest issue of *Supers*. They'd been able to get in a write-up about Transcendant just before it went to print, apparently. I started reading it, but found myself too depressed to continue. So I stuffed the magazine into my bag and watched people, instead.

Mostly, I watched the children. I loved the sense of wonder on their faces. Airports were still awesome to them. A boy of about four passed by with his father. In his hand was a plush airplane. I don't know why, but I found this stupidly endearing. Little girls pulled their tiny luggage bags behind them, brightly colored vinyl things adorned with My Little Pony and Barbie.

Across the walkway, other passengers waited for a flight to Orlando. The kids there were giddy with anticipation. Bound for Disney World, no doubt.

Among them was a little girl with sandy blond hair wearing a purple shirt with a giant image of Tinker Bell. She stood in front of her parents, fidgeting between them. She looked like her mother, who reminded me of someone. And then my breath caught as a third person joined them. Another woman, both stately and exotic. She handed the little girl a drink before sitting next to the one I'd taken to be the girl's mother.

I watched them, my pulse racing, frozen to my seat. The little girl caught my eye and saw that I was staring. She stared right back, then offered a cautious wave. I returned the wave. Then she turned to the exotic woman, said something to her, and pointed at me. The woman looked over at me. Our eyes locked.

An eternity later, she reached over and touched the mom's arm. She, too, looked over at me. And her mouth hung open, as mine would have, had I not been clenching my jaw so tightly.

The little girl said something to them and, getting no reaction, took it upon herself to bounce on over to me. This pulled me from my stupor. I looked down at her as she fetched up against my thigh, her eyes fixed on my white hair. "Hi, there," I said.

"Are you Dynamistress?" she said, straight to the point.

I nodded, trying to remember how to breathe. "I sure am, sweetie."

Her face lit up. "I'm named after you!"

"No way! You're named *Dynamistress*, too?"

She giggled, bending her body over my leg and smiling at me, nearly upside-down. "No, silly! My name's *Dinah*!"

My heart nearly stopped when she said the name. "So how old are you, Dinah?"

"Five and a half," she said. Then she righted herself and looked at me seriously. "My mommies say they went to college with you." All I could do was nod. My voice didn't want to work. "Come see them!" she said, pulling on my hand.

So I did.

Sharon and Jackie stood as we approached. I tried to smile, but have no idea whether I succeeded. Theirs seemed sincere, though. I stopped in front of them, little Dinah still holding my hand. "Daddy," she said, "it's *her*!"

Her father smiled and came over, taking her hand from mine. "Come on, honey. Let's give them a minute alone." He gave a friendly nod as they wandered off.

We were alone. Surrounded by a few hundred people, but alone. I was the first to speak. I'd imagined for years seeing them again and had practiced the speech in my mind a million times.

"Hi," I said, nailing it.

Jackie stepped up and wrapped her arms around me, squeezing tightly. "Hi," she whispered in my ear. Then she let go and Sharon had her turn. Not as tightly, but warmly. Her cheek on mine was like an electric shock. Even after eighteen years.

We stood there, just looking at each other. It was wonderful. It was awkward. "So," I said, trying to put us at ease, "you have a daughter."

"Jackie is the birth mother," Sharon said.

"And the father?" I indicated with a jerk of my thumb the man who'd walked off.

"That's Michael," Jackie said. "He's not the biological father, though. We did the sperm donor thing before we met him. But he's been with us since Dinah was two, so as far as she's concerned, he's always been here."

"*Dinah*," I repeated. "She said you named her after me."

"Yeah," Jackie said.

"That doesn't bother you, does it?" Sharon asked.

"Bother? No. Surprise? Yes. I mean, after how things ended..."

Both women frowned. "What do you mean?" Sharon said.

Jackie answered. "She means that we didn't keep in touch for long after we moved to Pittsburgh. And she thinks this is a reflection on her."

"Says the psychologist," I said with a smirk.

"It was us," Sharon said, "not you. At first, we were overwhelmed with grad school." I sure understood that one, since I experienced it a year later.

"And then there was our rough patch," Jackie added. "We were separated for about a year, and getting back together was a bit rocky. Took some time."

"Oh," I said. "I'm sorry."

Sharon shrugged. "Ancient history."

"And then you moved to San Francisco," Jackie said, "and became a superhero."

"So, that was that," Sharon concluded.

I was stunned. "How did you know?" I asked. "About me moving. And the other thing."

"The lab fire," Jackie said. "And the lawsuit."

"We heard about it, and that you were involved, from one of our friends back in State College," Sharon added.

"It wasn't hard to put two and two together," Jackie said. "In school, you were always a bit evasive about what you wanted to do with your degree. But you talked about genetic manipulation and metabolism."

Sharon jumped in. "And when the news reported that you'd been working on a personal project without the lab's knowledge, we figured it had to be something outside the norm."

"And you talked all the time about metas," Jackie said with a shrug.

I was overwhelmed. They'd actually followed my career. They hadn't forgotten about me. They'd never stopped caring. I could feel my heart in my throat and tears threatening.

"Dinah's been begging us to contact you," Sharon said. "But we figured you were too busy."

"I don't know what to say," I managed to spit out. "Now I feel bad for not following your careers."

Jackie snorted. "Not much to follow. I'm a school counselor."

"And I teach developmentally disabled kids," Sharon said. "Different schools," she added, "but near enough for easy commutes."

"And, um, Michael? What's he do?"

"He's a photographer," Jackie said. "Works for the *Post-Gazette*, but does the occasional show of his own work, too. And he's wonderful with Dinah."

"Sounds nice," I said.

"Well, yeah," Sharon said. "But he's not perfect." When I looked questioningly at her, she explained. "He doesn't like Turkish coffee."

"That's because it's disgusting," Michael said as he and Dinah returned. The others formally introduced us and he shook my hand warmly. "I've heard so much about you," he said. "A pleasure to meet you."

"I have a poster of you!" Dinah said, inserting herself between me and her dad.

"Is that right?" I said, not realizing there were posters of me in existence.

"One of the photos from *Supers*," Michael said. "I did a high-rez scan and blew it up for her. It's the only non-Disney decoration in her room."

"Daddy, take a picture of us!"

"Excellent idea, Tink," he said, moving to his camera bag under his seat. "Gather up, ladies."

Dinah insisted that I hold her in the picture. I lifted her so her face was next to mine. Her mothers scrunched in, flanking us. Big, cheesy smiles. A bright flash. One perfect photograph.

And then my flight began to board.

I handed Sharon my card, telling them to stay in touch and to email me the photo. We said our farewells. Dinah wrapped her arms around my neck in a fierce hug. "You're my third mommy," she said in my ear before smooching my cheek.

I managed to wait until I was walking away from them before letting the tears flow.

Twenty-Three

"One half of knowing what you want is knowing what you must give up before you get it."
~ Sidney Howard

I think one of the traits that indicates maturity is the ability to make difficult choices with a minimum of equivocating and an absence of whining. It involves the ability to understand and accept that many of our desires conflict with one another, and then to prioritize, to appropriately place values, in order to make the best decision. It involves the ability to accept that sometimes the best choice isn't the one we want most. And sometimes, it's simply being able to recognize that a choice needs to be made at all.

"So," Invictus said as we sat drinking tea in his office, "I take it you're ready to come off of medical leave."

I placed my cup gently on the saucer, avoiding eye contact with this man I'd grown to respect so much. "Well, yes. But that's not why I asked to see you."

"All right. What's on your mind?" he said, cradling his tea in his palms.

"I want to say first that it's been an honor working with you and the rest of the Gatekeepers," I said, looking at him. I saw his eyes narrow. "But I'm afraid it's not something I can continue doing."

"I see," he said, leaning forward, putting down his cup and looking at me in concern. "And why is that?"

"There are a few reasons," I told him. "But it boils down to not being particularly comfortable in the group."

"Dyna, I know there are a few members who've never really accepted you—"

"Oh, it's not that," I said. "A group this size, that's probably true for many members. The size *is* one of the factors, though. Speaking only for me, I find it too large and cumbersome. As I've said to others, it sometimes seems as though the Gatekeepers is really several smaller groups under one banner, rather than a unified team."

Invictus nodded. "I understand how you could feel that way."

"And there's nothing wrong with that," I said. "It's worked well for you for decades. I just think I personally need something smaller."

"So you're looking for another team, not going solo? I could recommend a few."

"Thank you, but that won't be necessary." I nervously took another sip of tea. "I'm forming my own."

He seemed surprised. "Interesting."

"And in fact, the inspiration for it came partially from you."

Invictus raised an eyebrow. "Indeed?"

"It was about a year ago. You and I were discussing Lily. You told me you were impressed by my dedication to her, but pointed out that we're not social workers."

The big man nodded. "I remember."

"It's just..." I hesitated, hoping I could adequately convey what I was thinking. I took a deep breath and plunged in. "Have you ever thought about what happens to the people we save? After we leave?" I didn't wait for a response. "Even the ones who are physically unharmed often have difficulty recovering from the psychological trauma. And then there's the homeless, who are frequent victims. They don't have the support system others do."

"So you *want* to be a social worker."

I shook my head. "No, but there are things that need to be done after the costumes are gone. These people often need things we can't provide, but we can – and I think *should* – advise them on how they can get these things in the aftermath of whatever has befallen them. I want to know, inasmuch as is possible, that they're going to be okay in the long term." I looked at Invictus again, and felt self-conscious.

He was quiet for a long while, just looking at me. I couldn't read his expression at all. Finally, he shook his head slightly, a faint smile touching the corners of his mouth.

"What?" I said.

"Just thinking of how much you've changed. You're so different from the woman who joined us not so terribly long ago."

I felt my cheeks flush. "Suppose I have," I said. Though in truth, I think Dana said it rightly. I was shedding the fake persona that had taken hold of me in my teen years, returning to the girl I'd been before I decided I was the center of the universe.

"Are you intending to recruit any Gatekeepers?"

I measured my response carefully. "Invictus, I would never want to undermine your team by doing that without your permission. But obviously, there are some I'd love to have with me." I cleared my throat. "I'll certainly tell them what I'm doing, since they'll be wondering why I'm leaving. And if some of them want to join me?"

Invictus shrugged. "Then we will miss them. I will not hold it against them. Or you."

"I'm relieved," I said.

"It's not the first time such a thing has happened."

"Oh?"

He nodded. "Years ago, a friend of mine in the Gatekeepers decided to start his own team. Like you, he felt our group was too large. I believe there were four members who went with him."

"I didn't know that. How did it work out?"

"In my opinion, quite well. Until they were disbanded after a particularly high profile event in which my friend was grievously injured."

I frowned at him. "Wait..." Invictus just nodded. "Scoutmaster? The Bay Scouts broke off from the Gatekeepers?"

"Not common knowledge, these days."

"Son of a bitch," I said. "I wonder why he never mentioned it."

"Will you find it relevant to tell your future members?" Invictus asked casually.

"Well, perhaps not. Though it's not something I'd ever hide, either."

"I don't believe Daniel was hiding it from you. It was quite a while ago, after all."

"I suppose."

"How soon will you be resigning from the team?"

I offered a tiny smile and placed my Gatekeepers-issued comm unit upon the table between us.

When I got home, I stood in my bedroom, staring at my blue and white costume lying on the bed. It was a beautiful thing. I remembered how much I'd hated the idea of the skin-tight fabric. But I'd grown to love the feel of it. Even the silly circlet I wore on my forehead had become dear to me. I admired the twisted DNA pattern stretching down the sides and on the cape. It was the costume of a hero, no question.

And that's why it had to go.

I carefully folded it up and placed it in a small garment bag. I zipped it shut and tucked it away in the bottom drawer of my dresser. Then I stretched out on my bed.

I had Dynasonic's four CDs spread out in front of me. I always enjoyed reading liner notes and whatnot, but today I found myself just staring at the covers. The band's first, eponymously-titled release had a vibrant image. It was a series of off-centered circles, beginning with a solid disc of golden yellow, then alternating rings of that color and black, each one thicker than the one before. On later releases, this became the "O" in the logo of their name.

Their third album, though, was the cover that captured my attention the most. On a pure black background was a grayish line drawing of a woman's head, tilted back, hair spread, mouth open in a scream. The band's logo was at the bottom. The title of the album sat at the top – *Pariah.*

Yes.

That would do just fine.

That evening, we had a meeting at the apartment. I sat anxiously as the others got drinks and snacks. It was a full house. Kit and Lily were there, as were the regular Gatekeeper Girls – Jasmine, Kim, Jennifer, and Vicky, who'd brought Bridget along. I even managed to get Jack to show up.

Once everyone was seated, I thanked them for coming. "So," I began, "this morning, I met with Invictus. Tomorrow, he will announce that I have formally resigned from the Gatekeepers."

This elicited the expected astonished reactions from the group, save for Sinta, who already knew. The only other one who didn't seem surprised was Jasmine, who wore a tiny smile as she gazed at me.

I explained my reasons to them, as I'd done with Invictus, and assured them that it was a very amicable parting of ways. And I told them that I had something planned. Something different.

I gave them the same spiel I'd given Invictus, about there being more to helping victims than stopping the bad guys. "But mostly," I said, "I want a group with autonomy. Not limited to what the government says is okay to pursue or what isn't." I glanced at Vicky, who smiled back. I saw the nods of the others. They got it. "A new friend of mine told me once that one of the reasons for her professional success was that she surrounded herself with others who shared her vision. She made her own environment, to use her words. And that's what I want to do. That's why you're all here. I want you with me."

"Even me?" Bridget asked, surprised.

"Absolutely," I said. "Look, I don't expect any immediate answers, especially from those of you still attached to the Gatekeepers. Though you should know that Invictus is okay with it if you do join me."

I leaned over and picked up a box, pulling out a stack of books. "This is a guide to consensus decision-making. This is how we'll be running the group." I passed them around.

"I thought consensus just meant everyone agreed," Kim said.

"Well, basically, yes. But there's a structure for streamlining the process," I said, "and types of consensus that don't require one hundred percent agreement, but are still far better than simple majority rule."

For the next hour, we discussed how I envisioned this new group, what it would do, how it would operate, and so on. When they were all seemingly satisfied, I said, "If you do decide to join, come back here on August first, at eleven o'clock. I'll order pizza and we'll formally put the group together."

"One last question," Vicky said. "This all sounds brilliant, but no one has brought up the most important thing."

"Which is?" I asked.

Vicky nodded seriously and said, "Will there or will there not be a hot tub?"

I blinked at her, then the others erupted in laughter. "Possibly," I said as Vicky grinned at me.

"Dyna," Lily said, "what are we going to be called?" Others nodded expectantly.

"Well, that's something we'll have to vote on," I said.

"No," Jasmine said. "Your idea. You get to name it."

There was no opposition to this, so I nodded. "Well, you know the reasons I wanted to form the group in the first place. I felt like I didn't fit other groups. And I know some of you have also felt out of place, for one reason or another. I wanted our group to be home to all those who didn't fit. The name I like is the Pariah Project."

As expected, this drew confused looks from some. Jack was the one to speak up. "Doesn't 'pariah' mean 'outcast'?"

"That's the common meaning, yes. As I said, it's a group for misfits. Not literal outcasts, but ones who sort of feel like it, even if that feeling is self-inflicted." That seemed to satisfy them. "The word itself comes from the Tamil word for 'drummer.' And I guess you could say most of us, to paraphrase Thoreau, march to our own drums."

This actually elicited some nods of approval, so it was time to unveil our logo. I picked up a piece of paper. I'd recreated the Dynasonic logo on the computer and printed it.

"This is the logo I suggest. The center circle represents the drum head. The rings, of course, being sound waves, compressed on one side, expanded on the other."

"Then why aren't we the Doppler Project?" Kit said.

"I knew you'd say that," I said, mock-glaring at him. "It's off-center because most of us are. Especially you," I said with a wink.

"So we'll all be required to wear that thing?" Vicky said.

"Not at all," I said. "Purely optional."

There was more discussion, which eventually moved off the topic of the team and into general chatting. By the time it broke up, several of them looked pleased, some unsure. Jennifer in particular seemed conflicted. She hung around until the others were gone.

"What's up?" I said as Sinta began cleaning up.

Jennifer smiled slightly. "Just a bit torn. I mean, it sounds like a great idea, and you know I really like y'all. Includin' you," she teased, "even though you're not very funny."

I laughed. "Jen, there's no pressure. I understand if you're not comfortable leaving the Gatekeepers."

"Haven't really been a member all that long, y'know? Would kinda feel – I dunno – inconsiderate."

"I get that. I would love to have you with us, but I couldn't blame you a bit for staying where you are. It's a great team. And it pays well. This won't." I smiled at her. "Look, if I see you on the first, fantastic. If not, we'll do lunch soon. Always friends, regardless."

She nodded and forced a smile again. "Right," she said. "Then I'll see ya when I see ya."

Real estate prices were low since the crash, so it was a good time to shop for a property to serve as my new team's headquarters. In my online browsing, one property stood out.

Three stories, about 3,500 square feet, zoned for combined residential and commercial. It had an unusual floor plan, with half-floors and a small penthouse with a deck on the roof. And it was "priced to move," as agents like to say. I called and arranged to see it, though I already knew I was going to buy it. I'd seen it before, after all.

When I arrived for the tour, I asked if we could start in the basement. As Dynasonic had said hers had originally been, the basement here was a full kitchen. Four familiar wooden pillars split the center of the room, lengthwise, with the kitchen on one side, space for dining, and I saw just where I could put a small bar.

The main floor was the living and dining area. This was a lavishly decorated room, with beautiful wooden bookcases lining it, a gorgeous fireplace on one side, and a small conference table in the center. There were even stained glass windows. At the far end was a glass-walled entry area and the door to the street.

The master bedroom was on the second floor. Skylights were set in the ceiling in two rows. In the middle of the room's parquet floor, a groove was cut in a large square. "What's that?" I asked. In reply, the agent just smiled and stepped over to the wall, where he flipped a switch. I watched in fascination as the entire square section began to rotate, flipping over completely, revealing a hidden bed. Like a Murphy bed, but in the floor, rather than a wall.

The next floor up held a tiny room, which in turn opened out onto the rooftop deck. It was smallish, but nice enough. I couldn't help but notice, though, that the roof itself was flat and unused. The only things there were the skylights. Should be easy enough to convert it into something functional.

Yes. This would make an acceptable headquarters. And a fine home.

I put half down and financed the rest at a rock bottom interest rate, giving me mortgage payments in the area of five thousand a month.

With any luck, we'd be able to close in a month or so, since the sellers had already done the third-party reports, such as the appraisal, the engineering report, etc. They were ready to get it done quickly.

So it was official. I was moving back to familiar territory, just north of the Tenderloin.

My imminent relocation was going to leave Sinta effectively homeless, since she couldn't afford the rent on our apartment by herself. I mentioned this to Daniel on one of my visits to see him.

"She can have her old place back," he said. And seeing the confusion on my face, he said, "Never sold it."

"But you could have gotten a lot of money for it," I said.

He shrugged. "Didn't need it. Between my speaking engagements and my disability pension, I'm fine. Won't live in luxury, but won't want for much, either."

"I'm glad."

"But speaking of money," he said, "how will you pay your new team members? You won't have the resources of the Gatekeepers."

"I'll be applying for grants," I told him. "Given the nature of our team, I think there are several we'll qualify for."

"Enough to pay salaries? To cover health insurance?"

"It'll be tricky," I admitted. "Some of the prospective members are financially well-off. I plan to ask them to voluntarily suspend a salary until we have the means to pay it steadily. Also," I added, "there's no requirement that this needs to be someone's full-time gig. I expect Jack to continue his work at Wonderland, for example."

Daniel nodded, draining his iced tea. "Sensible. If they're okay with him taking leave when you need him."

I took our empty glasses to the kitchen for refills. "Right. And that leads me to the main reason for my visit."

"You want me to come out of retirement."

I smiled hopefully as I poured the tea. "Would that be so terrible?"

"Not sure what use I would be to you."

"I'll find something."

"I don't know. Would cut into my social life."

I chuckled. Then I saw his face as I returned to the living room. "Seriously?"

He nodded. "Something I never allowed myself to have, before. Was too focused on the Scouts."

"Look," I said, "I know I've brought this up before, but I really want you to think about it. Ever since your injury, I've been following the literature. And we're getting close, Daniel. Soon, we'll be able to regenerate spinal nerves. It's not my specialty, of course, but I know we could get you into a program."

Daniel was quiet for a moment before saying, "When we reach that breakthrough, let me know. And sign me up. But I won't be an experiment in the meantime."

That was something, at least. "Okay," I said.

"As for being part of your new team," he continued, "how about I just make myself available as a consultant to you?"

"Oh, well, you didn't really have any choice, there," I said.

Daniel laughed. "Figured."

The following weeks were filled with planning. And spending. I ordered the components of my laboratory. I emailed Jasmine the building's schematics. She'd be in charge of our security and defenses. I dutifully ordered the items she'd need. Ping Song agreed to set up our computer network and our communications system, including our portable smart-comm units. I bought all that, too. By that point, my bank account was hurting.

When I wasn't spending money, though, I was figuring out how to bring some in. I'd researched a large number of grants, including ones from state and federal governments and those of independent associations. The application process was time-consuming, but would ultimately be worth it.

I hoped.

On August first, Sinta and I waited anxiously to see which guests would arrive. She stood next to the video unit on the wall, watching, excitedly announcing everyone who appeared at the door.

By eleven-fifteen, we had our team. And it was everyone who'd been at the meeting, with one exception. Jennifer wasn't there. Sinta and I supplied our guests with beverages. Just before we sat down to begin business, there was a buzz at the intercom. Sinta and I exchanged hopeful glances. She bounced over to the door – and let in the pizza delivery guy.

Sinta took the stack of boxes as I paid him. "Have a good one," I said.

"Thanks. You, too," he said, turning to leave, nearly tripping over someone behind him.

"Caught the door after him," Jennifer said. "Sorry I'm late. Overslept."

"Understandable," I said, barely able to keep from grinning stupidly. "Bats are nocturnal."

"Still not funny," she said, stepping past me and greeting the others.

The meeting itself didn't last long. "There are a few things we need to discuss," I said as we ate, "but will require you guys to do some reading, first. For example, the organization structure. We need to decide whether to remain as an unincorporated nonprofit, with or without applying to be a 501(c)4 as a social welfare organization, or to incorporate. I've put together information to help you get up to speed on all that and will email it to you later today."

"Cool. What's next, boss lady?" Bridget asked.

"Uh-uh," I said. "I'm not the boss. We're all equals."

"Whatever you say, boss," Bridget said with a smirk.

"What's next," I said, "is focusing on specialties. Each of us will have a particular area of expertise. For example, Jasmine is our security expert. I will be the group facilitator and the one to handle all the annoying details, like the financials, including applying for grants and whatnot." I handed a clipboard and pen to Sinta to hand around the room. "I've made a list of other needs we're likely to have. If you see something you're interested in, put your name next to it. And feel free to list something else, if you have it in mind."

As they passed around the form, I marveled at my luck. Everyone had signed on. All of them. I'd hoped for half, at best. Things were really looking good.

When the clipboard made its way back to me, I looked it over. Then I said, "There's one other thing I want you to all give some consideration. Some of you know that I do volunteer work as a suicide prevention counselor. Now, volunteer work is exactly that – voluntary. But I think it would be fantastic if more of us would do that."

Bridget spoke up. "I'd love to help at an animal shelter!"

"Awesome," I said. "I think all of us have things that are important to us, and could manage to donate some time and effort to them."

"Wonderful idea, Dyna," Jasmine said, and others nodded in agreement.

We talked over other general things for the next hour, which included me telling them about our headquarters. I expected to close on the property sometime during August. By mid-September, if not sooner, we should be ready for occupancy.

After the meeting ended, everyone went their separate ways. Kit and Lily went home, next door. Jack went to the lab. Jasmine, Kim, and Vicky went out for coffee, while Sinta, Jennifer, and Bridget went out for ice cream.

Vicky hung back as the others filed out. She kissed me on the cheek. "Well done, hon."

I smiled. "Yeah, I think we've just built a good team."

"Dyna, you didn't build a team," she said, squeezing my hand. "You created a family." Another buss on the cheek and she headed out to catch up with Jasmine and Kim.

When everyone was gone, I fixed myself a drink. For the life of me, I couldn't stop smiling. I had such a good feeling about the Project and needed to share my excitement.

First, I called Dana. I'd already run the concept by him but told him now about the meeting and the reactions of the others. After that, I called Macy. This was certainly big news and she should find out about it directly from me. But her phone dumped me straight into voicemail. I left a message for her to call me.

This reminded me that it had again been a while since I'd checked my email, so I fetched my laptop. After deleting all the obvious spam, I worked my way through all that weren't from the website. Once those were all dealt with, it left a couple dozen messages. Most of them were ones Macy had forwarded from website visitors. The remaining six were auto-forwards from the stalker. I read these, first.

The first four were typical of earlier messages. Pleading, demanding, but with a rising sense of urgency as they went on. The fifth was outright threatening. It said, "If I don't hear back from you by Friday, you'll regret it." The final message said simply, "You had your chance. See you soon."

That message was dated July 13. Close to three weeks ago. I checked the date of the last message forwarded by Macy. July sixteenth. Nothing since then. A sinking feeling hit me.

I jumped onto my website and looked at the "Contact Me" page. The contact email wasn't mine. It was "webmistress@dynamistress.com."

I realized, my blood chilling, that the stalker's messages had never addressed me by name. Because they weren't for me.

They were for Macy.

TWENTY-FOUR

"People don't change. Only their costumes do."
~ Gene Moore

One winter, when I was about nine years old, Dana and I were outside, playing in the snow. We had saucer sleds and would slide down the flood control dike across the road from our house. Scooter was with us, occasionally bounding down the short, steep slope alongside us, neck deep in the drifts.

At one point, I stood atop the dike, catching my breath. I looked around for the dog, but didn't see him. Then I looked at the creek.

Scooter had padded out onto the frozen surface of the water and fallen through a thin patch in the ice. He was scrabbling at the ice, trying to pull himself out. I remember the panic on his little face.

I was terrified. I screamed out his name, tears flowing and freezing on my cheeks. My dog was going to die.

But before I knew it, Dana was down the slope and onto the ice. I began to follow, but he told me to stay back. I just knew I was going to see him fall through. He was so much heavier than a small dog.

But he made it. He slid easily over to the hole, reached down, and lifted the dog out. In minutes, they were back on land, and we headed in to dry off Scooter and warm him up. It was the most incredible thing I'd ever seen, and Dana had treated it like it was no big deal.

Years later I would realize that he'd never been in any danger. Nor had Scooter, once Dana saw him. Had I not been there, he would have lifted the dog out telekinetically, from a distance. But because I was, and he needed to maintain the illusion of being "normal," he was able to do it all invisibly.

He stabilized the dog so he wouldn't go under, all while sliding over to him *above* the ice. Of course, being able to accomplish all that while keeping me oblivious was an impressive bit of meta-multitasking.

I didn't know where Macy lived, but fortunately knew her parents' names, and they were listed in the phone book. I mapped it on the computer, then called the detective who'd been working on the case and told him what I'd figured out. I gave him Macy's address and told him I was on my way.

I'd been dressing as I spoke to him. I wasn't sure why, but it seemed fitting to go as Dynamistress, rather than Dinah. It wasn't the blue and whites I put on, but my new outfit, a sort of hybrid of my original leathers and the "hero" uniform. The top was dark blue Lycra, sleeveless. The Pariah Project emblem would eventually be sewn on the chest. The bottoms were fitted cargo pants of the same color, tucked into calf-high, black, combat boots with buckled straps, made from energy transparent materials. I'd commissioned the boots after seeing Quanta's at Transcendant's memorial. My hair was in a ponytail with a dark blue bandanna. Black and gold sport sunglasses, a similarly colored tactical belt, and a floor-length, black, leather trench coat finished the ensemble.

Macy's house was just over two miles due south of my own place, in the Westwood Highlands neighborhood. The streets there are terraced on the hillside. Her home sat in the middle of the avenue, crammed against the neighboring houses on each side. The back of the house was up against the hill, shaded by trees.

A patrol car sat in front of the house as I approached. Two officers were climbing the flight of stairs from the street to the front door. I landed behind them, causing them to turn.

"You're Dyna... um... Dynasomething?"

"Yeah."

"You called this in?" the other officer said.

"I did."

"Then you might as well keep us company," the first said, resuming the climb.

We reached the door and rang the bell. I wanted to just blast inside, but knew that was exactly the wrong thing to do, just as I knew no one was going to answer the door.

But then it swung open. Macy stood inside, back from the door, hidden partially in shadow. I was shocked. Relieved, but shocked.

One officer gave me a look that said I was wasting their time. The other said, "Macy Zhang?"

"Yes?"

"We were asked to do a welfare check. Is everything okay, here?"

"Why wouldn't it be?" she said. But as she said this, she shook her head no.

I took off my shades, and Macy's eyes widened as she recognized me, but she said nothing.

The officer nearest the door sniffed. "What's that smell?"

"I, um, made a frozen pizza. Kinda burnt it." She answered the cop, but her eyes remained fixed on me.

"Mind if we come in and take a look around?"

"I'd really rather you didn't," she said, still looking at me. There was fear in her eyes.

"Are your parents at home?"

Good question, I thought, and immediately began scanning the house with my energy vision.

"No, they went out to dinner," Macy lied. I saw three distinct energy signatures deeper in the house.

"Miss, please let us come in."

I put my hands on the shoulders of the cops and silently indicated the need to back off.

Macy closed the door on us as I led the cops down the steps. "There are three people in there besides her. Her parents, I assume, and her stalker. He probably threatened to kill them if she didn't get rid of us."

"You got X-ray vision or something?"

"Or something," I said as we reached the street. "Look, it's important that he thinks we've left. You two need to drive off."

"I'll report a hostage situation," the younger officer said.

"Do what you have to do," I said. "And so will I."

The older officer looked askance at me. "And that would be what?"

I just frowned. "Not really sure, yet. Now go."

The cops nodded, got in their cruiser, and drove off. I took to the sky, where I watched them turn the corner at the end of the street, then backtrack up the hill to the next avenue up. I met them there.

"SWAT and negotiation teams will meet here," said the younger officer.

"I'm going in," I said.

"Negative," the older officer said. "You'll wait for the negotiation team to arrive."

"You need me for reconnaissance. Give me a radio and fifteen minutes."

After a brief staring match between us, the older officer grumbled, "I'll give you ten. But after that, we send in our crew." His partner grabbed a two-way radio from the car and set it, then handed it to me.

"Okay," I said. I jacked in an earpiece and inserted it, then nodded my thanks before soaring over the roof of the nearest house and onto the steep slope behind.

I wished I felt as confident as I was pretending to be. Truth was, I was terrified. I couldn't help but remember my last hostage situation, and how I'd choked. Maybe I should just wait for the police. They had experience with this sort of thing.

But no. This was Macy. I couldn't risk anything happening to her or her family. I couldn't assume the police would be quite as careful about it as I would be. Or at least, that's what I told myself.

There was no direct line of sight between my vantage point and windows of the house, so I approached from the west and soon reached the back of Macy's house. I slipped over the wall from the neighboring property and dropped lightly to the deck.

There were no blinds or drapes over the window and door, and I could see that it entered into the master bedroom. A quick scan revealed that all four occupants were on the lower level. I tested the door and found it locked. There were two windows to the bedroom, both of which would be too high off the steeply sloping ground for anyone to access without a ladder. I took to the air and hovered in front of one of them. Thankfully, it wasn't locked. I slowly slid it open far enough to slip inside.

"I'm in," I whispered into the radio. "They're downstairs."

The bed wasn't made and ropes were tied to the rails on the headboard and around the legs at the foot of the bed. There were blood stains on the ends of the ropes at the headboard, and on the sheet corners there.

Heart pounding, I crept out of the bedroom and toward the stairs. Walking on cushions of energy, I made it down in almost complete silence, listening to their conversation the entire way.

"Don't be stupid," came a male voice that wasn't Macy's father's. "Of course they'll be back, so this *is* necessary."

"It's not," Macy pleaded. "Aaron, please... just give yourself up."

The voices were coming from the kitchen. A quick scan showed three energy patterns at one side of the room, the fourth on the opposite side. Of the four, three were quite still, two at one end of the room, the third near the other side. The fourth, whom I assumed to be Aaron, moved around near the first two, then crossed the room to the fourth.

"Just stop," Macy begged. "Let them go."

"It'll all be over soon," he said.

Finally, I reached a corner from where I could see into the kitchen. And what I saw made my stomach knot. Macy's parents were seated at the kitchen table. They were bound in their seats, mouths gagged, plates of burnt pizza crusts in front of them. They sat perfectly upright, their heads held perfectly still. The father had a black eye. The mother had a split lip. Both looked beyond exhausted.

I looked closer and saw that the undersides of their chins were puckered and bits of blood dripped down onto their rumpled and stained clothing. I looked above them and saw an eye bolt screwed into the ceiling. The stalker had looped razor thin piano wire around their throats and up through the bolt, from where it led off to the other side of the kitchen.

This was a very sick kid. And, I realized, not stupid. He'd been stalking Macy for months, but waited until now – when school was out on summer break – to take any actions. No school absences to draw attention.

I stepped around the corner, into full view of her parents. Her mother's terrified eyes widened and she let out a small sound. I froze. I had the radio in my hand and locked the button in transmission mode so the police could hear what was going on.

"See?" the man said. "Told you they'd be here. Think it's your friend? I think it's your friend." Then, in a suddenly angry voice, "Talk to her!"

Macy's voice quavered as she said, "Dyna?"

I said nothing, hoping he'd think they were still alone. But after a moment, he yelled, "Don't fucking pretend you're not there!"

"I'm here," I said.

"Just so you know," he said, "I have a gun. And Macy."

"Okay," I said. I took a deep breath. "So... Aaron... how about you tell me what you want?"

"I *have* what I want." His voice was ragged, stressed.

"Right," I said, taking a careful step forward. Under the smell of burnt pizza crust was the odor of ripe garbage. "You've been here a while, haven't you?" I was nearly to the doorway and could now see bags of trash stacked against a wall. "Hope that wasn't your last frozen pizza. Be a shame to burn the last one. I've got some cash on me, if you want Macy to run out and get more."

"How stupid do you think I am?"

"I don't think you're stupid at all," I said. "Which is why I think we're going to end this peacefully."

"Then you're the stupid one."

"Mind if I come in?"

"Not a bit. Come join the fun."

I removed the earphone and tucked it with the radio into a pocket in my trench coat. Then I stepped slowly into the kitchen, hands up in front of me, fingers spread. The boy stood in the corner of the kitchen, Macy in front of him, a gun in his right hand, held to her head. His left hand was hidden behind his back, probably holding another weapon, I figured.

I looked at Macy. The wire filament came down from the eye hook, looped around Macy's neck, and was tied around Aaron's waist. It was taut, so any big movement – such as him falling to the floor – would cause the wire to cut into all three of the hostages.

"Hey, kiddo," I said, far more casually than I felt.

"Hey, D," she said, a tear rolling down her cheek. The girl was terrified, and for good reason. For that matter, so was I. I truly had no idea what to do. This was a brutally ugly situation.

In the bright kitchen, I could see much more than in the shaded doorway downstairs. There were no noticeable bruises on her, but she looked awful. Her clothes were dirty and torn and she seemed broken in spirit, if not in body. I could also see now that she wore make-up, not applied very well. Eye shadow, mascara, and lipstick. I got the feeling she hadn't put it on, herself. I tried not to think of what that implied, even though the thought had been in my mind all along.

As for her captor, he appeared a couple/few years older than Macy. He looked to be maybe seventeen. He had dark circles under his eyes, and was slightly manic and twitchy. He continually adjusted his grip on the gun, as though it were uncomfortable. He wore jeans and a Team Dyna shirt. "Like what you see?" he taunted.

"Everyone's alive, so, yes."

"That could change," he said.

"In the blink of an eye," I replied, glaring at him. "But we're going to avoid that, aren't we?"

"I see you've got a new super-suit," he said in a mocking tone. "Trying to give the impression that you're actually tough?"

"Something like that," I said. "I like your shirt."

"Wore it just for Macy," he said with a smile of contempt.

"You know, we both thought your emails were meant for me," I said.

"That's because you're stupid!"

"You go to school together, right?"

"None of your business."

"He does," Macy said.

"Shut up!" he said, kicking her foot.

"Hey, it's cool," I said. "Really." I looked at Macy again. She seemed to be more alert, paying more attention to me.

The gun never wavered from its position against Macy's head. "You're going to leave, now," Aaron said.

"You know I really can't do that," I said.

"Sure, you can. Just turn and walk out."

"Aaron, look," I said, as soothingly as I could, "I'm here to try to end this peacefully. But in a minute or two, you're going to have a SWAT team surrounding this house."

The fact that he'd been there so long without killing anyone was encouraging. But he hadn't felt threatened, before. And now here he was with a gun to my friend's temple. He was sweating and his gaze darted around the room, at me, at Macy's parents, and at the doorway. His desperation was clear, but how desperate was he?

"You're going to tell them to get lost," he said. "Or else this gets even uglier." And then he pulled his other weapon out from behind his back. To my shock, it was a grenade. He held it around in front of Macy's body. "Pull the pin," he said, answering any question about his desperation.

"No!" Macy said. "Are you nuts?"

He pushed the gun deeper into her cheek. "Do it!"

"Aaron," I said calmly, "how do you expect to survive that?"

He shrugged. "Got myself a Macy shield."

"Please," I said, "there's no need for this."

"*I* say what's needed!" he yelled. "Pull it, Macy!"

Looking at me fearfully, she did as he said, pulling the pin on a grenade that I sincerely hoped was fake. I watched as it lurched free of the weapon. Thankfully, Aaron kept firm hold of the safety lever.

I'd had the beginnings of an idea of how to end this confrontation, but the grenade added a level I wasn't sure how to account for. But I was out of time. My ten minutes were almost certainly up. The cops were going to come in, any minute. I stood there, staring at Aaron and his grenade, adrenaline surging in me, energy wanting release.

I'm startled by the click of a SWAT officer's gun. My blast erupts, thrown off by my surprise, and—

No. Not this time.

This time, I was going end things as smoothly as my brother rescuing a dog from an icy creek.

Macy hadn't stopped staring at me, and I hoped she'd get the meaning in what I was about to say. "Look, Aaron. I really think you should just *drop* this..." Macy raised an eyebrow. "...on *account* of *three* things." Her eyes narrowed a little. She looked worried, but then gave a minuscule nod. She trusted me.

"And what things would those be?" he sneered, adjusting his grip on the gun again.

"*One*," I said, holding up a finger of my right hand, my arm canted out at the elbow, "you don't really want to be doing this." Macy licked her lips, glancing at her parents, whom I could barely see in my peripheral vision. I was glad I hadn't taken off the sunglasses. I didn't want him to see where I was looking.

"*Two*," I said, showing another finger and further extending my arm, "you know it really can't end the way you want it to." Macy looked at me expectantly, and her gaze held such confidence. She believed in me, even though I was scared shitless. Macy's timing needed to be just right on this. As did my aim. Energy surged, building up in my hands.

"*Three—*"

I shot blasts from each hand. The one from my right blew a hole in the ceiling, freeing the eye hook and the wire it held. Simultaneously, Macy's knees buckled and she dropped, her head now clear of the gun. A split-second later, the blast from my left hand knocked the gun from Aaron's grasp.

I sprang forward, reaching for the grenade. But I was too late. The safety lever released and shot away as Aaron lobbed the grenade.

Time slowed.

I followed the arc of the tiny bomb, having no real clue how long I had before detonation. A few seconds, at most. I reached out and felt its heavy metal weight as it smacked into my palm.

The only window in the kitchen was directly behind Macy's parents. I couldn't risk throwing it in their direction, nor trying to blast through it. So I did the only thing I could think of to protect them all. I dove to the floor, curling up with the grenade buried under my ribcage, putting all my energy into my protective shield.

"No!" Macy screamed, just as my hopes of it being a fake grenade were destroyed.

The blast was louder than I'd expected. Searing pain ripped through me. And it was hot. Really hot.

Seconds later, I uncurled and sat up, ears ringing and chest, abdomen, and thighs stinging. Fragments of grenade shell tumbled to the floor. To my shocked relief, fragments of my body did not follow, although a glance down confirmed that my clothing was not bomb-proof.

I looked over at Macy, to see her standing over Aaron, who writhed on the floor, holding his groin. I stood and stepped over to her, removing the loose wire from her neck. Then I checked to make sure the wire hadn't gotten her. It had, but it was a shallow cut. Then I went to her parents, who sat stunned in their seats, covered with plaster dust from the ceiling. I untied them, removing their gags and assessing their injuries. They were, thankfully, also slight.

Macy rushed past me and embraced her mother and father as I pulled out the radio. "Come get him," I said, "before I punch him through a wall."

I stared at the boy, absently rubbing my stomach. I wanted to feel something toward him, but I wasn't sure if it was anger or sympathy or a combination of both. But I felt nothing other than a tremendous relief. Maybe once the shock of the situation was past, I'd feel something.

The police arrived and hauled Aaron away. EMTs checked the family more thoroughly for injury. Mr. and Mrs. Zhang looked at me with gratitude. Macy squeezed me in a hug. I knew we'd be talking about this at some point soon, just as I knew Aaron's abuse had almost certainly gone beyond what I'd seen. But I'd have to wait for the details. I slipped out as the police sat down to talk with them.

After giving my statement to another officer outside, I flew home, my mind racing. The reality of the situation was settling in. If anything had gone awry, or if he had killed any of them at any point, I would never have been able to forgive myself.

And I now had something to add to the new team's mission. Each member, I decided, should be trained in crisis intervention, including hostage negotiation. The team would have to approve this, of course, but I'd make a solid case for it.

"Wow," was Dana's assessment of the hostage drama when I called and told him about it. "So they're all okay? Physically, anyway?"

"Yeah," I said. "I know they'll get counseling, and hopefully they'll not be too badly affected by it in the long run."

"And what about you?" Dana asked.

"What about me?"

"I know you. You'll find some way to pull a negative out of this positive resolution and feel guilty about it."

I took a deep breath. "I'm trying to be better about that," I said. "But truthfully, there's something I did do wrong. I just got lucky."

"What was that?"

"I'm not trained as a hostage negotiator. I didn't really know the right things to do."

"I don't know about that," he said. "You had pretty good training when you became a suicide prevention counselor."

"What?"

"Active listening skills. Listening is often more important than what you say."

"Interesting," I said. "Makes sense, I guess."

"Oh, before I forget, you need to clear your calendar for a few days in October."

"Because?"

"We're going to Lake Tahoe. Alice Cooper is appearing there on the sixteenth."

"Okay, you're officially my favorite brother."

"I always suspected."

The following weeks were busy ones. Sinta and I packed for our respective moves. Jasmine and I talked a lot about the logistics of the Pariah Project. Vicky and I spent time together.

One day in early September, I met Macy at her house. Her parents greeted me and expressed their appreciation again. Then Macy and I went for a walk around her neighborhood. We stopped at a deli and picked up some drinks, then just walked the residential streets and talked.

She spoke vaguely of the things Aaron had done to her parents, which were limited to mild violence. The things he did to Macy were bad, though not quite as bad as I'd feared. But she was getting counseling. It was helping, she said.

"I don't want to see him again," she said.

"I know. But you'll have to."

"You'll have to be there, too, huh?"

"It's one of the less glamorous responsibilities of my job. Most times, a deposition is enough. Defense lawyers don't generally want the costumes there live and in person, y'know?"

"Yeah."

"But I'll be there for this one, believe me. Even if they don't require me on the witness stand, I'll be there for you."

"Thanks, D," she said, looking up at me with a slight smile.

We spent at least an hour just wandering the neighborhood and talking about trivial things. By the time we arrived back at her house, her spirits were improved, and I'd even coaxed a laugh or two out of my foremost fan. Macy would be forever scarred, but she didn't strike me as the sort of person who'd allow this to cripple her. She was strong. She'd get through it. In time.

I dropped her off at her door with a hug and a promise to get together again soon. Then I took to the sky and soared toward home.

As I flew, I mused on the events of the past couple years. So many terrible things had happened. Macy's whole ordeal. Vicky's kidnapping and molestation by her father. My other-self's sacrifice. Jack losing an arm. Transcendant's death.

There were good things, too, including some recent ones that were pretty big deals for me. My visit home had started healing the rifts between my mother and me. Seeing Sharon and Jackie ended a pain I hadn't even realized had been hurting me for so long. I couldn't stop thinking of little Dinah, either, which once again put thoughts of motherhood in my head.

I had my own team, now. It would be a rough thing, keeping it together and making it financially stable. But I knew it was going to be successful. As Vicky said, the Project was our family. It would undoubtedly be dysfunctional, but I had high hopes.

And that was really how I was feeling: hopeful. For the first time in a long while, I had a good feeling about the future. Just as I knew Macy would eventually be fine, I knew I would be, too. Scars and all.

My dues had finally been paid. The future was filled with possibilities, and I was going to make the most of them. It was time for Dynamistress to become what I knew she could be.

I couldn't wait.

Afterword

As is probably evident from this volume, it was during this time that I was contacted about being Dinah's ghost writer for her memoirs. And, as mentioned in the previous volume, I initially balked at the request. But in November of 2009, the publisher sent me photocopies of a few selections from Dinah's journals and, after reading them, I was definitely intrigued.

My anxiety was mainly a concern about how to present the material. There were many options, and I was urged to meet Dinah to discuss them with her. But the holiday season was upon us and, before I knew it, we were into 2010. I contacted her in January, but Dinah was unwilling to meet. She didn't say why, though what happened a month later made it obvious, and confirmed my involvement in this project.

The story of that horrific event, and its aftermath, will be presented in the final volume of this series. Until then, live well.

Vincent M. Wales
August, 2014

About the Author

Vincent M. Wales was raised in the small town of Brockway, Pennsylvania, where he frequently complained about the weather. Since then, he has worn many hats, including writing instructor, suicide prevention crisis counselor, essayist, Big Brother, freethought activist, wannabe rock star, and award-winning novelist.

He spends most of his writing time in coffee shops, since his cats fail to grasp the entire concept of "writing time."

He currently lives in Sacramento, California, where he frequently complains about the weather.

www.vincentmwales.com

www.ingramcontent.com/pod-product-compliance
Lightning Source LLC
Chambersburg PA
CBHW030424310726
48979CB00009B/1605/J

* 9 7 8 0 9 7 4 1 3 3 7 6 8 *